RAVE REVIEWS FOR
DEBUT AUTHOR BETH PATTILLO!

"*Princess Charming* blends fantasy and reality to create an exciting love story from a fresh new voice."
> —Jo Beverly, *New York Times* bestselling author

"*Princess Charming* is a fresh and delightful fairy tale, full of wit and sparkling intelligence."
> —Barbara Samuel, three-time RITA winner

A PRINCE'S KISS

Nick loomed before her, broad and well-muscled, like the forbidden fantasy he was. Without thinking, Lucy let her tongue dart out to wet her lips. He saw it. She realized that immediately. His eyes narrowed on that small, betraying movement of her tongue. Lucy looked away.

"You had to do that, didn't you?" His voice was gruff, his body tense with restrained energy. "It's not enough to crack my head open, force me to fight your villains, and make me endure an entire night handcuffed to temptation. Oh, no. You had to do *that*." He gestured toward her mouth, his eyes fixed on her lips as well. "By Jove, princess, a man can only endure so much."

His hand reached out and grasped her wrist, using the contact to draw her closer, until she could no longer see his chest, only the deep brown of his eyes. His nearness sent tremors down her spine that settled in her knees. Where was her resistance? Why wasn't she flailing away at him for his audacity?

The first touch was feather soft as his mouth skimmed over hers, but she felt the contact all the way to her toes.

Princess Charming

Beth Pattillo

LEISURE BOOKS   **L**   NEW YORK CITY

A LEISURE BOOK®

January 2003

Published by

Dorchester Publishing Co., Inc.
276 Fifth Avenue
New York, NY 10001

ISBN 0-8439-5141-9

The name "Leisure Books" and the stylized "L" with design are
trademarks of Dorchester Publishing Co., Inc.

Printed in the United States of America.

Visit us on the web at www.dorchesterpub.com.

Princess Charming

Once upon a time . . .

Prologue

Santadorra, 1803

Nick St. Germain dug his fingers into a crevice in the rocky ledge. Beside him, his mother and sister huddled against the cold stone. He refused to give in to the tears that threatened as he searched for his mother's face in the darkness. The thick black night of the Pyrenees shadowed all but the outline of her form. His little sister, Josephine, sniffled in the crook of his mother's arm. Jo was only four, eight years younger than he, and still a baby. Too young to understand why they had fled the palace and now clung to an unforgiving wall of slate beneath the mountain's towering pines.

In the midst of the darkness, he felt his mother's hand on his shoulder. Her fingers trembled where they rested against his coat. "Your father thinks us headed for the northern coast of Spain. He cannot help if he does not know we've turned westward." Nick could hear the indecision in her whispered words. He had pleaded with her for the last hour to let him return to the palace for help,

1

but his mother had wavered, unsure of the safest course.

"I can bring the guards, Maman. They will have defeated the rebels by now. I will fly, fast as the wind." The sounds of pursuit grew louder, the rustlings giving way to the clop of horses' hooves against the hard-packed earthen trail below. Nick shivered. "You and Jo must hide in the caves until I return."

His mother's hand left his shoulder and moved upward to cup his chin. Tears stung his eyes as he fought for control. At that moment, the clouds parted and a moonbeam penetrated the gloom. He could see her now, Her Serene Highness, Queen Eleanor, her blond hair gleaming almost silver in the moonlight, her expression fierce.

"Without the royal family, Nicholas, our people have no hope. They will fall into the hands of that tyrant, Napoleon. Santadorra is merely a stepping stone to Spain."

Bile rose in Nick's throat. " 'Twas the peasants, not Napoleon, who revolted. Let the rabble suffer the consequences."

"Nay!" His mother lifted his chin higher. "This was no people's rebellion. This night's work can be laid at the doorstep of the French *provocateurs*. Santadorrans will come to know that soon enough. They will need their king."

Nick choked back a sob at the mention of his father and shook his head, freeing himself from her touch. "The people have chosen their fate, just as Father chose to stay and fight. I care only for you and Jo."

Pinpoints of light appeared below, and sabres rattled mere yards away. Nick could hear the methodical *thwack, thwack* as the men began to search the undergrowth below the ledge. Jo whimpered again. Fear coursed through him; the hairs of his neck stood on end.

The look in his mother's eyes frightened him further, a look of love and longing and despair that scared him more than the soldiers below. "Oh, Nicholas." Her words were thick with grief. "You are indeed our only hope."

A cry rose from their pursuers, as if the men were

hounds who had caught the scent of the fox. "Jo and I will find a hiding place in the caves. Run, Nicholas. By all that is holy, run."

His mother's hands were pushing him, and he found himself on his feet. His legs must have had some will of their own. Without stopping to kiss his mother or sister, he shot off as fast as he could. The ground was a carpet of slick, wet leaves, but still he ran, stumbling to stay upright and grasping tree limbs and thick gorse bushes as he scrambled up the side of the mountain. His heart pounded in his chest. He would cross the ridge and then race down the valley on the other side. From there, he could follow the road, if he was careful and the other French patrols had made camp. How long? An hour? Perhaps two? He could do it, if he tried very, very hard.

And then he heard the screams. A high-pitched one: his sister. The other a low moan. His foot slipped, and he went down in the thick loam of the forest floor.

Oh, God, he must go back. He scrambled to his feet and began to slide downward on the slick covering of decaying leaves and loose stone.

A shot rang out. And then another, followed by shouts of triumph. Nick felt his blood turn to ice.

The cold, unforgiving darkness of the mountain closed around him like a thick, wet cape, and the Crown Prince of Santadorra knew he had failed, and that he was alone—except for the marauding French soldiers not a hundred yards below.

Chapter One

London, 1819

Nicholas St. Germain paused from his labors, leaned against the handle of the gardening hoe, and eyed the obese blond pug stalking him as a lion would an antelope.

"If you're going to savage me, Wellington, do it now. It will save me having to weed the rhododendrons."

Wellington, who more resembled a wrinkled, over-stuffed pillow than the famous general, sniffed with disdain.

Nick raised his eyebrows. "You took the idiotic notion to dart into the middle of Bond Street. Crispin wagered I could not go twenty-four hours without playing the hero and, traitor that you are, you proved him right in less than twelve."

Wellington growled in umbrage. Nick snorted and lifted the hoe to attack a weed. At least he thought it was a weed. "I should have let you be trampled by Coverley's grays." He whacked at the offending stalk, and it broke off just above the ground. "Never perform a heroic act for a dog."

4

Wellington barked in indignation.

"Don't look innocent, you mongrel." Nick glanced down at his stained smock and rough wool trousers. "Crispin is no doubt peering down on us right now, enjoying the sight of me mucking about in his grandmother's garden." He grimaced. "And talking to her dog."

Nick looked toward the house and, as expected, caught sight of his friend waving heartily from the drawing room window. When the urge to throw down the hoe and throttle Crispin had passed, Nick wiped the sweat from his brow with his sleeve.

"I'm done with wagers, Wellington. And no more heroism. Ever. It's devilishly hard on my boots." He surveyed his ruined hessians with dismay. The cards had not been falling in his favor of late, and his credit was stretched beyond hope of repayment. His father had said he would see him barefoot before he sent him another farthing, and the King of Santadorra's prediction might soon come to pass.

Wellington responded to Nick's declarations by sidling closer, lifting one leg, and relieving himself on the scuffed brown leather.

"The devil!" Nick cried.

Wellington shot off down the gravel path and Nick sprinted after him. The dog veered around a statue of Diana, skirted a small fountain, then leaped through a bed of irises. Nick crashed after him, cringing at the destruction his hessians left in their wake, but he was determined to corner the blasted pug at any cost. Wellington reached the rear wall and skidded to a halt.

"You're trapped now, you overbred cur." Nick stooped to grab the dog, intent on retribution. At that precise moment, the door in the garden wall swung open, and with a thwack, the weathered wood knocked the Crown Prince of Santadorra unconscious.

"Ahh." Nick winced at the light touch of a hand at his temple, and his stomach lurched. Stars danced behind his

5

closed lids. The last thing he remembered was stooping over to grab that canine menace, Wellington, as they skidded to a stop at the back of the garden.

A female voice, light and airy, penetrated the haze of pain enveloping his head. "Drat! I've murdered a gardener."

Nick wanted to object that he was in too much pain to be dead. The owner of the breathless voice, whoever she was, ran soft fingers through his hair—soft, that is, until they brushed the spot where his skull felt as if it might explode.

"Ow!" His eyes flew open. His vision was still a bit fuzzy, but his sight was clear enough to register the blue-eyed, blond goddess biting her lip and looking at him as if he were in need of last rites.

"Who the devil are you?"

The goddess bristled. "I might ask you the same thing, although I suppose you were hired by Lady Belmont to replace young Whitley, who ran off to sea. What an idiotic notion, putting your head in the way of the door. I could have killed you."

Nick groaned. Self-righteous and dangerous. A complication he didn't need, even if the package included skin like Devonshire cream and pink, bowed lips. Wellington barked in agreement with the chit's scolding and Nick winced. "Pipe down, both of you. My head feels as if it's been run over by a carriage wheel."

"And well it should, if you intend to go about colliding it with doors."

Nick stared at her. "If I intend? Colliding it with doors?" Was she a lunatic?

The girl rose, her limbs tensed for flight. She was small, a pocket Venus, the very kind of woman who always brought out his damnable heroic tendencies. She was looking anywhere but at him, as if he were of less consequence than Wellington.

"Fortunately, you seem to have recovered, and I'm expected home. Good day."

"Whoa!" He grabbed the much-turned hem of her skirt as she passed. Did she think he would let her trespass so blithely through a private garden? "One moment, princess." Princess? What bit of madness had made him utter that endearment, even in mockery? He cleared his throat. "You may leave the same way you entered." He nodded toward the garden door, expecting the movement to bring sharp pain, but thankfully there was only a dull throb.

The girl hesitated, and then she glanced toward the door through which she'd come. Nick's eyes followed her movement. His sight was still a trifle bleary but not blind.

"Is someone following you?"

She jumped. "Following me? Certainly not."

Nick lumbered to his feet, and to his surprise, the girl grasped his arm to steady him. The warmth of her touch penetrated the rough sleeve of his gardener's smock. He gained his balance and she dropped her hold as if his arm was on fire. Their eyes locked, and Nick felt the ground shift beneath his feet. Surely not. Surely it was only his injured head, woozy from the door's attack. This girl was anathema—beautiful, troubled, obviously in need of a hero. The Almighty had seen his vow to Wellington as a challenge and had responded immediately by sending the ultimate temptation.

Nick, though, would not be so easily undone. He had sworn an oath, even if it was only to the most troublesome dog in Christendom, and by Jove, he intended to keep his word.

And yet the part of him that defied his best intentions made the damning questions tumble from his lips. "Have you run away from your employer? See here, if you're in trouble, I can—" He stopped abruptly. "No," he heard himself mutter, as if watching the too-familiar scene from a distance. "No. Not—"

Before he could finish the thought, the garden door swung open and a pair of burly ruffians stepped through the portal.

Wellington erupted into a frenzy of barking and made a dive for the boots of the closest intruder. The stocky man gave Wellington a kick that sent the pug flying. The girl cried out and started toward the dog, but Nick grabbed her arm and thrust her behind him. With his other hand, he reached for a scythe propped against the wall. He cursed his own stupidity, for he should have expected this from the moment he'd noticed her eyeing the door.

"Aw, look, 'Ector." The first man smirked, revealing a great quantity of rotten teeth. "She's gone and found 'erself a protector."

Nick's shoulders tightened in anticipation of battle. Two against one, and the one's head still felt as if it had connected with a cricket bat. Behind him, he could feel the tension thrumming through the girl as surely as he could feel his own pulse. The second man, larger than the first but somehow less menacing, cast an uncomfortable glance around the garden as he shifted from one foot to the other.

"Get on with it, Tully. Somebody might 'appen along."

Nick tightened his fingers around the handle of the scythe. If there was one thing he had learned, it was how to play the part of a hero, right down to the lines of dialogue.

"Whoever you are, you are trespassing on Lady Belmont's property. I suggest you leave." His voice sounded firm even as he trembled with the effort of holding the unwieldy scythe as he would a rapier.

"All right, all right." The stocky man turned toward the door. "C'mon, 'Ector. 'E's too much for the likes of us." Suddenly, though, the ruffian whirled about and lurched forward, making a grab for the scythe.

Nick feinted and parried with his awkward weapon, thrusting the blade beneath his attacker's nose. Behind him, the girl gasped, for he had stopped just short of cutting the man. His attacker grunted in surprise and stepped back.

" 'Ow'd you learn to fight like a nob?" The ruffian wiped his nose on his filthy sleeve. "C'mon. Put up yer fives, and fight me fair, man to man."

Nick groaned. That was it, then. The challenge he'd never been able to resist: not merely to play the hero but to stack the deck against himself, to make his task as difficult as possible. After all, wasn't that what true heroism required?

He tossed the scythe to the ground and squared his shoulders. "Man to man it is, then."

Behind him, the girl bit back a cry of exasperation. The second ruffian sank down onto a nearby bench. "I'll just rest meself 'ere a bit, Tully, until you're done with poundin' 'im to a bloody pulp."

The first thug shot his fellow blackguard a disparaging glance. "Demme, 'Ector, you'd still be hanging at your mother's teat if she'd let ye. If you've not the stomach for a fight, make yerself useful and fetch a rope to tie her. This bloke won't take long to bash."

"Aye, Tully. 'Tis just what I'll do." The squeamish giant looked delighted at the opportunity to escape from the garden and in a moment, he was gone. Nick breathed a sigh of relief. The ruffian's arrogance had at least evened the odds.

The girl stepped forward and bent to retrieve the scythe, but Nick caught her arm. "No." Despite his years away from the palace, the word held the imperial authority of a monarch's command. The girl flushed with fury.

She shook off his grip. "There's no need to play the hero."

Her words caught him like an uppercut. She looked magnificent in her righteous indignation, despite her obviously laughable belief that she could fend for herself. "Princess," he drawled, "where have you been all my life?"

Princess? *Princess?* If any of the matchmaking mamas that haunted London's *beau monde* ever heard him murmur that endearment to their daughters, he'd be wed within a week. Nick's stomach sank as he realized the depth of his attraction to her. No woman was as irresistible to a would-be hero as one who spurned his aid.

Out of the corner of his eye, he caught a sudden flash of movement. The ruffian had retrieved the scythe and now raised it above his head like an ax.

"Watch out!" the girl cried and then she shoved Nick backward into the thug. The contact threw his attacker off balance and they fell into a heap on the path. Nick felt the air rush from his chest with one quick *whoosh.* The scythe flew through the air and landed at the girl's feet, the blade mere inches from the tips of her half boots. Nick, truly afraid for the first time since the men had entered the garden, fought to regain his breath. The first thug, who lay beneath him, roared and shoved Nick aside as he came upright. The fiend spied the scythe at the girl's feet and lunged forward.

Just in time, the girl reached down and snatched the handle. The scythe wavered precariously in her grasp but her expression showed not the slightest tremor. Breathless, Nick could only watch—fascinated, intrigued, furious—as she attempted to brandish the weapon.

"Well, wot 'ave we 'ere?" Blood trickled from the corner of the ruffian's nose and his smile was truly evil. " 'Tis me lucky day. I like 'em young and blond as a guinea." He turned and spat, and Nick could have sworn he saw a tooth go sailing through the air. The girl shuddered at the vile words but she held her ground.

Nick had dreamed such scenes before, in the haunting combination of memory and nightmare that stalked his sleep. Only this time he would not awaken to find himself in his own bed, the linens twisted and soaked with sweat.

"Back!" She waved the scythe as menacingly as she could, but Nick could see that her arms were tiring quickly.

"More like 'on yer back,' " the man smirked. " 'Tis where you'll soon be, you—"

Nick sucked in a deep lungful of air and rolled to his feet. Glancing about, he spied a small stone urn on the potting bench along the wall. He grabbed the vessel and raised it above the ruffian's head. The thug, unaware of Nick's recovery, continued to advance on the girl. With all the force he could muster, Nick brought the urn down on the man's crown with a resounding blow. A second thud followed the first as the ruffian dropped to the ground.

The girl stood immobile, stunned by the violence and more than a little bit green beneath that creamy complexion. Nick looked down. At his feet, the thug lay in a crumpled heap, blood oozing from his crown. This skirmish was over, but how long until the other villain returned with a rope—or reinforcements?

Nick knew the best antidote for the shock of battle was practical action. "He'll come round before long. We should toss him out."

The girl exhaled and then squared her shoulders, and Nick knew, from that one small movement, that she was tenacity to the backbone. She looked up, capturing him again in those clear blue eyes before she turned her attention back to the man at their feet. "Can we manage? He looks heavy."

"He's not likely to grow any lighter." Nick leaned down and grasped the thug under the arms. Without waiting for instructions, the girl took hold of his ankles.

"One, two, three." In unison, they inched the man's dead weight across the path and to the door. With a grunt of satisfaction, Nick shoved the man's torso across the threshold and then set his hands on the girl's shoulders to slide her aside. The brief sensation of her flesh beneath his palms sent a shiver down his spine. Nick dropped his grip on her shoulders, grasped the man's legs, and swung them out the narrow portal. With a final shove, he rolled the thug onto the cobblestones and shut the door. The girl threw home the bolt and dropped the crossbar like a chatelaine preparing for siege.

Nick took a long look at his undoing and could only suppress a groan. Curse it, why couldn't she have been plain and wan? "Care to tell me why those two ruffians had you so firmly in their sights?"

The girl feigned innocence. "I have no idea why those men followed me," she protested, and Nick had to allow that she was a credible actress, just not enough to fool him. Again, she squared her shoulders—those shoulders that had felt so right beneath his hands. "Men see a female servant alone and take a great many notions. Thievery. Or rapine." She shuddered at the thought, and Nick did as well. He was all too aware of the vulnerability of a woman alone.

"Indeed," was all he said.

She knotted her fingers in her skirt and shifted from one foot to the other. "I do thank you, sir, for your assistance and will trouble you no further." She bobbed a curtsy and her eyes darted toward the other door in the garden's eastern wall.

"Trouble?" He was irritated, intrigued, and foolishly reluctant to let the hoyden leave. "Pray tell, princess, what makes you think you've been any trouble?"

She flushed a becoming shade of pink, and Nick's body responded with alacrity to her beguiling combination of brazenness and embarrassment. She spread her hands in front of her in a gesture of apology.

"See here, I'm dreadfully sorry about your head, but how was I to know you were waiting just this side of the door? And I'm sorry for the thugs, too, but it's not as if I asked them to follow me. Now, if you'll excuse me, I'll be on my way and we can forget this small incident."

"Small incident?" Nick eyed her in disbelief. "I am struck unconscious, the most repulsive villain ever dredged up from the Thames attacks us, and it's a *small incident*? Remind me, my sweet, not to be present when you become ensnared in anything large."

The girl bit her lip, her features white, and Nick cursed himself for a cad. While she obviously prided herself on her independence, she clearly wasn't accustomed to street brawls. An apology formed on his lips, but before he could utter a word, the girl burst into tears.

Blast and damn! Instinctively, Nick grabbed her and pressed her against his chest. With an awkward, hesitant motion, he stroked her hair, for he was far more used to fighting on behalf of fair maidens than comforting them. "C'mon, now, don't cry, princess. I abhor when women cry."

For one long moment, she clung to him as if he were the only thing afloat in a stormy sea. Her need was a siren's call. Every inch of her pressed against him, and Nick fought the urge to turn his head and seek out her lips with his. The fierceness of the desire scared him more than the scythe-swinging ruffian. Rescue but don't respond, he had always pledged to himself. The words had never proved problematic before.

Suddenly, the girl shoved at his chest and stumbled away, leaving his arms empty and a strange, unsettled feeling in his midsection.

"I do not cry." She wiped her eyes with the back of her hand, her appearance at odds with her defiant words. "It is merely some dust in my eyes."

He didn't argue further; he couldn't really, because his mind wouldn't form the proper sentences. Instead, he produced a handkerchief from his pocket and extended it to her. She frowned and then took it, careful not to let their fingers touch. Without a thought for feminine delicacy, she blew her nose with a resounding honk. She flushed when she realized what she'd done, looked about in embarrassed indecision, and finally shoved the handkerchief into the pocket of her worn dress.

Nick refused to be enchanted. If he wanted the truth about what she was up to, it was time to collect himself and take advantage of her flustered state.

"Do you really expect me to believe that you've no idea why those men were following you?" He stepped forward, and she instinctively stepped back. He didn't think he truly scared her, but if she was intimidated, he was not beyond pressing his advantage. "I'm afraid, princess, you give yourself away rather easily. You didn't appear surprised to see those thugs. No more dissembling. What intrigue are you involved in? Thievery? Smuggling?"

"Neither," she protested. He continued to advance and she fell back, step by step.

"Princess—"

"Please don't call me that." Her fingers twisted her skirt into knots.

"Why? Is it not every young girl's dream to be a princess?" She continued to retreat until her back met the stone wall. Nick felt a swell of triumph. He had her cornered.

"Dreams of being a princess?" She laughed derisively. "Not for those of us belowstairs."

"Belowstairs," he murmured, and his eyes searched hers. Her speech was far too refined for a lower servant. "I would have thought you a chambermaid at least." With a quick movement, he caught her hands from her skirts and examined them. Her palms were red and chapped, the knuckles scraped raw.

"You're rather a puzzle, aren't you?" He dropped her hands, leaned closer, and planted his own hands against the wall on either side of her head. Her breath was coming in tiny gasps, and she seemed as intensely aware of him as he was of her. Nick knew he should stop. He should let her go before he became any more involved than he already was. How many minutes had it been since he'd sworn off heroism? Ten? Twenty? But who would have expected temptation to be as entirely delectable and confounding as this mysterious girl?

"I'm no cipher," she protested, but Nick wasn't paying attention to her words. He was leaning closer, drawn by the irresistible lure of a damsel in distress.

"The devil you're not," he murmured as his lips moved toward her ear. He felt her breath on his cheek, and that soft caress weakened his knees far more than the blow to his head. "And unless I miss my guess, you're involved in some sort of hum all the way up to your delicate little neck." His lips paused a mere inch from the neck in question.

"Wellington!"

"What?"

In a flash of movement, the girl ducked beneath his arm and dashed across the gravel path. Nick cursed and turned his head to watch her, his hands clinging to the wall for support—and for the strength not to follow her. He watched as she found the pug beneath the small white blooms of the solomon's seal, its little body motionless. She laid one tender hand on the dog's side, but the pug showed no signs of distress. Instead, he snorted in his sleep and twitched his hind leg.

"With any luck, he's frolicking in a heavenly meadow, but I suspect you couldn't kill him with an ax."

She raised her chin in defiance. "Wellington is well, thank you very much for your concern." She stroked the pug's round belly. "At least he tried to protect me."

"That mongrel? Protect you?" Nick snorted. "And what do you call what I did?"

The girl's spine stiffened, straight as a poker. "Your actions were foolish. And unnecessary. Even the rawest recruit knows never to throw down a weapon. Honestly, I'd have been better off—"

"Cease!"

The girl jumped as if she'd been slapped. Anger and frustration tightened his stomach like a vise. Nick was glad he'd not moved from the wall. His fingers curled in the ivy. Why did it have to be this girl? Why not some grateful wench who would appreciate and facilitate his heroism? Or who would leave him out of her predicament altogether?

Instead, she glared with the defiance of the young and naïve and dismissed his ire with a wave of her hand. "You don't have to stand like that. I'm not your prisoner anymore."

"Princess, I'm holding on to this wall so that my hands

don't decide to wrap themselves around your neck, which they are itching like the devil to do."

"Oh." She paled, which salvaged his pride a bit.

"Go." He barked the word like a commanding officer. He needed her to leave. She was too vulnerable, too beautiful, too tempting.

"But—" She hesitated, and he realized with a shock that felt like a blow to his solar plexus, that she did not want to leave him either. Anger mingled with attraction in her eyes, and Nick swallowed an oath. Whatever sparked between them, the girl felt it as well.

Nick clung harder to the ivy. "Go! Or I'll not be responsible for the consequences."

The girl stood unmoving for a long moment. Nick felt his knees sag, and he swayed toward her. His fingers flexed and then renewed their grip. *Hang on, old boy. Hang on.*

Finally, with a small sigh, she took a step backward. "Yes, of course. You're right. I should go." She paused and bit her lip, which only drew Nick's attention to its fullness and delightful rosy hue. "Good-bye."

His eyes met hers, and their gazes locked. A connection, almost a bond, arched between them and the feeling shook Nick to the core. The girl turned and fled. Nick watched her go, not sure whether the tightness in his throat was evidence of relief or regret.

Lord Crispin Wellstone watched the entire scene from behind the shelter of the drawing room draperies and cursed his friend for a lucky dog. Nick never had difficulty finding female companions, and this one looked a fit match for the arrogant prince. As the girl ducked through the gate that separated his grandmother's garden from that of Nottingham House, the sun caught her golden hair. Crispin started, and the curtain almost slipped from his fingers. He had been mistaken. The chit was not a maidservant at all, but the seldom-seen Lady Lucinda Charming, daughter of the late Duke of Nottingham and stepdaughter to the aging schemer next door who styled herself the duchess.

Lucy Charming. Hmm. Crispin rubbed his chin and looked toward Nicholas St. Germain, Crown Prince of Santadorra, who was softly pounding his head against the garden wall.

Or might it be . . . Princess Charming? He smiled at the delicious irony. Just as Nick always played the hero, Crispin could never resist acting as matchmaker. He dropped the curtain and rubbed his hands together in gleeful anticipation. Any addlepated fool could see that Nick and Lucy Charming were a match made in heaven—or at least in his grandmother's garden. Now they only needed to realize it.

And perhaps a bit of help from Crispin.

Chapter Two

Lucy raced across the garden of Nottingham House, her cheeks aflame. Anger and attraction combined to fuel her embarrassment. Her heart still pounded, more from her encounter with Lady Belmont's new gardener than from the contretemps with Sidmouth's spies. Of all the arrogant, wrong-headed, interfering . . . *heroes*. The word sprang up uninvited, but she couldn't deny its truth. No, she would deny it. She had no need of a champion, and she refused to depend upon anyone but herself. What's more, she would not succumb to the lure of a handsome face, even if he looked more like Guinevere's Lancelot than a gardener. Nor would she be drawn in by a strong pair of arms, never mind that they offered shelter in a world spinning out of control.

Lucy paused outside the kitchen door and listened. None of the servants would mention her clandestine comings and goings, but still she was careful. Her stepmother was no fool. Lucy sank onto the bench outside the doorway to catch her breath.

With the toe of one half boot, she scraped mud from

the leather of the other. She would put the gardener from her mind entirely, even if his brown eyes had been as seductive as her morning cup of chocolate and his defense of her had created a beguiling warmth in her heart. Above all, she would not recall the delicious shivers that had raced through her when he'd looked into her eyes. No, she would not think of any of that. She need only remember that she was no princess, and he was no prince.

Lucy sighed, rose from the bench, and entered the kitchen. She had no need of a hero, especially one who would throw down a perfectly good weapon in the name of honor. For eight years since her father's scandalous death, she had depended on her own ingenuity and resourcefulness. No, she had no use for a hero. Nevertheless, that traitorous part of her that still felt the clasp of the gardener's hands on her shoulders wished that she did.

Lucy slipped through the kitchen door and descended the stairs to the lowest regions of her father's Mayfair town home. *Please let them be here.* While her birth and family lineage might offer her the smallest of protections against Lord Sidmouth, the Home Secretary, and his persecution of the reformers, her friends would have no such shield.

"Mr. Selkirk?" She lifted her candle higher and peered into the dim corners of the little-used storage room. "Tom?"

A soft rustle came from behind a row of casks, and then two figures emerged into the light: an older man and a boy on the verge of manhood, both of whom shared a strong chin and a decided family resemblance.

"Lady Lucy." The younger of the pair doffed his cap and ran his hand through an unruly shock of hair. "Is it trouble?"

Her stomach twisted. "Sidmouth's men followed me as far as Lady Belmont's. There was an altercation." She forced herself to ignore the disturbing images of the gardener who had come to her defense. "They are indisposed, for the moment, but there isn't much time."

"You are well, Lady Lucy?" Tom twisted the cap in his hands.

"Yes. Please, do not worry. Help arrived from an unexpected quarter." Unexpected and unwanted. Definitely unwanted.

Mr. Selkirk frowned. The older man had been her father's gamekeeper until her stepmother had turned the family off the Charming estate. Now the family eked out a meager existence in the hills above Nottingham. The wizened servant reached out, and Lucy took his hand gratefully. Soft understanding shone from hazel eyes that had seen too much of the world's cruelty. "We must leave, then, Lady Lucy. We have put you in danger long enough, asking you to carry our messages and papers."

Mr. Selkirk's words were sensible, Lucy knew, but the thought of losing her connection to the reformers made her ache. Her father had believed that England must change if revolution were to be avoided, and that only by giving all men the vote would the country he loved remain the country that he loved. Now, his cause was all that remained of him. Yet the late duke would have been the first to say that her involvement must be sacrificed for the greater good. Lucy reached into her pocket and pulled out a tightly folded piece of parchment.

"Sidmouth's men will not be thwarted so easily, so I will not attempt the Blue Barrel tonight. Here is the list of contacts in the midlands." Lucy wanted to scream at the injustice, for at long last she had earned the confidence of the reform leaders and had been invited to attend a meeting of the inner circle. "Plans are to be made tonight for the suffrage rally at Spitalfields, and for Nottingham as well. The names of key reformers in each of these shires will be needed." Tears welled in her eyes.

Mr. Selkirk squeezed her hand. "You have more than done your duty, my lady. 'Tis only this list that keeps us safe from Sidmouth's infiltrators. Your father would be proud of you."

Mr. Selkirk's words pierced her heart. Unbidden, images of the library at Charming Hall rose in her mind, the Axminster carpet spattered in blood and her father lying twisted behind the massive teakwood desk. Swamped by the memories, she couldn't respond, could only press down the dangerous thoughts that lurked at the edges of her consciousness. Rumors had flown after the duke's death, rumors of suicide and scandal, but her stepmother had quickly squelched them. His Grace had only been cleaning his pistols. Tragic, really, for he was a man in his prime. Lucy's knees shook so much she pressed them together, afraid that Mr. Selkirk and Tom would see her trembling. She had seen the gun in her father's hand. She had seen the blood, and she had hotly denied the rumors whenever they reached her ears. If only she could make a convincing denial of them to herself.

"Tom and I will find another bolt-hole," Mr. Selkirk said, attempting to reassure her. "I only hope they have not discovered your identity. Perhaps we should remain, for your father, God rest his soul, would never forgive me if anything happened to you."

Lucy forced herself to breathe, to appear normal. "My father, sir, would applaud my activities." She squeezed Mr. Selkirk's hand. "As he would your protection of me these last years."

Lucy envied Mr. Selkirk his ability to adapt to the harsh realities of life. Her father had always told her she was destined to tilt at windmills, that no less could be expected of the daughter of Lord Charming, the populist duke. The remembrance brought a tightness to her chest. If that was her fate, she could have used a generous measure of Mr. Selkirk's patience, for the dream of suffrage seemed a distant reality indeed. Tories such as Lord Sidmouth were determined that the common man should never gain the vote.

Lucy smiled to reassure her friends. "I may need to skulk in the kitchen for a fortnight or so, but I shall be safe enough." She rarely lied, but she did so now without a single pang of conscience. She would not rely upon the Selkirks to see to her well-being, any more than she would depend upon her dark-eyed hero.

Mr. Selkirk's eyes searched her face, and Lucy held up well under the scrutiny. Tom disappeared into the dark corner of the room and returned with a small haversack.

"Don't fash yourself, Lady Lucy," Tom consoled her. "We'll find quarters elsewhere."

Lucy tried to swallow past the lump in her throat. Her life was a lonely one at best, caught between her role as Lady Lucy and her passion for reform. She ached to see the Selkirks go. "I imagine any hiding place you find will be an improvement over these accommodations," she said, gesturing to the cold stone around them. She wanted to hug them both, but though they were in many ways like family to her, the invisible barriers of class and birth kept a certain distance between them.

"God go with you." She gave them a blessing instead of a hug, and the two men nodded.

"With you as well, my lady."

She wanted to linger in the damp confines of the basement, but there was little else to say. "Send word where you are staying," she admonished them, "and if someone carries messages to Nottingham, give my love to Mrs. Selkirk." The portly woman had been her father's cook and her childhood confidante. A sudden pang of longing for Mrs. Selkirk's maternal presence shot through her.

"We'll relay the message, my lady. Now, go. The duchess will be wanting her tea."

Nick leaned against the stone wall of Lady Belmont's garden where he had slumped to the ground after the girl's departure. His head felt as thick as a log, his chest tight even under the loose-fitting gardener's smock, and his legs trembled with relief. He hardly knew what to think of the events that had just transpired, but he did know what to think of the girl. Trouble. Quagmire. Bottomless pools . . . no, dash it, those were her eyes. Bottomless pit.

Yes, that was it. A bottomless pit of temptation.

He straightened and stepped away from the wall, and almost tripped over Wellington, who was eyeing him with reproach.

"I am not going after her, so you can find another victim for that mournful gaze of yours." Nick stepped over the dog and moved toward the house, but his stride was hampered by the ache in his head. Wellington caught up with him and padded along at his side, but Nick refused to look at him. He was not going to be manipulated by the canine menace for the second time in less than a day.

Enough was enough. He would find Crispin and inform his friend that the frolics were done. He wanted his own clothes, his own snifter of brandy, and his own choice of bed partner at Madame St. Cloud's. He would not look over his shoulder to the spot on the gravel path where he'd collided with the door; he would not even glance toward the gate on the eastern wall he'd heard close behind her. He would not dwell on the fact that she must be one of the Duchess of Nottingham's servants. Not for a moment.

Crispin was still in the drawing room, and he looked pointedly at Nick when his muddy boots left a trail of prints across the carpet.

"My grandmother may be rusticating, Nick, but she'll slice me to ribbons when she returns if her carpet looks like the show ring at Tattersall's."

"Don't start, Crispin." Nick had endured enough for one day without having to suffer his friend's good-natured interference.

Crispin feigned an innocent look. "Me? Whatever would I start, Nicky?"

"I'm not going after her." The tension in his jaw made the declaration difficult, but not impossible.

"After whom, Nicky?"

"The confounded girl from the confounded garden." His gut clenched.

"Oh? There was a girl?"

Nick wanted a brandy, ached for a brandy, but he stood rooted to the spot in the middle of the drawing room. "Devil take it, you know there was a girl. I saw you at the window."

Crispin grinned. "Hmm. Yes. A rather pretty piece, too. Shame you're not going after her. Say, if you're not interested, perhaps I could—"

"No." The word escaped without conscious thought.

"But, Nicky, I thought you said you weren't interested." Crispin grinned.

"I'm not. Neither are you." He wouldn't wish such an impudent baggage on his worst enemy. Only on himself, apparently.

Crispin sighed. "Aren't you even a little curious? And can we be sure she arrived home safely?" He paused, relishing the drama. "Once that stocky little thug awakes he won't be well disposed toward either of you."

Nick grunted and eyed the decanter on the sideboard gleaming ruby red in the sunlight.

"And, of course, there is the question of what deep game she's involved herself in," Crispin continued. "I shouldn't wonder if she's in over her head."

Nick stared at the scuffed, stained toes of his boots. *I shall be firm of purpose,* he reminded himself.

Crispin moved toward a sofa and plopped down on it, propping his boots on the small table opposite. "To be sure, she's only someone's chambermaid . . ."

"Scullery maid," Nick inserted without thinking, and then almost kicked himself.

"Ah, well, then, there you have it. How can she possibly be in need of any assistance if she ranks as high as all that?"

"It won't work, Cris." His throat tightened, as if a noose were closing about it. He stood straighter to relieve the sensation.

"What won't work, Nicky?"

"I'm not going after her. I'm through playing the hero.

Let someone else be the sacrificial lamb." The protest lacked conviction, even to his ears.

Crispin sighed, and the teasing light in his eye vanished. "But you can't help it, can you, Nicky? No matter how you try, you cannot exorcise those ghosts from your past. You crave heroism like an opium eater craves his drug, and have done so since the first day you arrived here from Santadorra. What's more, you can't scrape together more than two farthings without bestowing them on some lost cause."

Nick started to deny the charge, but Crispin was right. Every waif he encountered, every desperate young buck who had lost the family fortune at faro only served to stoke the memories of when his best efforts had been insufficient. So if he was out of funds, it was not because of profligacy on his part, although he did have his moments. No, it was this damnable tendency of his to try and rescue every alley cat, mongrel dog, climbing boy, and scullery maid who crossed his path.

"I must stop, Cris, but I can't seem to help myself."

His friend frowned. " 'Tis a question of moderation, Nicky, of purpose. You must pick your battles more carefully. The world is full of problems you cannot solve."

"Most of them my own," Nick said with despair. "But I swear, Cris, even when I try to avoid these situations, they invariably find me."

"Like the girl," his friend offered.

"Yes, like this girl. And now I'm standing here in your grandmother's drawing room, ruining her carpet, knowing I should avoid the chit like the plague, and it's all I can do not to run outside and leap the garden wall." Only through sheer dint of will was he keeping his hessians firmly in place.

"Hmm. Well, as I said, the thought of that odious little ruffian is distressing. Especially if he should find her alone. I should think he'd have rather a lot of revenge on his mind."

Nick's hands curled into fists. "Stop."

Crispin smiled at him, his blue eyes innocent. "I'm only putting words to your thoughts."

"No. I'm thinking no such thing." Yet the suffocating feeling of inevitability descended over him like a fog. "Her employer will see to her welfare."

"The Duchess of Nottingham?" Crispin snorted. "The only welfare that concerns her grace is her own. And perhaps that of her two unfortunate daughters. I doubt she'll give a moment's thought to the kitchen maid, unless of course her pots are not properly scrubbed or she needs water for her bath."

The image of the girl lugging buckets of water up the wide stairs of Nottingham House caused a heavy weight to settle in Nick's stomach.

"I'm not going after her."

"No one said you should."

"It's none of my affair."

"Indeed, it is not."

"She may launch herself into the very mouth of hell itself, and I should have no obligation."

"Of course not."

Crispin's agreeable responses had their intended effect. Nick took a deep breath and let his shoulders slump. "Front door or kitchen door?"

"Definitely kitchen door," Crispin replied.

"Yes, I suppose so." Nick glanced at his boots. "No need to clean up, then."

"No, I'd say not."

"You'll provide the necessary distraction in the drawing room?"

"With pleasure."

He eyed his friend. "You're enjoying this immensely, aren't you?"

Crispin laughed. "Of course."

"Go to the devil," Nick said and strode from the room.

The kettle was whistling when Lucy entered the kitchen, but Cook, a pale imitation of the redoubtable Mrs. Selkirk, dozed peacefully in her chair, a half-empty bottle of sherry dangling from her hand. Lucy swiped at her skirts and smoothed her hair, hoping that despite the events of the afternoon, her appearance would not be too remarkable.

She grabbed a cloth to wrap around the handle of the kettle and with trembling hands poured water into the waiting teapot. What she needed, of course, was to disappear for a day or two to throw Lord Sidmouth's bloodhounds off the scent, but the chances of that happening were remote at best. Even more, she wished that the two thugs might disappear themselves, before they could report her activities to the Home Secretary, whose persecution of reformers had made him the most hated man in England. Wishing for such things, though, was like wishing for the attentions of Lady Belmont's new gardener—seductive, but far too dangerous and not likely to lead to any good result.

Setting the delicate china pot on a tray, she added cups and saucers. She willed her hands to stop shaking as she sliced the last bit of cake, adding it to the sandwiches Cook had managed before the sherry overcame her. *I will not go to pieces.* Instead, she would address her difficulties one at a time, as each obstacle presented itself. Until the thugs appeared again, she would maintain the pretense of normalcy.

Overhead, a bell clanged, evidence that someone in the drawing room tugged impatiently at the pull. Lucy left the kitchen and trotted up the stairs, balancing the tray with an experienced hand. The door to the drawing room stood ajar. Lucy nudged it open with her hip and, squaring her shoulders, entered the room.

"There you are, you wretched girl!" The Duchess of Nottingham reclined on a sofa, her sal volatile close at hand. The weight of her turban alone with its affixed plumes and jewels would have bowed most women's heads, but the duchess's languid pose was as assumed as her gentility. "Where have you been? We have waited an age for the tea."

Lucy feigned meekness and set the tray on the low table in front of her older stepsister, Bertha, who eyed it greedily. The younger of her stepsisters, Esmerelda, sat in a chair at the opposite end of the room with her nose buried in a book.

"I was in the garden," Lucy replied. No need to say whose garden.

The duchess sniffed. "Grubbing in the dirt, no doubt!" She turned to her two daughters, only one of whom was attentive to her invective. "Let this be a lesson, girls. Young ladies of true gentility may take a turn about a garden on the arm of a gentleman, but they would never actually *dig* in it!"

"Of course not, Mama." Bertha shifted her bulk as she reached for a piece of cake. "Flowers aren't edible. Of what use is a garden?" She narrowed her eyes at Lucy. "Where is the rest of the cake?"

Esmerelda paid no heed to the conversation, merely turned the page of her book and continued to read.

Lucy shrugged and turned to her stepmother. "If there's nothing further?" She was anxious to return to the kitchen and watch for Sidmouth's men.

"Wait!" Bertha snapped. "She cannot have been in the garden all the while. I looked there before." She eyed Lucy with triumph, her mouth curving into a satisfied smile that reminded Lucy of an overfed cat.

"Indeed?" the duchess intoned. "Pray tell, Miss Lucy Charming, where else have you been this afternoon?"

Anger rose within her, but she tamped it down. It would do no good. Just as it would do no good to point out that she was not Miss Lucy Charming. She was Lady Lucy Charming, daughter of the late duke, and she outranked everyone in the room save for the duchess herself.

"I daresay she's been fraternizing with the servants," a new voice drawled from near the window. Lucy started and looked up to find the cold green eyes of the Reverend Mr. Whippet staring her down. His gaze lingered on Lucy's modest bosom as he left his position by the curtains and moved toward the duchess. Lucy suppressed the shudder that rippled through her. The vicar had repulsed her even before the night he'd found her father's body in the library of Charming Hall. Since then, his insinuations about her father's death had frightened Lucy even more than his lecherous looks.

"Indeed, it is a good thing you have kept her out of society, your grace," the clergyman added. "Before one could circle a ballroom, she would be belowstairs preaching revolution to the servants."

Lucy bit her tongue with all her might, or at least with as much might as the tender appendage would allow. The Reverend Mr. Whippet held the living of the parish of Charming Hall in Nottingham, but he was scarcely to be found at his duties. He had become more of a personal chaplain to her grace than anything else, and her stepmother consumed his every toad-eating word like manna from heaven. The woman might be a duchess, but she'd been born to the shop. Mr. Whippet, on the other hand, was genteel by birth, even if he was only the grandson of an earl.

Her stepmother sighed dramatically. "You have the right of it, my dear Mr. Whippet. An embarrassment to the family, to be sure, but what else is to be done? She is, after all, her father's daughter, willing to give every laborer and tradesman the vote." The look she turned on Lucy did nothing to conceal the malice that lay at the duchess's core. "At least in our kitchen she has no one with whom to foment revolution."

A sharp retort sprang to Lucy's tongue, but she refused to give the duchess the satisfaction of goading her into indiscretion. Bertha giggled, revealing bits of sandwich caught between her teeth. "Indeed, Mama, she can hardly breed discontent belowstairs," she trilled. "Unless, of course, the pots and pans can be given the vote."

Lucy swallowed. "Suffrage is the right of every man."

"What was that?" Mr. Whippet barked. The duchess swiveled her head toward Lucy as fast as her turban would allow.

"Yes, Lucy, what did you say?" Her eyes narrowed, but Lucy refused to flinch. If she were going to be made a martyr, she refused to go meekly.

"I said—"

The drawing room door swung open, and Scarborough, the ancient family butler, stepped inside with a small silver platter in hand, a white calling card resting atop the tray. "Viscount Wellstone, madam," he intoned, his voice resonating in the sudden silence.

Lucy blanched. The dratted gardener had obviously gone to his employer forthwith, and Lady Belmont had dispatched her grandson to find the offending maid at Nottingham House. Bertha squealed at the news of the viscount's arrival and brushed the crumbs from her bosom, tugging the neckline of her bodice lower with startling effect. Esmie glanced up from her book. The duchess actually rose from her reclining position and set both feet to the floor. Mr. Whippet bristled, angry that his lone masculine status in the room was now challenged.

Lucy watched with apprehension as the elegant Lord Wellstone entered the room and moved toward her stepmother. "Good day, your grace." He smiled and bowed, and her stepmother's face flushed with pleasure. Lucy's stomach knotted.

"My lord." The duchess inclined her head. The plumes on her turban waved perilously close to Lord Wellstone's face. "This is a surprise. And a pleasure, too, of course. Do sit down."

Bertha giggled again, and Lucy waited for the ax to fall. Lord Wellstone nodded to her stepsisters, including the silent Esmie in his acknowledgement. "Miss Esmerelda. Miss Bertha. Mr. Whippet, I believe," he added with a brief nod to the other gentleman. He took the chair opposite her stepmother's sofa. "I do hope my call is not ill-timed, but your man assured me that you were at home."

Her stepmother and stepsister launched into twitters of denial of any inconvenience. Their compliments and effusions would have overcome most men, but Lucy watched in morbid fascination as the viscount appeared to encourage them in their outrageousness. Oddly, he ignored Lucy just as Esmie ignored them all, and Lucy breathed a small sigh of relief. Perhaps he had not come to denounce her after all.

"Would you care for tea, my lord?" her stepmother asked.

The viscount considered the teapot for a long moment. "I would, indeed, your grace." He paused ever so slightly, his handsome face troubled. "Unfortunately, I can only do it justice when it is piping hot."

"Lucy!" The duchess snapped her fingers. "You will bring more tea straightaway."

Lucy's head snapped up and her cheeks colored. She started to refuse, but to her surprise, Lord Wellstone turned toward her and, beyond the view of the others in the room, gave her a surreptitious wink.

"This moment, Lucy." The duchess made a shooing motion. Something very strange was happening. Lucy's stomach churned.

"I don't want to trouble you," Lord Wellstone said rather insincerely, but her stepmother shushed him.

"It is no trouble, my lord. *Lucy,*" she stressed, "will be glad to fetch a fresh pot of tea."

"Yes, yes, of course," Lucy agreed, still confused as to the viscount's intent. Deciding that retreat was the better part of valor, Lucy bobbed a curtsy and left the room. She clambered down the back stairs as she tried to puzzle it out. Despite the fact that his grandmother lived next door, Lord Wellstone had never before paid a visit. If he was not here to denounce her for the contretemps in Lady Belmont's garden, what could the man be thinking by establishing such an acquaintance and raising expectations?

31

Belowstairs, Cook still snored in her chair and the fire burned low. Lucy reached for the scuttle to replenish the coal and then picked up the poker. Surely her life had grown complicated enough for one day. She was strategically arranging the coals among the embers when there was a knock at the open kitchen door. She turned, and moaned softly under her breath when she saw her handsome, would-be hero standing on the threshold. Her dratted heart raced at the sight of him.

Nick cringed as the girl whirled around, clutching a poker in her hand. Having seen her wield the scythe in Lady Belmont's garden, he knew to proceed with caution. After all, she had been rather adamant before about not wanting to be rescued.

"Hello." Nick winced. Not a brilliant opening. The girl arched one pale eyebrow incredulously. Nick fought to hide a smile. She was a woman of spirit, he would certainly give her that. "Somehow I didn't think you'd be cast into rapture at the sight of me." He decided to take a chance and step inside. His eyes traveled around the room, taking in the spare furnishings and an older woman, most likely the cook, snoring in the corner.

"Why are you here?" The girl hadn't lowered the poker an inch. Nick ignored the fact that the sight of the hoyden sent his pulse skittering. It was only nerves. And battle fever, brought on by the altercation in Lady Belmont's garden.

"I don't believe those men are finished with you, princess, and I don't fancy the idea of leaving you as easy prey for the likes of them."

She turned away, and Nick wondered if she found something amiss with him physically, for she had avoided his gaze more than once in the garden, and she was now doing so again.

"You speak rather well for a gardener." Despite the fact that he had come to her rescue earlier, suspicion was etched in every line of her body.

"And you speak rather well for a kitchen maid." He admired her profile. Her cheek was flushed from the warmth of the fire, and her corkscrew curls formed a golden cloud around her head. It would help matters considerably if she weren't so damnably appealing.

"I can imitate my betters," she shot back. "And you?"

"My betters took pity upon me," Nick improvised. "Thought some elocution lessons might improve my standing in the world." That was true, to a certain extent. When he'd arrived in England, his native Santadorran accent had been thick as treacle. Crispin had made it his personal crusade to render Nick's English comprehensible.

"It doesn't appear to have improved your lot, since you're still a gardener." She lowered the poker the merest bit.

"Ah, but I wasn't even a gardener before," Nick said. His eyes moved to the length of iron in her hand. "Do you suppose you'll put down that weapon anytime soon?" She looked at the poker, as if noticing it for the first time, and then her eyes rose to meet his. Their gazes held, and again Nick felt the ground shift beneath his ruined boots. Once more she looked away, and, by Jove, the disconcerting sensation ended as abruptly as it had begun. With a shrug, she returned the poker to its stand beside the fireplace and reached for the kettle.

"I don't need your protection." The words were sharp, defensive. "I can manage very well."

His jaw clenched. "Princess, I have no doubt that you could hamstring both of those ruffians and the Home Secretary as well," he said, referring to the vastly unpopular Lord Sidmouth.

She jumped, dropping the kettle. A spray of boiling water flew from the spout. Nick bolted forward and yanked her toward him, away from the scalding stream. She collided with his chest, and he stumbled backward before finding his balance.

"Are you hurt?" The indescribable sensation of this

golden-haired kitchen goddess pressed against him pierced him to the core. Every curve of her fit perfectly against him, and his body responded as it was meant to. Hastily, he set her back. Her eyes, soft and unfocused, mirrored his confusion.

"I'm f-fine," she sputtered and pushed his arms away. "A silly mishap, nothing more."

"Well, then, aren't you two a fine pair o' lovebirds?" a familiar voice said from the door. Nick turned to see the thug, Tully, standing in the threshold, Hector looming behind him with a length of rope in his hand.

"Confound it," Nick muttered under his breath.

The girl tensed and slid toward the fireplace, where the poker still leaned in its stand. Nick started to stay her movement, but it would do more harm to call attention to her.

"Have you come back for another thrashing?" Nick mustered as much bravado as he could into the question.

"We want as wot we came for in the first place," Tully said, jerking his head in the direction of the girl. "There's those what wants to talk with 'er."

"And you think I'll stand here and let you take her?" Nick actually laughed at that. Once he embarked upon a rescue, he brooked no interference. With deliberate nonchalance, he rolled up the sleeves of his smock. Clearly this day was not meant to be an easy one. "I thought we'd settled this once before."

Tully rubbed his head. "Not to my liking."

In the corner, the cook snorted. The sherry bottle dropped from her fingers and rolled across the room, spreading a stream of liquid in its wake. It rolled between Nick and the doorway until it bumped to a stop against the grate, where the girl's fingers were closing around the handle of the poker. She looked at Nick, and then at the length of iron in her hand.

Nick was no idiot. "Now!" she cried, and he was ready when she tossed the poker through the air. He caught it and brandished it before him like a sword. The poker made a much better rapier than the gardener's scythe.

Tully started forward, lust for revenge distorting his face. His foot hit the sherry coating the stone floor and suddenly he seemed to be flying through the air. Nick turned, changing his grip, and swung the poker like a cricket bat. The iron connected with the thug's midsection with a satisfying thwack, and the miscreant doubled over before falling to the floor.

"Aw, now," Hector grumbled from the doorway, "when ye 'arm Tully, then I'm the one wot 'as to do somethin' about it." He reluctantly crossed the threshold. "Why don't ye just send 'er with us, peaceful like, and no one 'as to be 'urt."

The giant moved toward the girl. Nick cast about for a weapon, since Tully was now wrapped around the poker, but the only thing at hand was the kettle the girl had dropped. Deciding that hot cast iron made as good a weapon as any, Nick snatched the kettle from the floor and, with one heave, sent it flying in a perfect arc that struck Hector on the temple.

The reluctant thug shot him a look of surprise before he crumpled to the floor.

"Hmm—what?" snorted the cook in the corner, rousing at last. Just then two more shapes loomed in the doorway, and Nick knew it was time to flee. He grabbed the girl's wrist and towed her toward the stairs that led to the main part of the house.

"Stop!" commanded the voice from the doorway, but Nick refused to heed it, fully intent on carrying out the course of action he had only that morning sworn to avoid. They dashed up the stairs and into the wide hallway that ran the length of the house. Nick spotted the front door.

"Wait!" The girl pulled against his grip, but he was brooking no arguments. They passed an open doorway, and a glance inside revealed the Duchess of Nottingham and her daughters, as well as Crispin and another gentleman dressed all in black. But even his friend's presence was not enough to keep Nick's boots from moving toward the front door. He wanted this hellion somewhere private, somewhere quiet, and when he got her there, he was going to find out what in Hades those men wanted of her.

"Let me go," the girl hissed, angry and not afraid.

"Lucy!" a shrill voice rang out, only it rang with exasperation and disdain, not panic. The black-and-white tile of the marbled foyer echoed under their feet as Nick hauled her along. He threw open the front door and, despite the girl's protests, pulled her down the steps after him.

He was going to rescue her whether she liked it or not.

Chapter Three

Ominous gray clouds gathered over Mayfair as Nick towed the angry scullery maid down the steps of Nottingham House. He was glad there were no scythes or pokers lying about the street, for he was sure she would quickly see to it that he met the same ignominious fate as the ruffians who were pursuing her. Well, she had a rescuer now, a known hero, and he intended to give her the full measure of his efforts.

Yip! Yip! Wellington appeared on the steps of Lady Belmont's town home, his gelatinous torso trembling with excitement.

"Stay, Wellington," Nick ordered as they passed by, but it was a hopeless cause. The little dog tumbled down the steps and hit the pavement at a dead run. Nick glanced over his shoulder to find Wellington barreling along behind them.

"Wait for Wellington," the girl admonished him, but Nick ignored her and instead wracked his brain in an attempt to formulate a plan. The cobblestones passed quickly underfoot, yet he had no idea where he was headed. He could hardly take the girl back to his rooms at the Cromwell, especially since she believed him to be a gardener, and the only other respectable residence he frequented was Lady Belmont's. But what of the disreputable ones? His boots pounded the pavement, and he could hear Wellington's asthmatic wheeze hot on their heels. Well, why not the disreputable ones? It was not as if the scullery maid whose wrist fit so neatly in the circle of his fingers had any high-born sensibilities that might be offended, or a reputation that would be compromised.

At that moment, the clouds burst and rain poured forth in a torrent, drenching Nick and his companion in a matter of moments. The soggy turn of events decided the matter, and he headed in the direction of an establishment he knew all too well.

Lucy wiped the rain from her face and, for once in her life, wished for a bonnet. There was only one way to deal with a man determined to rescue, and that was to let him believe himself the hero. He would tire of his antics soon enough, and until he did, she would try to think of a plan, for with two of Sidmouth's thugs lying unconscious in her stepmother's kitchen, disaster loomed even larger than before, and her chances of emerging from this bumble-broth unscathed were diminishing as rapidly as Parliament's efforts at reform.

The gardener led her through a jumble of London streets, the fingers encircling her wrist strong but gentle. The very possessiveness of the gesture irked her. He doubled back and then ducked through an alleyway while Wellington grunted with the effort of keeping pace. She lost track of time when she began to tire. The rain drenched her hair and seeped down her spine until she was thoroughly wet.

Lucy glanced behind them and could see no sign of pursuit. "We can stop now," she said to the gardener, her voice low so as not to attract attention.

"We're not stopping until we're safe." He didn't turn

to look at her, just plowed ahead through the downpour and the growing foot traffic as they approached the old part of the city. Lucy fumed and eyed the passing carriages, praying that Wellington would not feel like chasing a barouche.

"The only thing endangering us now is this forced march through the middle of London," she muttered. "It's high-handed tactics like this that make women dream of suffrage."

His shoulders tightened for a brief moment, but he didn't break his stride. "Only a bit further now."

"Where?" They were leaving the respectable part of the city, and ahead lay the East End and its squalid uncertainties. She knew the area well enough. The reform meetings were held in its smoky taprooms and she had ferried messages back and forth between most of them.

The gardener stopped so suddenly that she collided with his back. Beneath his wet homespun smock, his muscles were like iron, and Lucy felt the shock of the contact all the way to her toes. Their momentum threw him against the waist-high iron gate that stood guard in front of a shabby row house, the worn brick facade clinging to its last vestiges of gentility.

Lucy caught the rain-dampened post and steadied herself. She would not be distracted by the longing that rose within her at the reminder of his strength. Wellington collapsed at her feet and his eyes rolled back in his head as he wheezed.

"Here?" she asked. The house was rather unremarkable, with only a few windows lit in the face of the darkening sky.

"Yes, here." The gardener swung open the gate and led her up the short walk.

The polished bronze knocker on the door appeared well worn, as if a great number of guests had made use of it. Lucy shot a glance at her rescuer as he lifted the heavy bronze and gave three quick raps, wondering at the man's audacity. He was a servant, and so was she, as far as he knew. What were they doing on the front steps?

They waited several long moments for an answer, and then the door opened to reveal a beautiful young woman in a mobcap and apron.

"Nicky!" Her eyes lit with pleasure when she saw the tall gardener. She threw back the door. "Oh, Nicky, it's been ages!" She launched herself across the threshold and into his arms. Wellington barked when the young woman pressed her lips against the gardener's mouth, and Lucy felt the unwelcome urge to strike someone. Or at least snatch off her mobcap and pull the woman's hair.

"You naughty boy, where have you been?" The beauty stepped back and gave his arm a playful swat. "Shame upon you, Nicky."

"Hello, Henny." The gardener smiled without the least embarrassment at the maid's forwardness. "I'm afraid I've been occupied elsewhere of late."

Lucy rolled her eyes and snorted, but the maid only laughed. "I'm sure you've been a busy boy." Her eyes traveled suggestively over his smock and breeches, and Lucy blushed on his behalf, or maybe her own. The maid's mouth formed a petulant little pout. "Dressed in that costume, you are irresistible."

"As are you," he said, indicating her attire, and he smiled in return, a lazy, indolent smile. A smile that Lucy had not yet seen, and made her knees go decidedly weak, even though it was not intended for her. Lucy decided perhaps she would hit him instead.

"Ahem." She cleared her throat. It was time to remind the two moonlings that another party was present, not to mention an impressionable dog. "This reunion is quite touching, I'm sure, but wasn't the idea to escape notice?" Lucy was proud that her voice held all of the asperity and none of the jealousy she felt.

The maid turned, as if noticing her for the first time. "Oh, hello. Are you the new girl?"

The exasperating gardener gave a shout of laughter. "No, Henny. Never the new girl. Listen, we must get out of sight." He glanced over his shoulder. "Surely Madame St. Cloud could allow us the use of her drawing room for a bit?"

"But Nicky, have you forgotten? It's Tuesday. The drawing room is always used on Tuesdays." Her suggestive laughter grated on Lucy's nerves. What could be scandalous about a Frenchwoman using her drawing room on a Tuesday?

"Then someplace else," the gardener said. "It doesn't matter where."

The maid turned her attention to Lucy, her eyes traveling up and down, taking note of Lucy's wet, faded dress and disheveled appearance. Henny's eyes lit with a low flame of spite, but Lucy refused to cower.

"Well, there is one room that's not in use." The maid smiled at Nicky, looking like a cat promised a dish of cream, and a knot of unease tied itself in Lucy's chest.

"Now, Henny," the gardener protested.

"It's that or nothing, I'm afraid."

The gardener slanted Lucy a sidelong look, and Lucy met his gaze with defiance. Whatever the problem, clearly the pair believed Lucy was not up to the challenge. "Are we to stand here until night falls?" They would never see her flinch, just as she had never allowed her stepmother to force her into showing fear. "Or shall we stand about as if we were foxes waiting to take tea with the hunt?"

Henny smiled with satisfaction, and the gardener sighed. "Very well, then. Lead on, Henny." He turned to Lucy. "Just remember that you agreed to this."

The maid stepped back, the gardener took Lucy's arm, Wellington heaved his bulk up the last step, and much to Lucy's apprehension, the four of them entered the house.

Although the faint sound of voices could be heard from behind closed doors, Lucy breathed a sigh of relief when she saw the foyer was deserted. Perhaps this unremarkable home was as good a place as any to hide until she could sort through her difficulties and arrive at a plan. Her willingness to fall in with the gardener's scheme had nothing to do with his maddening heroism or personal attractiveness. She was not depending on his help but merely being practical.

The maid led them up the main staircase, and Wellington moaned dramatically as he heaved himself upward, until Lucy bent down and scooped his wet little body into her arms. They followed the maid down a corridor, and when they reached the end, Henny stopped at a mahogany door. She turned the knob, and the gardener gestured for Lucy to enter the room first. She caught the glance he shot the maid, and the hairs on the back of Lucy's neck snapped to attention. After a slight hesitation, though, she complied and stepped through the doorway.

Lucy took one look inside the chamber and gasped. The room was a terrifying menagerie of leather, steel, and wood. Henny gave a throaty laugh at Lucy's shock and for a moment, Lucy's feet failed her. Then the pressure of the gardener's hand on her arm jolted her into action. She moved forward, fascinated. Morbidly so.

"It's a torture chamber," she breathed, too stunned to be afraid.

The only remotely recognizable items were a large bed that dominated the center of the room and a huge wardrobe standing in the corner. Her stomach clenched with fear, and she frantically cast about for another exit. She glanced at the man beside her, who regarded her with amused brown eyes.

Instinctively, Lucy pulled her arm free from his grip with a sharp tug and turned toward the door. One step, then two—she was almost through the open doorway when his fingers closed around her wrist once more.

"Wait!" In her panic, Lucy lost her balance, but the gardener steadied her and then took the squirming Wellington from her arms. "It's not what you think."

Henny snorted. "It's exactly what she thinks, Nicky."

The gardener shot the maid a silencing look. Lucy wondered if he were distracted enough for her to break free again, but she couldn't leave without Wellington, whom the gardener was clutching like a sack of flour. "I mean the situation. The situation is not what it appears to be."

"Wellington and I want to go home." Lucy kept her voice firm so that it did not betray the fear that knotted her gut. She should never have trusted him. Servants who used the front door. A room that resembled a medieval chamber of horrors. Perhaps they were white slavers. Perhaps . . .

The heavy tread of a man's footsteps sounded on the stairs. "Someone's coming," Henny hissed. She darted to the doorway and peered out before turning back toward them. "Lock the door behind you. I don't want to get thrown out on my . . ."

"Enough." The gardener silenced her with a sharp motion. "Tell Madame I've taken the room, and that I don't wish to be disturbed."

"You, taken this room?" Henny's grin revealed uneven teeth, the only blemish in her otherwise attractive face. "Madame will never believe it, Nicky." Henny gave him a saucy wink and left, closing the door behind her. Lucy bristled at the flirtation and despised herself for it. She could only pray that this nightmare would end soon, because her life had gone horribly wrong from the moment this infuriating man had put his head in the way of Lady Belmont's garden door. She'd thought this might be a temporary sanctuary, but once more, she'd landed in the soup.

The gardener shoved Wellington into her arms and moved to turn the key in the lock. At the moment, Sidmouth's thugs didn't appear so threatening, not compared with the aggravation this man elicited. Perhaps she could imprison him in one of these contraptions and . . .

He turned around. "Don't call me Nicky." His dark eyes flashed with warning. "I despise that name."

"What shall I call you, then?" She cradled Wellington closer, more than willing to offer a few choice suggestions of her own.

"Call me Nick. Or Nicholas, if you must." He cast a look of scorn at Wellington. "Ungrateful beast." Nick circled the hard leather settee in front of the cold marble fireplace. Lucy watched as he sank down on the unforgiving cushion and tried to find a comfortable spot. Remembering his battered head, which must surely ache, she felt a twinge of sympathy for him, but then this rescue was his idea, not hers. He was the one who had landed them in the midst of this chamber of horrors.

"Where are we?" Lucy would have liked to sit down as well, but the only other chair in the room was a monstrous wooden contraption. She didn't even want to think about what it might be used for. "This is the strangest house I've ever seen."

"Shh." Nick sat up and motioned for silence. Then Lucy heard it, too—the sound of booted feet in the corridor outside the room. Over the footfalls came the sound of Henny's distinctive giggle, and her voice, clear as a bell. "In here, sir. Your pleasure awaits."

"Damn her eyes! Quick!" Nick jumped to his feet, grabbed Lucy's wrist, and towed her across the room toward the enormous wardrobe. "In here."

Lucy balked. She was not about to climb into the dark confines of a wardrobe with a man who sparked such dangerous feelings within her. "But you locked the door," she protested.

The doorknob rattled. A deeper voice sounded in the hallway. "Step lively, wench. I've not got all day. The duchess had to attend to a contretemps in her kitchen, but she will expect me back to dine."

Lucy gasped. Mr. Whippet! Wellington recognized the impatient masculine voice outside as well and growled again. Understanding dawned, clear as a summer morning. The macabre bedchamber, the drawing room that was being used by a . . . Lucy gulped. By a *group* of people. The maid, who was no maid at all. And the lecherous Mr. Whippet.

"This is a . . ."

She looked toward the gardener, who had opened the door of the wardrobe and cleared a space inside, and her spine tingled. "This is a . . . that is, it's a . . ."

Nick grinned. "Yes, I know."

Lucy felt the heat of anger flood her body from head to toe. Was it possible to kill a man while trapped with him inside a large piece of furniture? The scoundrel didn't appear the least bit embarrassed. A key rattled in the door again, and Lucy found herself caught between the proverbial devil and the deep blue sea. Yet her decision was not a difficult one; better the devil that thought himself a hero than being discovered by Mr. Whippet.

She didn't protest when Nick hustled her and Wellington into the wardrobe. Nick followed her inside and shut the door, drenching them in blackness as thoroughly as the rain had drenched their clothing. The well-made wardrobe allowed not a sliver of light to penetrate the dark interior. Nick shifted his weight toward her, and the wardrobe, which had looked so enormous from the outside, suddenly grew far too small for Lucy's comfort. By necessity, they sat side by side, the outside of her leg brushing his, his shoulder rubbing against hers, the smell of damp rising from the rough wool of their wet clothing. A slow ache grew in her midsection. For a moment, Lucy let herself remember what it had felt like in Lady Belmont's garden when he had trapped her against the wall, his body moving inexorably closer, closer . . .

She heard the door to the bedchamber open, and Henny and Mr. Whippet entered the room. Lucy could hear their voices, slightly muffled, through the walls of the wardrobe.

"Take off your clothes." Surprisingly, the voice was Henny's, not Mr. Whippet's. The instructions were followed by a sharp crack that made Lucy jump. Wellington roused and snuffled, repositioning his head against her shoulder. The gardener gave a muffled laugh, and a second wave of understanding washed over Lucy. Another loud crack sounded, the snap of a whip.

45

"Now, down on all fours." From the rich pleasure in her voice, Henny was enjoying herself quite thoroughly. Mr. Whippet protested, but the whip cracked a third time. "Now, slave boy. Bark like a dog."

Beside Lucy, the gardener shook with silent laughter, and Lucy felt the movement where their bodies pressed together. She suppressed the giggle that rose in her own throat. Nick shook harder, and Lucy gave his leg a pinch.

"Shh." She kept her voice low, although Mr. Whippet's antics might have drowned out a small cannon. "We'll be found out."

"Ow. Stop pinching me." He captured her hand in his, and the urge to giggle died in her throat, quenched by the warmth of his fingers as they captured her own. His touch felt familiar and yet strange, like a lover dreamed of but never met. Alarmed at her thoughts, Lucy tried to shift away from him. Her other hand cradled Wellington, and so she could only tug at Nick's grip to try and free herself. He refused to release her, though, his strong fingers entwining with hers.

"*Woof, woof,*" Mr. Whippet barked, and Lucy could tell he was enjoying the odd encounter. Wellington stirred in his sleep at the sound. When the Reverend Mr. Whippet actually howled, neither she nor the gardener could restrain themselves, and only by squeezing Nick's hand with all her might could Lucy keep her laughter from escaping. Their shared mirth warmed her as much as his touch.

"Drat that Henny." Nick's sotto voce words barely reached her ears. "I'll see if there's another way out. I'd not be surprised if there was."

She refused to feel disappointed when we released her hand. With slow, deliberate movements, he turned himself and slid deeper into the wardrobe while the vicar's howling continued. A moment later, Lucy felt the brush of air against her neck.

Nick didn't say anything, just tapped her on the shoulder and she knew she was meant to follow him. He took

Wellington and, struggling against the restrictions of her heavy, wet skirts, she clambered after him.

"Here," Nick said, the word echoing in the ebony darkness. She wondered if the blackness bothered him, for his voice cracked slightly. "Thank God I've found a door." Lucy wondered if darkness made him nervous.

A sliver of light appeared. Perhaps this man had his uses after all. Lucy blinked as she followed Nick into the next room, still clinging to his hand.

Where the first chamber had been one of horrors, this one was the stuff of dreams. Light, gauzy fabrics were draped everywhere, as if by an angel's hand, and the bed on the raised dais looked like the bower of a fairy queen. Each tabletop held a vase of fresh flowers, and in the corner, a pretty screen depicted cherubs frolicking in a garden. The room was fit for a princess, and its beauty took Lucy's breath away.

Nick crossed to the other door of the chamber and quickly turned the key in the lock.

"That didn't keep Henny out of the last room," she said. He was far too appealing, and she was growing to like his heroic tendencies, even though they tempted her to depend on him. She needed to distance herself.

"Henny has special skills, a product of her childhood in Seven Dials," he said with a wink, one conspirator to another, and she flushed. "I doubt many of the other young women at Madame St. Cloud's are as proficient at picking locks. Besides, I imagine Henny thinks us still in the wardrobe listening to Mr. Whippet."

Lucy was surprised that he knew the vicar. "You are acquainted with the man?" As soon as the words left her lips, she knew she'd made a mistake. The gardener's handsome features showed no curiosity, but the sudden tension in his body betrayed his interest in her response.

"I know who he is. Perhaps you do as well?"

Lucy feigned nonchalance, afraid she'd tipped her hand, and turned to examine several gilt-framed paintings on the wall. "Mr. Whippet is vicar of the Charming parish. He is a frequent visitor in the duchess's drawing room."

The gardener stepped away from the door and approached her, his expression ominous, but Lucy held her ground. "Has he . . . bothered you?"

The hard line of the gardener's jaw almost proved Lucy's undoing. Oh, heavens, he cared that the repulsive vicar might have taken liberties with her. Drat all gardeners, especially the brown-eyed ones! She must put a stop to this silly attraction.

"The Reverend Mr. Whippet may cast me all manner of looks," Lucy hedged, "but he will never lay one finger upon my person."

"Indeed, he will not," Nick agreed, and Lucy forced herself to ignore the pleasure his words caused to dance along her skin.

"You didn't need to rescue me." She should divert him from his preoccupation with Mr. Whippet, for such thoughts might lead him to her identity. "In fact, you've only made things worse."

"Worse? Pray tell, princess, how much worse do you believe this situation can be? Our friends Tully and Hector are no pleasant picnic at Kew."

"You've been to Kew?" Perhaps she could turn the subject.

He hesitated, the pause of a man deciding whether to lie, and a frisson of apprehension crawled up her spine.

"I'm a gardener. Of course I've been to Kew." He said the words with authority, perhaps too much so.

"But . . ."

"I think it would be in our best interest to remain here for the night." He crossed to the window where the heavy clouds had brought an early end to the long summer day. "We can leave in the morning, when the servants go about their business. It shouldn't be difficult to blend in." He looked toward her. "Unless, of course, you can think of a better hiding place."

"I shouldn't stay here." Lucy shivered, not from her wet

clothes but from the danger she knew remaining in this man's presence would bring. Yet she had nowhere else to go in her rain-soaked dress. Her sense of self-preservation, though, was strong enough to realize that each moment spent in this man's company tempted her to forget her hard-won independence. "My step . . . that is, my employer will be searching for me," she hedged. Perhaps dodging Sidmouth's thugs would be preferable after all to spending a night with a man she was tempted to depend upon.

He cast aside her concerns with a dismissive wave. "Your employer will have to wait until we rid ourselves of those ruffians. They won't have much difficulty tracing our steps to this house. In the morning, we can slip past them without them being any the wiser." He cautiously lifted the draperies a mere inch. "Ah, it is as I thought. We have uninvited guests."

Wellington snuffled against Lucy's neck, but it was the thought of Sidmouth's spies outside that caused icy tendrils to snake through her. She bent down and placed the sleeping pug on one of the large cushions. Wellington twitched and then began snoring in earnest. "Can you see them?" She moved to join the gardener by the window, but he waved her away.

"Let's not confirm their suspicions. Our new friend Tully is wedged between two houses across the street. I wonder if he's considered that a red cap is not the most inconspicuous choice." He paused for a moment. "I don't see the other one. No doubt he's in back, watching the stables."

Lucy wiped her damp palms against her even damper skirt. Thank heavens she had given Mr. Selkirk the list of reformers' names. "They found us rather quickly."

"It seems they have incentive." He strode to the middle of the room and, stepping onto the dais, pulled back the bedclothes. Lucy eyed him warily. The best course might be to pretend to go along with his plan. Once he was asleep, she could quit the house under the cover of darkness. Perhaps she could steal his clothes and contrive somehow to disguise herself. But then where would she go? She could not return home now that Sidmouth's men knew where she lived, and she refused to endanger any of the other reformers by seeking shelter with them.

He waved toward the painted screen in the corner. "No doubt Madame keeps nightrails and such back there. Make yourself as comfortable as you like."

Lucy paled. What an idiot she was. In an instant, the veneer of heroism she had painted upon him washed away and she saw his actions for what they were: a blatant attempt to seduce her into intimacy. She was such a fool, to have been tempted to rely on him even a little.

"I will do no such thing." Lucy bristled. She would leave, and immediately. In one quick motion, she scooped Wellington from the pillow where he was happily twitching in his sleep and started for the door. "Your rescue, sir, is at an end. Good evening."

He reached the door before she did, blocking her way. "Are you daft? Mr. Whippet is still in the house, and those imbeciles outside are eager to work their best villainy."

"I will not share that bed with you." No point in beating around the bush, even if the declaration did make her blush a fiery red from head to toe. "Your attempts at heroism are poor cover for your true intentions."

For a moment, he did not respond. Whatever he was thinking, he did not allow his features to reveal his thoughts. They stood mere inches apart, both as unbending as two bars of iron.

"You needn't worry," he said, his dark eyes unreadable. "You may be the most exasperating female I've ever met, but you're perfectly safe, despite our rather . . . unusual circumstances."

Lucy hesitated. "On your honor?" It seemed a rather foolish promise to extract from a man who was not a gentleman.

"On my honor. Now, let us prepare for bed. We'll need to rise with the dawn if we want to slip out of here among the servants going about their morning rounds." He reached for her shoulders and spun her about. With a little push, he propelled her toward the screen in the corner. "Do whatever you like about the nightrails, but shed those wet things. I don't fancy playing nursemaid if you contract pneumonia."

Lucy trembled at the image of this man cradling her in his arms and trying to tempt her with a cup of broth. She had always wondered about the secret world of men and women, a world she had not explored beyond a few kisses. The most dangerous quality about her would-be hero was that he made her want to explore the feelings between them in a way forbidden to young women of good birth.

Lucy refused to entertain temptation, though. Instead, she squared her shoulders and ducked behind the screen, thankful for its protection. She shed her wet dress and her ablutions took only a few moments. Several thin nightrails of satin and lace hung on pegs behind the screen, and Lucy considered them, each more revealing than the one before. She heard the sound of Nick's boots falling to the floor and apprehension knotted her belly. Was she ten kinds of a fool to think that she was safer in this room than in trying to escape on her own?

She plucked a piece of rose satin from a peg and slipped it over her head. A matching wrapper followed, which she cinched tightly at her waist. There. They were the most conventional of the lot. Lucy drew a deep breath and emerged from behind the screen.

The gardener turned, clad only in his breeches, his chest shockingly bare. From one hand dangled a shiny piece of metal—a pair of lightweight manacles he must have found in the trunk at the foot of the bed. As Lucy watched in disbelief, he clasped one of the irons around his wrist and snapped it tight. With a determined look on his face, he stepped toward her. Lucy shrieked and bolted for the door, but he was too quick. He caught her around the waist and snatched her tight against his chest.

"Sorry, princess. I said you were safe, not trustworthy. It's the only way I'm going to get any sleep." She struggled against him as he placed the other cuff around her wrist and snapped it shut. The metal gave a soft click.

"Where's the key?" she demanded, afraid of the sudden weakness in her limbs. She pulled against the restraint. Her eyes flew over him, ignoring his bare chest as she looked for a possible hiding place.

"The key? I have no idea where it is," he said with a smile, and Lucy's knees trembled even more. "Now, shall we get some rest before we make our daring escape in the morning?"

Lucy strained again at the metal cuffs that bound them. "You are a fiend, and I would not share that bed with you if my life depended upon it."

His eyes turned molten with a combination of amusement and challenge. "Princess, you should know better than to throw down the gauntlet in front of a dedicated hero."

Lucy shivered at the intensity of his gaze, for she recognized determination when she saw it. Her stomach lurched, and she knew without a doubt that she should have chosen Sidmouth's thugs after all.

Chapter Four

The mere sight of his scullery maid in a thin wrapping of rose satin almost deterred Nick from his foolhardy heroism, but some instinct, a self-destructive one most likely, compelled him to see his plan through as he snapped the other cuff around her delicate wrist. Her beguiling blue eyes snapped with fury—rightly so, he supposed, since she was the most fiercely independent wench he'd ever met—but she would capitulate to the inevitable. Women always did.

"You are a despicable cad. Release me."

Nick wondered that he didn't but refused to consider the matter any further. "Sorry, princess. As I said, there's no key." He nodded toward the bed. "Accept your fate and we can both rest more easily."

The look she gave him was hot enough to melt the wrist irons that bound them together, but she was intelligent enough to know he had won. With a sniff, she raised her chin and climbed on to the bed. He followed as the chain pulled at his wrist. In seconds, she had scooted as close to the opposite edge as she could without falling off and lay stiff as the poker she'd tossed him in the duchess's kitchen. With a snort, she closed her eyes and pretended to sleep.

Nick settled into the mattress beside her and decided that of all the idiot notions he'd entertained in the past few hours, this one was the most harebrained of them all. He rubbed his temples with his free hand. Why was he so determined to rescue someone who obviously didn't want his help? He was hopeless, it was true, when it came to his heroics. Just as some men could not pass by a bottle of brandy, Nick could not fail to come to someone's aid. Yet never before had he foisted his help on such an unwilling soul. Something about this girl compelled him, even though she must have spent most every moment since they'd met wishing him to the devil.

Brief images flashed before him of another dark night, spent in the Santadorran mountains, huddled in a cave and afraid to cry. The fact that the kitchen maid and his sister would have been the same age meant nothing. Nick banished the thought. Besides, his attraction to the girl was anything but brotherly.

The sound of her breath from the pillow next to his should have relaxed him, assured him that she was safe for now, but instead his muscles tensed with anticipation. Not that he had anything to anticipate. Perhaps it was merely Madame St. Cloud's establishment that set him on edge. Surely his restlessness stemmed from the sensuality that had seeped into the walls, not from the exasperating girl who lay next to him in the broad bed.

Nick shifted his weight against the mattress, careful not to rattle the slim chain that bound them together. Why in heaven's name hadn't he used the irons to secure her to the bedpost instead of to himself? Dash it, but she was warm. Invitingly so. Even though he wasn't touching her, Nick could feel the heat radiating from her body. He tried not to look at her, tried to keep his eyes averted from the temptation he knew he'd find, but desire overcame will and he turned his head.

Much to his surprise, he found that she truly was asleep. Framed by the lace-trimmed linens, she looked like a royal princess instead of a scullery maid. Masses of golden curls tangled about her face, her delicate features relaxed in slumber. The natural arch of her eyebrows suggested strong pride, but the softness of her mouth and fine shape of her nose rendered her beauty approachable. If he had not known better, he would have thought her the daughter of some titled aristocrat, for her appearance spoke of breeding and bloodlines. Perhaps that was what had led him to call her princess from the moment he'd seen her. What name had the duchess yelled when they'd fled the house? He closed his eyes and allowed the memory to come floating back. *Lucy.* The shrill screech of the dowager's voice could not disguise the aptness of the name. *Lucy.* It suited her, at once both innocent and independent.

Nick lay motionless among the pillows, watching her sleep and trying to curb his unwelcome desire for the hoyden at the other end of the wrist irons.

He was awakened at the crack of dawn by the faint rap of the front door knocker. His muscles tensed. While gentlemen might depart Madame St. Cloud's in the predawn hours, very few arrived then. He heard the murmur of voices but could not quite make out the words. Nick knew that the odds were good, though, that whoever the hunter was, the beautiful kitchen maid and he were the prey.

The sound of footsteps on the stairs sent his protective instincts into action. With one quick turn, he moved to cover the girl's body with his own. He chose the position deliberately, so that all that would be visible from the door was his back. Perhaps the appearance of intimacy would be enough to send whomever it was on their way.

He heard doors open and shut down the length of the hallway, each time with a mumbled apology and angry words from a disturbed gentleman or a screech from one of Madame St. Cloud's irate girls. Nick waited, arms aching with the demands of holding himself close enough for illusion and yet keeping some semblance of distance from the enticing body beneath him. His chest ached as well, oddly enough, but that feeling bore no connection to his physical efforts. He heard Madame St. Cloud's softly accented voice and as the footsteps moved closer, he recognized the second voice.

Crispin.

The key rattled in the lock. Briefly he wondered if any of the locks on Madame's doors actually worked, but he had no time for further thought. The door swung open, and a familiar chuckle traveled across the room.

"Good morning, Nick," Crispin said from the doorway.

At that moment, he felt the girl move beneath him. She gasped, and her body went still. Nick looked down. Her blue eyes were awash with fear, and then, in an instant, recognition. The brief flash of sensual awareness almost made him forget the presence of Crispin and Madame, but her words snapped him back to reality.

"Get off me, you great oaf."

Warm male flesh. Muscles and sinew and heat, and the smell of bay rum and something smoky. Lucy had never been this close to a man before in her life, and for one long moment, she couldn't breathe. Trapped between Nick's body and the soft mattress, she fought against the seductive lure of both.

"*Cheri!*" A soft, disembodied voice, promising and sensual, came from beyond Nick's shoulder. "You naughty boy. I did not know you were here. Which of my girls hid this information from me?"

Lucy heard the woman move closer, and then her face appeared over Nick's shoulder. She was beautiful in the elegant way of mature French women. Even at this hour of the morning, a perfect coiffure complimented her classic features, and the strands of gray at her temples did not mar the allure of her amethyst eyes and generous mouth. Nick rolled away, and Lucy gulped in air.

"Good morning, Madame," he said, smiling disarmingly at the woman. "Privacy seems to be in short supply today."

Lucy flushed. "Please, Madame." She held up their wrists, displaying the lightweight iron cuffs. "Is there a key?" She thought she might die of embarrassment, but distancing herself from the tempting gardener was worth every bit of humiliation. The Frenchwoman's eyes lit with delight, and the gardener, despite his bravado, actually flushed a dim red beneath his olive complexion.

"Nick, *cheri*, how foolish of you! I may indulge men's pleasures, but I do not put my girls in danger." The woman stepped forward and with a quick movement of her long fingers, she sprang open the cuff. "All of my customers know how to work the irons. You could have been free at any moment."

Lucy rubbed her wrist where the iron had scraped a raw place. The gardener's eyes met hers, and in their brown depths, Lucy saw the truth. He had known all along how to release them, the rat!

"You lied."

"Not quite." He reached over to undo the cuff that held his wrist, the movement bringing him uncomfortably close once more. "I said I had no idea where the key was."

"You wretch!" Hot color flooded her cheeks. Lucy grabbed a pillow from behind her and swung it at him, but he scrambled away. He climbed from the bed and off the dais. Lucy felt another blush stain her cheeks at the sight of Nick in nothing but his breeches.

The gardener crossed to the middle of the room and then stood immobile, as if uncertain what to do next. "This is not what either of you are supposing." He frowned at the Frenchwoman and looked toward the door, and at that moment, Lucy realized that a second person had entered the room.

Her heart sank when Lord Wellstone's eyes met hers. His grin was amused, not lewd, but Lucy pulled the sheet up to her nose nonetheless. She glanced at Nick, who was regarding the viscount's perusal of her with some consternation. Nick propped his hands on his hips. Heaven preserve her, but her rescuer's protective instincts were riled again. Why did his response have to trigger that strange fluttering in her stomach?

"It's not what it appears," Nick repeated. His stance sent some sort of unspoken message to the other man, much like a tomcat staking his territory. Only she wasn't territory. And with the dawn, it was time to face the tangled mess her life had become, to reassert her independence and move on. Alone.

"But Nicky, I do not understand," the Frenchwoman said. "You know it is against the rules to bring a companion from outside."

Lucy grew hot at the implication, especially when Nick made no move to defend her reputation.

"*Oui*, Madame." He dropped the wrist irons onto a low table. "I would never have thought to impose upon your hospitality if we had not been in dire need of help."

"Help?" The woman looked amused. "Pray, Nicky, what help have you ever needed in one of my boudoirs?"

The woman's words confirmed Lucy's worst suspicions about Nick's familiarity with the house.

"Yes, Nicky, do tell us," Lord Wellstone said. "I, too, should like to know." He leaned against the door frame, one boot crossed over the other as if he might stand chatting all day.

Nick sank down on the small sofa to pull on his boots. "Go to the devil, Wellstone."

Lucy gasped at the gardener's effrontery, and Madame chuckled. "My girls would be most disappointed if word of your defection were to spread."

Nick slid on his second boot. "If you're both finished amusing yourselves at my expense, we have serious matters to discuss."

Lucy felt the Frenchwoman cast her a questioning glance before she frowned at Nick. "*Cheri*, should you not allow the young woman a moment of privacy? And you, too, my lord." She arched an eyebrow at both of the men. "I think something is not right here. This girl is no *femme de la nuit.*"

Finally, someone with a clear head. Lucy could only hope that Madame would send her along her way as soon as possible, and she could be free of her self-appointed hero. Although at the moment the prospect of such freedom was a bit daunting, for to her mortification she'd fallen asleep almost as soon as her head hit the pillow, as if she'd believed herself safe and protected. She was no nearer contriving a plan than she'd been the night before.

"I'm not letting the girl out of my sight." Nick's tone brooked no argument. "Why do you think I used the manacles?" He rose from the settee. "I appreciate your concern, Madame, but it will be sufficient if you and Lord Wellstone allow us a moment alone."

Madame's eyes narrowed, and Lucy realized she was not a woman to be taken lightly. "Have a care, Nicky, even if you are a favorite. Though it is small, this house is *my* kingdom, and I alone rule here."

Lord Wellstone laughed. "Well said, Madame. I'm not leaving either, Nick. You need someone in this room with two clear thoughts to rub together." He threw an apologetic look at the Frenchwoman. "Besides Madame, that is."

"I will not stay where I am not appreciated." The woman's generous lips pouted quite effectively. Lucy wished she could employ such a trick without appearing foolish. "What? Do you think I rose from an empty bed to deal with the likes of you two *enfants?*"

Nick and Lord Wellstone ducked their heads, appearing more like contrite schoolboys than men who frequented such an establishment, which made Lucy smile in spite of her predicament. The viscount stepped aside as Madame swept from the room. He closed the door after her, and his devil-may-care façade vanished. Lucy wished she could sink through the mattress, for the time to pay the piper had come.

"By all that's holy, Nick, what have you done now? I've been searching all night. It finally occurred to me that you might come here."

Lucy watched in fascination as the two men met as equals. The gardener snorted. "Give over, Crispin. You put me up to this. It only wants your playing the innocent to become a complete farce." He moved across the room and peered through the curtains. "Did you see the one in front?"

"The only person in London who hasn't is the blind beggar in Covent Garden." Lord Wellstone moved to stand beside Nick and the two of them studied the street below. "That red cap lacks subtlety."

"Exactly," Nick replied with a grin, and Lucy realized that these men were not aristocrat and servant. They were friends, evidently of some long-standing nature. As Madame had intuited, something was not right. The two men were absorbed in their perusal of the street, and Lucy knew a better opportunity for escape might not come. She was accustomed to relying on no one but herself, and though she had no idea how her current difficulties would be resolved, the time had come for her to take her fate back into her own hands.

Out of the corner of her eye, she gauged the distance to the secret door. Silently, she pulled back the bed linens and slid to the opposite side of the mattress. The small steps leading to the dais held under her weight without any telltale creaking. She slipped behind the screen and lifted her old dress from the peg where she'd hung it to dry. With quiet stealth, she traded Madame St. Cloud's satin for her own patched and mended woolen.

"We'll slip out among the servants," Nick said from the window.

"Um." Lord Wellstone's voice was thoughtful. Lucy moved from behind the screen and eased her way toward the door. "I don't know, Nicky. What we really want is to lock them up right and tight, so they don't spill news of yesterday's events. It's the only way to protect . . ."

"Lucy!" The gardener's tone rang with imperial command.

She froze, her hand on the doorknob, and in that instant, the strength of her attraction to him and the need to depend upon him hit with all the force of a gale at sea. Heart in her throat, she yanked open the door and sped into the darkness of the secret corridor as if her life depended on her escape.

Her advantage was not as great as she'd hoped. A moment later he was behind her, his boots clattering against the stone. Her fingers brushed along the wall, frantically seeking the door to the wardrobe. They brushed against the knob and she tugged it open. Just as she lifted the hem of her skirt to clamber inside, a pair of strong hands grasped her waist.

Was she deliberately torturing him? The blasted girl squirmed in his grasp, every part of her body in contact with his. If she did not hold still, he wouldn't be held responsible for his body's response. After all, he was only human. A mere mortal grasping a very enticing, exasperating woman who made his head spin, not that he would admit it to anyone but himself.

"Let me go," she demanded, but he kept his grasp firm. "I should be happy to throw you to the lions, you ungrateful little baggage, but not until I'm ready."

"I can take care of myself," she protested and drew back her leg to kick him in the shin. Nick stopped her by scooping her into his arms. The moment he did, he realized his mistake. The sleepy, warm scent of her washed over him, completely at odds with the spitfire that wriggled in his arms.

Nick strode briskly down the corridor, eager to rid himself of his tempting burden, and reentered the room where Crispin waited. He summoned all the indifference he could manage. "If you're determined to sacrifice yourself on the altar of whatever cause you're pursuing," he admonished her, "then at least have some breakfast first. I'd hate to face those thugs on an empty stomach."

He set her on her feet and stepped back. It was a gamble, he knew. Given her stubbornness, she was likely to turn and flee once more, but he wasn't going to follow her again. If she ran from him this time, he was going to let her go. Truly.

And if Crispin could read his thoughts, he would be howling with laughter.

Thankfully, she didn't run. With a mutinous look, she moved toward the cushion where Wellington stretched and yawned.

"As I was saying," Crispin drawled from the settee, "I have a plan, if the two of you are willing to listen."

Nick scowled, and the girl made no answer.

"Well?" Crispin propped up his feet on the table opposite.

"Let's hear it," Nick answered grudgingly, still distracted by the most infuriating scullery maid in London.

Ignoring him, the chit turned toward Crispin. "What sort of plan, my lord?"

"Rather simple, but rather daring, I should say." Crispin preened under her attention, and Nick clenched his fists. Why should he care that the girl was focusing her attention on Crispin? "We walk out right under their noses," Crispin said, as if it weren't the most obvious scheme in the world.

"Which would be a smashing plan," Nick drawled, since he'd already thought of it, "except that once we're out of sight, they'll run straight to their superiors."

Lucy eyed him warily. "Their superiors? Do you believe them some sort of spies?"

Nick laughed. "Princess, we both know who they are. Delectable as you may be," he said, and then wished he hadn't, but it was too late to unsay the words. "Delectable as you may be, they haven't hung about on account of your golden curls."

"Quite right," Crispin added with a winning smile, "although it only proves what great heathens they are."

Lucy blushed, and Nick cursed under his breath. He caught Crispin's eye and lowered his brows, warning him. "The plan?" Nick prompted.

"Oh, it's quite simple, really. We make it look as if we're sneaking away, but in reality, it's a trap. We'll lure them somewhere and then lock them up. Once we've got them, it should be a small matter to put them on a ship bound for Australia or the Americas. With the pair of them off the scent, no one is the wiser, and we can all return to our lives."

"That is brilliant, my lord." Lucy smiled warmly at Crispin, and Nick wanted to throttle him, except that she was right. It was a good plan.

"And the particulars?" he asked grudgingly.

"Quite easily managed, actually, if the two of you are willing to cooperate."

Nick looked at Lucy, who was regarding him as if he were the lowest species of insect. "The sooner we leave this place, the better," he said. He kept his eyes still, his face impassive. With any luck, in a few hours she'd be safely ensconced at the Duchess of Nottingham's kitchen and he could go on with his life.

The thought should have cheered him. Instead he found it completely depressing.

"Well, then, that's it," Crispin said. "Now we simply need a corset."

Lucy blushed. "My lord!"

Crispin laughed. "Don't worry, love, it's not for you. It's for Nick."

Nick swore that he would revenge himself against Crispin, even if it took his last breath. He adjusted the train of the gown's skirt with one hand and tried not to breathe, since the restrictive undergarments he wore didn't allow for such non-essential movement as expansion of his lungs. The moment this charade was finished, he was going to

Gentleman Jackson's boxing salon and pummel some poor soul into the ground. Perhaps he could convince Crispin to come along.

His friend was adjusting the jaunty cap on Lucy's head. "Don't look about," Crispin instructed her. "Just keep your head down like a proper groom." He tweaked the shoulders of the short jacket that did nothing to conceal the way her shapely hips filled out the snug trousers. Nick had protested those trousers, but Crispin had waved him off with a laugh. Outside, a hackney waited at the curb. The thug with the red cap still lurked about the building opposite Madame St. Cloud's establishment, and the ruffian was about to be treated to a rare show.

Lucy handed Wellington to Henny and sniffed back a tear. "Someone will take you home soon, poppet." Wellington looked unperturbed as he burrowed his head against Henny's bosom.

"We'll spoil him dreadfully," Henny said by way of consolation.

Lucy eyed her warily. "Not too many sweetmeats," she said. "And absolutely no cake."

Henny pouted, and Nick decided it was time. The sooner he got out of this ridiculous outfit, the better.

"Let's go." He offered his arm to Lucy and then, realizing how ridiculous he looked dressed in the borrowed morning gown and pelisse, his hand fell to his side. Lucy giggled and his temper began a slow burn. He knew in all his heroics he played the fool often enough, but rarely did he so accurately dress the part.

Henny opened the door for them and Wellington yipped a farewell. Nick stepped over the threshold and descended the steps, his head held high and the plumes in his bonnet waving.

Lucy skipped down the steps beside him in a fair imitation of a young groom. She opened the door to the cab and held out her hand to assist him inside. For a brief second he balked, wondering how on earth he was supposed to launch himself into the hackney.

"Pull up the hem," Lucy whispered. He reached down and hiked up the skirt beyond the bounds of modesty and launched himself into the carriage. Lucy scrambled in after him. In a falsetto voice, Nick trilled orders to the driver. A moment later, the cab moved off down the road.

"Do you think Tully took the bait?" Lucy peered out of the window but Nick pulled her back.

"If he didn't, he's a bigger idiot than I took him for. We are the most unconvincing pair ever to trade skirts for pants, or vice versa."

A sharp whistle rent the air and Nick relaxed, at least as much as a man could relax while wearing a bodiced petticoat. "There's his signal to the behemoth around back." He opened the reticule Madame had given him and drew out a small mirror. "Hold this out the window, just so." He demonstrated the angle and then handed her the glass.

Nick watched as Lucy placed the mirror. "A little to the left. Yes, that's it." He had a clear view of the cobbled street behind them and of the man in the red cap loping along after the carriage. In a moment, he was joined by the taller of the two thugs. "Excellent. You can draw it in now."

She did and paused for a moment to study her own reflection in the small glass. "I rather like this outfit," she said, smiling at herself in the mirror as she adjusted her cap to a more rakish angle.

Nick's temperature rose. "That outfit is as temporary as it is indecent. You're in enough trouble without slinking through London in trousers."

She turned her smile on him, and Nick's stomach clenched. "With such an efficient rescuer," she taunted, "I needn't worry." She was teasing him, and he liked it qas much as he despised it. "Especially one who is so . . . à la mode." Her eyes sparkled as they traveled over him, and she sat up straighter, as if preparing for battle.

Nick felt his groin tighten. Before this little adventure was over, he was either going to have to kiss her or kill her, and he wasn't sure which might prove the more satisfying.

Chapter Five

Lucy squeaked in surprise when the hackney drew up in front of Lady Belmont's town house. "The trap is to be laid here?"

"We couldn't chance losing them. Even those idiots would have come sniffing back here if they'd lost sight of the hackney. Now open the door."

Lucy bristled. "Please," she prompted. For a rare moment, she had the upper hand with this infuriating man and she meant to enjoy it.

He raised one eyebrow—really, he would have made a very fine aristocrat—and looked her over as if she were a crust of molding bread. "When a man is wearing a skirt," he said, his voice dangerously low, "he is not required to be polite."

Lucy was wise enough to know when she had pushed him too far. She opened the door and set out the steps, hopping lightly to the ground before turning to offer her hand to Nick. If Crispin's plan worked, Sidmouth's men would soon be well out of the way, and she could return to Nottingham House and continue her activities. The thought brightened her considerably.

She almost laughed out loud as Nick emerged from the cab. His disguise could not have fooled anyone for above half a minute. The plumes on his bonnet knocked against the doorway of the carriage as he refused her hand and maneuvered on his own. His skirts tangled around his hessians and he stumbled to the pavement.

"There she is!" a rough voice cried out, and Lucy turned to see the familiar pair of spies almost on their heels.

"Run," Nick ordered. "And remember the plan."

Lucy balked, resenting his arrogant tone.

"Go!"

She hated it, but she responded to his command. Instead of dashing up the stairs to Lady Belmont's front door, she turned aside and scampered down the service stairs to the warren of rooms below. The cook and two scullery maids cried out in astonishment when she dashed through their midst, Nick close behind her. "Which way?" she called when she reached the far end of the kitchen.

"Left," came the breathless reply. She turned around long enough to see Nick gasping for air.

"Corset too tight?" she called as she took off again, secretly enjoying his predicament, exhilaration and fear pumping through her chest and limbs. From behind her, she heard the scullery maids scream again as the spies followed close behind.

"Corset? Not a bit tight," Nick ground out. He drew closer and Lucy redoubled her speed. When they reached the end of the hallway, she stopped short.

"This way." He grabbed her wrist, a gesture she was coming to despise, but she would have to divest him of his dictatorial attitude at some future date. He led her through an open doorway into a small anteroom that held several crates and casks stacked in neat rows against the walls.

"I hope Lord Wellstone arrives in time," she muttered as they moved through the anteroom and into the darker chamber beyond.

Nick swung the door closed behind them, lowered the rather flimsy crossbar, and leaned against it. "If Crispin doesn't arrive promptly, we're done for. I can barely breathe in this contraption, much less take on those two villains again."

Lucy looked at Nick and her heart softened. Really, for a misguided hero, he wasn't so terrible, and he was certainly attractive.

The air in the room smelled of smoke and earth, and a fine gray powder coated the walls. Lucy stepped nimbly around the stray bits of coal on the floor as she surveyed her surroundings. A small window next to the coal chute provided the only light.

"I'm surprised Lord Wellstone remembered this place."

"I'm not," Nick replied. "As a boy, he spent more time in this house than his own." He patted the crossbar. "Told me he put this up so he could shut out the world when he needed to."

"And his grandmother approved of skulking in the coal cellar?" Lucy's heart ached at the thought of Lord Wellstone's solitary childhood, for it reminded her of the years since her father's death. She understood loneliness well enough.

The harsh clatter of boots sounded in the anteroom. "We've got 'em now, 'Ector."

"Come help me brace this door," Nick said. "I don't know how long this will hold."

Lucy hastened to comply. The door was rather narrow, and when they leaned their backs against the wood, their shoulders brushed. She looked up, and her eyes met his, her heart making that infuriating leap to her throat.

Wham! The ruffians' first assault on the door rattled Lucy almost as much as the look in Nick's eyes. She pressed harder against the wood and scrambled for firmer footing.

"If they break through, stay behind me," Nick ordered between clenched teeth.

"If they break through," Lucy countered, "let them take

me. They'll let you alone once they have what they came for."

Nick shot her a look that would have melted steel. "By Jove, you are the hardest woman to rescue I've ever met. Do you think I put on petticoats for nothing?"

Lucy felt her cheeks flush with anger, but that was preferable to the vulnerability and the attraction she felt in his presence. "You're the most obstinate rescuer I've ever had the misfortune to encounter," she shot back, teeth clenched with the effort of holding the door closed as the thugs pounded on it. "I don't need your help." But she did, and what's more, she hadn't felt lonely from the moment he'd towed her down the steps of Nottingham House.

The next blow to the door slid it open several inches and fear closed her throat. Where was Lord Wellstone?

Then, suddenly, as if she'd conjured him, she heard his voice outside. "Gentlemen, gentlemen. Why are you assaulting my grandmother's coal cellar?"

The ruffians gave two loud bellows and then Lucy heard the unmistakable sounds of fisticuffs as Lord Wellstone and his footmen engaged the enemy.

"Just let us know when you're finished, Crispin," Nick called, and Lucy could see the tension flow out of him as he leaned against the door. Relief coursed through her as well, her muscles sagging so she could hardly stand.

"One moment, St. Germain," Lord Wellstone's voice came back, followed by the sound of a well-delivered blow and a cry of outrage mixed with pain from one of the spies.

Lucy looked at Nick again. Their eyes met once more. She drank in the sight of the incredibly handsome man next to her, outfitted in a walking dress and chipstraw bonnet, and she couldn't stop the giggles that spilled forth. "You've bent your plumes," she said, pointing toward the broken feathers.

Fortunately for her, he began to laugh as well. They stood side by side, shaking with mirth, until the grunts and thuds from the other side of the door ceased. Lucy wiped her eyes with the back of her hand. "I'm sorry. I shouldn't laugh, after all you've done." She looked up, and he was gazing at her with an unfathomable expression—not exasperation or hurt, but a sort of well . . . fascination.

"I think," he drawled, faint lines appearing around the edges of his smile, "I may have met the one woman I'm quite incapable of rescuing."

Lucy's heart stopped, and she watched as his deep brown eyes turned even darker. The force of her attraction to him seized her once again, her knees sagging even further.

"You can come out," Lord Wellstone called from the other side of the door, breaking the spell Nick's gaze had cast. "The footmen have carted off your two admirers."

The words were sobering, a summons back to reality, and Lucy lowered her gaze and stepped away from the door. Just like that, then, it was over. The last day and night had been a chain of events she would never forget, nor would she forget the strange feeling of camaraderie that had sprung up between them, but it was done now. Time to return to her home and her own difficulties. To her solitary life. To her independence. "We'd best go," she said, nodding toward the door.

"Lucy." He reached for her hand, but she neatly sidestepped him. Better to end the charade before she felt more than attraction for the man.

"I must return home. The duchess will be furious."

"I'll speak with her," he said, and Lucy laughed at his audacity.

"I'm sure the testimony of Lady Belmont's undergardener will carry a great deal of weight with her grace." She moved around him, heart aching, and reached for the crossbar. "Thank you, but no. I will deal with her on my own." She had learned to fend for herself, and no man, however extraordinary, could be allowed to change

71

that. Especially this exasperating gardener who kindled a hopeless longing in her breast.

He stepped back and Lucy opened the door, refusing to meet his eyes, although she felt their gaze quite keenly. She emerged into the anteroom just in time to see Lord Wellstone disappear into the hallway. To Lucy's consternation, he shut the exterior door, trapping her and Nick inside the storage room.

"Lord Wellstone?" she called, confused.

"Crispin, what the devil are you up to?" Nick demanded from behind her as the key turned in the lock. Lucy rushed toward the door and turned the knob, but the stout oak refused to budge.

"Crispin! Let us out of here at once," Nick ordered.

"I'm afraid that's not possible, Nicky. The key seems to be stuck." Lord Wellstone's voice was heavy with laughter. "I'll fetch a locksmith. Don't worry, though. There's port in the casks, and you might find some biscuit in there as well. I'll be back as soon as I've dispatched our friends to a ship."

Panic rose in Lucy's chest.

"Crispin, don't do this," Nick called, but the only reply was the sound of Lord Wellstone's boots moving down the hallway.

Lucy stared at the locked door in disbelief. Why would Lord Wellstone lock them up? It made no sense. Unless . . . But, no, surely he wouldn't go to her stepmother. Not when he had seemed to conspire with her against the duchess the day before, when he had given her that conspiratorial grin in the sitting room, and when he had helped them trap Sidmouth's spies.

She turned round in time to see Nick sink down on one of the crates. With a quick yank, he pulled the ridiculous bonnet from his head and flung it against the opposite wall. "Damn him."

Lucy flinched at his language, but he had reason to curse. She would have liked to curse herself. For the first time, she realized that Nick would most likely lose his position because of their escapades. Perhaps Crispin had gone to inform Lady Belmont he had the errant gardener under lock and key. Yet, remembering the camaraderie between the two men, that seemed unlikely.

Nick reached behind him and fumbled with the buttons on the walking dress. Lucy hesitated, unsure whether to offer her assistance. When she heard the sharp rip of fabric beneath his impatient fingers, she stepped forward.

"Here. Let me." Surprisingly, he complied, rising from the casket. "Turn round," she ordered him and he did, presenting her with the daunting width of his shoulders.

One by one, her trembling fingers slipped the small buttons through their holes. His nearness flooded her heart with unwanted pangs of longing. To rest her cheek, even for the briefest of moments, against his strong back. To feel his body pressed against hers, as it had been when she'd awoken in Madame St. Cloud's fairytale chamber. To feel the warmth of his fingers twining through her hair, instead of wrapped around her wrist in a domineering grip—

Before Lucy could complete her task, he tugged the garment off, and it slid down his lean hips to puddle on the floor. The white linen of the bodiced petticoat stood out in stark contrast to the olive smoothness of his skin. Wary of such temptation, she quickly undid the petticoat's hooks. He shucked it off his arms and down, stepping out of the ridiculous garment.

Lucy tried to will herself to move, to step away from him, but her feet proved leaden and her muscles weak. Wearing only his breeches, Nick tossed the clothing to join the bonnet on the floor and turned toward her. Her breath caught in her lungs at the sight of his bare chest.

"I wouldn't wear skirts for just anyone." He loomed before her, broad and well-muscled, like the forbidden fantasy he was. Without thinking, she let her tongue dart out to wet her lips. He saw it. She realized that immediately. His eyes narrowed on that small, betraying movement of her tongue. Lucy looked away.

"You had to do that, didn't you?" His voice was gruff, his body tense with restrained energy. "It's not enough to crack my head open, force me to fight your villains, and make me endure an entire night handcuffed to temptation. Oh, no. You had to do *that*." He gestured toward her mouth, his eyes fixed on her lips as well. "By Jove, princess, a man can only endure so much."

His hand reached out and grasped her wrist, using the contact to draw her closer, until she could no longer see his chest, only the deep brown of his eyes. His nearness sent tremors down her spine that settled in her knees. Where was her resistance? Why wasn't she flailing away at him for his audacity?

But she didn't want to push him away, she acknowledged to herself. As his head tilted, and his mouth moved closer to hers, Lucy waited patiently, expectantly, like the prize idiot she was.

"Lucy?" he whispered, but her only response was to abandon all good sense and reach for his lips with her own.

The first touch was feather soft as his mouth skimmed over hers, but she felt the contact all the way to her toes. His kiss wound its way from her lips to her heart and then throughout her body. His breath slid across her cheek as he raised his head, hesitation in his eyes.

Lucy didn't want him to hesitate. She wanted him to kiss her properly, and she didn't want to think about why. Not now. That could be saved for later, when she had time to scold herself for this indiscretion, for the folly of believing that he was the one who could change her life, her loneliness, the one man on whom she might depend.

"Kiss me," she ordered, and he arched one eyebrow.

"Please?" he prompted, just as she had done in the carriage.

Mutiny rose within her, but evidently Nick was wise enough to forestall her rebellion by the simple expediency of reclaiming her lips with his own. As the tingling shock of his kiss turned her bones to porridge, her control slipped away. The intimacy of the contact frightened her, but the pleasure of it made her arms steal around his neck as his mouth pressed more firmly against hers. When she felt the tip of his tongue brush against her lips, her knees gave way entirely and his arms came around her to hold her upright.

It was like the bonfires she remembered from the country fairs of her childhood, warmth that began with a small flame and grew with each passing moment until one must back away or be singed. Her pulse pounded in her ears and her body flamed with awareness. He opened his mouth, slanting it against hers, and Lucy welcomed the deepening of his kiss. He pulled her closer, and she gasped at the contact. It was far too intimate, and yet every part of her felt that it was right, this conflagration that Nick had started within her.

"I should stop," he breathed against her ear when he'd deserted her mouth to trail kisses down the sensitive skin of her neck, but Lucy didn't want him to, could no longer remember any reason why he should. She could have kissed him forever, or at least as long as he managed to hold her upright. Her body felt at once strong and weak, as though he had cast some magic spell over her limbs. As if in response to her thoughts, he settled her more closely against his chest, and both of his hands sank lower until they clasped her bottom.

Lucy froze.

Fear, stark and bold, coursed through her, dousing the flames of passion. He was so close she could have crawled inside his skin, and what frightened her was how much she wanted to do just that. Not because he was handsome or strong, but because he was Nick. Lady Belmont's gardener. A man who would rout villains or even wear a bodiced petticoat on her behalf. Oh, heavens.

"Lucy?" His hands slid upward to catch her shoulders, and he stepped back. She forced herself to look at him even as she pushed away the feelings his touch evoked. Longing was futile, as was desire. There was no place for such things in her life, even less since yesterday's disasters.

"I have to go." She only just managed to keep the words from sounding as desperate as they felt.

"And I should be happy to oblige you, but I'm afraid, for whatever reasons, Crispin has other ideas." He was looking at her carefully, and Lucy knew he was no fool. He dropped his hands from her shoulders and moved back. "Perhaps I should say I regret what just happened, but, at the moment, I find myself unable to mouth such falsehoods." His eyes were still fixed on her, and they burned with the same intensity that his touch had carried.

Why did he have to have those beautiful, beautiful eyes that were the exact shade of chocolate? "I have to go," she repeated, rather like some dull-witted parrot.

"Yes, I believe you mentioned that."

Lucy forced her feet to move somewhere, anywhere. Without thinking, she walked backward into the coal cellar and came to a stop in the middle of the room. She spun around, once, twice.

And then the light from the window fell on her, and she saw her escape.

With a practiced eye, she judged the distance to the window, as well as its dimensions. She would never have made it in a skirt, but wearing breeches, she stood a chance. If Nick would help her.

Nick had followed her into the room, and he now leaned against the door frame, his chest and shoulders only a few shades lighter than the wood. "Lift me up." She gestured toward the window. "If it latches from inside, I can get through. Then I'll come back through the house and unlock the door."

She saw him eye the window, mentally measuring as she had done. "It will still be a stretch, even if we manage to get you on my shoulders," he countered. "And it will take the skill of a climbing boy."

"I can manage. Besides, it's better than waiting for Lord Wellstone to return."

She could tell by his annoyed expression that she'd somehow hurt his feelings, but she hadn't meant to. Surely he had no more desire to be trapped with her than she had to be trapped with him. Except, of course, for that kiss. There was entirely too much desire in that kiss.

He moved away from the door and came toward her. Her heart raced, but she resolutely willed herself to stand still.

"I'll strike a bargain with you, Lucy."

Why did his mouth have to be so intriguing? Why couldn't his shoulders have been stooped and narrow, instead of strong and broad? And why, oh why did her heart pound like heavy summer rain on the stable roof whenever he said her name?

"A bargain?"

"Yes. You tell me why those two ruffians were following you, and I'll be happy to lift you up to the window."

Lucy's stomach sank. "That's not a bargain. That's blackmail. Besides, it's none of your—"

"Don't say that this is none of my affair. It became my affair the moment you struck me on the head with Lady Belmont's garden door."

She paused. He did have a point, but, still, the truth was not something to be shared lightly. Most reformers had prices on their heads, and in these desperate times when a single loaf of bread cost half a week's wage, the lure of money could turn the noblest of working men into informers.

"I can't tell you."

"Then I suppose we'll have to wait here until Crispin returns. Perhaps, when I escort you home, I can share our little adventures with the duchess. I'm sure she would be most interested to know how you passed the night."

"You wouldn't!"

"Oh, indeed, I would."

She hated smug men. They crossed their arms across their muscled chests, smiled with self-satisfaction, and watched one dangle like a worm on a hook.

"Very well." She paused, uncertain where to begin. "What do you know of the Luddites?"

"Rabble-rousers," Nick replied shortly, his brow furrowed in disdain. "Framework-knitters in Nottinghamshire who terrorized their employers when they would not meet their outrageous demands."

Of course it had been too much to hope that he would see beyond the propaganda the government had spread. "Good, honest men," she shot back, "who starved while their employers engaged in ruinous speculation and destroyed the quality of their work."

Nick frowned. "There was no excuse for their lawlessness. The militia were called out, and the dragoons. They disturbed the public peace, and if they were treated harshly, it was no more than they deserved."

"Their children were starving!" Maybe it was better that he didn't comprehend the justice of her cause, since his lack of sympathy for the poor rendered him far less attractive. A thick heaviness settled in her stomach.

"What have you to do with the Luddites?" His frown had disappeared, to be replaced with a look of doubt.

"Nothing. The fictional Ned Ludd is long departed, but there are some who still believe in reform. If Parliament can be brought to see the need for universal suffrage—"

His jaw dropped. "Allow every field laborer and vagrant the vote? We have only to look across the Channel to France to see the consequences of that." He began to pace in front of her, and Lucy felt a strange lurch in the vicinity of her heart. She had been right, after all, to put a stop to his kiss.

Lucy took a deep breath as she marshaled her arguments. "We have only to look to France to see the truth of it. Every man should have the right to participate in the government that rules over him. You, of all people, should understand that. Lady Belmont will probably sack you once she discovers what has happened."

His face had gone white, but Lucy didn't wonder at his response. Sometimes the strongest opposition to reform came from the very people it was intended to help.

"I don't believe you." His words were clipped, his spine straight and unyielding. "Even those crackbrained reformers would never allow a young woman to put herself at such risk. Suffrage is the prerogative of men. Why would you fight for rights you will never share?"

Her answer was little more than a whisper, a wish locked so deep in her heart she rarely ever let herself dream it. "Perhaps one day I will."

"You are a fool." He said the words as calmly and as plainly as if he were commenting on the weather. "Reform can never succeed, not until human nature changes. Reform is merely a clever word to conceal the real purpose—revolution."

His contempt was better for her purposes, she knew that, but it hurt nonetheless. She struggled against the need for his good opinion. He was a means to an end, nothing more. She couldn't allow him to be more. Lucy glanced toward the window and then at Nick again, refusing to cry. She hated that she felt disappointed in him. "We will never resolve this, and you did make a bargain."

Small white lines fanned around his mouth. "Yes. I suppose I did."

When he came toward her, it was as if he could barely stand to be in her presence, and though she knew his distaste shouldn't hurt her, it did. He moved next to the wall and laced his fingers together, reluctantly offering her his help. "I'll boost you up. If you can open the window, then we can be rid of each other that much sooner."

This time when Lucy stood next to him, she felt no anticipation, no tingle along her spine, just a deep sadness. She placed her foot in his joined hands but held back from touching him elsewhere.

"You'll have to put your hands on my shoulders," he pointed out, his voice detached and almost bored. Resolutely, Lucy did as he said, and he hoisted her up. Her fingers scrambled for the lock on the window and flipped the catch. With a shove, she lifted the sash.

"Can you lift me higher?" She needed only another six inches or so to be able to pull herself through the window.

"On the count of three," he instructed, his voice still cold. "One, two—"

It was like flying. She managed to duck under the sash, but her momentum scraped her shoulders against the window frame. She ignored the pain and pulled herself through the opening. When she stumbled to her feet, she found herself near the service entrance where she'd entered the house. No one was about on the street above. She turned back to the window and knelt. Nick had moved to the middle of the room, and she could see him clearly framed in the morning light.

"Can you find your way back round?" he asked. From that height, he looked smaller and much less formidable. "I can only hope that Crispin left the key in the lock."

"It's of no account," she said, and he looked up in surprise.

"Of course it is of some account. I've no desire to remain in here any longer than necessary."

"No, I mean it's of no account, because I'm not coming back for you." She watched his face as her words registered.

"You little—"

"I'm sorry, Nick. But given your feelings toward the reformers, it's time we parted ways." She paused, wanting to say something, wanting to take away the sting of what she knew she had to do. "Thank you, though, for everything."

It was a feeble peace offering and one he brushed aside. "Lucy," he warned, his hands clenching into fists, "don't do this. You'll regret it. I swear you'll regret it."

This was the second time she had cried since the day before, and she never cried. "Good-bye, Nick."

She looked at him one last time, taking in the memory of his face as if she were drawing her last breath of air. Something shifted deep within her, something breathtaking and important, but Lucy refused to analyze the feeling. She stumbled to her feet and ran, but even the pounding of her half boots on the stairs did not drown out the deep voice furiously calling her name.

Chapter Six

Lucy peered around the hedge she'd chosen for concealment as she surveyed the garden of Nottingham House. Her heart still raced from her mad dash around the corner and through the mews at the back of the house. She'd only stopped long enough to shed her boy's attire and trade the breeches for an old dress and shoes she kept hidden in the stables. She'd often donned a boy's attire in her reform efforts, and the habit of concealing a change of clothing in the stables had served her well more than once. The duchess was sure to be livid over her absence, much less her unorthodox costume, and Lucy was not certain what punishment she might mete out.

With one hand she brushed back her hair, but that simple action reminded her of the gardener's touch and her susceptibility to him. Lucy sighed. She had allowed herself to believe in his heroism, had allowed herself to be rescued, had allowed herself to be weak, to depend upon him. But despite his myriad attractions, Nick was no knight in shining armor, no prince disguised in a gardener's smock, although his response to her passion for reform had been worthy of any aristocrat. No, he was not the man of her dreams. He had responded to her as he would any young, reasonably attractive scullery maid. The thought made her ache. Indeed, he had been repulsed by the very mention of her beloved reform, and if she had any sanity left, she would firmly remind herself of that fact.

Voices floated across the garden, interrupting her reverie. Her stepmother and Bertha appeared, marching across the path in her direction.

"You claimed to have searched quite thoroughly yesterday," the duchess snapped. They were within a few feet of Lucy now and she hardly dared breathe.

Bertha crossed her arms over her prodigious bosom and pouted. "I searched the entire garden not an hour ago, Mama. Perhaps she is gone for good, and we shall all be the happier for it. You always say she is a millstone about your neck, as mad as her father before her and as likely to bring ruin upon us. With any luck, she has sunk to the bottom of the Thames."

Lucy bristled at the slur against her father's memory, but prudence held her tongue.

"Hush, you foolish girl." The duchess was eyeing the little folly she'd ordered built in the center of the garden. To make room for the picturesque eyesore, she'd had Lucy's mother's roses removed. "If you had any sense, you would know that Lucy's presence in our home accounts for many of our social invitations. She is a Charming by birth, a fact that these high sticklers in London make a great deal of, even if her father was a madman. If we lose her, you may no longer have the opportunity to snare a marquess."

"A marquess?" Bertha snorted. "You have overused your *sal volatile* again, Mama. After three seasons, neither Esmie nor I have received an offer from so much as a *mister*."

Lucy would have laughed at Bertha's shrewd answer,

but the duchess's attack upon her father lit a flame of anger. The duchess shot her daughter a withering look. "Do you think I am made of pound notes? If it were not for the duke's heir allowing us to use this house in his absence, we should find ourselves returned to Nottingham, where you would be obliged to simper at Squire Barnston. You take my meaning very well, I am sure."

Lucy's fingers trembled where she grasped the branch of the hedge. With a deep breath, she stepped from behind the shrubbery. "Yes, madam. We all take your meaning quite well. We always do."

"Lucy!" her stepmother shrieked and grasped Bertha's arm for balance.

"Lucy!" her stepsister echoed, her face pale. At least Bertha had the grace to appear shamefaced at the sentiments they'd been expressing. Her stepmother, however, recovered quickly, drawing herself up to her full height.

"You have gone too far this time, Lucy Charming." She dropped her grasp on Bertha and seized Lucy's arm instead. "As if your father had not blackened the family name sufficiently, you will bring scandal down upon us all. We can only hope that you were not seen fleeing my home with a servant." Her fingers dug into the flesh of Lucy's upper arm. "If you are compromised, if you ruin my daughters' prospects, I will beat you black and blue. I swear it."

Lucy winced at her stepmother's grip and stumbled along the path behind her as the duchess towed her toward the house. "I have not been compromised," she protested, although her heartbeat skipped with guilt at the lie. If her escapades of the last day and night were known, society would indeed consider her virtue beyond repair. They entered the kitchen, and Cook looked up in surprise, her pale, rheumy eyes widening when she saw Lucy in the duchess's grasp.

"Lady Lucy," she said, smiling. " 'Tis good that yer back, ma'am."

"Yes, it is very well that she has returned," the duchess

barked, "but it is no concern of yours. I am afraid that Lucy will not be able to help you today, Cook. I have need of her elsewhere."

Lucy sputtered a protest but her stepmother continued up the stairs, dragging Lucy in her wake. It was only when they had climbed to the attic, the duchess having ordered Bertha to return to the sitting room, that Lucy realized her stepmother's intentions.

"No." She strained against her stepmother's grip, but the duchess's hand had the strength of a vulture's claws.

"Yes, indeed. And you will remain here until you are prepared to give a full account of your whereabouts since yesterday."

The duchess threw open a door and thrust her into a dark, narrow room. "Here you shall stay until you divulge the secrets you have been hiding, Lucy Charming." Her eyes must have widened in surprise, for her stepmother smiled with evil satisfaction. "You think me unobservant, but I, too, have my tricks and stratagems. Something is afoot, and I intend to get to the bottom of it."

Lucy swallowed. Thank goodness the Selkirks had departed. "There is nothing to tell."

"Indeed. I seem to have made a grave error in leaving you so much to your own devices. Are you prepared to tell the truth?"

Lucy hesitated. Despite Nick's abominable sentiments about reform, she still felt the need to protect him. Likewise, there was no possibility of admitting to her stepmother what had been going on beneath her very nose for the past three years.

"Any truth I have is my own, and I choose not to share it."

Her stepmother's eyes narrowed. "Very well, then. I shall leave you with your precious truth, and you may dine and drink upon it. I daresay when it fails to satisfy your hunger or your thirst you will be ready enough to give it up."

The duchess backed out of the room and shut the door

behind her. Lucy heard the key turn in the lock. With a large sigh, she flung herself on the bed. She was utterly tired of the sound of doors slamming, for somehow she always seemed to be on the wrong side of them.

For as long as he lived, Nick was never going to rescue anyone again. Especially not blue-eyed scullery maids who tasted of a volatile combination of temptation and suffrage.

Seated on a wooden crate, he leaned against the casks of port in the anteroom, the discarded walking dress wrapped around his bare shoulders for warmth. Crispin had yet to return, but when he did, Nick was ready to give him an earful.

Complete, unmitigated disaster. Day and night from Hades. Humiliation and wounded pride. And those were the good parts of his encounter with the hellion disguised as a kitchen maid.

No, that was a lie. He loosened the dress about his shoulders, warmer at the thought of her. To be brutally honest, the best bits had been when she'd been so close he could smell the unique scent of her, and he could feel her body pressed against his own. Even now, angry and disillusioned, he could scarce forget the sensation of her arms wrapped around his neck and her breasts soft and enticing against his chest.

It should be easy to let her go. Her desertion was motivation enough, but given her political views, he should have no problem relinquishing this quest for her safety. Call it reform or revolution or any manner of names, her cause was still what had killed his mother and sister, and he wanted no part of it. There was no point in trying to change the world. He knew that deep within, which was what made his penchant for rescue so ridiculous. It was like trying to empty the English Channel with a teacup. The Channel remained eternally full, and the teacup ended up dashed to bits.

Nick shivered. Long minutes passed as he waited for

Crispin's return, and he was on the verge of tapping a cask of port when the lock turned in the anteroom door and it swung open.

A grinning Crispin peered around the corner. "Where is she?" he asked in a conspiratorial whisper. "I trust you made good use of this opportunity, old man. I had a devil of a time convincing Grandmama's footmen to leave you here. The poor lads thought they'd all be carted off to a Santadorran dungeon to rot."

Nick stood. "The footmen have no cause for concern. You, on the other hand, might think long and hard before returning to Santadorra in the near future. For you, there just might be a spot on the rack."

Crispin laughed. "Give over, Nick. You can thank me later. Now, where is she?" He looked genuinely puzzled, and, for a moment, Nick considered giving his friend a taste of his own medicine and locking him in the coal cellar. Fortunately for Crispin, Nick knew that his friend had meant to do him a good turn, however misguided his actions.

"The girl in question is gone." Nick strode out the door without looking back. A moment later, Crispin followed.

"What do you mean she's gone? There's no way out other than the door."

"She went out the window."

Crispin sighed. "You must have helped her, then. Are you daft?"

Nick stopped in the middle of the hall and swiveled on his heel. "Don't push, Crispin. I'm only inches from thrashing you as it is. Yes, she's gone, and yes, I helped her, but she lied. She said she'd come back round and unlock the door for me."

Nick would have liked to wipe away the broad grin that stole over his friend's face, but at that moment, two scullery maids appeared at the other end of the corridor. With a look of understanding, he and Crispin took the shortest route to the kitchen, emerging onto the street just below the main entrance.

"So, she outsmarted you, did she?" Crispin chuckled. "You must be losing your touch, St. Germain. There was a day when women actually ran toward you instead of away from you."

Nick stood in the shadow of the stairs, uncomfortably aware of his half-dressed state. "This one may run as far away as she pleases. In fact, the farther she runs, the better."

Crispin's eyebrows lifted in surprise. "Those didn't appear to be your sentiments this morning at Madame St. Cloud's."

Nick refused to acknowledge the tightening in his midsection. "This morning, I didn't know she was a revolutionary."

"A what?" Crispin's jaw dropped.

"Close your mouth, man. You heard me correctly. Actually, she called herself a reformer, but we both know there's not a farthing's worth of difference between the two."

"A reformer? Are you sure?"

"I heard it from the girl herself. She's for universal suffrage. Wants the vote for all the poor working men who've been trod upon by the aristocracy. Thank heavens she didn't know my true identity. She'd probably have cracked my head open with a coal scuttle and been on her way."

Crispin snorted in disbelief. "Hardly. I've seen enough females smitten with your charms to recognize the symptoms. Really, Nick, I thought you'd use this chance to full advantage. She's a lovely girl."

Nick lifted a hand in protest. "Even if she weren't a revolutionary, she's a kitchen maid, and you know my feelings about dallying with servants."

Crispin was quiet for a moment. "Quite so." He appeared to be lost in thought, and Nick debated for a moment whether it might not be the perfect opportunity to draw Crispin's cork for the trouble he'd caused. He was, however, standing in the middle of Mayfair with a woman's walking dress wrapped about his shoulders.

"Where's your carriage?"

"Over there."

"Then the least you can do is take me home."

The two men crossed the short distance to Crispin's stylish barouche. Once they were inside and moving, Crispin spoke.

"Look, Nick, I didn't intend to cause trouble. I suppose I thought there might be a chance that—"

"That what?" Nick snapped, although he knew perfectly well what Crispin meant.

"You know. You and the girl, trapped together . . ."

Nick turned away to look out the window. "Crispin?"

"Yes?"

"Don't take any more chances on my behalf."

Evidently it was not sufficient humiliation for Nick to arrive at the Cromwell in such an outrageous costume. He crossed the foyer of the small hotel where he rented rooms and climbed the stairs, and with Crispin on his heel, opened the door to his sitting room only to be stopped by his valet. Phipps actually looked perturbed, and not by his master's outlandish attire.

"You have a visitor, Your Highness."

"A visitor? Did you not tell him I was away from home?" The valet was usually adept at rebuffing the toadeaters and other social climbers of the *ton*.

"I did try, Your Highness, but I'm afraid he insisted." The older man's thin lips showed his disapproval, but Nick knew that he, as well as the unwanted visitor, was the subject of Phipps's censure.

"I see, Phipps. Never mind. Our visitor, whomever he may be, will remove himself at my instruction, you may be sure."

Nick was spoiling for a fight. For all his bluster, he couldn't take out his frustrations on Crispin. His friend had meant well, and he'd had no idea that *she* was a public nuisance who should be locked up at the earliest convenience. Nick pushed past Phipps only to find, much to his surprise, the King of Santadorra standing before the windows that overlooked the street.

Behind him, Phipps took a deep, wheezing breath and announced, "His Royal Highness, Leopold, King of Santadorra."

Nick smothered a curse. "Yes, Phipps. I'm aware of who my father is."

The king stepped forward, looking well turned out in a bottle-green coat and buff pantaloons. His father's attire only served to make Nick more aware of his own dishabille.

"Well, son, I'm pleased to see you looking so well." The king stepped forward to examine him, one eyebrow arching in the very way Nick knew his own did. "I have been worried about you. Silly of me, I suppose. What father would worry about a son who returns home mid-morning wearing a *woman's gown!*" During this speech, his father's famously deep voice swelled to a bellow.

"Hello, Father. Delighted to see you as well." Devil take it! Of all the times for his father to arrive unannounced. He hadn't known the king had left Santadorra. With a calm he didn't feel, he turned to the valet. "Phipps, would you be so good as to ring for the tea tray? I'm sure my father finds himself in need of refreshment."

"What I find myself in need of is a son who is fit to be the heir to my throne!" The king could not hide the flush that underscored his aristocratic cheekbones.

"Yes, well, then you'd best marry again, hadn't you, Father? I suppose it's not too late. You are not, after all, completely past your prime."

His father failed to even wince as that barb struck home. The older man was as tough as boot leather, and Nick would do well to remember that. He hated being caught at a disadvantage, but it seemed that when it came it his father, he was always at a loss. "Perhaps you would care for something a bit stronger than tea?" he asked, strolling to the sideboard. "Sherry? Or brandy? As I recall, that was always your favorite. Or if you like, I can send Phipps to the cellar for a particularly fine Madeira I won recently on a wager."

"It's not yet noon." The scorn in his father's voice was as familiar to Nick as his own face in the mirror. He knew he did it purposely, this antagonizing of his father, but if there was no approval to be found, then he might as well make himself deserving of the disapproval.

"Yes, well, all the more reason to start," Nick replied. "It makes the rest of the day so much more palatable." With a casualness he did not feel, Nick removed the stopper from the brandy and poured a large amount into a glass. He could feel his father's eyes upon him as he arched his neck and downed it in one long swallow.

The impact almost gagged him, but no one would have ever known. He turned back to the door where Crispin hesitated, half in and half out of the room.

"You'd best come inside, Crispin. Perhaps if you are present, my father and I will behave with more civility than usual."

"Yes, Crispin, do come in," his father echoed, "if only to let me gaze upon the kind of man I wish my son could be."

"Hello, Your Highness." Crispin, that model of rectitude, bowed to Nick's father. "I'm pleased to see you again, though I daresay you overrate my virtues."

The king laughed and walked toward Crispin, extending the hand that he had not proffered to Nick. "Yes, well, do not let it go to your head. It does not take a great deal of character to look virtuous next to my son. I had just relented and sent him his quarterly allowance, and I understand from the bankers it is gone."

Crispin's smile faltered. "I think you might be surprised, Your Highness, to learn that—"

"Crispin," Nick interrupted, "would you care for a brandy?"

"No, thank you, Nick." Crispin glowered at him, but Nick turned away. If the king chose to think ill of his only son, then Nick was determined to let him do so. He had long ago learned not to defend himself.

"Then perhaps you had best make yourself scarce after all." He knew he was being unpardonably rude, just as he knew Crispin would understand.

"Yes, of course." Crispin might be outrageous at times, but he was also forgiving of Nick's occasionally autocratic behavior. "However, Nick, there is one small matter that I really ought to—"

"We can meet for a light nuncheon, Cris. At White's? I'm sure my father would be delighted to join us."

"Yes, certainly, Nick, it's just that I needed to tell you something with regard to Lucy."

"Lucy?" his father asked. "Who is Lucy?"

"No one," Nick snapped, and then wished he hadn't, for his abrupt response was too revealing. "We'll speak later, Cris."

"But, Nick, I really believe you ought to know that—"

Nick interrupted him by virtue of grabbing his arm and hauling his friend to the door. His father trailed behind them, an interested and interfering spectator.

"Lord Wellstone does not look as if he is yet ready to depart," the king admonished his son, but Nick ignored him.

"At White's," he reiterated.

"But Nick—"

"Are you sure you don't want your friend to hear my news?" the king asked.

"News?" Nick froze in his steps. There was a note of satisfaction in his father's voice that made him instantly wary.

"Yes, news of the Regent's latest whimsy."

Nick felt a prickle up his spine. His father generally had little use for the Prince of Wales, a dissipated roué who ruled in the mad English king's stead.

"You have come all this way because of Prinny?"

"No, but I have come all this way to attend a ball at Carlton House."

Nick stared at his father in confusion. The entertainments at the Prince Regent's home were legendary, but hardly the stuff to draw his father all the way to England.

"What makes this ball so unique that it would entice you from your lair?"

"Why, its purpose of course."

"And that would be . . ."

"To find you a bride. Once you make your choice, we'll arrange for a wedding straightaway."

Nick felt the blood rush to his head. "You can't be serious. You are not some medieval despot, and I am no prize to be won."

"Indeed, I am quite serious." His father wore the look of a victorious warrior. "The invitations went out this morning. I have just come from Carlton House where the Prince Regent and I have been consulting about the menu."

"The menu?"

"Yes, of course. We expect to seat several hundred at dinner, but the ball will include considerably more. After all, we couldn't invite just the young women, could we? Had to round out the company."

Surely it was a jest. Nick looked at Crispin and saw a guilty tinge of red around his friend's ears.

"You knew." The accusation was soft.

"I didn't know precisely. That is, your father did write to me in the most general terms . . ."

Nick looked at the pair of them, first one and then the other. Betrayers, both of them.

"I will not cooperate. You might as well rescind the invitations immediately."

"Very well," his father said, disturbingly agreeable. "I shall give you a choice. You may choose to participate in these festivities or you can return with me at the end of the week to Santadorra. The choice, of course, is yours."

But it was really no choice at all, and his father knew that. When he had left Santadorra, after he had cried over his mother's grave and mourned the lack of even his sister's remains to bury, he'd sworn to his father with the feverish passion of childhood never to return.

"And what must I do to fulfill my part in this scheme?" He felt his father's machinations tightening like a noose around his neck. Much as he'd felt in the presence of his exasperating scullery maid. The comparison made him shudder.

"What must you do, Nicky? Ah, only something quite simple." His father smiled with satisfaction. "All you must do, my dear boy, is choose a bride. After all, it is more than past time to insure the succession of the Ivory Throne."

Nick knew he was trapped. His father would not balk at enlisting the Santadorran Guards to kidnap his own son. If he failed to comply with his father's wishes, he would feel his native soil beneath his feet before many days had passed.

"You have planned this very carefully, I see."

"Indeed, sir, I have. For the last seven years since you reached your majority, I have left you to your own devices, but no more. Now I have taken matters into my own hands."

Nick forced himself to breathe, for he knew his father had him at *point non plus,* just as he knew that the only woman he'd met in a great while who even interested him was a golden-haired chit with a penchant for reform. "Then carry out your plan, sir, and I wish you joy of it. As for myself, I expect to find none."

He turned toward the bedchamber, leaving his father and Crispin in the sitting room, and with a weary heart, a growing sense of doom, and a woman's walking dress still wrapped about him, he crossed the threshold as if headed for the gallows.

Chapter Seven

Lucy must have slept several hours upon the rickety cot in the corner of the attic room, for when she roused, bright midday sunshine fell across the scarred planks of the floor. For a moment, she gazed at the unfamiliar surroundings, and then memories came flooding back, vivid pictures of the heroic gardener and his chocolate eyes and the awful mistake of depending upon him that she'd nearly made.

Angry warmth stole through her veins. He had insisted on rescuing her, had clapped her in irons, and then, when he'd discovered her passion for reform, he'd turned cold as ice. Lucy pounded the thin mattress beneath her with one fist. Like so many others, he wanted no part of the true Lucy Charming, of her passions and dreams. Drat the man, anyway. She'd not asked for his help, had never sought his good opinion. But, oh, how she ached when she recalled the coldness that had dropped over him like a curtain as she'd expounded on the glories of reform.

Her anger, though, quickly gave way to a bone-deep

weariness. She had done her best in the last eight years, since her father's death, to be true to her heart, and now the heart she'd always depended upon for guidance had proven fallible. She'd been tempted by the promise of a hero—someone to share her burdens and her goals, someone to depend upon. She'd been tempted, and she'd succumbed, and the cost of her weakness was the even deeper sense of loneliness that settled over her like a blanket.

Lucy rolled onto her back and contemplated the cracks in the low ceiling above her head. The escapades of the last day and night had made one fact perfectly clear: She was neither a true reformer nor a true aristocrat. Had her father felt this way, she wondered, never truly accepted by the working men he championed and shunned by the privileged men he challenged? Had he, too, existed in some sort of strange netherworld? And, finally, the most bone-chilling question of all, were her stepmother's insinuations correct? And was this very feeling the reason he might have taken such a drastic step? Lucy's stomach rolled at the thought. Had her father's death indeed been a horrible accident, a mere slip of the fingers while cleaning his dueling pistols, or had the discharge of the weapon been deliberate?

With an angry hand, she swiped at the tears that pooled in her eyes. No, her father would never have left her alone by choice. And yet, after the events of the last day and night, she understood why he might have despaired. Her future, which only yesterday she could have outlined so clearly, suddenly seemed hazy indeed.

Footsteps sounded outside the door, and Lucy scrubbed away the last vestige of her tears with the sleeve of her dress. The key turned in the lock. She sat up and braced herself for another battle with her stepmother, but let out a sigh of relief instead when Esmie appeared, carrying a tray of food.

"You're awake, then."

Lucy eyed her stepsister with caution. Although Esmie

was not actively vicious, as Bertha and the duchess often were, Esmie usually complied with their wishes. Her only love seemed to be for her precious books.

Esmie didn't bring the heavily-laden tray to Lucy but set it down on a small table near the door.

Lucy swung her legs over the side of the cot. "I'm surprised to see you."

Her stepsister eyed her speculatively. "Yes, I'm sure you are. Are you hungry?" She gestured toward the tray. "I brought you some nuncheon."

"Does your mother know you're here?"

"Mother? Why, of course." Esmie looked surprised. "It was her idea."

So, Esmie had been sent here for a purpose. The duchess was not relenting, merely changing tactics.

Lucy rose from the bed and moved toward the tray, but Esmie stepped in front of her before she could reach it. "There is one small matter."

"Which is?" With the duchess, there were always strings and conditions, even for a matter as simple as a cold collation of bread and cheese.

"We received an invitation an hour ago. A very important invitation." Esmie made the pronouncement as solemnly as if she were delivering a philosophical lecture.

Lucy was instantly wary. "What has that to do with me?"

Esmie shifted uncomfortably from one foot to another, an unusual state for her stepsister, and avoided Lucy's eyes. "Actually, the invitation was addressed to you, and it as much as says that Mama and Bertha and I may not attend without you. Not that I would wish to go, but Mama and Bertha . . ."

Lucy sighed. Small wonder, then, that the duchess had sent Esmie with a peace offering. "It must be from someone quite important if the duchess is willing to humble herself by including me in the party."

Esmie looked distressed. "It is only *the* event of the season, and at Carlton House, no less." Her obvious dismay at the prospect almost made Lucy smile, except that Lucy shared her stepsister's dismay, if for entirely different reasons.

"Carlton House?" The home of the Prince Regent was as legendary as the lavish entertainments held there, and neither she nor her stepmother had ever been included in its circle of guests. The thought of the Prince of Wales spending hundreds of thousands of pounds on frivolity while his subjects starved filled Lucy with indignation.

Esmie's frown deepened. "A bride-finding ball, no less, given by Prinny and King Leopold of Santadorra, for his son, the Crown Prince. Mama says if you will cooperate, you may attend. But she makes two conditions." Esmie ticked them off on her fingers. "One, you must not put yourself forward to any gentlemen, and two, on no account may you dance with anyone but Mr. Whippet."

Lucy almost laughed. Did her stepmother really know her so little? She had no use for the spectacles of the *beau monde*, but the despair that had settled upon her lifted at the intriguing idea that rose in her mind. What the reformers truly needed were allies—well-placed, influential allies who could introduce the necessary bills for suffrage into Parliament, men such as her father had been. And where were such allies to be found, if not at Carlton House? Perhaps it was time to make use of her family name and parentage. Perhaps—she hardly even dared think the thought—perhaps with her father gone, she might speak to the Regent in his stead.

Lucy's heart pounded, but she refused to reveal her agitation. Deliberately, she made her face fall. "So I am to play the wallflower."

Esmie looked truly puzzled. "You are to be included in the party. Surely that is sufficient?"

Lucy ignored her comment and tried to brush by her stepsister toward the breakfast tray. Esmie scooted back and grabbed the china teapot from among the dishes. She lifted a cup and saucer and poured. Lucy felt her knees weaken as the rich scent of chocolate assailed her nostrils.

"Have we a bargain?" Esmie held out the cup. The duchess must have promised her an entire new library, for rarely was her stepsister willing to stand her ground so firmly.

Lucy hesitated for effect, and then, finally, with a nod, accepted the cup from her stepsister.

"Are you sure we are agreed?" Esmie's impatience betrayed her anxiety.

Lucy hesitated, drawing out her response. Even those with very little power liked to exercise it when they could. "Very well."

Her stepsister nodded. "For once, Mama will be pleased," she called over her shoulder as she left the room, off to claim whatever prize the duchess had promised.

Lucy sat down on the cot with her chocolate and began to plan. She was feeling rather pleased herself at the prospect of approaching the Regent.

One o'clock found Nick waiting patiently amid the mahogany splendor of the dining room at White's. He'd regained his aplomb during the course of a vigorous scrubbing in the bath, and he was now prepared to mount a counterattack against his father. The king might believe he had devised a foolproof scheme to trap his son into marriage, but Nick was far more determined to avoid the parson's mousetrap than his father realized. Crispin arrived a quarter of an hour past the appointed time, looking quite sheepish.

"Hello, Nick." His friend stood awkwardly before him for a long moment and then sank down in the chair opposite. "Sorry to be late. I got caught in a throng that sighted Prinny's carriage and pelted it with vegetables." Because of his extravagance and his unfeeling treatment of his popular wife, the Prince Regent was not always a beloved figure.

Nick concealed his natural shudder at the thought of the mob and its potential to turn violent at the drop of a handkerchief. "I see that you escaped. Did the prince?"

Crispin shrugged. "I confess I did not wait to find out. I am sympathetic to the plight of the poor, but I doubt they would be as sympathetic toward me."

"Yes, indeed." Nick knew he must turn the conversation quickly, for the mere topic was enough to unsettle his stomach. He knew all too well the capacity for violence among the peasant class when their passions were stirred. "Shall we order our meal?"

Despite the familiar solace of beef and ale, neither man seemed quite comfortable. Crispin looked anywhere but at Nick, and Nick, for his part, chewed vigorously to keep his thoughts at bay. Finally, Nick pushed back his chair and threw down his napkin. A waiter immediately appeared to remove his plate.

"Give over, Crispin. Fortunately for you, I've decided not to hold your behavior against you, since you did manage to rid London of those thugs. But I must warn you I'm at my limit. There are intrigues afoot, and I am weary of surprises." Since Lucy had knocked him on the head with Lady Belmont's garden door, his life had been spinning steadily out of control. The effect was not to his liking.

Crispin tossed back half a glass of ale in one long swallow, wiped his mouth with his napkin, and looked Nick in the eye.

"I have a confession to make, Nick."

"Spare me from confessions and reformers," Nick muttered.

"What?"

"Nothing. I suppose you'd better get on with it, before this extremely heavy nuncheon has me slumbering in my chair. What deep, dark secret must you divulge?"

Crispin's hand nervously smoothed his cravat, which had the unfortunate effect of demolishing its smartly tied perfection.

"Yes, yes. Right. Of course. Get on with it, certainly." He drew a deep breath. "You above all people know, Nick, that I am something of an inveterate matchmaker."

Nick snorted. "Happily for you, you have never turned your talents toward me. What poor fellow's life have you gone and ruined now, Crispin? No, don't tell me. Let me guess." Nick settled back in his chair, ready for the first time since the previous morning to enjoy himself. The prospect of some other fellow's misery always did wonders for lightening one's own.

"Is it Lord Warmouth? But I must tell you that he is head over heels for Dunley's youngest chit."

"No, not Warmouth," Crispin answered, nervously tugging at his cuffs.

"Ah, then it must be my expatriate cousin, Prince Stephen. He has no prospects of a throne, 'tis true, but there might be an impoverished earl somewhere willing to part with a daughter if the settlement is large enough."

Crispin's hands now moved to pluck at his napkin. "No, Nick, not Stephen."

"The Earl of Ashforth perhaps? The paragon earl is said to be looking about for a bride."

"Not Ashforth either. Besides, he has those five children, all still in the nursery. Even I cannot find any advantages for a young woman in such a match."

"Well, then, who is it?" Nick found himself growing weary of this guessing game, impatient with his friend's reluctance. They had often shared their amusement over Crispin's unusual talent, for to date none of his "matches" had yet to turn unhappy, a fact in which his friend took excessive pride.

Crispin tossed the napkin into the middle of the table. "As you know, my methods are normally quite straightforward. An introduction here. A discreet meeting there. But I'm afraid this time I used a bit of concealment on the parties involved."

Nick grinned, glad for a bit of amusement in the midst of the complications of his own life. "How very romantic of you, Cris. I hope the pair turn out happy."

Crispin's gaze flitted about the room. "I am sure they

will—turn out happy, I mean—once they sort things through."

So a happily ever after was not assured? Nick pitied the poor chap, whomever he was. "Well? Who is it? Don't keep me in suspense, old man."

Crispin flushed, and Nick felt a small twinge of anxiety. "The thing of it is, Nick, . . . what I mean to say is . . ."

"Yes?" Really, this was carrying the drama a bit far, if all they were going to do was laugh at the prospect of some poor chap acquiring a leg shackle. "Who is your latest victim, Cris?"

Crispin turned a dark red and looked as if he might strangle before he blurted out, "You."

For a moment, the import of the word failed to sink into Nick's brain. "Me?" he asked blankly, casting about for some explanation and then hitting upon one. "Oh, of course. The ball. But I have decided to forgive you that part in my father's scheme. I know you meant well." The stiff points of Nick's shirt collar suddenly felt a bit tight and he ran his finger around his neck to loosen his cravat.

"No, Nick. Not the ball. The girl."

"The girl? What girl?" Nick waited, confused, and yet at the same moment aware of a sense of inevitability engulfing him.

"*The* girl." Crispin paused, and Nick's world teetered in the balance. Then Crispin said her name; two syllables that pronounced Nick's doom.

"Lucy," Crispin said.

"Lucy, the scullery maid?" Nick had spent last night tossing among the bedclothes, trying to escape unwanted memories of blond curls, bright blue eyes, and passion for reform.

"No, not Lucy the scullery maid," Crispin answered slowly, as if speaking to a very small child. "Lucy, the daughter of the Duke of Nottingham. Lady Lucinda Charming, actually, not to put too fine a point on it."

Nick sat immobile, the beef and ale in his stomach turning to lead. "*Lady* Lucinda?" Time stood still, and then, with a rush, reason returned. And humor. Nick burst into laughter. "Oh, I say, Cris, well done. Clever enough to fool even me for a moment. Lady Lucinda. Yes, very funny." He chuckled again and reached for his glass of ale, draining the last bit.

Crispin paled. "I'm not joking, Nick. Not about this."

But Nick was not to be taken in. "It won't wash, Cris. I saw her hands, as work-roughened as the lowest servant. And her dress, faded and patched everywhere." Nick ran a hand through his hair in relief, and yet his insides felt strangely hollow. Despite his words, he was not quite ready to joke about Lucy because he was not impervious to the temptation she represented.

Crispin leaned closer, lowering his voice. "On my honor, Nick. She is Nottingham's daughter."

But Nick was not a man to surrender without a fight. "Natural daughter, perhaps. I wondered about that myself."

Crispin leaned forward. "No, his legitimate daughter, by the first duchess."

But Nick would not give over. Not on something this important. "Then why have I never seen her? She is older than twenty, is she not? Why has she not made her come out?"

"She did, after a fashion. The season you were squirreled away at my hunting box with that bird of paradise, just to infuriate your father."

Nick shifted in one of White's usually comfortable dining chairs. "Then why does she never attend any of the *ton* affairs?"

"Her stepmother has put it about that she is not quite right in the head. Given the rumors about her father's death, the duchess was readily believed."

Nick barked with laughter. "Not right in the head? I will attest to her attics being to let, but only on the subject of reform. Otherwise she is as sane as you or I."

"Nick." Crispin caught his eye, and in the green depths of his friend's honest gaze, Nick read the truth he had been denying. "I'm sorry, Nick. It's just that . . . well, you know my nature."

Nick could see regret etched in the lines about his friend's mouth. Crispin was contrite, and that very expression convinced Nick of the veracity of his words. Suddenly, he found it quite difficult to breathe. They sat in silence for a long moment, for both men knew the consequence of Crispin's revelation.

"I didn't know about her involvement with the reformers," Crispin offered at last, "else I would never have concocted this scheme. But when I saw the two of you in Grandmama's garden, that feeling I sometimes have came over me, and it occurred to me you would make a very good match."

Nick saw his friend look at him closely, watching for any signs of forgiveness, and Nick was not sure that he would be able to produce them. Because despite his good intentions, Crispin had, in the space of less than two days, ruined Nick's life. Compromising a duke's daughter meant marriage. Marriage meant children, and children meant an heir for Santadorra, and an heir meant returning to the country he'd sworn never to set foot in again. Even he felt that much duty to the royal line.

A thought occurred to him, one that settled like a pool of lead in his stomach. "Has she known all along?"

"Known what?"

"My identity. Was her ignorance a ruse to trap me?" He thought of Lucy and her sensual response to his kiss. How sad to think it had all been playacting designed to capture a prince.

Crispin hesitated, this time reaching for the carnation that stood solitary guard in the small vase on the table. With careful, deliberate actions, he began to shred the flower into minuscule pieces. "Actually, Nick, she has no idea who you are. No, that's not true. She thinks you're one of my grandmother's undergardeners. And a rather cheeky one at that."

Crispin's words eased some of the tightness that knotted the muscles beneath Nick's breastbone. So, her response to him had not been feigned after all. He had always wondered how a woman might react to him as simply Nick St. Germain rather than as the Crown Prince of Santadorra. Nick crumpled his napkin into a ball. Now he knew. She would abuse him, torment him, and force him to burn with desire, damn her eyes. And all the while she would believe him to be a gardener.

Nick threw his napkin onto the table with an oath. There was no question now that he would have to make an offer for the chit. Crispin had tied his hands. Nick slumped back in his chair. Still, there was one thing Nick could do. There was time to see if she might truly come to care for him, and not the crown he would one day wear. The deep appeal of that thought hurt. Would Lucy be willing to throw away her passion for reform for a mere gardener? And was Nick the man to persuade her to do it? The challenge of discovering the answer to these questions gave him purpose.

He straightened. "I believe, Cris, that Lady Lucinda must be invited to the ball at Carlton House." He smiled, suddenly feeling much more certain of himself.

Crispin's ears turned red. "Actually, she has been."

Nick stared at his friend for a long moment. "You realize that when we leave here today, we are going straight to Gentleman Jackson's and strap on a pair of gloves."

Crispin blanched, and then nodded. "Yes, Nick. Perfectly understandable thing to do, given the circumstances."

Nick eyed his friend carefully. "And you've no objection to my pummeling the daylights out of you?"

Crispin smiled weakly. "Of course I object, but I doubt it will do any good."

Nick nodded. "Quite right."

They rose and quitted the room. As they stepped through the portals of the exclusive club and descended the steps, Nick turned to Crispin.

"You will see she has an appropriate gown? I doubt her

stepmother will have her fashionable interests at heart." Lucy might be a reformer, but she was a woman as well. Finery should not be neglected merely because of her misguided political principles.

Crispin nodded in agreement. "I'll visit Madame Paradis today. My grandmother mentioned that the Duchess of Nottingham patronizes her, much to the modiste's dismay. With any luck, she may have Lady Lucy's measurements."

Nick halted. *Lady Lucy*. The title rang through him with the clarity of a church bell, much like the wedding bells that would seal his fate.

Chapter Eight

Lucy's extraordinary dress had been the last to arrive at Nottingham House the morning of the Carlton House ball. In fact, her stepmother barely noted the delivery of the fourth and final parcel from the exclusive shop of Madame Paradis. Indeed, the duchess and her daughters were too enraptured with their own mysterious gifts to pay any mind to Lucy's delight. She had stood at the window of the salon as her stepmother, Bertha, and Esmie untied strings and ripped away brown paper to reveal three elegant ballgowns, far superior to the made-over gowns they'd spent the last few days piecing together. Other packages within had held fans, ribbons, and dancing slippers. Even Esmie could not keep from fussing over their largesse, and Lucy swallowed her disappointment while chiding herself for her vanity. She did not need a new length of silk, transformed at the cost of some poor seamstress's eyesight, to accomplish her purposes at Carlton House. Her ancient gray bombazine would serve.

But her high-mindedness had melted when her fingers pulled back the paper on her own parcel to reveal the

most extraordinary gown she'd ever seen. She shook it
out, and the gleaming folds of white satin streamed out
around her. An overdress of silver filigree followed, as
well as a white evening cloak trimmed with ostrich feathers. Silk dancing slippers and a pair of long white silk
gloves, together with a rope of brilliants for her hair and
an ivory fan, completed the ensemble.

"What is this?"

From her position on the floor, Lucy looked over her
shoulder to find that she'd garnered her stepmother's
attention at last.

"Our mysterious benefactor has included me in his beneficence as well." Lucy held her head high and looked
the duchess in the eye. She could see her stepmother
considering whether to reject the gifts, but greed overcame spite, and Lucy was allowed to keep the dress.

Now, as Lucy climbed the steps of Carlton House on
trembling legs, she knew that when it came to advocating
for reform, the extraordinary dress would have to work
the magic that plain Lucy Charming could not, for she
was frightened to death. When she glanced up to take in
the overwhelming grandeur of the Corinthian columns
that lined the porte cochere, the feathers on her cloak
tickled the edges of her face. Heart racing, she clutched
the ivory fan in her gloved hands and willed her nerves
to depart.

"Keep your chins up," the duchess advised her daughters as their party, which to Lucy's dismay included the
Reverend Mr. Whippet, entered the grand foyer. The
black-and-white marble tile and heavy gilt furniture left
no doubt as to the royal status of the house's owner. Lucy
trailed behind the others as they crossed the vestibule to
the magnificent circular staircase and descended. The
ball was to be held on the lower level in the huge conservatory that adjoined the Prince Regent's massive dining room, overlooking the gardens. Liveried footmen
lined the corridors and anterooms as they descended,
and the sound of music and laughter grew louder.

"Dinner will have been served," the duchess said in an undertone. "Several dinners, in fact. The Prince Regent had four dining pavilions erected in the garden just for this occasion." She sniffed. " 'Tis a pity we were not accorded the honor of an invitation to dine. At the fête honoring his regency, there were more than one hundred dishes."

"More than a hundred dishes? For a thousand people?" Lucy was aghast.

"Enough food to feed the East End for a fortnight," Mr. Whippet boasted. "But I daresay tonight's entertainments were scarcely less extravagant."

Lucy blanched, thinking of the cost of this ball and feeling guilty for her anticipation of it, even if it were only a means to an end.

They had reached the dining room, and Lucy could see the entrance to the conservatory. They stopped just outside the doors where footmen took their cloaks, and then they moved forward, crossing the entrance to the conservatory cum ballroom. Mr. Whippet gave the major-domo their names.

The elderly, periwigged man nodded as solemnly as if the clergyman had just conferred a knighthood upon him. "The Duchess of Nottingham, Lady Lucinda Charming, the Reverend Mr. Whippet, and the Misses Fortunes," he intoned, his voice resonating over the raucous noise of dancers and musicians.

A few heads turned, and the duchess nodded to several acquaintances as they made their way into the ballroom. Lucy trembled at the sight of such costly elegance. Hundreds of people crowded beneath the high, gothic arches of the conservatory. The open-air reform meetings Lucy had attended with her father as a child had made her comfortable with crowds, but still her pulse skittered as her stepmother steered them around the edge of the room. A profusion of flowers, candles, and silks in the Santadorran royal colors of ivory and sapphire covered every available surface. Matching ribbons had been threaded through the orange trees, and even the birds in their cages sported sapphire and ivory plumage. Overhead, the fan-shaped wrought-iron and glass ceiling reflected the whirl of color and movement.

Lucy could feel the curious stares of the guests. The duchess drew Lucy to her side and whispered in her ear, "Stop staring. And try not to look mad as a hare. They're all thinking of your father, you know."

The duchess's harsh words reminded Lucy that the Charming name was still the object of public speculation. The thought galvanized her. Lucy forced herself to relax and appear as natural as possible, even though she was tempted to leap for one of the chandeliers and swing back and forth. How dare complete strangers gossip about her, or believe the worst of her father?

Her stepmother was gesturing to Mr. Whippet, but it was a moment before comprehension dawned. Lucy could hardly stand to look into his florid face, and she could not suppress the memory of him barking for Henny while she and Nick hid in the wardrobe at Madame St. Cloud's.

"Lady Lucinda." He bowed formally over her hand. "You will want to dance. Let me be the first to engage you."

Lucy started to refuse, but her stepmother trod upon her toe. "Ouch! Very well," she agreed and tried not to shudder when she laid her hand on the vicar's arm. He seemed not to notice her distaste as he pulled her into the steps of the gavotte.

"You acquit yourself very well," Mr. Whippet said after they had settled into the set. Lucy nodded and tried to discourage conversation, but Mr. Whippet would not cooperate. "I suppose your stepmother has given you the news."

"News?" Lucy's spine tingled. "What news would that be, sir?"

He smiled, only his expression was more like an eel writhing across his face. "I am surprised you have not been informed. But, I suppose the duchess saw no need to consult you, since it is really not your decision to make."

"Decision? Pray, what decision would that be, sir?" Mr. Whippet's pudgy hand caught hers as she pirouetted around him, and Lucy wanted to snatch it away.

His eyes dropped, and Lucy could feel him ogling her bosom. "Your stepmother has given me permission to pay my addresses to you, my dear. In fact, she has agreed that there is no reason the wedding cannot occur as soon as the banns have been read."

"Wedding? Whose wedding?" Surely not. Even her stepmother would not dare, but the thought did nothing to quiet the sudden pounding of her pulse in her ears.

The dance brought her into Mr. Whippet's arms. "Why, our wedding, Lady Lucinda. It was rather difficult of your father to settle such a large dowry on you instead of leaving it to the duchess, but in the end it will not matter. Your stepmother and I will split the money between us. And I will have you, of course." His hand slid down her arm and brushed her hip, making Lucy's flesh crawl. "I'm sure you will provide ample compensation for the blunt I've sacrificed to her grace."

Lucy was so horrified she could not speak. Instead, she looked up from the steps of the gavotte to find two sets of eyes watching her every move. The first set of eyes, a frosty gray pair, belonged to her stepmother. The second, a deep green, belonged to Lord Crispin Wellstone, his satisfied smile very broad.

Crispin had to admit to himself that the trap had been neatly laid. And now Nick's future bride danced with grace in the most exclusive ballroom in the land. Nick was watching from the shadows, where Crispin had banished him as soon as the majordomo had announced Lucy's party, and Crispin could only hope Nick was appropriately befuddled by the sight of his scullery maid in all her finery. With her silver-and-white adornments, she looked exactly like a dove, the royal bird of Santadorra. The symbolism would not be lost on Nick.

At that moment, the music ended. Before the duchess could make a move toward her stepdaughter, Crispin approached the cluster of men that quickly gathered around Lucy and the odious Mr. Whippet. He arrived in time to hear Lord Eisley's youngest pup requesting the honor of a dance.

"Certainly not," Crispin said and planted himself between Lucy and the dandy in question. He nodded to Mr. Whippet. "Good evening, sir. If you do not object, I will steal away your young charge. She did promise me this dance."

Mr. Whippet sputtered in protest, but Crispin ignored him. He bowed to the lady in question. "Lady Lucinda."

"Lord Wellstone." Lucy looked uncomfortable as she placed her hand on his arm, but she accepted his invitation to dance with no resistance. That was good, for Crispin was afraid that shortly she would be putting up a great deal of resistance indeed.

Poor Nicky. It was said that truth was painful, and the Crown Prince of Santadorra was soon to find out exactly how much so when he revealed himself to Lucy Charming. With his free hand, Crispin rubbed his still-sore jaw. He for one planned to enjoy every moment of it.

If Lucy had been any more mortified by the viscount's notice, she would have turned to stone on the spot. Her stepmother would be furious. Even now, over Lord Wellstone's shoulder, she could see the duchess hustling forward with Bertha and Esmie in hopes of catching his eye. Lord Wellstone led her into the country dance that was forming, and she had little thought to spare as she was propelled up and down the line of dancers. Lord Wellstone did not try to converse when the pattern of the dance brought them together. Instead, he smiled as if to reassure her, or to brace her for something unpleasant. Lucy's spine tingled.

The dance went on forever, the fervor of the dancers increasing with each pass up and down the reel. When the final turns were complete, Lucy was breathless and face to face with Lord Wellstone at the far end of the conservatory. A few steps away, the glass doors stood open. The gardens beyond were lit with a profusion of Japanese lanterns.

"I should return you to your stepmother, Lady Lucinda, but perhaps we could both use a bit of fresh air?"

If another man had issued the invitation Lucy might have doubted his intentions, but the viscount's interest in her seemed brotherly, not loverlike. Perhaps he felt sorry for her, for the complete jumble she had made of her life by involving herself with his grandmother's gardener. Still, she didn't need his pity. What she needed was an introduction to the Regent, and despite the risk of her stepmother's displeasure, Lord Wellstone might be the key.

Lucy nodded. "A bit of air would be lovely." The viscount offered her his arm and they slipped, unnoticed, from the conservatory.

Chapter Nine

"I will take the blame if the duchess scolds you," Lord Wellstone reassured Lucy as they ventured across the lawn that sloped down to the gardens. "I'm quite adept at blame-taking, having had years of practice."

His smile was really quite nice. If she had not met Nick, she might find Lord Wellstone very attractive, actually. But somehow his well-bred English air paled next to that of Nick and his rougher peasant ways.

Taking her silence for acquiescence, Lord Wellstone led her deeper into the garden until they had passed the last string of lanterns. Lucy wondered if it might be a good time to broach the subject of the Regent. Her stomach rumbled, both from nerves and hunger, for she had been too nervous to eat earlier.

"Really, Lord Wellstone, perhaps this is far enough. I doubt the air could get any fresher."

"Have you seen the maze?" He tugged her onward and she thought about resisting, but Lord Wellstone radiated affability.

"The maze?"

"Rumor has it that the Regent had it built so that he could hide from Princess Caroline if she ever called at Carlton House," he said, referring to the prince's estranged wife.

Curious, Lucy followed him into the twisting corridors formed by thick hedges. Lord Wellstone had clearly been there before, as he seemed to know his way quite well. She could hear the soft fall of water into a basin and guessed there must be a courtyard ahead. A few minutes more and they stepped into the center of the labyrinth.

Several torches burned around the edges of the courtyard. In the center, a small fountain cascaded into a large marble base. Stone benches stood guard at precise intervals around the circle.

"Charming, isn't it?" Lord Wellstone said and then winced. "No pun intended, of course."

"It's very pretty," Lucy replied, her unease growing. She was realizing what she'd done. At the most fashionable party in the kingdom, she had left the ballroom with a man who was not her husband and she was alone with him. Heavens, she would be a social pariah before she ever met the Regent.

"I should return to the duchess." Lucy edged back the way they'd come. She glanced over her shoulder and eyed one of the openings into the courtyard. That was the way, wasn't it? All of the portals now appeared frighteningly similar.

"Her grace will not worry. She knows you are with me." Lord Wellstone exuded patience, but Lucy's instincts told her not to take his demeanor at face value.

"Of course she will not be worried, but I did so want to meet the Regent and his guest, the Crown Prince of Santadorra," Lucy said. "Perhaps you could introduce me?"

Crispin smiled very strangely, which set Lucy's nerves farther on edge. Lord Wellstone was up to something, she was sure of it. And yet she did not sense any danger.

"I suppose you wish to discuss reform with Prinny," he

said. Lucy winced. Clearly she was a very transparent female.

"Yes," she replied honestly. "I wish to persuade him to throw his support behind the Whigs. It was the only real way I could think of to help. Somehow yelling 'huzzah' at secret meetings seems rather ineffectual."

Lord Wellstone smiled indulgently, as if she were a small child who deserved a treat. "My dear, women far more ingenious than you have attempted to persuade the Regent around to their way of thinking for years. What makes you think you will succeed where they have failed?"

Lucy refused to be cowed. "I doubt those women ever stood in the midst of a Luddite rally. I doubt they ever nursed wounds made by a soldier's pike."

Lord Wellstone nodded, more serious now. "Indeed, I'm quite sure they have not. As you know, I am not unsympathetic to your plight. Perhaps I can be of some help. If you will wait here, I will see if I can entice the Regent to take a turn in the garden. No promises, mind you, but I'll do my best."

Lucy could hardly believe it. His compliance seemed too good to be true. "Very well," she said cautiously. "I will wait here, but no longer than a quarter of an hour."

Lord Wellstone bowed. "A quarter of an hour it is, then." He slipped from the courtyard, and Lucy noted the corridor he had taken. She only hoped he would be successful in bringing the Regent to her, for she did not relish the prospect of finding her way out alone. She shivered, and, wishing that she'd brought a shawl, sank down on a bench to await her rendezvous with what was surely her destiny.

Nick stood behind the shrubbery and fumed. Why would Crispin make such a ridiculous promise to Lucy? Certainly his friend had no intention of fetching the Prince Regent and dragging him into the maze. Even if she was the most misguided female Nick had ever met, she did not deserve to have her hopes elevated when there was no chance of them being fulfilled.

Peering around the corner, Nick watched her as she settled onto a marble bench near the fountain. With her silvery gown and her hair piled high atop her head, she looked as if she had been spun from his recent dreams. He had still not quite recovered from his first glimpse of her in the ballroom, for in the midst of the pageantry and splendor, she had seemed the ultimate in feminine elegance. But, here, wrapped in a cloak of darkness, she appeared as ethereal and timeless as a moon goddess.

Nick snorted at that thought. He of all people knew how deceiving Lucy Charming's appearance could be.

Cautiously, Nick stepped into the courtyard. His evening slippers moved noiselessly over the grass until he was within a few paces of her. He saw the exact moment she sensed his presence, for she tensed and then leaped to her feet.

"Good evening, princess."

Lucy's eyes reflected surprise, then shock, and finally bewilderment. "Nick?" She took in his attire, her gaze traveling from the sapphire stickpin in his snowy cravat to the ivory stockings and silver-buckled evening shoes. It was a far cry from the gardener's smock and his old boots. "Oh, Nick," she wailed, crestfallen. "What have you done?"

"Done?" he echoed, confused. Lucy was frantically looking about and wringing her hands.

"Nick, you'll be caught. This is mad, impersonating a gentleman. Whatever possessed you to do such a thing?"

Nick stopped himself from grinning. Even though she held his heroism against him, she still didn't want him to land in the soup. Definitely a good sign. He decided to play along for the moment. Pressing his advantage, he stepped closer.

"Would you believe me if I said I came so I might see you?"

She hesitated, and he saw understanding dawn in her

eyes. "You know who I am." It was not a question but a statement of fact. Her hands fluttered at her sides, reflecting the sudden panic in her eyes. "I suppose Lord Wellstone told you. The two of you seem to have an unusual bond."

Not ready to reveal the exact nature of his friendship with Crispin, Nick sidestepped the implicit question. "Lord Wellstone thought I should know the truth."

"Why? It serves no purpose." She dropped her gaze. "We are nothing to each other."

"Really, Lucy? Nothing?" Even if she hated him for his actions or his lack of sympathy for reform, he would hardly call the sparks they struck off each other "nothing."

She turned away so that he couldn't see her face. "Why did you come, Nick, especially after the trick I played on you? The risk is too great."

The truth tumbled easily from his lips. "I came to see you."

She was trembling. Nick's chest tightened at the realization. "To see me?" She laughed. "How ridiculous. All you had to do was venture through the garden door. You've known where to find me all along."

Nick instinctively rubbed the back of his head. "The last time I ventured near a garden door, you knocked me on the head with it. Besides, Lady Belmont's gardener couldn't very well mount the front steps and ring the bell of Nottingham House."

Nick could only see her profile but he couldn't miss the deep blush that rose in her cheeks. Her embarrassment gave him hope. So, she was not adverse to seeing him again, even after the way she'd abandoned him in Lady Belmont's coal cellar.

"What are you really doing here?" She repeated the question as if he were the village idiot who could not quite comprehend things on first hearing.

"I told you. I came to see you, and it was worth the risk. You are breathtaking."

"This is all Lord Wellstone's doing, I feel sure," Lucy

said defensively. "Someone sent gowns to Nottingham House this morning. Given the proper finery, anyone can be beautiful."

Nick snorted. "Have you seen your stepmother and stepsisters this evening?"

"I said, given the *proper* finery."

"Lucy, you could send those three to the finest modiste in Paris, and they would still look like a sow and her piglets rolled up in silk."

Lucy couldn't help but laugh. The tension eased from her shoulders, and Nick found that strangely satisfying. Lucy Charming might be the most infuriating woman he'd ever met, but she had a tender heart, one that had apparently been abused for some time. Beneath her bravado and derring-do and her misguided feelings about reform, she was surprisingly vulnerable. He knew he should use that knowledge to his advantage, but it was difficult to plot strategems when he was standing with Lucy in the moonlight.

"Esmie doesn't look like a pig," Lucy said. "She's too thin."

"She's the runt," Nick shot back and was pleased to see Lucy hide a chuckle behind her fan. The light wind had shifted, stirring the tops of the shrubbery and bringing on its wings strains of music from the conservatory. "Have you enjoyed the dancing?" Nick asked, studying her face. Lucy was good at hiding things, and he wanted to know if she had at least gained some pleasure from the ball. If she was to become a part of his world she would need to be able to move comfortably in the *beau monde*, and despite her status as the daughter of a duke, little in her background had prepared her for such a role.

"I'm afraid I was too nervous to truly enjoy it," Lucy replied. "I've never danced before."

"What? Not even at home?" Surely she had been given lessons for she acquitted herself well on Crispin's arm.

"Especially not at home. I was only allowed to observe when the dancing master came."

119

Nick murmured some choice imprecations in Santa-dorran.

"Did you say something?" Lucy asked. She had turned back toward him, and Nick took that as a sign to move closer.

"No, nothing." He held out his hand. "Would you like to dance here? No one is watching, and I shall not complain if you tread upon my toes."

Lucy eyed him warily. "Where did you learn to dance?"

Nick was not to be so easily caught. "Why from the same fellow who cured me of my country accent, of course." He smiled at the memory of stumbling about his room at Eton as Crispin showed him the proper English steps.

Lucy looked as if she might decline his offer, so Nick stepped forward and took her hand before she had the opportunity to refuse him. The feel of her gloved hand in his shouldn't have the power to weaken his knees, but, alas, it did.

"It's a waltz," Lucy argued. "I've not been given permission to waltz."

"Do you think one of the patronesses of Almack's will see you out here?" Nick teased, referring to the society matrons who monitored the behavior of young women of good *ton*. "If so, I think they would be far more concerned that you were in the arms of a gardener than that you were indulging in the wicked decadence of the waltz."

"I shouldn't." She was going to refuse him. Nick scrambled for some way to keep her from returning to the ballroom.

"Ah, I see now. You are too polite to speak the truth, of course. I am a mere peasant, and you are a lady of quality. Certainly you would have no wish to dance with me."

"That is not true!" Lucy's eyes blazed, and Nick's body responded in kind. Once they were married and he persuaded her to shed these ridiculous notions of reform, their marriage should be a lively one, within the bed-chamber and without.

"But it is true, Lady Lucy." He had certainly picked the right gauntlet to throw down. "You may be a reformer, but at heart you value the distinction of social class as much as any aristocrat. Otherwise why remain at your stepmother's beck and call? You have not rid yourself of all your ties to privilege."

Compliments and words of seduction would have had little effect in bringing Lucy into his arms, but challenging her dearest beliefs worked like a charm. She straightened her spine, pulled back her shoulders, which drew Nick's attention to the daring cut of her gown's bodice, and reached for his hand.

"All men are equal," she proclaimed and moved stiffly into his arms. "And I will dance with whomever I like, regardless of his position in life."

Nick needed no further prompting. Lucy in his arms was cue enough. He pulled her close, too close, really, for a proper waltz, and swung her into the pattern of the steps. It was awkward, for her inexperience kept her from trusting his lead. The grass beneath their feet was not the polished oaken floor of the conservatory and she stumbled. Instinctively, Nick molded her against him, and Lucy gasped.

Their feet stilled, but neither one dropped their hands. "It's not a good place to waltz after all, is it?" Nick asked. Although they were standing still, he was as short of breath as if he'd run a foot race. How could he have forgotten, in a few short days, what it felt like to have Lucy pressed against him? He could gladly spend the rest of his life in the center of the Regent's maze, performing the most awkward waltz in the world, if only for the pleasure of holding her in his arms.

"Do you like me even a little, Lucy Charming?" The top of her head came to his chin. She was not looking at him, feigning interest in some object over his shoulder. With one finger, he tilted her face until he could look into her eyes. "Do you like me in spite of my gardener's smock?"

"Don't," she protested and pushed against him. He had thought she would cry. Most women would. But Lucy was frowning, and fury lurked beneath the downward curve of her lips. Nick knew he shouldn't look at those lips for too long, but he seemed unable to stop himself. After all, this was part of what he'd come tonight to discover. Would Lucy Charming fall prey to Nick the gardener as easily as she would to Nicholas St. Germain, Crown Prince of Santadorra?

"Don't what?" He had too many choices. Should he trace the curve of her jaw with a string of kisses? Or perhaps her eyelids and the delicate arch of her brows? Would his best tactic be simply to capture her lips beneath his own and remind her of the attraction that flowed between them?

He felt her muscles tense, and her arms tightened on his shoulders. She was preparing to push him away, but Nick was ready to prevent that from happening. To his surprise, Lucy's hands rose not to deny him but to clasp behind his neck. With almost grim determination, she exerted enough force to bring his head down to hers. Nick could have laughed with delight, but he had a stronger sense of self-preservation than that.

"I shall kiss you," Lucy whispered fiercely, "to show you that the differences between us do not matter to me. But I shall only do so if you agree to leave immediately. I don't know if Carlton House has a dungeon, but I'd prefer not to visit you there."

Nick would have agreed to anything at that moment. He nodded, and the next thing he knew, Lucy's mouth was pressed tightly against his. She kissed him as if she was preparing for war, but he enjoyed the touch of her lips in spite of this. He waited patiently until her patriotic fervor lessened, and before she could pull away, he seized the chance to turn the kiss from defiance to desire.

For once, Lucy seemed inclined to follow his lead. When he slid his tongue along the seam of her lips, the taste of her was as rich and mellow as he remembered. She sighed, and he deepened the kiss. All sense of time and place fled as he kissed her. It was a dangerous pastime, making love to Lucy Charming. Thought receded until only instinct remained, and Nick's instincts were as strong as any man's.

He wanted to feel her—with his mouth, with his hands, with his body. And evidently she wanted the same thing, for she pushed herself more tightly against him and her tongue pressed against his. Clearly she'd never kissed a man so deeply before, and Nick had to admit that she was not a natural. Despite her lack of inborn talent, though, he bravely soldiered on, and when he lightly stroked her tongue with his own, she caught the rhythm and responded so beautifully he almost lost control.

He reached for something to steady himself, but his hand found her breast, which only complicated matters further. The low-cut ball gown proved wonderfully accommodating as he slid his fingers against her skin, reveling in the feel of her. Slowly, he maneuvered his hand around the fullness of her bosom and cupped it in his palm. She froze, and Nick was reminded of how abruptly she'd broken off their embrace in the coal cellar. He held his breath as he waited for her reaction to this new intimacy.

"Nick," she whispered, her voice a mingling of desire and confusion. It would have been better if she had slapped him. Anything would have been more conducive to gentlemanly control than the way she breathed his name against his lips. He'd never dreamed one syllable could have him teetering on the brink.

With a groan, Nick dropped his hand, for her voice reminded him who she was and where they were. Besides, they must leave something for the wedding night. Mustn't they?

Lucy was looking at him with those big blue eyes that stole more bits of his soul with each passing moment. As he watched her, he saw the exact instant she realized what she'd done, and with whom she'd done it. She struggled valiantly, but even his little reformer was conscious of her station in life, however much she might try to deny it.

"Don't, Lucy." He refused to release her while she looked so distressed. Clearly the moment to reveal his identity had come. "It will all work out in the end." He paused, gathering his courage. "I only need to know . . . that is . . . it seems we have, well, this attraction between us, and . . ."

The torment in Lucy's eyes gave him hope. She was tortured, which meant she did care for him. At least, he thought she did, from the way her mouth had formed a little "o" at his words and the way her fingers were digging into his shoulders. "What I mean to say is . . . No, what I mean to ask is, if the differences in our stations were not an issue, would you . . ."

He could feel her, too, hovering on the brink. Her mouth moved to speak, and Nick waited with bated breath.

Marriage was not going to be so bad after all.

"Nick . . ." Lucy paused, and then she smiled so sweetly he thought he might melt into a puddle in the grass. "It's impossible. I shouldn't. You are the most infuriating, high-handed, opinionated—"

"Yes," he interrupted, not liking where her thoughts were leading her. "I admit to all that. But I want to know about you, Lucy. How you feel. Is it foolish to hope that your feelings toward me might be, well, tender?"

Nick winced. What idiotic words to choose. Who could ever tell, watching his feeble attempts with Lucy, that he had charmed most of the women in London?

"Tender? My feelings?" A teasing light gleamed in her eye, and Nick knew he'd just handed her another weapon. Not that she needed any more in her arsenal. He was hopelessly outgunned as it was. "No, I don't believe you could call them tender," she replied, but her eyes sparked with both passion and glee.

Nick had never expected to find this kind of happiness,

and he had certainly never expected the source to be an infuriating little reformer who dragged him from one end of London to the other in pursuit of her cause. It was almost a shame that her activities would end with their marriage, but she would come to understand what was due their position. Just as he would need to instruct her in lovemaking, he would also tutor her in the reality of political reform. In the end, she would be the better for it, and they would both be happy.

"I know it will not be easy for you to give up what you love so dearly, Lucy." Perhaps if he could simply channel her desire to do good deeds into a more socially respectable arena, the transition would not be too difficult for her. After all, he himself had a weak spot for lost causes. "It will be a new world for you, but it is not so very bad, once you grow accustomed to it. Some of the people are quite entertaining, provided one has had enough to drink."

Lucy frowned. "A new world? But I have spent my life among common people, Nick. It will not be new for me." She nodded in the direction of the conservatory. "I would far rather give up all *that*," she replied, "than the world of gardeners and scullery maids."

With a jolt, Nick realized the enormity of what his charade was about to cost him.

Lucy patted his shoulder. "I have no ties, except for my stepmother and stepsisters. My father's heir is a distant cousin. If I disappear from the *beau monde,* few will notice. If I am not there to be punished, my stepmother can do nothing."

Nick again felt the noose tightening around his neck. Surely she would forgive him, perhaps in a day or two. Or a week. Or a lifetime. "Lucy," he began, searching for a way out of the muddle he'd created, "I'm not sure you take my meaning."

"Oh?" She stiffened in his arms.

"Well . . . that is . . ." The music had stopped, and in the night air he could hear the sound of people approaching.

125

Laughter rang out. A large party had entered the maze, and it would be only a matter of moments before he and Lucy were spotted. Once the guests identified them, their fate would be sealed and Lucy would be thoroughly and publicly compromised.

Frowning, Lucy pushed at his arms again. "I think I see. You are not talking about marriage at all, are you?" Heat rose in her cheeks, but this blush alarmed rather than enticed him, for this was the color of anger, not embarrassment.

"Marriage?" he echoed. The word was enough to weaken his knees, and not in a good way. "Well, actually . . . to be perfectly honest . . . that is to say . . ."

The voices were coming closer, and above them all Nick heard the shrill tones of Lady Jersey, one of the patronesses of Almack's and the most inveterate gossip in London.

Lucy was struggling against him in earnest now, but Nick tightened his hold. There was nothing else to do. She was his road to ruin, the road back to Santadorra, the worst woman in the world for him, but his own heroism had brought him to this point, not to mention Lucy's myriad attractions as well. He looked down at her, his headstrong, willful, infuriating, beautiful, misguided Princess Charming, and sealed his fate by kissing her again.

Chapter Ten

Nick had made the decision to seal his fate, and so he wrapped his arms around Lucy and kissed her as if his future depended upon it, which it did. Judging by the ardor of her lips against his, she was unaware of the audience that had entered the little courtyard. The onlookers gave a collective gasp. Nick was determined to enjoy every nuance of this embrace, because once Lucy lifted her head and learned the truths he'd been hiding, she might never kiss him again.

"Nicholas!" His father's stern exclamation would have snapped a lesser man to attention, but Nick took his time ending the kiss before he lifted his head and looked defiantly into his father's eyes. He glanced at the spectators who were about to witness his descent into matrimony, their faces aglow with delight at the prospect of fresh scandal.

The King of Santadorra strode forward, his face set in hard lines. "Young man, I will have you horsewhipped for this."

The Prince Regent appeared amused, Lady Jersey was

127

taking in the sight with a shrewd lift of one eyebrow, and several other ladies of the court were fanning themselves. At the back of the group stood Crispin, hands lifted in helpless apology.

Like a lioness prepared to defend her cub, Lucy turned in his arms and placed herself between him and his father. "If you harm one hair on his head, sir, I will . . . I will . . ." She sputtered to a stop, evidently realizing that she had little with which to threaten such an elegant, imposing gentleman as his father. Clearly she had no idea who the furious older man was.

In contrast to the snowy white of his hair, the king's cheeks were a dark red. "Young lady, this scoundrel deserves everything that is about to happen to him. Luring you out here, taking advantage of you. Your reputation is destroyed."

Nick could only grin as Lucy's spine stiffened. It was nice, for once, to see someone else on the receiving end of her wrath.

"I was not lured," Lucy snapped. "I was escorted. By Lord Wellstone." She nodded at Crispin, and the entire company swiveled to stare at him. Crispin flushed before he recovered himself and rose to the occasion.

"That is true, actually." Crispin moved forward through the crowd until he stood between the Prince Regent and Nick's father. "I did escort her out here, but only . . ."

"Silence!" The command came from the Regent, whose amusement had dissipated. He turned to Crispin. "Is this the favor you asked of me? To trap your friend into marriage?"

"No," Crispin protested. "Not at all, Your Highness. I brought you out here to meet Lady Lucy."

"Lady Lucy?" The Regent turned toward her, and Nick squeezed her arm in a warning he was sure she had no intention of heeding. "And you are she, madame?"

Nick watched with pride as Lucy refused to cower before the Regent. "Yes, Your Highness. I am." Nick also breathed a sigh of relief when she failed to launch into a diatribe on the inhuman treatment of the working class. Perhaps this situation could be saved.

The Regent lifted his quizzing glass to one eye and studied her from the top of her golden curls to the hem of her gown. "My friend Lord Wellstone informs me that you have something very particular you wish to say to me, Lady Lucinda." Nick blanched. So the Prince Regent knew who she was. "I believe Wellstone said you wished to speak to me on the matter of reform?" His ennui in relation to the subject was evident.

Before she could open her mouth to speak, Nick interrupted. "Perhaps another time might be more opportune for this conversation," he said, "when Your Highness's attention is on matters of state rather than matters of pleasure."

The Regent bristled. "Are you suggesting, Nicholas, that I have not the mental capacities to entertain and rule simultaneously?"

Nick's father jumped into the breach. "Of course not, Your Highness. My son would never imply such a thing. However, given the circumstances, perhaps it would be best if we all adjourned to the house. We can sort matters out in a more private manner."

"Nicholas?" Lucy asked, looking at the Regent in puzzlement. "Your son?" she echoed, turning toward his father. She paled and then stepped away from Nick. He watched, a hard knot forming in his stomach. Those remarkably fine blue eyes narrowed, and Nick knew the time had come to pay the piper.

Lucy's cheeks had gone bright red. "You are not Lady Belmont's undergardener."

He winced. The words were a greater indictment than any that could be handed down by a court of law. "No, I am not." It was too late now for private explanations. "At least, not on my better days."

Lucy's very kissable lips pursed with distaste. "A gentleman's son. That explains your accent. And your ability to dance." She paused, and tears gathered in the corners of her eyes, and Nick felt her pain as if it was his own. "And your familiarity with Madame St. Cloud's house, of course." Lady Jersey and the other women gasped in shock, but Lucy did not appear to hear them. The flush on her cheeks traveled downward, staining the graceful curve of her neck. "From the moment we met, you have played me for a fool."

If anyone else had put that look in her eyes, Nick would have strangled him with his bare hands. Instead, he could only stand helpless as the consequences of his actions came home to roost.

"I was not aware of your identity at first, either," he said. "I thought you a servant, and you gave me no reason to think otherwise. You deceived me as much as I did you." The words were half explanation, half accusation and did nothing to soothe Lucy's temper.

"And tonight?" Lucy demanded, her voice tight. "Was this to be the culmination of your plans? This public humiliation?"

"No!" Nick stepped toward her, but she backed away. "It was meant to be a very private unveiling of the truth. You are the one who beguiled Crispin into drawing the Regent out here. I meant to meet you alone."

"It was my chance," Lucy said softly, her eyes as bright as her flushed cheeks. "My chance to help. Not just by applauding speeches and passing round petitions, but making a difference for the common man."

She turned toward the Regent, and Nick's stomach sank. Not now, Lucy. Not after they'd been caught in such a flagrant indiscretion. But his soon-to-be bride was never one to let a golden opportunity pass.

"Your Highness, if you knew what your people suffered, you would act. I know you would. If only you could see beyond this world," she said, waving to indicate the courtyard and the elegant men and women gathered there, "and realize the struggles and burdens of your subjects. I know you would not leave them to the mercies of Lord Sidmouth and the Home Office."

Filled with a sense of impending doom, Nick watched the portly Regent. For a long moment, the only sound was the splash of water in the fountain. Finally, after what seemed a lifetime, the prince responded.

"Lady Lucinda," he drawled, and the entire company stood motionless, hanging on his every word as if suspended in time, "I would advise you that reform is a waste of your apparently considerable energies. England is a prosperous nation where a man may determine his own lot in life. If he works hard, he should not know want. And if he is idle, well, then, he receives what he deserves, don't you think?"

Nick's stomach knotted. How many times had he uttered much the same words? But now, hearing them from the Prince of Wales's mouth, he was struck by their arrogance and lack of human feeling.

"Oh no, Your Highness!" Lucy protested. "Surely you cannot ignore facts! The price of bread is beyond the reach of most laborers, and enclosure has taken away their gardens and grazing for their cows. Why, in Nottinghamshire . . ."

"Nottinghamshire?" the Regent echoed, looking alarmed. "Madame, in the past we may have been forced to tolerate Luddites in the midlands, but we refuse to entertain them at Carlton House!"

Nick knew the situation was careening out of control. "She is no Luddite, Your Highness. Merely a soft-hearted creature who does not understand the complicated nature of politics."

Lucy swung around and glared at him. "Not understand? Of course I understand. I understand very well that royalty would rather enjoy the privileges of ruling than take up the responsibilities entrusted to them. I know that this," she waved her arm at her surroundings, "was built with bread taken from the mouths of children."

Their audience gave another collective gasp, and Nick resigned himself to the fact that he would shortly be courting Lucy in a dungeon somewhere. He waited for the Prince of Wales to explode, but instead, the Regent chuckled.

"Well, well, Nicholas. You have certainly picked a fiery filly to draw your phaeton. Not your usual sort of queen, is she?"

"Queen?" Lucy echoed, confused.

"No, Your Highness." He glanced toward his father. "Fortunately, the king is very healthy and Lucy should have a great deal of time to accustom herself to her future role."

"King?" Lucy had the wild-eyed look of a fox cornered by the hounds.

"I am glad that your bride will be English, as your mother was." The Regent moved forward, stays creaking in protest, as he offered Nick his hand. "The Santadorrans were our staunchest allies against Boney, and now we will be joined by the blood of marriage and not just the blood spilled in Spain and France. And in Santadorra, of course."

"Bride? Who is going to be a bride?" Lucy glanced from one man to the other, and Nick felt another prickle along his spine. He walked toward her and took one of her hands in his.

"You are, my dear. You are going to marry me. As soon as the banns can be read."

"I'll do no such thing." Lucy lifted her chin, which was always a bad sign. "Why would I want to marry you?"

Crispin chortled, and Nick shot him a silencing look. "Because, my dear Lucy, you have been hopelessly compromised. We must make it right."

"Make it right?" She laughed. "By doing something so wrong?"

Nick winced and tried not to mind being publicly ridiculed. He could feel every eye in the courtyard upon him. "Is the thought of a royal marriage so distasteful?"

Lucy paled and pulled her hand from his. "That is not amusing, Nick. I've had enough of your tricks and stratagems. You are no more a prince than I am a princess."

"But you are, Lucy. Or you will be, very shortly."

Nick felt someone at his elbow and looked around to see his father standing beside him, a look of concern on his face. "It is true, young lady. He is my son, and the prince."

Lucy looked from one man to the other, as if testing the resemblance. "And you, sir, you claim to be a monarch? Next you will try to convince me that Lord Wellstone is Napoleon's heir."

This was not how Nick had envisioned asking Lucy to be his wife. In his more fanciful moments, it had involved the satin nightrail she'd donned at Madame St. Cloud's, and even the wrist irons.

"Crispin?" Nick paused, distracted by the image of Lucy clad in nothing but satin. "Actually, he does have some cousins on his mother's side from Corsica, and—"

"Stop!" The command came from the Prince of Wales. "I have heard enough of this nonsense." He glared at Lucy. "Young woman, you have been made a very rare and valuable offer. Santadorra is a small principality, it is true, but its location is strategic and its wealth adequate. You could do worse than to wed Prince Nicholas."

Lucy looked at his father. "And that makes you?"

"King Leopold, madame. At your service." His father gave a courtly bow, and Lucy wilted.

"Oh no." Her eyes darted around the crowd. "And you all knew? You knew he was the prince?" Someone giggled, but no one replied.

In the past two weeks, Nick had often wished to see the infuriating Lucy Charming humbled, but now that it had come to pass, he regretted it deeply. She turned back to him, her head bowed. "I will never forgive you. Never." Her words were low, pitched to reach only his ears, but despite that, they fell like thunder. "You have destroyed everything I have worked for. I can only hope you have great satisfaction of it." She spun on her heel and before he could stop her, she fled the maze.

"Go after her," Crispin whispered, but Nick was welded

to the spot. Lucy was right, and he was immobilized by the sudden, clear picture of himself as seen through her eyes. Surrounded by wealth and privilege, even when he had considered himself impoverished, he had cavalierly assumed that nothing could compare to what he could offer Lucy. But misguided as it was, she felt deeply about reform. Perhaps he was a bit jealous, for since his mother's death, had anyone ever cared as deeply about him?

With Lucy gone, the onlookers disbanded, trailing along in the Prince Regent's wake as he departed the maze. Nick's father threw up his hands in disgust and went after the Regent, presumably to calm the troubled waters. Crispin crossed to Nick's side and nudged his shoulder. "Go after her, man."

"Why?" His feet felt like two great blocks of lead. "She's right, you know. I have ruined any hope she had of working for what she believes in. She wants no part of my world."

"But if she doesn't agree to marry you, the duchess will throw her out on the street. Or marry her off to someone like Mr. Whippet. She told me earlier that her stepmother had given him permission to pay his addresses. Becoming the Crown Princess of Santadorra is the more attractive option, even if it means marrying you."

Nick snorted. "Your tact is legendary, Wellstone."

"As is your arrogance, St. Germain. You wanted to play the hero. You wanted to rescue Lucy. Well, now the really difficult part lies ahead—you have to save her from herself."

Nick's shoulders sagged. "If she rejected me publicly, I hardly think she's likely to change her mind in private."

"You must make her change it, Nicky. Use your persuasive powers."

Nick snorted. "My persuasive powers, as you call them, seem to be singularly ineffective with Lady Lucinda."

"Well, you'll never know unless you try. And for once

in your life, Nick, you've chosen a woman worth persuading."

The truth in Crispin's words was difficult to swallow. Once accepted, though, they seemed to take on a life of their own. He felt his feet begin to move as he started after Lucy. He had spent his whole life avoiding the mistakes of the past. On his own, he would never have chosen to pursue someone as ill-suited for him as she was. But when she was near, he felt alive, as he'd not felt since before those dark days when he had fled the Ivory Palace with his mother and sister.

Nick gained speed with each step until he was racing through the maze. As luck would have it, she'd chosen the one corridor that wasn't lit by torches, and so he stumbled along in the dark as quickly as he could.

Lucy fled into the night, avoiding the lights and laughter of Carlton House as tears tumbled down her cheeks. Her face burned with shame. Had any woman in the history of England ever looked so unspeakably foolish?

Her fan had been lost in the maze, and somehow she was wearing only one slipper. She thought of her beautiful feather-trimmed cloak lying unclaimed in an anteroom of the conservatory. The only finery that remained was the rope of brilliants in her hair.

Lucy avoided the conservatory and found a dimly lit pathway that led around the side of Carlton House's looming edifice. In the darkness of an alcove, she collapsed against the stone, gasping for breath and allowing the tears to flow.

Fool! she scolded herself between sobs. Trusting, gullible fool! Nick had played her like a fish on a hook, and, oh, how he must have laughed at her notions of reform. Of course he was appalled, for he and his ilk were the very people the movement targeted. No wonder, then, that he had gone pale in Lady Belmont's coal cellar when she'd poured her heart out to him, or that he'd then turned cold as ice. How he must have laughed at her, he and his friend, Lord Wellstone.

And what had tonight's charade been about? To humiliate her? To seduce her? And what an idiot Lord Wellstone had been to lead all of those people into the maze. Lucy's face burned with shame as she remembered the look of bored condescension on the Prince Regent's jowly face.

She had known not to depend on Nick, and yet she had done it in spite of herself. With a bitter laugh, she pushed away from the alcove and continued down the path, following it up the slope until she emerged at the front of Carlton House. Before her, a vast array of carriages crowded the drive. Taking a deep breath, she plunged into their midst, moving as quickly as she could. She wanted only to be home, safe in her own little room and far removed from this disastrous evening. Several coachmen called out to her as she darted between landaus and barouches, but Lucy waved away their offers of assistance, swallowing back tears as she continued to run. Limping unevenly, she finally paused and removed her remaining slipper, which was filled with bits of gravel from the pathway.

"Stop that woman!" The shout came from behind her, and she turned to see Nick standing in the driveway, flanked by several men mounted on horseback, their tall fur hats and dark cloaks lending them a menacing air. Panicked, Lucy dashed away again, her legs and arms churning as quickly as the skirts of her beautiful gown would allow. She yanked the train up and flung it over her arm. The hem was filthy with mud.

Nick shouted again. "A reward for the man who stops her!" Just ahead, a coachman leaped down from his box and planted himself in Lucy's path.

"Now, miss, you don't want to run through Lunnon alone." He reached for her arm, but Lucy feinted and slipped around him. "What? Why I'll be . . ."

Lucy dared not stop. Nick's commands and the pounding of horses' hooves rang in her ears. Her first instinct was to flee toward the east where she could lose herself in the warren of streets near the river, but good sense prevailed. Instead, she cut across St. James Square, heading north toward Mayfair. It was not far to the duchess's home, and the mounted men had been slowed by the need to wend their way through the maze of carriages. If she were clever, she could evade Nick and his horsemen long enough to reach South Audley Street.

Glancing around, Lucy spied the broad steps of an imposing town home. With a frantic look over her shoulder, she dashed around the edge of the steps and down the short flight of stairs that led to a lower servants' entrance. She huddled against the cold stone of the building as overhead the horses' hooves pounded by. The men called something to one another in a language she assumed was Santadorran, and then quiet settled over the street once more.

Lucy leaned against the stone wall and drew a deep breath. She'd been an idiot to trust Nick, a fool to believe him to be a gardener. All the signs had been there, but she'd willingly overlooked them because she enjoyed his company. Enjoyed his kiss. Enjoyed the way he made her heart race and the veil of loneliness lift from around her. Now she would pay the price for such foolish fancies. Hadn't she known, since the day six years ago when her stepmother had dragged her into the study to see her father's lifeless body, that she would always be alone? That there was no one on whom she could wholly depend?

Such thoughts, though, did nothing to help her in her present situation, so Lucy banished them as she stood concealed in the dark shadows of Mayfair. Besides, eluding her pursuers had bolstered Lucy's confidence for the moment. She was not quite ready to accept her fate so meekly. Surely when it came to her ruined reputation, she had another choice besides marriage, one that did not involve Nicholas St. Germain. And one that certainly did not involve becoming a crown princess.

Lucy reemerged onto the street and turned toward home. She was almost to Piccadilly when a dark shape materialized out of the shadows. A flash of steel glinted in the moonlight, and Lucy's heart leaped to her throat. Even the West End of London was not safe from footpads. Lucy hesitated, unsure whether to retreat or to try and outrun the man.

"Give me the jewels," he hissed, gesturing toward the rope of brilliants in her hair. Lucy felt a brief pang of regret that she'd eluded Nick and his men so easily. For once, she wouldn't have minded him being around to rescue her. Lucy fingered the brilliants in her hair. To be sure, they were only paste, but she'd had so much stolen from her already this night.

"I will give you nothing. Let me pass." Her bravado was convincing, even to her own ears. The man hesitated.

With her rational mind, Lucy knew that she should just snatch the cheap bauble from her hair, fling it at the man, and run for her life, but she had lost so much tonight. Her shoes, her fan, her future. She was not ready to part with anything else.

Gathering her skirts in both hands, she feinted and then darted past the man. For a moment, he looked confused, as if no one had ever before denied the power of six inches of polished steel, much less a gentry mort with no cloak or shoes. Lucy moved quickly, and just as she was poised to break into a run once more, he grabbed her wrist. His fingers were as cold as the steely knife. "Give me the sparklers," he demanded and yanked her toward him.

Something within Lucy snapped. She was mortally tired of people grabbing her. She was tired of clawing hands and wrist irons and handsome princes who yanked her to and fro. She was tired of men with knives and scythes and pikes. Most of all, she was thoroughly tired of being at the mercy of others because she was a woman.

Lucy was not wholly unschooled in the art of defending

herself. With one quick motion, she stepped forward and lifted her knee, driving it into her assailant's groin. He shrieked and dropped to the ground as if he'd been struck by lightning. The knife clattered against the pavement and Lucy kicked it away, sending it skittering into the shadows on the opposite side of the street.

"Women are not always the easy prey you think," she said to the prostrate form of the footpad, resisting the urge to kick him again. "Good evening, sir."

Lucy was smart enough to flee while she could. She dashed toward Piccadilly and then, hovering in the shadows until the street was momentarily empty, she ran across the thoroughfare and toward her stepmother's home. Once across, she paused to look back, and to her surprise, she saw Nick and the troop of Santadorran guards standing stock still, watching her in disbelief.

Lucy hesitated, and, to her surprise, Nick lifted his hand in a salute. So, he had seen her altercation with the footpad after all but had been too far away to intervene. Surely her actions would prove that she didn't need his help.

She couldn't make out his expression in the darkness, only the outline of his form. He made no move to come toward her, and so they stood, immobile, watching each other across the width of the Circus. Lucy knew that while he'd been tempting as a gardener, he was even more so as a prince. For he had announced his intention to marry her, and she could have him, if she wanted. If she were willing to give up what was most dear to her. She could have a hero, to protect her from the villains in her life. She could depend upon him, and the cost would be the merest trifle in his eyes, only everything that made her who she was.

It was too great a price to pay, even to assuage the ache of loneliness in her breast. Without returning Nick's salute, Lucy turned and started for home. For the rest of the way, she could hear the faint sound of horses' hooves behind her as Nick and his men followed at a discreet distance.

Chapter Eleven

Lucy reached the safety of Nottingham House without further incident. The pain of her humiliation still stung, her dreams of reform lay in ashes, and the pulse-pounding fear of her encounter with the footpad had yet to subside. More than any of those things, however, the memory of Nick's kiss fed the restless agitation within her. How unfair that someone so despicable could kiss with such alarming thoroughness. Lady Belmont's gardener, indeed! He had played her for a fool, but she had let him as she ignored the warning signs and depended on him against her better judgment. She would not make that mistake again, no matter how much his eyes reminded her of her morning cup of chocolate.

The house was quiet at this late hour. Lucy changed into her oldest dress and descended to the kitchen carrying her bedraggled ball gown. Cook must have come around long enough to bank the fire. After lighting a lantern, Lucy draped the mud-stained garment over the scarred trestle table and set about rebuilding the fire and heating water. If she attended to the dress right away, she might remove the worst stains. Her magical evening might have ended in disaster, but that was no reason to neglect the beautiful work of an exploited seamstress.

Her solitude, however, proved all too brief. Scarcely a quarter hour later, she heard the clatter of a carriage and footsteps on the floor above. She sighed and put away her rags, dumping the bowl of water she'd been using into a waiting bucket. She was folding the damp dress when the door at the top of the stairs flew open and her stepmother entered. Lucy cringed as the heavy oak banged against the wall. She tensed for the onslaught of the duchess's wrath.

"There you are, you darling girl!" The duchess stumbled over her skirts in her haste and grasped the stair railing just in time to prevent a tumble. "Whatever do you mean, skulking down here in the kitchen?" she asked, as bright as a counterfeit guinea. "If there is work to be done, Lady Lucy, you must ring for one of the servants, never mind the lateness of the hour."

Her stepmother's smile was more ferocious than her frown. Lucy eyed her with caution. "I supposed I was one of the servants."

The duchess laughed, a cackling sound that would have been at home in a hen yard. "Don't be silly, dearest. I have indulged your desire for domesticity, but no one has ever mistaken you for a maidservant."

Lucy thought of the endless hours she had spent brushing out her stepsisters' hair or polishing the gleaming woodwork in the drawing room. "You have shown great forbearance, I am sure, madame, to indulge my lower nature."

The duchess looked puzzled, as if unsure whether Lucy was jesting. "Yes, well, you have always been like that, you know. Even from the first. Always vanishing into kitchens and stables at the most inopportune moments."

Lucy wanted to laugh at the irony. From the day the duchess had entered her father's house, Lucy had known her stepmother's malicious nature and had fled her presence whenever possible.

"But that is neither here nor there," continued the duchess. "The past is gone, I daresay, and we must move forward. And what a brilliant future it will be for you, too, my dear. The Crown Princess of Santadorra! I daresay the jewels alone will make you a wealthy woman."

Lucy stiffened. "There aren't going to be any jewels."

Her stepmother laughed. "Of course there will be jewels, my dear. There always are when princes are involved. They seem to have piles of them stashed away in those drafty castles. I daresay Prince Nicholas will be sending some over as soon as it is light enough."

Lucy shuddered at the thought. Other women might envision breathtaking strands of diamonds and pearls, but to Lucy they would be little different from the wrist irons Nick had used the first night they met. "Madame, you seem to be under the mistaken impression that I am planning to marry. I assure you I have no such intention."

For a moment, all was still. The duchess paled. Her tight lips thinned even further while her beady eyes narrowed until they were two small jet buttons.

"Of course you will marry him!" Her screech echoed against the cold flagstone floor and rebounded off the crumbling plaster on the walls. "He is a *prince*, for heaven's sake."

Lucy had thought her stepmother would be disgusted by the scandal, perhaps send her away to live in disgrace. It had never occurred to her that the duchess would be in favor of the match.

"There is no need for us to marry. It was only a kiss, nothing more." Her stomach tightened at the flagrant lie.

"Only a kiss?" The older woman's hand clutched the banister behind her for support. "In front of the Regent himself and the King of Santadorra? Not to mention 'Silence' Jersey? You might as well have been frolicking in the fountain in your shift."

As she'd worked on her dress, Lucy had convinced herself that the scandal would blow over, a seven-day wonder no one would recall past midsummer. The reformers would not ostracize her because of a bit of gossip in the *beau monde*. But her stepmother's words brought her fears rushing back. She had not bargained on the duchess actually desiring her to accept Nick's suit. "I care nothing for propriety or my reputation," Lucy said to forestall her stepmother's schemes. "You have already convinced the *ton* that my attics are to let. Given the gossip about my father, it will not be difficult to attribute my behavior to instability of mind."

"Why on earth would I do that?" The duchess's eyes held the gleam of a starving woman at a feast. "This is what I have waited for. Your ridiculous behavior will trap you a prince, and nothing could be better for Bertha and Esmie. Why, they will move in the very highest circles. I believe that a duke is not beyond reach for either of them, now that we are related to royal blood."

She had seen that greedy look in her stepmother's eyes before, and Lucy knew that once the duchess determined a course of action, there was little that could dissuade her. "I have declined Prince Nicholas's offer and the matter is at an end," she insisted.

Her stepmother moved toward her, and though Lucy had never been afraid the woman would do her physical violence, now she was uncertain. Venom, pure and green, shone in the duchess's eyes. "I think not. By the end of the season, you will be married. In fact," she paused and smiled coldly, "I will even grant you a choice of husbands. You may accept the Crown Prince's proposal. Or you will marry Mr. Whippet."

Lucy knew better than to show fear. She leaned forward and laid a hand on the scarred wood of the trestle table. "I will do neither of those things. We live in a more enlightened age. No one can force me to wed."

Her stepmother smiled slyly. "I understand Mr. Whippet has already informed you he has my permission to pay his addresses. I wondered if you might be difficult about him, but I never dreamed that you would catch Prince Nicholas. How fortunate that I took precautions on the way home and sent one of the grooms to Whitehall."

"Whitehall?" The name unsettled her, as the duchess had intended it to. "Surely the government could have little interest in this scandal?"

"They will not be interested in the scandal, but they will be delighted to learn that I have uncovered a plot to conceal radical reformers in my home."

Lucy's eyes flew to the door at the far end of the kitchen.

"I had no way of knowing when the information might be helpful, but it appears that time has come."

With those few words, Lucy felt herself trapped as neatly as a hare in a gamekeeper's noose, for even though the Selkirks had departed, they would not be difficult for Sidmouth's men to find, given the right information. Lucy's mind churned frantically, searching for any strategy that would overpower her stepmother's weapons, but the sinking feeling in her stomach told her it was a hopeless cause. She could never allow Mr. Selkirk and Tom to be arrested, for guilty or not of any crime, most reformers either met with the gallows or found themselves transported. The duchess held the winning hand, and Lucy's fate was the prize.

Or was it? A sudden memory of Mr. Whippet barking like a dog filled her thoughts. The idea forming in her mind was risky, but perhaps it might work. "If I agree to marry, then you will let my friends alone?"

Lucy hated the look of satisfaction that spread across her stepmother's countenance. Fortunately, the duchess would not be smug for long.

"Of course." Her stepmother raised one hand to adjust her turban. "Though the government will trap all of the radicals eventually, I suppose. It is only a matter of time."

"But their freedom from harassment requires only my

agreement to marriage?" Lucy wanted the terms of their bargain to be quite clear.

"Yes. Haven't I just said so?"

Lucy laughed. Her stepmother thought her neatly trapped, but the duchess had unwittingly left a loophole, an oversight that Lucy planned to use to her full advantage. "Then I consent. And thank you, madame." Impulsively, she leaned over and kissed the duchess's cheek.

The duchess jumped back in surprise and rubbed her face in annoyance, smearing the liberal application of rouge. "Whatever was that for?"

"Why, for helping me to make a sensible decision," Lucy replied. "Good night, madame."

Lucy bounced up the stairs, her earlier despair forgotten. She need not depend on Nick, or on anyone else, for that matter, for she herself could save the day. All was not yet lost.

The next morning, Nick stood before the Duchess of Nottingham's town house, a bouquet of early summer roses in hand. His father and Crispin stood behind him like seconds at a duel. While it was early yet to pay a call in the fashionable part of town, the deed must be done, and Nick wanted it behind him as soon as possible. Despite Lucy's protests and her abrupt disappearance the night before, she was not likely to refuse his suit. By now she would have had the opportunity to come to her senses, and he could not endure another episode like the one the night before. He'd been a hundred feet away when the footpad had pulled the knife on Lucy, and that old feeling of helpless panic had ripped at Nick's gut. No, he was going to secure his ties to Lucy and then keep her under lock and key for the rest of her life. He was determined to find himself betrothed before luncheon, and one step closer to a return to Santadorra. The thought sent another swell of emotion through him. His attempts at heroism had led him full circle, it seemed, straight back to the past he'd been running from all these years.

"There's naught to be gained standing here on the street," his father said and nudged him forward. Nick's feet seemed to have a will of their own, carrying him up the steps and into the waiting arms of fate. Crispin wisely said nothing, merely rubbed his jaw at regular intervals.

The butler escorted them to the formal drawing room. Again, Nick hesitated at the threshold, but his father, using his silver-tipped walking stick as a prod, prompted him forward. The butler, who looked as dry and withered as an autumn leaf, bowed to all three of them. "Your Highnesses, your lordship. I will inform the duchess of your presence."

Nick's father raised a hand. "It is not the duchess we desire to see, my man. We have come to speak with Lady Lucinda."

The butler's eyebrows lifted a fraction of an inch, a flagrant display of emotion for the stolid servant. "Very well, Your Highness. She is entertaining a visitor in the morning room and will attend you shortly." The butler disappeared, leaving the door ajar.

Nick wondered who else might be calling on Lucy at such an early hour. Probably one of her fellow radicals. He glanced longingly at the brandy decanter on the sideboard but decided against it. It was best to have all his wits about him when dealing with Lucy Charming.

"I have never heard of a proposal by committee," he said, pacing around the room. "I daresay I could be trusted to do this properly on my own." He cast a withering look at his father and Crispin. The king was studying the paintings along one wall, and Crispin had gone to prop himself against the fireplace, one hand on the mantel and one boot propped on the grate in a classic pose.

Crispin ignored his gibe. "I wonder who Lucy is receiving at such an early hour."

The king frowned. "Not much burdened by propriety, is she? That will change, of course, when she is your wife, Nicholas. You will see to it."

Nick thought the chances of making Lucy conform to propriety seemed remote indeed. He would rather try his hand at something simpler, like handling venomous snakes. "I have no doubt that Lucy and I shall suit each other, sir." Especially after he had molded her impulses to his liking. "As for suiting the rest of the world, that is another matter altogether."

The conversation was interrupted by the sound of a man's voice in the hall. Curious, Nick stepped toward the doorway in time to see the butler handing Mr. Whippet his cloak, gloves, and cane.

"Who is it?" Crispin asked, but before Nick could answer, he was forced to step back from the doorway and Lucy entered, trailed by that canine menace, Wellington. She lifted her chin and ignored Nick, going straight to his father. The little pug ignored Nick as well.

"Good morning, Your Majesty." She turned and nodded at Crispin. "Lord Wellstone. Thank you, sir, for sending my old friend to keep me company." She reached down and scratched Wellington behind his ears. Her greetings stopped there as she pointedly refused to acknowledge Nick's presence in the room. "Would either of you gentlemen care for some refreshments?"

Nick stepped up behind her and Wellington growled at him. "Hello, Lucy."

She tried to conceal the shiver that ran down her spine. If she'd been facing him, he might never have seen it. The involuntary reaction lit a warmth in his midsection and gave him hope. Any emotion, even hate, was better than indifference, especially in a wife.

Lucy slowly turned. "Oh, it is you, Prince Nicholas." She looked at him as if he were a particularly sticky glob of mud that had adhered to her half boots. "Forgive me. I did not notice you."

Nick breathed a sigh of relief. If she were totally set against him, or if he had proved himself beyond redemption in her eyes, she would not be treating him to such a spectacular show of indifference. Apparently he still had hope of winning Lucy's agreement to the marriage. Like most women, she was signaling her willingness to be coaxed out of her megrims.

"An understandable oversight, Lady Lucy, since I am standing behind you." He reached out and took her hand, even though she had not extended it to him. Wellington growled a second time. Lucy wore no gloves, and her hands were like ice. So she was nervous, despite her smile and calm demeanor. He raised her fingers to his lips and brushed them with a kiss.

Lucy responded as if he'd slapped her. She snatched her hand away and stepped back, narrowly avoiding Wellington as she fled to a nearby sofa. The little pug followed and tried to heave himself up onto the cushion.

"Very fine weather today, is it not, Your Highness?" Lucy asked his father brightly as she reached down and lifted Wellington onto the sofa. Crispin groaned and sank into an armchair by the fire. Nick's father cleared his throat twice and stared at his future daughter-in-law in confusion.

"Ahem, ahem. Yes, my lady. Certainly. Fine weather, and all that, but we're here to talk about—"

"Reform!" Nick interjected, and Lucy's eyes snapped toward him. She paled, and when she spoke, her voice was low.

"Have you not humiliated me sufficiently? Must you come into my home and mock me here as well before your vanity is satisfied? I suppose this is all because I did not recognize you from the first for the *prince* that you are."

Nick unclenched his jaw and tried to remember it was his behavior that had been in the wrong the night before, but Lucy had the ability to goad him into a temper when no one else could.

"Madame, this has little to do with my vanity and more to do with your conduct. We would not be in this situation if it were not for your total lack of decorum. Reform is a base business for a man, even more so for a woman."

Her shoulders stiffened. "I beg to differ, Your Highness. We would not be in this situation if you did not feel the need to parade about in servants' clothing!"

"Children, children," Crispin interrupted. "Squabbling will resolve nothing. Lady Lucinda, Nick has come to say something very particular to you, and given the events of last night, I should think you would be eager to listen."

Lucy shook her head. "It is not necessary. None of this is necessary."

Nick moved forward and seated himself on the sofa beside her, Wellington standing guard between them. Lucy glared at the prince as if he were a plague carrier.

"Your hasty departure last night was unfortunate," Nick said, leashing his own temper. Whatever Lucy's failings might be, he was the one who had publicly compromised her and it was up to him to set matters to rights. "We left an important matter unfinished."

"Did we?" Lucy looked at him with wide-eyed innocence. "I don't recall."

Nick glanced at his father, who frowned and looked meaningfully at a spot on the floor in front of Lucy. Crispin coughed in a vain attempt to muffle his laughter. With a deep sigh of resignation, Nick slid from the sofa until he was kneeling in front of her. He thought about taking her hand again. It would certainly be a good strategy, in case she decided to slap him, but the feel of her hand in his was likely to wreak havoc on any good sense he still retained.

"Lady Lucinda, I have come today to ask you to make me the happiest of men."

He had thought she would laugh at him or grow angry, but instead she smiled with satisfaction, and for a moment Nick wondered if she'd played him for a fool. Had she, in her perverse way, been angling for a proposal after all?

"What are you saying, Your Highness? I am not quite clear on how I might be the source of your happiness, but I will do whatever is in my power to send you into transports of joy."

Nick hesitated. What did she have up her sleeve?

"You will make me the happiest of men, Lucy, if you will agree to be my wife and my future queen." Nick was warming to his subject now, gaining confidence, for he had practiced this bit in the mirror several times that morning. "I can offer you everything that a woman dreams of: position, wealth, a title. I know that our . . . um . . . courtship has been rather unorthodox, but, well, surely we can manage to rub along quite well together."

Rub along quite well together? Had he really said that? That was certainly not how he'd practiced it. He watched Lucy for any sign as to her thoughts, but her face was smooth as glass, her eyes politely interested, with a gleam of triumph in them. That gleam worried Nick, made his collar feel far too tight.

Lucy pulled Wellington into her lap. "What a charming offer," she said, and then smiled. "No pun intended, of course."

That was when Nick realized he was in a great deal of trouble, and his breathing became quite shallow. Lucy was far angrier than he'd thought.

Her blue eyes bored into his. "It is good of you, Prince Nicholas, to sacrifice your life, your happiness, even the future of your country so that I might not be burdened by a blight upon my good name. But, then, you are of a rather unique disposition, are you not? Rescuing damsels in distress—for that matter, anyone in distress—seems to be a rather integral part of your nature. Unfortunately, your attempts to rescue me seem to have had some rather disastrous consequences."

Nick eyed her with caution. "It is not my attempts to rescue you that have caused this difficulty, my lady. It is the very public kiss we shared at Carlton House, and I believe you were a partner in that indiscretion."

She flushed a becoming shade of pink. "My indiscretion, sir, was committed with a gardener, and while it would have led to my disgrace, it would never have imposed upon me a sentence of marriage!"

It was absurd to be jealous of himself, but Nick felt the prickles of that unwanted emotion. "Your indiscretion with a gardener is a direct comment upon your morals, I am sure," Nick said before he could stop himself.

Her cheeks grew bright red. "I am not ashamed to associate with common men, sir. There is more decency in the fields and cottages of Nottinghamshire than in all the ballrooms of London. And if lo—that is, if feeling affection for someone of the lower classes is a sign of low morals, than mine are scarcely up to my ankles."

"Affection?" Nick shouted, ignoring the other word that she had almost said, since it caused his muscles to tense for flight and made it difficult to breathe. "And you display your affection by humiliating its object in front of the most esteemed personages in the land?"

"I did not humiliate you. I defended you."

"You rejected me. You ran from my proposal so that the guards and I had to follow after you for your protection. Do you know how frantic I was when you fled through St. James Square? Whatever I might be, Lucy, I am not a worse prospect than that ruffian who accosted you. A woman, alone at night—I can only thank God that someone taught you how to defend yourself, and that you arrived home safely."

She was quiet for a moment, and Nick realized his words had made some sort of impression upon her.

It was Crispin who decided to jump into the breach. "Nick is not so bad, Lucy, once you become accustomed to him. Even now the scandalmongers are printing their morning editions. Your situation is shortly to become much worse, I'm afraid. If you and Nick can settle things this morning, you will perhaps be insulated from the worst of it."

Lucy eyed him narrowly, unappreciative of his concern. "You knew all along! When you came to my stepmother's that first day . . . and when you locked us in the coal cellar . . ."

Crispin tugged at his cravat. "Well, yes, of course. I

151

knew . . . that is, I wanted to . . . oh, dash it all, Lucy, I could see straightaway that you and Nick were perfectly suited for each other. I just afforded you the opportunity to see for yourselves."

Her cheeks flamed. "Perfect for each other? Are you mad? I've never heard anything so ridiculous in my life."

"I agree," Nick said, and then wished he'd kept his mouth closed, for now Lucy was eyeing him furiously.

She turned on him. "So you will marry me anyway, even though I am ridiculous? Merely for the sake of appearances and reputations?" She rose abruptly, setting Wellington aside. Nick rose, too, and followed her across the room to stand in front of the windows overlooking the street.

"Now, Lucy." He must placate her, for her hands planted on her hips meant that things were going from bad to worse. "You know what I mean. We find ourselves in a ludicrous situation." He stepped closer to try and shield his next words from Crispin and his father. "We'll sort it all out, Lucy. I promise you. It will not be so terrible."

She had gone quite pale. "How could it possibly be any worse? My every move would be scrutinized," Lucy hissed. "I should be useless to the reformers."

"Of course you would," Nick agreed. "But life as a royal princess would have its compensations, don't you think?"

She looked at him, eyes wide with disbelief. "Compensations? What could ever substitute for the loss of my freedom and my cause?"

"Me?" Nick offered with a small smile, in an attempt to be winning, but he was sorry as soon as he uttered the lonely syllable. When it came to Lucy Charming, he had evidently come to enjoy rejection, even crave it.

"You want me to sacrifice everything?" Her blue eyes widened. "Merely to be a princess?"

Why did Lucy Charming have to be the one woman in all of England who had no desire to become royalty? "Not just any princess. My princess. And, someday, my queen."

Join the Historical Romance Book Club
and GET 4 FREE* BOOKS NOW!

A $23.96 Value!

Yes! I want to subscribe to the
Historical Romance Book Club.

Please send me my **4 FREE* BOOKS.** I have enclosed $2.00 for shipping/handling. Each month I'll receive the four newest Historical Romance selections to preview for 10 days. If I decide to keep them, I will pay the Special Members Only discounted price of just $4.24 each, a total of $16.96, plus $2.00 shipping/handling ($23.55 US in Canada). This is a **SAVINGS OF AT LEAST $5.00** off the bookstore price. There is no minimum number of books I must buy, and I may cancel the program at any time. In any case, the **4 FREE* BOOKS** are mine to keep.

*In Canada, add $5.00 shipping/handling per order for the first shipment. For all future shipments to Canada, the cost of membership is $23.55 US, which includes shipping and handling. (All payments must be made in US dollars.)

NAME: _____

ADDRESS: _____

CITY: _____ **STATE:** _____

COUNTRY: _____ **ZIP:** _____

TELEPHONE: _____

E-MAIL: _____

SIGNATURE: _____

She laughed. "And leave England?"

Nick squirmed. "Well, not straightaway. Someday, perhaps."

"Perhaps?" His father, who had clearly overheard every word, sounded puzzled. "What do you mean, perhaps?"

"You want me to give up everything I believe in," Lucy continued, color returning to her cheeks, "to become something I despise, and do so knowing that I will never have a chance to make a real difference to anyone or anything. Is that what you are offering me, Nick?"

"You would make a difference to me, Lucy." The words sounded like cannon shot in his own ears.

She stilled, and her eyes searched his. "Why? Why would I make a difference to you?"

But he couldn't answer that. Not now. And certainly not in front of Crispin and his father. "Be realistic, Lucy. We have no choice, other than the kind of public scandal that would make mockeries of us both."

"But we do, Nick. We do have a choice." Lucy was edging away from him, but he was determined not to let her elude him again. For better or for worse, Lucy Charming was his destiny, and one that he did not want to escape. Only alter a bit.

"We cannot go back," he argued. "From the moment you knocked me on the head with that blasted door, our fates were sealed."

Her face whitened. "No. We have a choice. There is always another choice."

Nick knew that he had to say his next words. "Do you really think your fellow reformers will welcome you with open arms when they realize what association with the infamous Lucy Charming will bring? Your notoriety will render you useless. How many delegates can you hide beneath your stepmother's nose, or the noses of the *ton*, once they realize what you're about?"

"No," Lucy protested. "It won't happen. I won't let it."

"It's too late, Lucy. It's too late to change anything. We can only move forward and make the best of it."

"And that's what I would be to you?" she asked. "The silk purse you fashioned from a sow's ear?"

Nick stilled. "No. You would be my wife. My princess."

His answer was not good enough. He could see that in her eyes. "That is all?" she asked.

He would not allow her to be anything else, to work her way any further beneath his skin. "What more is there? What more can there be? It has to be better than living as a virtual servant in your stepmother's home."

She looked away. "Except that in this house, I have had a certain freedom that has meant a great deal to me. Would I have that with you, Nick?"

He could not lie. "Your life will change, Lucy, one way or another, but I am not an unreasonable man. I know your passion for reform, and you will be free to indulge it within certain boundaries. You will have as much freedom as any woman of your station could wish for."

"Hah! Boundaries set by you, no doubt?"

Blast! Could the woman at least appear to be reasonable about this thing? "Boundaries set by society, Lucy. You may have your choice of projects—climbing boys, half-blind seamstresses, whatever you like. Heaven knows there are enough unfortunates in London to keep you busy for the rest of your life."

She bristled. "That is not reform. That is applying sticking plasters to gunshot wounds. Until all men have a voice in the government of this country, there will never be any real change."

This remark sent his father into a coughing spasm so severe that Nick was forced to leave Lucy standing by the window and attend to the king. He and Crispin pounded his father's shoulder blades until the fit passed.

"Well, what say you, young lady?" his father demanded when he recovered his voice. "It is as fine a proposal as you are likely to receive today."

Lucy smiled and Nick's stomach tightened, for she appeared far too satisfied with herself. "Actually, I have already received a much finer offer this morning, and I have accepted it."

The words took Nick's breath away and sent his father into another coughing spasm. Crispin continued to pound on the older man's back, but Nick had endured enough. "This is not amusing, Lucy." His patience was at an end. How much longer would she resist the inevitable? "Come, let us name a date so that preparations may begin. I daresay you will want some time to buy wedding clothes."

She smiled brightly, falsely. "Certainly, but it will be none of your concern. My future husband has directed that any bills be sent to him."

Nick rubbed his temples, for a sudden headache had appeared there. "Lucy, I am your future husband. There is no other choice."

"But there is, Your Highness, and I have made it." She lifted her chin in a manner that would have done any actual princess proud. A cold shiver raced down Nick's spine.

"Oh, Lucy. You didn't." The image of Mr. Whippet in the foyer retrieving his things from the withered butler flashed through Nick's head. "You wouldn't."

"I would, and I did." She was trying to look pleased with herself, but Nick could see that underneath her bravura, she had some understanding of what it meant to play with fire.

"Are you mad? You know what type of man he is."

"And so will the rest of the world, if he fails to live up to our agreement."

Nick moved toward her, his hands clenched in frustration. "You are treading on very dangerous ground, Lucy."

Her eyes sparkled. "Mr. Whippet will suit my purposes, and I shall be perfectly safe."

The thought of Lucy married to the decadent vicar guaranteed a lifetime of sleepless nights. "What makes you so certain? What sureties has he offered?"

Lucy laughed. "Woof," she said, and winked at Nick.

He could endure no more. The woman was his personal pestilence, a plague sent from God to torment him for his wicked ways. He had thought an offer of marriage would see her thoroughly rescued at last, but she had outmaneuvered him again. Nick turned and strode to the sideboard. He poured himself a very tall brandy and downed it in one swallow.

Chapter Twelve

London society was agog with news of the now infamous Lady Lucinda Charming. Still, it was not her acceptance of the Reverend Mr. Whippet's marriage proposal that caused women to stare and men to ogle her on those rare occasions when she ventured into public view. Rather, it was the offer of marriage she had declined that caused a sensation and made Lucy the most talked-about woman in town.

The fact that the spurned Prince Nicholas haunted the Duchess of Nottingham's doorstep on South Audley Street did little to quiet the gossip. Nor did the fact that Lady Lucinda refused to see him. The rest of the *ton* might speculate it was her family history of mental infirmity that caused the mysterious miss to spurn the handsome prince, but Lucy herself knew the truth. She was tempted to depend upon Nick, and so she was wise to refuse him admittance when he lifted the knocker at precise, two-hour intervals to inquire if she were at home.

Besides, if she came face-to-face with him, she might begin to regret her actions. She was pointedly determined to ignore the lump that rose in her throat when she thought of Nick's heroism over the past week. She did not desire to rely on anyone else to be rescued. Not even by him.

In the days since she'd informed Nick of her acceptance of Mr. Whippet's proposal, the only difficulty with her decision had been that she couldn't seem to concentrate on anything or anyone but the ever-present Crown Prince of Santadorra, drat the man. She was thinking of him now as she sat fidgeting in a chair before the fireplace in the morning room, one eye on the ormolu clock on the mantel and the other on the duchess. Her stepmother lay prostrate on the sofa, smelling salts close at hand.

"You are a wretched, ungrateful girl, Lucy Charming. You, of all people, might have been a princess! Think what that would have meant for my girls."

Lucy held back a sigh. They'd been engaged in this conversation for the past half hour, and though there was no escape from the duchess's recriminations, Lucy did try to channel her stepmother's complaints into happier thoughts.

"Given the scandal, Your Grace, I do not think the match would have been to my stepsisters' advantage." Lucy dug the toe of her slipper into the carpet, idly drawing a map of the East End in the rich nap. She marked the location of Spitalfields by making an indentation with her heel. After her humiliation at Carlton House, she had known that it was pointless to try to assume her place among the *ton*. No, she had been right before to believe that her home was among the common folk, and from now on, among them she would stay.

The duchess lifted her fan and gave it a few weak waves. "The scandal, as you call it, would have been allayed if you had only accepted Prince Nicholas. You tricked me, Lucy Charming. Placing the engagement announcement in the *Times* before I had any knowledge of your underhanded dealings. Mr. Whippet has no money, and only limited connections—nothing of use to my girls."

Lucy stiffened. "I kept my word, madame. I agreed to accept an offer of marriage, and so I did. In the end, you will have your share of my marriage portion, as you desired when you bargained with Mr. Whippet. Surely that is some comfort." From the hall, the casement clock chimed the quarter hour. If she could not escape from the drawing room soon, she would be late for the reform meeting. It was a considerable distance to Spitalfields, at least on foot, but though Lucy had listened to the rousing speeches of Sir Frances Burdette and William Wilburforce, she had never heard the famous Orator Hunt. She did not mean to miss him this day. Surely there was no man in England who could speak more persuasively on the cause of reform.

"Money is no comfort," the duchess moaned. "No comfort at all. If those reformers had ever returned, I would have locked them in the cellars until the Runners came, and you along with them." She paused and took a large swallow from the glass of port that rested on the low table next to her. Her eyes narrowed. "You have made some sort of bargain with Mr. Whippet, have you not? He has been strangely absent for a newly engaged man."

If her stepmother only knew. "No doubt he has been out spending my dowry," Lucy said as she rose from her chair. "I must beg you to excuse me now, madame. There are matters that require my attention."

With a curtsy, Lucy slipped from the room. It was nearly time for Nick to ring the doorbell again, and his presence would only open a new round of complaints of ill-use from the duchess.

Lucy hurried up the stairs and toward the luxurious new bedchamber her stepmother had given her in hopes of tempting her into accepting Nick. The large chamber's embroidered curtains and bed hangings were by far the finest in the house. Lucy let herself inside and disappeared into the adjoining dressing room.

She reemerged a few moments later, clad in the

breeches and shirt she'd been given by Madame St. Cloud. Her curls were tucked up in the leather cap. She paused to check her appearance in the mirror and frowned. Too pristine. Too feminine. She crossed to the fireplace and rubbed her fingers across the coal in the scuttle. Back at the mirror, she smudged her face until she resembled an overgrown climbing boy. "There." She smiled with satisfaction, admiring her artistry. No women would stare now, and any men who ogled her would be thought very strange indeed.

Her route was a familiar one, so routine she paid little attention to her surroundings as she slipped out of the kitchen door. Lady Belmont's garden was quiet as well, but even so she was careful to walk lightly on the gravel path. She opened the small door—the very door that had been the cause of her recent troubles—and peeked out into the street beyond.

The normal foot traffic of servants and tradesmen bustled by, but Lucy saw no sign of lurking Santadorran guards or government spies. When a large dray rumbled past, she darted out into its wake. Soon she was far enough from home that she could turn back toward the east and Spitalfields.

In her haste, Lucy failed to hear the sound of pursuit until it was almost too late. The heavy footfalls drummed behind her with the rhythmic precision of one of His Majesty's regiments. Her heart raced, dreading what was to come. Crispin might have launched two of Lord Sidmouth's spies to the colonies, but there were always men willing to do the Home Secretary's bidding, no matter what the cost to their fellow countryman—or woman.

Without glancing over her shoulder, she spun about and darted down an alley. The footsteps behind her increased in speed, and very quickly she was running flat out. Drat and double drat. She would never be on time now. The alley took a sharp, narrow twist, and then came to a dead end. Lucy gasped and stopped short, glancing about for a place to hide. No casks or boxes of rubbish lay strewn about. Resigned, Lucy turned and prepared to confront her stalker, only to find Nick standing in front of her, dressed in his gardener's attire and smiling with an irritating satisfaction. The sight of him did nothing to slow the pounding of her heart.

He bowed, mocking her. "Lady Lucinda. Very kind of you to receive me. Strange, but your butler believed you were not at home." He glanced around the alley. "But, then, perhaps this might be more accurately characterized as your home away from home."

"Go away." Lucy saw no need to be polite. She stepped forward, thinking to slip past him, but he moved in front of her, blocking her way. Lucy went still as she fought the urge to lower her guard. He made her want to relinquish control, to give her fate into his keeping, much as she had surrendered control to him that night in the maze. The temptation to cede the reins of her life angered her as much as it tempted her.

"Your Highness, I weary of these games." Her heart was beating wildly, but not from fear. No, her pulse raced because he was there, standing in front of her, looking at her with those chocolate eyes and speaking to her with those supremely kissable lips. And in his eyes was a look of concern, so seductive in her loneliness, but concern she must do without. She needed no one, depended on no one. Being caught in his embrace by his father and the Regent had been embarrassing enough, but the weakness he made her feel was the most humiliating thing of all.

He didn't reply, merely reached out—he was breathtakingly close—and traced the tip of his finger across her cheek. When he pulled his hand away, she could see the black stain there, and she blushed. She had forgotten about that part of her disguise, but it was too late for vanity. Indeed, it was too late for a great many things.

"I can assure you, Lucy, that I'm not playing games." And he was not. She heard it in his voice, saw it in the stiffness of his spine as he stood before her. He was a man with a reputation for pleasure-seeking, but he appeared dead serious as he stood before her now.

"Can you not accept a 'no' when it is given to you, Your Highness? Do you think when someone declines your offer of marriage that she is not sincere?"

"Oh, no, madame, I believe you to be all too sincere. That is the problem."

Lucy wanted to stamp her foot in frustration. He made her feel childish, when really she was only being sensible. Could he not see that? "We are not compatible, Your Highness. Surely you understand that as well as I. We would make each other miserable within a fortnight, if we even managed to be civil for that long."

"Would we?" He raised one dark eyebrow. "I'm afraid I don't agree. True, we are very different, but one of us might change."

Lucy snorted. "And you intend for that person to be me."

He paused, a look of consternation spreading across his face. "Well . . . that is . . . I hadn't thought of it quite like that."

"But you have, Nick." His name came out, unbidden, but Lucy pressed on, hoping he would not notice the slip. "You have as much intent to reform *me* as I have to bring change to England. I can see it in your eyes, hear it in your voice. I have no intention of changing, so there is no need to keep pressing your suit. I absolve you of all guilt and will sort out my own life."

It was a brave speech and would have been much more compelling if her palms had not been sweating and if she had not been acutely aware of how she longed to fling herself into his arms. The seductive lure of a hero could weave its spell around even her jaded heart. To depend upon him. To be safe. To have one's cares and worries taken away, as if by a magic spell. But it was an illusion, for all that it was an attractive one. Lucy had learned that lesson at her father's death.

"You will not change your mind, then?" he asked quietly. He seemed rather nonchalant for a man determined not to be spurned.

"Definitely not."

He smiled then, that sinful, delicious smile that made her feel as if she were standing too close to a roaring fire. "Then I propose a wager," he said.

"A what?" Lucy blinked.

"A wager. One I think will be of some interest to you."

Her skin tingled, showers of sensation traveling over her body. He was too clever by half, and she would do well to be wary of princes offering wagers. "What is this wager?" she asked cautiously.

"It is a matter of my education." He was looking smug again, a sure indication that her wariness was not unwarranted.

"Your education?" She laughed. "Have I not heard that you took honors at Oxford? I perceive no lack in your education, Your Highness, only in your manners."

He stepped closer, if that were possible, until the only thing between them was a few inches of air. "Ah, but I am sadly lacking, my dear, in some important knowledge. Apparently there are compelling reasons for the cause of reform of which I remain blissfully unaware." He leaned toward her, almost whispering. "But perhaps if someone might educate me . . ."

"This is not amusing." Lucy stepped back. He had no right to be so attractive and so unfeeling at the same time.

The teasing light left his eyes. "I don't intend to amuse you, Lucy. I am quite serious."

"Then what is your wager?" It would be too outrageous, too preposterous for her to even consider it, but perhaps if she heard him out he would leave and she could be on her way to Spitalfields.

He smiled, much like a cat toying with a mouse. "If within the next fortnight you can convince me that reform is a noble and worthy endeavor, not mere rabble-rousing by treasonous malcontents, then I shall grant you your heart's deepest desire—at least as far as it is in my power to do so." He stopped, leaving her in suspense.

Lucy was skeptical. "What could you know of my heart's desire? What very great thing might you do that would entice me to accept this wager and to sacrifice my freedom?"

He leaned forward again, his smile already tinged with victory. "If you win the wager, princess, then when I am King of Santadorra, I shall grant universal suffrage within my realm."

For a moment, the only sound was the bustle of wagons and carriages from the street beyond. Tears pricked Lucy's eyes. Nick's words stung, and not just her pride. She wearied of people laughing at her dreams. "Your jokes fail to amuse, Your Highness." She brushed at her eyes and tried to slip by him once more, but his tall frame blocked her way again.

"My dear Lucy, I am not being droll." His hands gripped her shoulders to hold her in place. "If you can convince me to change my mind about reform, then you will be responsible for thousands of men receiving the right to have a voice in their own government."

She looked into his face, searching. "Can you do that?" Surely it was not quite as simple as all that.

"I don't know why not. I will be king, after all. Not all royal powers have been usurped by the parliament—at least, not yet."

Lucy eyed him dubiously. Clearly this was just another stratagem to try and win her agreement to his offer of marriage. "And if I cannot?" she prompted. "What forfeit must I pay?"

His eyes darkened, if that were possible. "If you cannot convince me of the worthiness of your cause, then you will jilt the good vicar and become my wife—agreeably, and without delay."

"What guarantee would I have that you would do as you say? Or for that matter that you would not lie and deny reform even if I convinced you of its value? There is no advantage on my side."

He glared at her. "Is my word of honor insufficient for you, Lucy Charming? I am no liar, and I honor my debts."

"With gentlemen, I am sure, but I am a mere woman."

The sharp crack of his laughter echoed in the alleyway. "My dear Lucy, I would shoot any man who so questioned my honor. Would putting a bullet through you convince you of my sincerity?"

She could tell from the way he resorted to sarcasm that she had wounded his pride. Men were so prickly about their precious honor.

"Then I will accept your word as a gentleman, though other guarantees would not be amiss."

"Very well. I will do this. I will swear out my intent in writing, and we may file it with a solicitor. That will be as legal an agreement as any in England."

Her spine stiffened. "And only binding in this country, Your Highness. Such a paper would do your countrymen little good if you chose not to honor it."

He nodded. "You have a point. Then let me take my offer a step further. If, within two weeks, you can convince me that the reformers are not a group of revolutionaries in sheep's clothing, then not only will the men of Santadorra receive a grant of universal suffrage, but I will include the women of my country as well. Perhaps that would provide you sufficient inducement to accept such a risky wager, even if it has no legal recourse attached."

Lucy gasped. He was a vile, low, dastardly fiend. "You mock me, sir. And that is unconscionable, even for you."

She pulled back, but his hands still grasped her shoulders, and now they moved upward, sliding to cup her neck. She should have shaken off his touch immediately but the warmth of his hands felt too good, and he had opened her heart and her dreams to the very core. She was afraid to move, lest she shatter into more pieces than could be put together again.

He willed her to look at him and she did. "I will swear an oath, Lucy, on anything you like."

"Anything? Then swear on what you hold most dear."

His mouth thinned. Deep grooves stood out around his eyes. "I will swear on the graves of my mother and sister."

She hadn't known he had a mother. Well, of course she'd known he must have one somewhere, but she'd never heard her mentioned. Or a sister, for that matter. Clearly, though, they had been of great importance to him, for the look of pain that haunted his eyes could not be feigned.

He was so near and so intent that Lucy's stomach knotted. "You are serious, aren't you?"

"Indeed."

"And all I must do is convince you of the worthiness of my cause?"

"It should be simple enough." His thumb climbed higher, over the ridge of her jaw and upward until it lightly stroked her lower lip. "If you are so passionate about reform, it should not be difficult."

But thoughts of reform were fast disappearing under the spell he cast with the touch of his thumb on her lips. The desire she felt surely shone in her eyes. She looked down, keeping her gaze level with his gardener's smock.

"I will convince you," she said, "if only to save us both from a mockery of marriage." The words were meant as a vow, more to strengthen herself than to warn him.

He laughed. "While I will try very hard not to be convinced. I will require you to be most persuasive."

It was no use avoiding his gaze. He seemed to see into her soul even when she could not meet his eyes.

"Lucy." He said her name softly. She heard the underlying question, but she did not want to respond. Just let him kiss her without asking for permission. Then she would not be responsible for her own heedless tumble into folly. Very sensual, very compelling folly.

She raised her eyes and met the look of desire in his. When she did not turn away, he bent lower and his lips brushed hers, feather light at first, and then his mouth slanted open, and she grasped his smock to keep from falling.

Since her father's untimely death, she had hidden from her feelings. The best antidote for grief was a vigorous crusade, and her father's reformist leanings had formed a natural path for her to follow. Her suffragist activities isolated her from both the glittering world of titled aristocrats and the daily labor of the working classes. But here, in this moment, with Nick's lips forcing her to feel alive, she could no longer hide. She was neither the put-upon stepdaughter nor the outspoken proponent of reform. Instead, she was simply Lucy. A young woman who had been lonely for far too many years.

She kissed him back. She couldn't seem to help herself. His arms came around her and pulled her close. He whispered her name and his light breath against her cheek sent shivers running the length of her spine. "Lucy, what have you done to me?"

His question echoed her own thoughts exactly, and that was disturbing enough to force her to lower her hands from where she'd clasped them about his neck. With one soft push, she was free of his embrace. They were both breathing heavily.

"If I've only a fortnight, then we best begin now." Lucy struggled to present an unaffected front. She fought the urge to raise trembling fingers to her lips. "In fact, I'm late for a meeting."

Nick nodded. "Let's be off, then." He looked as disturbed as she felt, but surely the kiss they'd shared would have to be classified as one of his milder endeavors in the pursuit of women. Lucy saw the smudges on his face that her own coal-blackened features had left but she did not reach up to wipe them away. In the distance, bells chimed the hour.

"Follow me," she said, and wished that she could not feel his eyes pinned on her as she led him out of the alleyway. The way he looked at her made her want to stay in the shadows and continue that kiss indefinitely.

* * *

Nick meant every word of the bargain he'd made with Lucy. It would not be a difficult promise to honor, since he knew she stood no chance of convincing him that reformers held any noble or sincere ambitions. In a fortnight, not only would she see the error of her thinking, but she would agree to become his wife. Propriety and his father would be satisfied, Lucy would be his, and his life could return to some semblance of normalcy.

In the meantime, however, he would have to endure fourteen days of a world he detested. The only thing that would make it bearable would be sights such as the one he enjoyed now. He smiled as he followed Lucy through the streets of London, her slim hips and bottom lovingly outlined by the trousers she wore. He would, of course, have to forbid her to wear them again, but today he was enjoying the view.

"How much farther?" They had reached the edge of Spitalfields, home to thousands of weavers. The spire of Christ Church loomed over the rows of houses thrown up to accommodate the influx of laborers. From these homes came some of the finest silks in England.

Lucy gestured toward the spire. "Orator Hunt will speak today, outside the church."

Nick had not heard of the man, but clearly others had. The narrow lanes leading toward the church grew thick with people. He found himself hurrying to keep pace with Lucy, who moved nimbly amid the burgeoning throng. He lost sight of her, and the crowd pressed in on him, jostling and pushing. The great mass of people possessed an energy like a living creature, and the hairs on the back of Nick's neck stood on end. He had felt this energy before, the night the crowd of Santadorran peasants, incited by French *provocateurs,* had stormed the palace.

Nick swallowed his panic and caught sight of Lucy's cap a short distance ahead. He pushed against the crowd until he was near enough to grasp her shoulder. She looked back and smiled, her face flushed with excitement and anticipation, and continued. Nick held on to her as tightly as he could without betraying his feelings.

The square before the church was a writhing sea of humanity. Disguised in his gardener's togs, Nick knew he had nothing to fear, but trapped in the midst of this ocean of peasants, he felt his royal title all but stamped on his forehead. He kept his cap pulled low and clung to Lucy.

Being Lucy Charming, she didn't stop until she was within twenty feet of the platform that had been constructed in front of the church. The speeches had already begun amid a great deal of bunting and several large banners proclaiming the need for universal suffrage. When Lucy stopped, he tried to stop as well, but the crowd pushed against his back, and it was all he could do to hold his ground. Not sure how else to protect her, he put his arms around her waist, clasping them over her belly. Even his discomfort, though, could not shield him from the shock he felt when Lucy leaned against him and briefly squeezed his wrists, her fingers resting on his forearms where they gently cradled her against him.

The speaker droned on, and Nick was satisfied to ignore the man. He worried about the crowd while still savoring the pleasure of holding Lucy in his arms. The man ground to a stop, and the mass of people offered polite applause.

"I remain unconvinced," Nick whispered into Lucy's ear. He smiled when he felt a tremor run through her body. Pressed this close to him, there was no way she could disguise her reaction to his nearness.

"You have not yet heard Orator Hunt," she shot back over her shoulder. "Look, he is next."

The man who strode to the podium was the epitome of an English gentleman farmer. He was tall, more than six feet, dressed in riding clothes, but his thin lips and pale eyes gave him an ineffectual air.

"This is the man who is to convince me of the error of my ways?" Nick chortled. "Perhaps you will concede right now, and we can make wedding plans."

Lucy stiffened. "I will certainly be making wedding plans, sir. But not with you. Orator Hunt will see to that."

Nick listened with half an ear as the man spoke, but he was distracted by the disturbing image of Lucy standing in front of an altar with Mr. Whippet. Orator Hunt's comments echoed the usual complaints—demands for an annual parliament, universal suffrage, and secret ballots, pleas for a repeal of the Corn Laws. "He would make a very good Frenchman," Nick whispered in Lucy's ear, but she shushed him, and Nick found there was nothing to do but actually listen to the man.

The reformer demonstrated more energy now. His gestures became larger, his voice growing in intensity. His pale eyes shone with an almost holy glow, like a martyr facing the lions.

"Let me ask you this question, my beloved friends and brethren," Hunt bellowed as his gaze swept the crowd. "If all are to be sacrificed to the cause of our nation's freedom, then should not all Christians enjoy the same rights?" Cries of "huzza!" filled the air. "Should not all who proclaim Christ be given the vote?" The crowd of weavers, largely French Catholics and Huegenots, broke into wild cheers. Nick shifted uncomfortably in his worn boots. Orator Hunt had chosen his subject well, for only men who were members of the Church of England enjoyed rights of suffrage. Because of their faith, even propertied immigrants had no voice in their own government.

"Should not all men of Christian faith participate in a government ordained by God?" Hunt's question threw them into a further frenzy, and Nick refused to squirm. Blast the man for hitting the one sore spot in Nick's love for his mother's native land. While his mother had once been Church of England, she had converted to Catholicism to marry his father. Nick had been raised a Catholic. Though he had never put much stock in religion himself, at least not since he'd been rescued from the Santadorran forest at age twelve, Nick had often been on the receiving end of taunts and jibes at Eton.

"Should not all qualified men hold office and vote? Should not all taxpayers enjoy the right to own property, regardless of their house of worship?"

Lucy applauded and cheered with the rest of the crowd while Nick tried to push his disturbing thoughts away.

"An end to divisions!" Hunt cried, and the crowd echoed his roar. "An end to privilege!" The other speakers on the platform stepped forward and applauded enthusiastically. "An end to tyrannies that deny men their inherent rights!"

Orator Hunt stepped back from the podium, saluted the cheering crowd, and followed the other speakers as they disappeared behind the platform. Lucy turned in Nick's arms.

"Well?" she asked, her face shining with the joy of the words that had washed over her. She was lit from within, as if a thousand candles had been placed inside her. "Confess that you were moved a little bit. No one could be indifferent to that, not even Sidmouth himself."

And it was at that moment, at that very moment, that Nick felt his heart open with a great, resounding crack. She was so sure, so confident—more resplendent in her passion for reform than she had been in a satin ball gown. He could no longer deny the truth. He did not want her because she appeared so very beddable. He did not even want her for the fire she sparked within him each time his lips met hers. What he wanted her for was this—this innocence, this belief in the goodness of men, this hope for the future. He had lost his own so very long ago.

Around them, the crowd was dispersing in bursts of song and general merriment. Lucy's eyes were still shining, and suddenly he could not stand another moment of the optimism and *bonhomie.*

"Hunt is a fool, as are you," he hissed. "You would give the vote to every criminal and lunatic who haunts the streets. All your dreams would lead to chaos, and who do you think would be the first person slaughtered in her bed? The daughter of the Duke of Nottingham, my dear. To believe anything else is a lie."

The harsh words cut across her face like lashes, but he did nothing to call them back. Her eyes, her damned deep blue eyes, filled with pain. Nick knew he was striking out from his own well of grief, but he could not stop. His feelings ran too deep, and he would save Lucy from her folly if he could. Governments were ordained by God for a reason—so that people could sleep in their beds without fear of having their throats slashed.

"You will not even try," Lucy accused him, and Nick agreed.

"No. Not when the stakes are the lives of men I know and respect."

"It is not their lives that are at stake," Lucy argued. "Only their livelihoods. That is the real issue. The Conservatives may argue on principle, but they act on gold."

Overhead, the clock of the church chimed the hour. It was growing late, and dusk would soon settle. They still had a long walk across London ahead of them.

"Don't despair, Lucy. You still have thirteen days left to change my mind. Perhaps you will yet succeed, but Orator Hunt leaves me unconvinced."

"I will succeed," she said, straightening her spine. "I know a little of your character. You cannot be as indifferent as all that."

Nick refused to respond. Instead, he took her arm and guided her away from the church. He could not answer her, because she was right. He was not indifferent. Not to her, not to the Catholics, and not to the sufferings of other people. But these feelings were ones he could not afford to indulge. Not and honor the past.

"Has no one told you, my dear? My indifference is the stuff of legend. As is my intolerance." He glanced down at her. "And never wear those breeches again."

Chapter Thirteen

Lucy refused to be defeated by Nick's closemouthed response to Orator Hunt's magnificent speech, just as she was determined to win their wager. Consequently, she mounted her next offensive by sending a note round to him, inviting him to inspect a school based on principles of reform. And so, a few days after their trip to Spitalfields, Lucy found herself seated across from Nick as his father's well-sprung carriage rolled smoothly over the rough, muddy roads out of London. Nick leaned into the thick cushions and smiled with satisfaction, which irritated Lucy to no end. She was glad Crispin had sent Wellington along with them. The mere sight of the little dog had brought a flush to Nick's otherwise sanguine expression.

The carriage conveyed them past Kew and farther along the Thames. After much deliberation as to what might earn Nick's good opinion, Lucy had settled on this expedition to a school for abandoned climbing boys. Once the boys grew too large to fit up the flues, their masters turned them off with nowhere to go and no way to earn their bread. Surely the valiant work done at the school would help Nick see the need for reform.

"With regard to the school," Lucy said, "you should be aware that—"

"I brought a picnic luncheon," he interrupted smoothly. "I thought we might stop at Kew on our return."

Lucy felt a prick of surprise. "What? Oh, well, yes. I suppose we could. Now, about the school—"

"My cook asked your favorites, but I didn't know so I instructed him to pack a bit of everything."

She groaned with frustration. He was taunting her, however charmingly, with his indifference. "I'm sure whatever your cook selected will be delicious. Now, let me tell you about the school."

"Did I mention my admiration for that specific color of blue?" He nodded toward her gown. "It does marvelous things for your eyes."

Lucy rolled the eyes he was admiring. Clearly Nick had no intention of allowing her to make her case. Very well. She would let the school speak for her. This would certainly be the day that Nick saw reason, because not only would he be introduced to the value of education for the lower classes, he would also meet the generous benefactor who gifted the school on a regular basis. Lucy did not know the gentleman's name, as his beneficence had been anonymous, but Mr. Cartwright, the headmaster, had assured her that the school's patron intended to visit that very day.

So Lucy gave up her attempts to lay out all of the school's good work and instead let Nick offer pleasantries about the weather and the state of the roads, only responding to his comments when necessary. Actually, she responded a good deal more than was necessary, which further irritated her. Nick was doing his best, or perhaps his worst, to charm her, and it was working quite well, for her stomach fluttered with the nervous energy that his presence always created. His smile and dark eyes alone would have lured her into a delicious sense of complacency, but when he added his quick wit and dry sense of humor, Lucy could not help but be captivated.

"You did no such thing!" she shrieked when he regaled her with a tale from his school days. "Where in England would one find an elephant to put in the headmaster's sitting room?"

Nick chuckled. "It pays to have friends in low places as well as high. The caretakers of the menagerie at the Tower do not mind if you buy them a pint or two. Or a dozen."

He laughed unself-consciously at the memory, and a great yawning pit opened in her midsection. She did not want to like Nick St. Germain. She did not want to find him captivating or handsome or any of the other things that might tempt her into regretting her refusal of him. She had accepted Mr. Whippet, and her blackmail kept the vicar neatly in hand. After all, Nick did not want her for herself. He wanted a royal bride who could take her place in society, not an inveterate reformer who had recently found how much she preferred the freedom of breeches to skirts. No, it was only Nick's pride and his sense of his own consequence, as well as his sense of honor, that made him pursue her still. His interest had nothing to do with her true charms. The thought only made the emptiness in her belly expand even further.

"Ah, it looks as if we've arrived." Nick nodded toward the carriage window. "A smart-looking place, I must say."

The carriage had brought them down the high street of the village before pulling to a stop in front of a picturesque cottage. Ivy climbed with gleeful abandon over the slate-gray stone, and the panes in the windows gleamed with polished care. On the small patch of lawn in front, two coltish-looking boys attempted to roll a hoop.

"I wonder that the children are not at their lessons," Lucy said before the two lads came running toward the carriage. Almost instantly, a dozen heads appeared in windows and around gateposts. The front door of the cottage was thrown open and a stream of shrieking, shoving boys came pouring out.

Lucy winced at the cacophony, and Wellington growled, angry that his nap should be summarily interrupted. She had hoped that Nick would find the boys diligently at their studies, perfect models of the highest aims of reform. With reluctance, Wellington rolled to his feet and barked at the pack of boys.

Nick stepped from the carriage and turned to offer Lucy his assistance. "My lady." He bowed over her hand and delivered her safely to the ground while she tried to ignore the way his touch sent warmth traveling up her arm and down her spine. He reached into the carriage for Wellington, who came growling in protest.

"Gor' blimey, it's him! The nabob! The nabob!" a young voice cried, and the others quickly took up the chant. Lucy looked around, thinking to find the anonymous benefactor, but no other carriages were in sight. At that moment, Mr. Cartwright appeared. The headmaster mopped his balding brow as he toddled down the path.

"Welcome, welcome," he said, wiping his forehead between effusive greetings. "What a delight to have two of our greatest supporters visit us in unison." He smiled at her and bowed over Lucy's hand. "Lady Lucinda. The boys always look forward to your visits."

Lucy opened her mouth to return the greeting, but Mr. Cartwright had dropped her hand and turned toward Nick.

"Your Highness." The headmaster bowed so deeply that Lucy was afraid he would not be able to right himself, but with a bit of wheezing, he returned to an upright position. Wellington, gingerly held in Nick's arms, sniffed the headmaster with disdain, but the little dog's disapproval did nothing to stem Mr. Cartwright's enthusiasm. "As always, it is a great pleasure, indeed, Your Highness. The boys have finished the tree house you helped them begin last week. They hoped to have a formal dedication ceremony after tea."

Formal dedication? Last week? Lucy looked from one man to the other, from the gleaming pate of the round little schoolmaster to Nick's tall, solid form holding Wellington as if he were some species of rat, and her heart sunk to the top of her half boots. Oh, no. Oh, heavens. Not again. She refused to be duped twice by Nick St. Germain.

Mr. Cartwright urged Nick down the path toward the cottage, and Lucy followed in their wake, battling her confusion. Only she knew the answer already. She knew from the way Mr. Cartwright directed Nick to the most comfortable chair in the drawing room. It was obvious in the way several of the boys approached Nick to have their hair ruffled and to give account of their progress in their studies. Nick called each boy by name and offered praise or encouragement, whichever was more appropriate, while Wellington huffily settled himself at Nick's feet for a resumption of his nap. Lucy sank onto a settee, too stunned to be furious, numb and yet aching, as she observed Nick in all the glory of his patronage.

Her numbness did not last long.

Heat kindled in her chest and then spread to her cheeks. The cad. The scoundrel. He had known their destination since she had sent him her note, but he had not breathed a word of his secret. No, he had let her make a fool of herself through the length of London and beyond. Tears of frustration sprang to her eyes.

She looked up then and Nick caught her eye. He was smiling, but not with the wicked triumph she expected. Instead, his mouth curved into gentle lines, as if inviting her to join in his secret. His chocolate eyes begged her indulgence, asking her not to reveal his deceit in front of the boys.

Lucy's stomach twisted. He was a rascal and a scoundrel, but she couldn't resist that silent entreaty. His pleasure in the boys was obvious, as was theirs in him. Lucy examined her heart and found she could not deny any of the males present the happiness they enjoyed. She would save her scold for later. After all, they were to picnic at Kew, and she could lambast him all around the pleasure gardens for the remainder of the afternoon. That thought was immensely comforting.

Mr. Cartwright, beaming benevolently, came to join her on the settee. "I had no notion that you were acquainted with the prince, Lady Lucinda. He is a fine fellow, is he not? Most generous to the school. If I didn't know better, I would suspect he sent us his entire quarterly allowance last month." The headmaster gave his brow one final mop before stuffing his handkerchief in his pocket. "With his generosity, we have purchased the cottage next door and filled it with aging seamstresses whose hands can no longer ply the needle. They will be motherly influences on the boys, or so we hope."

Lucy barely heard Mr. Cartwright's words, so intent was she on observing Nick. Now the boys were gathered in a ring around his chair as he regaled them with a tale of adventure in the wilds of his native land.

"Santadorran bears are far hungrier and far more fierce than French or Spanish bears," she heard him say. "And so, as I huddled against the back wall of the cave, with no way to escape and no weapon at hand, I knew all was lost." The boys alternately laughed and gasped as Nick's tale carried them to the pinnacle of danger and then back down again. Lucy smiled at his vivid imagination. She doubted whether the Crown Prince of Santadorra had ever been allowed to venture alone into the mountain forests, much less enjoyed the opportunity to slay a bear.

The wild tales in the drawing room were followed by a more formal ritual, the dedication of the tree house. This newest addition to the school was found at some distance from the cottage, down the sloping lawn that led to the river. Nick appeared on the verge of offering her his arm for the trek, but the boys quickly commandeered him and

Wellington and bore them off toward the river. Lucy followed more slowly at the side of Mr. Cartwright, who continued to lavish praise on Nick, eager for Lucy to murmur her approval at each new compliment.

The branches of a sturdy oak served as the foundation for the new tree house. Nick circled the tree, nodding and speaking softly to the tallest boy, while the others stood back and anxiously awaited his verdict.

"Well done," he finally pronounced, and there was a collective sigh of relief and smiles all around. "Very fine, indeed." Of course, then nothing would do but that Nick should climb the homemade ladder and admire the structure from within. Lucy held her breath as he mounted the wooden steps, mere bits of plank nailed into the tree trunk. A few moments later, he emerged on the small balcony that overlooked the river. He waved down at her, his face awash with pleasure, his manner enthusiastic, and Lucy could only wonder what had happened to the cynical, jaded nobleman he claimed to be. For here was a man who took as great a pleasure in the company of small, illiterate boys as he would in the society of England's most elite aristocracy.

There was that pain in her chest again, Lucy thought almost offhandedly. She had felt it before, in her midsection, on the occasions when she had been in Nick's company. That alarming but not unpleasant feeling had been born at their first meeting, when he had been laid out, unconscious, on the gravel path of Lady Belmont's garden. She had felt it, too, that night in the maze at Carlton House, when she had first seen Nick in evening clothes instead of his rough gardener's smock. Oh, she had felt this pain before in Nick's vicinity more times than she cared to count—at Madame St. Cloud's, in her stepmother's kitchen, amid the press of the crowd in Spitalfields. Indeed, she felt it every time she was anywhere near him.

And it was at that moment, as Lucy gazed up at a prince acting like an overgrown, overexcited boy, that she real-

ized she was in love with him—the one man in all of
England who was most ill-suited to her dreams and purposes. An ache sprung up in her head and her heart simultaneously. Stupidly, amazingly, against judgment and
common sense and reason, she loved him. And so she
could never marry him, for she could imagine no worse
fate than a lifetime spent with a man who did not want
her, but simply a woman to conform to his ideas of a wife.
Truly, she had no choice but to win the wager, or lose
her heart forever.

Nick so enjoyed the company of the boys that he was
tempted to linger at Mr. Cartwright's school. He also
wanted to postpone his explanation to Lucy. Once again
he had deceived her, but this had been a harmless deception, one perpetrated solely so that he might enjoy
the upper hand with her for a few brief moments. She
had been a good sport not to expose his fraud in front
of the headmaster and the boys. Instead, she had glared
daggers at him and smiled in a way that promised decidedly feminine retribution.

Oddly enough, Nick was looking forward to it for retribution meant she would have to get him alone to scold
him properly. And if they were alone, the odds were good
that he could maneuver her into his arms again. She had
not seemed to object the last time he had held her in his
embrace.

Their good-byes said, they left the boys behind to
mourn the loss of their idol, and Mr. Cartwright alone to
contemplate what to do with the small bag of guineas
Nick had pressed on him. Nick's recent fortune at the
faro tables should have been applied to a new pair of
boots, but when Mr. Cartwright mentioned the need for
cots for the seamstresses, the guineas grew too heavy for
his purse. If he could report some headway with Lucy to
his father, perhaps the king would relent enough to stand
for new hessians.

To Nick's surprise, the short drive to Kew proved quite

pleasant. It was a beautiful June afternoon, the kind of day that made the copious amounts of English rain well worth the bother. When Nick had first arrived in his mother's native land at age twelve, he had missed the mountains and pine forests of Santadorra quite keenly. The green beauty of England, though, had won another corner of his heart, and there was no place he loved as he did the royal gardens at Kew.

The carriage left them at the main gate. They passed beyond its pillars, and Lucy strolled at his side down the Broad Walk, evidently as willing as he to observe the natural beauty of the place in silence and to endure the uneasy truce that had fallen between them. A footman carrying the heavy picnic basket followed at a discreet distance and Wellington wheezed alongside them, his asthmatic lungs preventing him from venturing too far off the path.

Nick's heart soaked up the pleasure of a day in Lucy's company as readily as his bones soaked up the sunshine. The gardens at Kew had been planted two generations before by Augusta, the Princess of Wales, mother of the poor, mad king. Plants of every kind, from every corner of the world, found their place at Kew under the watchful eyes of numerous gardeners. It was a place of science, but Nick found it more a place of beauty. And as an adult, he had grown aware of its ideal setting as a place for the wooing of females.

"The day is very fine," he said casually, testing Lucy to gauge her temperament. She had not railed at him once they had left the school and gained the privacy of the carriage. He had anticipated a scolding that would leave his ears singed, but instead she had seemed distracted and disinclined toward conversation. Nick found himself strangely disappointed, for a row with Lucy was more engaging than flirtation with London's finest beauties.

"The day?" She looked up at him blankly before comprehension dawned in her impossibly blue eyes. "Oh yes. Lovely. The kind of day that inspires poets, I suppose."

He had offered her his arm at the gate, but she had declined, and now he found he could not walk as near to her as he wished. The Broad Walk seemed very broad indeed.

"I am waiting for my scolding." His words were meant to provoke her. He waited for the explosion and was disappointed when it did not come. For some inexplicable reason, she had softened toward him. Nick could see the change in her as she looked anywhere but at him in a fruitless attempt to maintain her distance.

Just when he had given up hope of engaging her in conversation, she spoke. "Why do you not return to Santadorra? Surely you must miss it. When you described it to Mr. Cartwright's boys, it sounded like heaven on earth."

Her question caught him off guard, as she had no doubt intended. He swallowed and gave careful thought to his reply—and whether he should make one at all.

"I prefer England, particularly London. Santadorra is the back of beyond, nothing in comparison with this country."

"And yet you described it for Mr. Cartwright's boys with great enthusiasm. Surely you miss it."

Nick was accustomed to prevarication about his past, and so he ignored the way his heart beat a sudden, nervous tattoo. "I miss a great many things from my childhood. Excessive amounts of cake. Rolling in the mud. But those things belong to another part of my life, as does Santadorra." Perhaps that would put her off the scent. Nick wished she would turn the conversation to casual remarks about the Orangery they had passed, or the pond in the distance.

"It's hard to envision the Crown Prince of Santadorra rolling in the mud." Her smile was warm, forgiving, when he really would have preferred her to be contrary. He was accustomed to placating Lucy Charming, not allowing her to relax him with her conversation.

"Yes, well, it was known to happen, my rolling in the

mud. Especially when my sister . . ." He stopped, the sudden tightness in his throat shutting off his words. He rarely spoke of Josephine—Jo, they had called her—always as ready for a bit of roughhousing or sport as he had been. Her hoydenish ways had distressed their mother to no end.

"Yes?" Lucy stopped and waited for him to finish, but Nick knew he could not. All this talk of Santadorra, his father's arrival in England, the prospect of a royal wedding made those long-ago events come alive once more. His sister would have approved of Lucy, he thought suddenly, while his mother would have immediately set forth a scheme to turn her into a proper young lady. God, he missed them still, and in many ways the pain was as fresh as it had been the day he first set foot on English soil. Nick had no choice but to turn the conversation if he were to keep his composure.

"Look how the pagoda looms over us from this distance," he said, pointing to the oriental structure. "Shall we consider it more closely? We can picnic in its shadow, if we have the stomach for it."

"I'm quite fond of the hideous thing, actually," Lucy replied. "It appears as out of place as I often feel." She stopped, and Nick realized he'd been given an insight into the puzzle that was Lucy Charming. For all her passion for reform, she did indeed mind that she lived in a netherworld between good society and its underclass.

Nick was so occupied considering this interesting piece of information that they walked the rest of the distance to the pagoda in silence. He led her to a shady spot beneath the wide branches of an ancient elm. With no breeze to cool the air, the day had grown stuffy. "Perhaps we should have settled by the pond," Nick said as the footman approached. "It's awfully still and warm."

"This day's charms lie in its imperfections," Lucy replied with a teasing smile. "I often find that to be the case with time spent in your company."

The impish light in her eyes made Nick's breath catch

in his throat. He coughed and turned away. The servant laid out the picnic cloth and unpacked the basket. Lucy had taken a few steps away, closer to the pagoda. Wellington followed her, looking miserable. Nick had no affection for the annoying little canine, but he did have the common decency to feel sorry for the fat, panting pug.

"I like it here," Lucy said over her shoulder. "It has an air of the exotic not often found in England."

Nick moved toward her and Wellington growled. Nick's level of sympathy dropped. "And are you a connoisseur of the exotic, madame? I would hardly have expected it of a reformer," he teased to lighten his own thoughts. "Are you not all seriousness and passion for your cause? I would never have expected an affection for chinoiserie."

Lucy laughed at his sally, and Nick felt gratified. Perhaps his dwelling on the past would not ruin the day after all.

She turned back to him. "After nuncheon I shall give you the scold you deserve. It was quite wrong of you, you know, to deceive me about your relationship with Mr. Cartwright and the school."

Nick did have the good grace to dip his chin slightly. "It was only a small deception, and besides, I enjoy your passionate diatribes on reform, even if I do not agree with them. Every woman should have some cause or person who can evoke that much feeling."

"As should every man," Lucy replied, arching her eyebrow.

"Touché."

The footman had withdrawn to a discreet distance, and Nick held out his hand. "Our feast awaits, Lady Lucinda." She placed her fingers in his—an action that awakened both tenderness and possessiveness within him—and he led her back to the picnic cloth. Wellington trailed behind, already drooling.

Nick's cook had outdone himself, preparing a feast far too generous for two diners. Cold beef, potted quail, and an assortment of cheeses were flanked by bread and muffins. A selection of apples and two oranges lay in a bowl and beside them rested a small platter of cakes. Two bottles of ale, as well as two of lemonade, completed the repast.

They sat down at the edges of the cloth a few feet apart. "It seems your cook mistook your directions, Your Highness," Lucy said, and Nick eyed her warily, for the curving lines around her mouth spoke of mischief. "Apparently he was under the impression that the whole of Mr. Cartwright's school was to join us."

Nick smothered a laugh and replied, with mock seriousness, "I thought it best to be prepared, in case you turned out to be one of those females with an endless appetite. Besides, Wellington could demolish this within minutes if we were to leave him unattended."

Lucy gasped in laughing indignation, on her own behalf as well as Wellington's, picked up a napkin, and swatted at Nick. Wellington barked his encouragement of her attack. Nick retreated, chuckling, and reached for the bottles of ale. Lucy looked as if she were considering swatting him again before her hunger got the better of her and she helped herself to bread and cheese, pausing between bites to slip Wellington a few morsels of cold beef.

Though it was not yet high summer, the droning of the bees had lulled the garden to sleep. Nick wondered if Eden had been as peaceful, and if Adam had enjoyed Eve's companionship as much as he enjoyed Lucy's. One could say what one liked about her want of propriety, but Lucy Charming was never dull. He had impressed her with his patronage of the school, he was sure. And when she forgot to hold him at arm's length, there was a warmth of feeling between them that bespoke not only physical awareness but similarity of mind. For all that they were worlds apart on the issue of reform, they were not so different at heart.

This was life at its finest, this leisurely picnic beneath the towering pagoda. The thought caused him to stop chewing the bite of muffin. Suddenly his mouth felt exceedingly dry. He reached for his bottle of ale and downed half its contents in one long swallow. Lucy looked at him curiously, her eyebrows raised.

"You appear excessively thirsty, Your Highness." She leaned forward, prepared to tease him, but something she saw in his eyes must have changed her mind, for in the next moment she became quite sober. "Are you unwell, Nick? You look rather pale."

Pale? Yes, well, he felt rather weak. Quite right that he should. After all, it was not every day that a man realized . . . That is, it was a rare moment, indeed, when . . .

The warm sensation that flooded over him was unfamiliar, little known in his life, and so it took a moment for him to understand its meaning. It was a sense of rightness. Of belonging. He had not felt it in so long.

By Jove, it was love.

By Jove and all that was holy, it was indeed love.

Wellington barked, demanding more cold beef, and Lucy turned to feed him while Nick attempted to refrain from panicking.

The return from Kew to Mayfair had never seemed so interminable. Lucy spent the entire ride trying to prevent Wellington from gnawing on the velvet squabs, and Nick could only be grateful for the distraction. At least the mangy pug diverted her attention and kept her from reading the guilty secret that must be plastered on his forehead. In love with Lucy Charming. Of course, it all made perfect sense now. It was inevitable, really, now that he looked back upon the days he had known her. How could one not love a beautiful, independent woman who introduced herself by knocking a man unconscious? It was his own fault for being on the other side of that door at the wrong moment.

Nick squirmed. By all that was holy, he was in love. Why else would he so determinedly pursue a woman who refused his help time and again? He craved heroism, it was true, but he had never been so insistent before. He'd thought it was merely the novelty of her refusal of his assistance that had goaded him into his pursuit of her. He'd persuaded himself that it was only the situation, not Lucy herself, that had fanned the flames of his protective instincts. He had misled himself, refusing to consider what motivation truly lay behind his actions. Now he could no longer deny the truth. For though he was a compulsive hero, he was not generally a fool. And, in his experience, there was only one thing that made men act so incredibly foolish. And that one thing was love. The kind of love that would make a man act against his better judgment, even against his own instinct for self-preservation. Only a definite case of love would make a man conceal his identity, rescue a woman who wanted no part of him, allow him to secretly rejoice that he must make an offer of marriage, and cause him to offer the object of his affection the most absurd wager—one he was not sure he could honor if he lost.

His realizations were like burning coals held to the bottom of his feet. He wanted to bolt, to escape as quickly as possible to some remote corner of the earth, but by sheer dint of will, Nick managed to maintain his composure.

At long last, the carriage pulled to a stop in front of the Duchess of Nottingham's home. Nick did not wait for the footman; he flung open the door and sprang to the ground. Impatient to be away, he did not even lower the steps, which was a mistake. Instead he urged Lucy into his arms and swung her down from the carriage.

That brief contact, her slim form so close to his agitated one, did nothing to settle his mind. When her feet touched the pavement, she looked up to utter her thanks, and it was all Nick could do not to settle his lips upon hers for a kiss she would not soon forget. The only thing that held him back was the panic that churned in his midsection.

Lucy was speaking to him but he could scarcely listen. The drumming of his own heart filled his ears. He tried to urge her up the steps so he could be rid of her, but she balked.

"Will you come or not?" she asked insistently. Nick, completely unaware of what she was requesting, nodded in agreement, willing to grant her anything in exchange for his escape.

"Yes, yes. Whatever it is, I'll come."

Lucy's eyes lit with surprise, and Nick wondered what he'd just agreed to do.

"Then we may meet Thursday morning at the Blue Barrel," she answered, obviously delighted at his acquiescence. "We can travel with the others, if you do not mind a bit of a rough ride."

"Rough ride?" Nick echoed tonelessly. "Where is it again that we're going?"

"To Nottingham, for the largest reform meeting in the history of England. Spitalfields is nothing to what Nottingham will be," Lucy answered with a smile whose very eagerness threatened Nick's self-composure. God, the next moment he'd probably be falling to his knees to declare his undying love for her, right on the pavement of South Audley Street.

"Reform meeting? Yes, of course." He backed away. "Blue Barrel, Thursday morning." Turning, he had almost gained the safety of his father's carriage when she called after him.

"Of course, I shall wear my breeches, since I will be traveling as a boy."

Nick refused to be provoked, if anything could provoke him more than the realization of his love for Lucy. He vaulted into the carriage. Thursday would be soon enough to worry about Lucy and her breeches. Today he had to come to terms with his damn fool feelings for the woman.

The carriage jolted forward, and Nick sank helplessly into the squabs.

Chapter Fourteen

The ox cart bounced over the rain-washed road as if the slow-moving animals purposely sank the wheels in the largest ruts. Nick gripped the side of the cart and resisted the urge to fling himself over the side and race back to London. Attending a potentially disastrous reform meeting in Nottingham was a damn foolish idea, but he had agreed of his own free will. Not that his will had been that free to choose. If he had refused, Lucy would have insisted on making the journey alone, and that was intolerable. If Lucy Charming were going to be compromised, ruined, or endangered, by Jove he would be the one doing the compromising, ruining, and endangering.

Nick made sure to keep Lucy close to his side during the journey, which, as a result of her boyish disguise, raised some eyebrows among their fellow travelers and earned Nick a few good-natured, if speculative, jibes. In the growing summer heat and the lashing afternoon storms, the only thing that had kept his sanity from slipping away entirely was the slim piece of paper tucked in the pocket of his leather vest. He had obtained the special license from the bishop before leaving London. With it, he and Lucy might be married by any clergyman willing to perform the duty. His wager with Lucy expired on Monday, and Nick fully intended to return from Nottingham a married man—at least in the eyes of the English government. A Catholic ceremony would have to wait.

Besides procuring the special license, Nick had taken one other step before leaving London. Late the night before their departure, he had paid a discreet call to Lord Sidmouth's office in Whitehall. His conscience had pricked him slightly, but in the end he could see no other choice. Lucy's safety was paramount.

Dusk was falling when they rounded the last bend in the road and saw the first signs of Nottingham. Nick eagerly anticipated the comforts—however dubious they might be—of a working man's tavern. To Nick's consternation, however, the ox cart avoided the town, skirting its edges and climbing a path that led up into the surrounding hills. In the growing dark, the countryside winked with unexplained light. As they rose higher, he saw the source of the illumination. The villagers had made homes for themselves by carving caves from the soft sandstone in the hillsides. Nick blanched. Although they were not as well known as Sherwood Forest, he had heard of the famous caves of Nottingham. Still, he had never actually considered people living in them. He shuddered at the thought.

"We've arrived," Lucy said, and squeezed his hand. Before he could offer his assistance, she jumped from the back of the cart. With a sigh of relief, she pulled the cap from her head and her hair tumbled down. In the darkening eve, her guinea curls glowed like bronze.

A young man emerged from the nearest cave. "Tom!" Lucy greeted the boy with enthusiasm, and Nick, feeling the pinpricks of jealousy, turned back to the cart to fetch their rucksacks.

Lucy appeared at his side with the fresh-faced youth in tow. "Nick, may I present Thomas Selkirk?" The boy nodded, his eyes probing, as if he were assessing Nick's measure as a man. "Tom, this is . . ." She paused and frowned in confusion. Nick didn't offer to assist her with her dilemma. Let her decide how much of his identity to reveal. After another moment, Lucy brightened and said, "This is my *friend,* Nicholas St. Germain."

Nick scowled. He did not want to be Lucy's friend. He wanted to be her husband. "Selkirk." He nodded at the lad but left his hands at his sides, clutching the rucksacks.

"St. Germain." The boy seemed as little thrilled with the introduction as Nick, as evidenced by the younger man's mouth turning down at the corners.

Lucy seemed oblivious to the tension. "I'm ravenous, Tom. Is your mother within?"

"Yes, my lady."

Lucy smiled sweetly at the boy, and Nick found himself resenting every nuance of that expression. Was he so ridiculously in love that he was jealous of her every word, her every look toward another man? Apparently so.

Lucy turned toward the makeshift house and Tom Selkirk followed her. Nick, rucksacks in hand, trailed the pair while trying to think of some plausible excuse he could offer for not entering the dwelling. Nick had few things he rejected out of hand, but caves were not on his list of places to be tolerated.

Lucy would not have expected it of him, but Nick had been cool and distant since he entered the Selkirks' home, thwarting her goal of furthering his conversion to reform. His every look, his every movement spoke his unease. Where was the man who had been so at home with the former climbing boys of London? He sat on the edge of his chair as if ready to bolt, his eyes moving at regular intervals toward the door. They had eaten little but dry bread and cheese since breakfast and yet Nick picked at his food, an insult to the rotund Mrs. Selkirk who kept trying to tempt him with choice bits of the stew. He gulped down several whiskeys in succession, leaving Lucy embarrassed and the Selkirks eyeing him with displeasure.

"The carpenters have finished the speakers' platform," Tom Selkirk informed the company. "Mrs. Trask has completed the bunting. The women will drape it on Sunday morning." In addition to the Selkirks, Lucy and Nick shared the simple table with Mr. Benton, one of the Nottingham reform leaders.

"What of the magistrates?" Mr. Selkirk asked. "Are they uneasy? I have heard reports the militia is to be called up."

There was a general murmuring, and Lucy shifted uneasily. Such a rally as they were planning had its risks, especially in Nottingham, which had been widely known for Luddite violence eight years earlier. Still, the region had been calm, if not entirely easy, for some time now. Surely the magistrates would realize that such a public gathering, with women and children in attendance, must be a peaceful one.

"A troop of dragoons has been spotted on the London road," Tom answered, "but they may be headed west. There has been some unrest in Gloucestershire."

"We shall hope so." Mr. Selkirk turned his attention to his stew.

Mr. Benton, the leader of the local reformers, laid down his spoon. "Even if we have no dragoons, you can be sure that Sidmouth's spies will be present. I am not entirely easy about this rally. I have a sense of something . . ." he trailed off, and Lucy looked at him in alarm. Mr. Benton was a quiet, unassuming man with considerable powers of perception, a quality that stirred him to leadership against his natural inclination for solitary pursuits.

"Change always brings risk," she offered, hoping to ease the minds of her friends. "This meeting will so obviously be a peaceful one that the authorities cannot feel threatened."

She felt Nick's eyes on her and could all but read his

thoughts. He did not believe that people of the lower classes could assemble without creating mayhem. Not for the first time, she wondered where he had acquired this notion.

Nick cleared his throat. "The reputation of this place is not in your favor." At these slightly slurred words, every head swiveled toward him. Mr. Benton grew pale.

"And what, sir, would you know of our reputation? The people of Nottingham are the most loyal subjects in the kingdom."

Nick was silent for a moment, as if weighing his words, and Lucy held her breath. She did not want to be forced to choose between her friends and Nick. Nick leaned back in his chair.

"I'm sure that the good folk of Nottinghamshire excel in every respect. The magistrates, though, have history on their side."

"On their side?" The normally placid Mr. Benton looked as if he might fall into a fit of apoplexy. "And what, pray tell, Mr. St. Germain, would you know of our history in this little corner of the world?"

"Only that there was much destruction of property, and even lives threatened, in past years. Only that men of business were forced to employ special guards and could no longer go around to the cottages of their employees to collect their rents and their finished goods from the framework knitters." Nick said all this in a moderate tone, but Lucy could see the whiteness of his knuckles where he gripped his wooden tankard. Her stomach knotted in apprehension.

Mr. Benton pushed back his chair and rose from the table. "Then there are a great many holes in your education, sir. For you say nothing of the laborers forced to pay exorbitant rents for their looms, receiving less and less recompense for the same work. You have told us nothing of bread prices that rose to such heights only the rich could afford a loaf. You have said nothing of children whose only food was potatoes and wild berries. Indeed,

Mr. St. Germain, I find you surprisingly ill-informed for a friend of Lady Lucy. But since you are her friend, I will bid you good night and leave you to Mrs. Selkirk's generous hospitality."

Mr. Benton laid his napkin gently on the table and bowed to the elder Selkirks. He patted Lucy on the shoulder as he passed by, and then he was gone. Lucy flushed with mortification.

Nick, too, rose from the table. "Mr. Selkirk, Mrs. Selkirk, I thank you for your hospitality and can only offer my apologies for ruining your joy in your dinner." He walked from the table to the corner of the room where their rucksacks lay in a heap. He slung the packs over his shoulder and looked at Lucy expectantly. "We had best make for our lodgings."

Lucy stared in surprise. Had he not realized? "Nick, our lodging is here. With the Selkirks." She felt hot with shame at his behavior. He had never acted so abominably, not even to her. Nick looked around the cave and shuddered visibly, and Lucy's eyes stung with tears that he would show such contempt for her friends.

"Nay, Lucy. I cannot remain here. We will find lodgings in town." He held out his hand to her.

Mr. Selkirk rose to his feet as well. "Don't be a fool, St. Germain. With the crowds that are gathering, do you expect to find an empty bed anywhere in Nottingham? And even if you could, I would not allow Lady Lucy to stay with you unchaperoned. I may be a simple man, Mr. St. Germain, but I know what is due a young lady. She will stay with Mrs. Selkirk and nowhere else."

"Then I shall sleep outdoors," Nick responded coolly as he withdrew his hand. "It will not be the first time." He dropped her rucksack and left the house, the makeshift door grating against its sandstone casing as it closed behind him. Lucy stood immobile, torn between her friends and worry for Nick. Whatever his faults, he was not normally ungracious. Something was amiss.

"It is June, and he will not freeze," Mr. Selkirk offered

as a conciliatory gesture, returning to his seat.

"Excuse me, please." Lucy laid her napkin on the table and rose from her chair. "Something is very wrong. I must go after him."

"Wrong?" snorted Tom. "I should say so. He may affect the airs of a prince, but he'll still be a commoner sleeping on the cold ground tonight. Good riddance, I say."

Lucy turned a deaf ear to Tom's imprecations and followed Nick out the door.

Nick strode out of the Selkirks' home and into the darkness. The longest night he had ever spent had been passed huddled in a cave in the Santadorran mountains, high above the Ivory Palace. His mother lay a hundred yards away beneath the crude tomb he'd fashioned from loose stones. His sister's body had been taken by the renegade soldiers who'd set upon them in their flight from the palace. At twelve, he'd not known what else to do, and so he had hidden in a crevice in the rocky hillside, not daring to weep for fear of discovery. Surely his father would come, but by the time the king and the Royal Guards had found him, morning had broken over the horizon.

Nick had not entered a cave since, until tonight, until he'd had to face his abhorrence or make his excuses to Lucy. If she had been a man, he could have offered the briefest of explanations and been left to his own devices. But a woman would never let a man escape without wanting to extract all the sordid details of his disgrace. A woman would want him to cry, would want to mend the great, gaping holes in his soul. The thought sent a chill through him. Nick liked his holes, thank you very much. They were as much a part of him as his disreputable boots.

He'd not gone a handful of yards from the Selkirks' door when he stopped, unsure which direction to turn. More than likely Mr. Selkirk was right and there would be no lodgings to be had in town. He turned and looked behind him, higher up into the dark hills, and pulled his cloak tighter. The shelter of the forest, however uncertain, was certainly preferable to a night of agony in a cave.

"Nick! Wait!" Lucy appeared in the doorway, the light from within the cottage surrounding her like an angel's halo.

He didn't want to wait. With newfound resolution, he turned toward an odd sort of staircase carved into the hillside between two of the houses. It led upward into the shelter of the trees.

"Nick! Please!"

He moved quickly, but she had broken into a run and was gaining ground. He longed to run himself, but then she would know that he meant to elude her. He had gained the top of the makeshift steps before she caught up to him.

"Nick! I know you heard me call." Her hand plucked at his coat, then at his pack. When she tugged on the rucksack, he let it fall from his shoulder, determined not to turn around, fully intending to keep going. Tears stung his eyes, and if Lucy Charming ever saw those, he would be a lost man. He didn't want tenderness, not now, not yet.

"I'll sleep out here," he said over his shoulder, using every bit of cool reserve he possessed to make the words sound convincingly neutral. "The cave is far too confined for my taste." She was still hard on his heels and now trying to grasp his arm.

"You can't sleep in the open," she protested. "Not without someone to share the watch."

He shivered in the darkness. God, he didn't want her to see his weakness. Women deserved only strength.

"Something's wrong, Nick. Tell me, please."

She was like an unrelenting mountain rain, washing away his willpower. "Nothing's wrong, Lucy. You've a vivid imagination. Go back to the Selkirks'. I'll return when it grows light."

They had reached a small grove of trees fifty yards

above the Selkirks' home. Away from the dwellings, it was completely dark and Nick risked turning to face her. In the inky night, she would not be able to read his troubled expression.

"Go back, Lucy. Leave me to my own devices." He sank down on a fallen log.

"I can't leave you alone."

"Neither can you stay. Mr. Selkirk will be up here at any moment, afraid that I've compromised the oh-so-proper Lady Lucy." He'd meant to hide the bitter sting to the words. His reserve, which had not betrayed him since his father and the guards had found him in the mountains so many years ago, felt alarmingly fragile.

"Mr. Selkirk may offer me the protection of his roof, but I will choose my own friends." Without waiting for an invitation, she lowered herself onto the log next to him. Her nearness twisted through him like a knife.

"Please, Lucy. Go back." Despite his best efforts, the words held a desperate undertone. "You worry needlessly. I shall be fine."

And he would be, once she was beyond arm's reach. Once she had removed herself and all the temptations that were Lucy Charming. It was not just her blue eyes and her curls and her wrongheaded crusade for reform that caused his palms to sweat like a boy plunged headlong into the throes of calf love. No, Lucy Charming's most tempting asset was her courage, a courage that he had lacked since the age of twelve, no matter how he might style himself the hero.

Lucy, though, refused to be so easily dismissed. She slipped her hand between his sleeve and chest and curled her fingers around his arm. Nick willed his pulse not to beat faster. Her touch was both heaven and hell. He wanted her, he could have her, but in the end, she would cost him what little remained of his soul, for marriage meant offspring and even he knew that he could not allow Santadorra to be denied its heir to the throne.

"Tell me." She said the words with soft understanding, and his stomach knotted.

"Tell you what? I've already told you to go away, and you don't listen. Would there be any use in telling you anything more?"

She ignored his caustic reply. "Tell me why you behaved so abominably to the Selkirks. For all your faults, you do not usually lack for polite address. Even if those around you are not your equals."

If he had not revealed so much of himself to Lucy over the last few weeks, she would not now understand so much of his character. She would have chalked up his behavior to princely pride or royal snobbery. To her, he was not Crown Prince Nicholas. He was simply Nick. The thought seduced him even as he fought temptation. He had never met anyone less intimidated by worldly consequence than Lucy Charming, but Nick remained silent. Let her make her own conjectures. Whatever they might be, they were less humiliating than the truth.

"I won't go back until you tell me why you were so rude." She squirmed closer to him on the log, and Nick's pulse accelerated despite his willpower.

"There's nothing to tell, Lucy. My motives are as base as you say. The Selkirks are beneath me, my inferiors in every regard. What does it matter if I insult them?" The whiskey he'd consumed with the dab of dinner he'd eaten suffused his brain. Nick was no stranger to strong spirits, but those caves must make for some powerful brewing houses. The steady year-round temperature would be ideal. No wonder the log beneath him seemed to tilt first in one direction and then the other.

"What does it matter if you insult them?" Lucy repeated his question, incredulous. "It matters a great deal to me, you . . ." She stopped. "No. I won't let you distract me. Not again. What is your objection to staying with the Selkirks? I have a right to know."

Nick laughed. "A right to know? What right?"

"The right of wager, I guess. You did agree that I might

select the means of your education about reform."

He snorted. "Sleeping under the Selkirks' roof is not part of that education. Attending the reform meeting is."

"It is all part and parcel of the same thing, Nick."

With each passing moment, he grew too exhausted to argue with her. "Go away, Lucy."

"All right. If you answer one question."

He paused. Agreeing to her request was a gamble, but if it would send her back to the safety of the Selkirks' abode it would be worth it.

"Very well. One question."

"Why are you afraid of caves?"

He slid farther along the log to escape the warmth that radiated from her body like steam from a Santadorran hot spring. "Afraid? How amusing. Is that what you think?" His tone was perfect—bored, distant, cynically detached. She would never push past his reserve, not while he was still conscious and upright, anyway.

"You are. You're frightened of the caves."

He gripped the end of the log with one hand, glad to have put some distance between them. "That's an amusing theory, Lucy, but hardly one with any merit. I simply prefer not to spread my bedroll among such common people."

"What happened to your mother and sister?"

"What have they to do with this?" His pulse pounded in his ears. Lucy followed him along the log. If he tried to move away from her again, he would find himself tumbled in a heap on the cold ground.

"The mountains in Santadorra—are there caves, as you told the boys?" Her hand slid down his arm, and her fingers claimed his. The warmth of her touch was his undoing. Or was it the warmth of her heart? Years of shame and humiliation mingled inside him and pressed against one another until they caught fire and burned in his breast.

"Yes, by Jove, there are caves." Flames rushed through him, scorching him with the shame of his memories. "Miserable, damp, cold caves. One of them overlooks my mother's tomb, princess. Perhaps another one holds the body of my sister. I have no idea, since I could never find her after the soldiers took her." With a jerky motion, he rose on unsteady legs, bile rising in his throat. Lucy moved with him, catching his elbow and holding him upright, and God help him, he let her. He leaned on her.

"And you? Was there a cave there for you?"

Thank God for the darkness. It hid this unmanly display. Thick tears coursed over his cheeks, tears that he had not cried since that awful night.

"A cave for me? Yes. Of course. A small one. One that only a twelve year-old boy could squeeze inside. The soldiers were less than a hundred feet away. They camped for the night there. I was afraid to breathe."

She would try to comfort him. She would murmur platitudes. Nick waited in dread, but Lucy was silent, blissfully silent. He wiped his cheeks with his sleeve. If he were a stronger man, he would shake off her grip on his arm, but that light touch—perhaps he could bear that. If she had tried to embrace him or fawn over him, he could not have borne it. But the gentle pressure of her fingers just above the crook of his arm could be tolerated. It would be so much easier if he didn't love her. Then he wouldn't care what she thought of him.

"I've never told anyone about that night." The words escaped before he could weigh their import. They echoed in his head and in the crisp night air, and he wished he could call them back. They revealed too much.

He could tell she was searching his face in the darkness. "Never told anyone? Not even Crispin?"

"No. Only my father."

"How long ago did it happen?" They stood quietly in the darkness, the lights of Nottingham scattered below them like diamonds on a queen's mantle.

Nick laughed bitterly. "Sixteen years. The poets like to deceive us by saying that time heals such wounds, but I have not found that to be the case." No, time had no such efficacious powers. Wagers and drink and women possessed much stronger medicine.

"Time does heal wounds," Lucy countered softly, "but only if we allow it to do so. You have kept this wound open purposely, Nick. No wonder it has festered."

Her implied criticism stung, and Nick shook off her grasp as he stepped away from her. What could Lucy Charming know of wounds and their healing? She lived the life she wanted, in the manner she desired.

"What could heal this, Lucy? And why should it be healed? They were my responsibility, and I failed. There is little more to be said." He wished he had never left the Selkirks' cave. Confession would never bring the absolution he sought, and once she had seen his weakness, Lucy would have yet another reason not to sign her name to the marriage lines that lay tucked in his vest pocket.

"And so you became profligate. A thorn in your father's side, so that he would not love you."

Nick winced. "It required little effort on my part to achieve that goal." The words had stewed inside him for so long that they were thick with anger. "My father is inclined to believe the worst of me. He does, after all, have history on his side."

"And what—or whom—do you have on yours?" she asked softly.

Nick's gut twisted. How could he answer that? He had Crispin, to some extent, but not beyond the bounds of the usual camaraderie between gentlemen. His tailor? No, for he had not paid his bills in some months. Not his boot maker either, obviously. Henny or Madame St. Cloud? For a price. The loyal subjects of Santadorra? It was their attempt to revolt, encouraged by the French soldiers, that had cost him everything he held dear. Whom did he have on his side? He supposed the former climbing boys in Mr. Cartwright's care might be bothered to consult him on the design and construction of tree houses.

"There is no one, princess." Grief rose up, inexorably,

like a stream fed by summer storms, filling every empty place inside of him. He should have known this would happen. From the moment he had opened his eyes that day in Lady Belmont's garden and had seen Lucy Charming hovering above him like some angelic visitation, he should have known this very moment would arrive, this confession would become necessary. "I am alone. It is what I like, and that is how I shall remain, even if I marry."

He had used similar words before with women, said in much more self-deprecating tones. If given the right mixture of haunting tragedy and masculine indifference, most women tumbled at his feet. He hated that Lucy would become just another victim in a long succession of casualties. Like all the others, she would want to heal him. Her instincts for reform would engage, and he would become a project, not a person.

She hovered a few feet away. He would bed her, he supposed, when she came to him. They would be married soon anyway, and he ought to gain some recompense for his confession. Surely he was due some salve to his pride.

With a deep sigh designed to draw her to him, he turned and even opened his arms. In the dark, she was hard to see. In fact, he could not see her at all. He listened. He could not hear her either. The soft breathing that had driven him wild that night at Madame St. Cloud's was not in evidence.

"Lucy?"

No answer. And then he saw her, farther down the hill. She stood poised at the top of the makeshift stairs.

"Lucy?" Damn, but there was the slightest hint of panic in his voice.

She looked back over her shoulder, and he couldn't read her expression. He had chosen the darkness to conceal his own feelings, but they hid hers as well.

"Where are you going?"

She stood silhouetted against the night sky by the lights from the caves below. "I'm returning to the Selkirks, as you wished. In my opinion, self-pity is more effective as a solitary occupation."

Self-pity? Her words hit him with the force of a blow. Nick stood stunned. How dare she? How dare she trivialize his most intimate secrets?

Suddenly, he was moving down the hill. He caught her on the stairway and grabbed her arm. "That is your response to my revelations? You walk away?"

She stopped and glared first at his fingers that held her prisoner and then into his face. They stood close enough now that even in the dim light he could see the color of her eyes, the blue of a Santadorran lake.

"Your Highness, I am mortally tired of being grabbed like some barroom doxy." She shook off his grip. "Do you never tire of trying to control me? Surely the sport must lose its freshness."

Nick stared at her in confusion, his heart aching. "I have never deceived myself, Lucy, into thinking I might control your behavior. I have only sought to remedy some of the damage you inflict upon yourself."

"And what of the damage that you bring upon yourself? Who will remedy that, Nick?" A soft night wind blew her curls into her eyes. He reached out to brush them back but she pushed his hand away. "I am sorry for your loss, but you are not the only person in the world who has ever suffered. You lost your mother and sister. I lost my father. The Selkirks lost their older son when so many of the Luddites were transported to Australia. We have all suffered, Nick, but you have had the comfort of money and position. You have had the security of education and breeding. You and I have never known day upon day of hunger. Nor have we watched our children starve before our eyes. Yes, our sufferings are real, but they are very little when compared with what occurs in the width and breadth of the world."

Nick wanted to breathe, but his lungs did not seem to be working. He wanted to protest, to defend his right to his pain, but the truth in Lucy's words rendered him speechless. He had indeed sought heedless self-indulgence as a remedy to his pain, while she had taken on the cause of reform. He had thought her foolish, but, not for the first time, he saw that he was the one who had been a very great fool.

Her expression was as hard and cold as the rock that surrounded them. "I bid you good night, Your Highness. You need not stay in Nottingham. I'm sure you will prefer to return to London in the morning. This wager is a charade that need not be played to its conclusion."

He would lose her. Nick knew it, felt it in the hollow ache that had taken up residence in his chest. If he let her go now, she would disappear from his life forever.

"No. I desire no such release. The wager still stands. Either you convince me of reform or you marry me."

"You will not release me from the wager?" she asked in disbelief. Their gazes held, locked in combat, but Nick refused to relent.

"No. I will not." He had already lost too much in his lifetime. He would not let her escape him so easily.

"Very well, then," she conceded, more graciously than he might have hoped. Was that relief he saw in her eyes? "I will see you at breakfast." She started down the stairs, and Nick stepped back to collect his rucksack and followed her.

"You need not see me to the door," she snapped, but Nick did not stop. He felt lighter somehow, as if by sharing his memories, he had divested himself of a physical burden. The prospect of the Selkirks' cavelike abode suddenly seemed less daunting now that he had shared the truth of his fears with Lucy.

"I'm not following you, princess. I've merely changed my mind about the desirability of a night among the trees. If the Selkirks will have me, I will make up a pallet on their floor."

His reward for his courage was the startled expression, and a dawning look of approval, in Lucy Charming's eyes.

Chapter Fifteen

Faint morning light stole through the slats in the wooden shutters, rousing Lucy from slumber. With the ease of much practice, she stole from the bed where Mrs. Selkirk lay sleeping, and in the dim light pulled on the dress and stockings she'd brought in her rucksack, and collected her half boots. Eager to meet the new day, she peered through the doorway that separated the sole bedroom of the cottage from the main room. The larger area held the three sleeping men: Mr. Selkirk, Tom, and Nick.

Lucy shivered in the cool air of the cave and reached for a shawl on a peg just inside the bedchamber door. Nick snored lightly, she noticed, apparently able to transcend the discomfort of cold night air and an even colder bed. For all his trepidation about the cave, he must have found some peace in the night, and she was glad for his sake. Perhaps she should have shown Nick more pity, but he seemed to have already ladled a generous helping into his own dish. Her heart had nearly broken at his story of that disastrous night in the mountains of Santadorra, but Lucy knew from experience that no matter how tragic one's history, life must go on. His tale, though, had helped her to see Nick in a new light. She had thought his need to play the hero resulted from his noble birth, from royal condescension. How could she have known that he was reliving his past again and again, seeking to change the outcome? Tears threatened, but she forced them back.

Half boots in hand, Lucy slipped past the sleeping men and let herself out the front door. The summer morning lay fresh on the hills, where the sheep had yet to devour the new grass, and overhead the sky stretched like an enormous aquamarine dome. A good omen, she hoped, for such an important day, for by sundown she would settle her wager with Nick one way or another. Either today's reform rally would convince him of the need for such measures, or she would agree to become his bride.

Both eventualities seemed as unlikely as rain clouds appearing in the crystalline sky, but somehow, Lucy knew she must win the wager before her love for Nick led her astray from what she knew was right. If she won the wager and convinced Nick of the necessity of reform, then he would be able to accept her but no longer be bound to marry her. And if she lost, then she would be forced to marry a man she loved who would never accept her for herself. Either fate seemed untenable, and yet Lucy knew that she could only make the one choice. Life without the man she loved would be far preferable to life with a man who did not love her.

"Good morning, Lady Lucy."

Lucy jumped at the sound, and her heart pounded until she realized that it was not Nick who had stepped through the doorway to join her in the sunlight. Instead, Tom Selkirk appeared, tucking his shirt into his breeches. Lucy was both relieved and disappointed.

"I'm too excited to sleep properly," she confided to Tom. Instinctively, they set off down the rutted road, two young people accustomed to each other's company. For a moment, the years fell away, and they were again the best of friends, tramping through the woods and walking the smoother paths near Charming Hall.

" 'Tis a shame your father's not here to see this day," Tom offered as they followed the track past dozens of other abodes. The little village of caves would begin to stir soon, its inhabitants eager to descend on the Market Square in Nottingham for the day's festivities.

"Yes, 'tis a pity." Her joy in the day faltered at the thought of her father. He had believed reform the only means for averting in England what had happened in France. In truth, he'd been rather traditional as an aristocrat. He'd not been hesitant to lend his strong back during the sheep shearing or lift a pint in the village tavern with his field laborers. He had known his station, but he had not looked upon the common folk as his inferiors. In a world where *noblesse oblige* was fast disappearing, her father had been a man who honored the responsibilities of his position.

Lucy's throat tightened as her last sight of her father rose in her mind, his body prostrate on the floor of the library, blood everywhere. Her stomach roiled, but her heart protested her even entertaining the possibility that her father's gunshot wound had been self-inflicted. He would not have committed an act of desperation as her stepmother insinuated. He held his principles too strongly. And yet . . . She had seen the growing despair in his eyes in those last weeks, when it became clear that reform was an impossible dream in Nottingham. And she knew that her dependence upon her father had left her exposed and vulnerable to the machinations of her stepmother. Never again would she depend on anyone, she'd sworn, and until Nick, she would never have imagined any difficulty in keeping her oath.

"Your father might have been the duke, but he never forgot his people," Tom said. The words caused a tightening in her throat. Yes, indeed, her father would have enjoyed this day, and Lucy felt both sorry and angry that he was not there to see it.

She did not reply, and Tom respected her silence, offering her his hand as he had done from childhood. Lucy grasped it and they continued forward, each preparing for the coming day. They were still hand-in-hand when they returned to the Selkirk's doorway, only to be met by a frowning Nick.

"Your mother wants you," he said to Tom, and the boy blushed at Nick's choice of words. Lucy frowned at Nick, but he ignored her expression. Tom gave her hand a squeeze and ducked through the doorway into the house.

"Tom is sensitive about his age," Lucy began, but Nick only rolled his eyes.

"He is but a boy."

"He's far older than you were when you fled to the Santadorran mountains."

Nick flinched, and at this sign of a direct hit, she scaled back the tirade she might have delivered. "There's no reason to torment Tom."

"You are a great defender of his." He sounded miffed, and even—could it be?—jealous.

"Tom will be a leader in the movement someday. He is intelligent and eloquent, two necessary skills for the job."

"In the meantime, he has you to hold his hand and coddle him." Nick sounded more like a petulant schoolboy than a worldly prince.

"You are jealous," Lucy said in wonder, delighting in the words as they rolled off her tongue. How ridiculous, but how satsifying, too. The Crown Prince of Santadorra jealous of an unseasoned Nottingham youth.

"I would never stoop to jealousy," Nick snapped. He looked wonderful in the golden morning light. Dark stubble covered his jaw, giving him the air of a pirate, and his clothes were rumpled. It was hardly fair that men should look so attractive first thing in the morning while women must spend time at their toilette merely to appear presentable. Then again, Lucy had spared no time at her toilette that morning. She lifted a hand to her hair. The results were probably quite evident.

"Of course you're not jealous," she agreed in false, bright tones. "Is it time for breakfast?"

A disgruntled Nick nodded. "I came to fetch you. Mrs. Selkirk has the porridge ready." She could hear the underlying resignation in his tone and wondered when was the last time that His Highness had eaten porridge. She almost asked but thought better of it. She had unearthed enough unpleasant memories from him the previous night. The day would be reserved for happier pursuits, or at least less haunting ones.

In less than an hour, they had eaten their meal, tidied the Selkirks' home, and begun the descent into Nottingham. Lucy walked with Tom, Nick trailing a few steps behind. As they drew closer to the town proper, the throng of people grew, swelling to fill the dusty road. The excitement in the air lent a spring to Lucy's step, but Nick's boots began to drag. For the first time, she thought about what it might feel like for a prince who'd been chased by a mob, and then by soldiers, to willingly join in such a mass of people. Her heart skipped a beat and she slowed her pace, allowing Tom to move ahead and Nick to fall into step with her.

"When we reach the square, you will remain close to me," he instructed as they walked. Lucy bristled at the command, but then his words of the previous night came rushing back. Nick had reason to fear, although there was no need. Still, she would humor him and allow him to see that not every popular gathering was a recipe for disaster. This peaceful rally would be the very thing to effect a change of heart in her reluctant prince.

"I want to hear the speakers," Lucy answered, not willing to let his command pass without any protest whatsoever. "We must be near enough to the dais to gain a sense of the speeches."

Nick looked down at her with a grave air. "You believe this will turn out well, don't you?" Skepticism marked every line of his face.

"It is a peaceful assembly, Nick. No one here intends any harm."

"You are too trusting. Not everyone's motives are as pure as yours."

Lucy laughed at the thought that her motives might in any way be called pure. She was no saint. Reform was important because it meant a better life for so many people. If more of society's elite truly comprehended the dire straits of the peasantry, they would act in quite a different manner. An image of the Prince Regent and his indifference flickered through her mind, but she pushed it aside. Peaceful rallies such as this one must attract the notice of Parliament, even if the Prince of Wales could not be brought to see the justice of the cause.

"My motives are as jumbled as anyone's," she teased him, and she was pleased to see his stiffness relax a bit.

As they entered the city, enormous crowds converged in the streets, pressing on toward the great square where the open-air market was held. Men toted heavy baskets of food or pushed small handcarts loaded with the day's provisions for their families. The women cradled babies or swung toddlers up in their arms. Older brothers and sisters dashed back and forth, adding to the general merriment and disarray in the crowd.

When they reached the square, the area was filled with banners and booths. Mr. Selkirk and Tom found an unoccupied corner between a cobbler's stall and a man selling ices. The wiry Mr. Selkirk set his basket on the cobblestones and Mrs. Selkirk began to unpack it. Tom immediately disappeared into the crowd, and Lucy longed to go with him. He would surely find his way to the very edge of the dais, but she held back out of concern for Nick. This spot, tucked away from the worst of the crowds, would be easier for him to endure and so more favorable to her cause.

"Was there ever any day such as this?" Mrs. Selkirk asked with a bright smile as she settled herself onto a cask, as comfortable a chair as anyone was likely to find.

Lucy grinned at her. "The hard work of the reformers has yielded great results. Parliament must listen to so many voices raised as one."

"Parliament will be more concerned about preventing revolution than with listening," Nick replied under his breath so that only Lucy could hear. She stilled, momentarily distracted, for Nick's words rang true. She was accustomed to accounting the common folk as her friends, but those who lived in the *haut ton* felt differently. And yet, Lucy thought, not for the first time, how could a gathering that included women and children be perceived as a revolutionary threat?

The speeches began, and Lucy's party was near enough to hear most of the words. Still, though, it was difficult to ignore the low buzz of conversation and the cries of babies. Lucy edged out from between the traders' booths.

"Lucy!" Nick hissed, but he didn't reach out to try and restrain her.

"Just a bit closer," she said and slipped out through the crowd. Nick could wait with the Selkirks. Her presence was not likely to change his mind if the speeches failed to do so, and she had waited so long to be a part of this day.

"No, Lucy." His voice rose slightly, but she ignored him and made her way toward the front of the crowd. Nick's voice had held a hint of desperation, but what was there to be concerned about? Lucy suppressed a pang of guilt. The rally was proceeding well, and there was no sign of the local militia, much less the king's dragoons. All would be well.

Lucy wove through the throng until she caught sight of the dais. It was draped in red and blue bunting, and the speakers' platform rose several more feet in the air. A man she did not recognize was holding forth with great eloquence on the need for additional poor relief.

"The parishes cannot rectify a problem that far exceeds their means," he shouted, and the crowd roared with approval. Lucy applauded, her heart full. The power of the common people was an amazing thing to witness. Justice, decency, and goodness radiated from the crowd in the market square up to heaven itself.

The speaker shook his fist in the air. "Parliament must hear! The Regent must hear! The men of England demand that their voices be heard!"

This time the roar that rose from the crowd was deafening. Lucy stopped applauding and clapped her hands over her ears. Suddenly, the ground beneath her feet began to rumble, further heightening the din. She looked around but could see nothing beyond the press of people. Then, to her right, there was a flash of metal in the sun. The crowd's roar died, and the ominous thundering of horses' hooves sounded against the cobblestones.

The screams began when the first line of dragoons appeared at the edge of the square. They rode straight for the dais, ignoring the men, women, and children in their path. Her heart in her throat, Lucy watched in stunned disbelief as the mounted soldiers in their bright uniforms passed within a few feet of her. One horse reared, and when the beast's hooves descended, a man fell beneath them. The woman next to her screamed and hit out at the soldier, who responded with a swing of his bayonet. Blood sprayed, fine as mist, and Lucy covered her mouth with her hand, holding back her terror as the genial mood of the crowd instantly transformed into absolute panic.

Chaos reigned in the square. For one frustrating, aching moment, Nick couldn't squeeze around Mrs. Selkirk's girth. The older woman struggled to her feet while Nick tried to slip past her and then finally grasped her shoulders and lifted her from the cask. She turned toward him, ashen.

"Lady Lucy. Tom." She mouthed the words over the noise of the fleeing throng. The sharp report of rifle fire echoed in the square and nausea rose in Nick's stomach.

He should never have let Lucy out of sight. Not for a single moment.

People of all ages—screaming women, crying children, angry men—flowed against Nick like a flooding river as he fought his way in the direction of the dais. He pushed against them, aware that to lose his footing would mean certain death. The king's troops showed little order or discipline as they plunged through the crowd. Nick ducked as a horse reared barely five feet from his head.

"Help me!" The plaintive cry came from his feet. He looked down to find a young woman thrusting a babe into his arms. She was bleeding copiously from her belly, and Nick could have sworn it was a bayonet wound. "Take him!" the woman pleaded. "Please, take my baby." He hesitated. Lucy. He must find Lucy.

"Please, sir," the woman begged, and Nick suddenly found the infant in his arms. He juggled the unfamiliar bundle as the crowd continued to surge past him.

"Come with me." He reached down for the woman, but she did not take his hand.

"No! Take the baby! Run! Run!"

Her words were frantic, but Nick felt a numbness stealing over him. He had heard those words—or similar ones—before, from another mother. His own.

Without knowing quite how he managed it, Nick reached down and pulled the young woman up beside him. "Hold on to me." With the baby tucked in the crook of his other arm, it was all he could do to keep the three of them from pitching to the ground and being trampled. Nick glanced over his shoulder in the direction of the speaker's platform and prayed for a glimpse of Lucy. A shadow fell over him and he looked up to find himself facing not a dragoon, but a local militiaman with a raised bayonet.

"Run, you filthy scum," the militiaman shouted. Nick watched as the man lifted the bayonet, and in that moment, he knew that all was lost. The baby began to shriek. He could not even protect an innocent babe from . . .

"You run, you bleeding coward." Tom Selkirk, appearing from nowhere, hoisted the soldier's stirrup and threw the man off balance. The momentary distraction was enough. Nick thrust the baby into Tom's care and then swung the woman into his arms.

It took them an eternity to cross the market square, fighting the panic-stricken crowd as Nick and Tom inched, inexorably, toward safety. "Have you seen Lady Lucy?" Nick shouted at Tom as they dodged bodies and soldiers. The baby wailed in the younger man's arms.

"I left her to your care," Tom yelled back angrily. "Damn your soul, St. Germain. Damn your soul."

If Nick had had any breath left, he could have told Tom that it was far too late. His soul had been damned long ago. They reached the shelter of an alleyway off the main square and Nick stopped. The sudden stillness was disconcerting after the pandemonium of the crowd. Gingerly, Nick laid the woman on a pallet of flour sacks on the pavement outside a bakeshop. Her pale skin and listless gaze reminded him of a death mask.

"Here," he said to Tom. "Give me the babe. Now fetch a surgeon, and be quick."

"Are you mad? There won't be a surgeon to be had, not in this catastrophe. And what about Lady Lucy?"

Nick wanted to scream at the boy, wanted to howl in pain at the fear clenching his gut, but neither response would save the woman at his feet or the woman he loved. "I don't care what you have to do, but fetch a surgeon! As soon as she is safe, I'll find Lucy."

Tom's nostrils flared, but Nick had no time for righteous indignation. "You know where to look. I do not. Now, Selkirk. Or we may lose them both."

These words, at least, were enough to spring young Tom into action. He took off without further protest. Nick could only pray there was a surgeon to be found. The screams of terror had subsided, but though he could not see the square from his vantage point, he could hear the moans and wails of the injured. Tom had laid the babe in the crook of the mother's arm, against her un-injured side, and the little one, reunited with the smell and warmth of his mother, gazed peacefully back at him. Nick ripped a large scrap from one of the flour sacks, brushed away the mold that clung to it, and bundled it into a compress to hold against the woman's wound. He pressed it firmly in place, the strength of his hands her only hope of survival. Nick sat, prisoner to the woman's need, and tortured himself with wondering whether any of the moans he heard were issued from the lips of the woman he loved, the woman he should have been protecting.

The clock in the church belltower chimed the hour before Tom returned with a surgeon in tow. Nick didn't pause to ask how Tom had obtained the man's services in the midst of such a melee. Instead, he yanked Tom down beside him, pressed the youth's hand against the woman's bandage, and leaped to his feet. Heart racing, he dashed around the corner and into the square.

The peaceful market lay in ruins, strewn with bodies like a battlefield. The soldiers had retreated, leaving carnage in their wake. Nick heard the sound of laughter from over his head and looked up to the wide balcony that spanned the front of an ale house. Several gentlemen, one wearing what appeared to be a mayoral seal, hoisted pints in the air, and with a jolt, Nick realized they were celebrating. The urge to climb the balcony trestles and wring their necks with his bare hands almost overwhelmed him. He started toward the ale house and then stopped. Lucy. She was still out there, somewhere.

Other once-jubilant reformers were now picking their way cautiously back into the square to recover the injured and the dead. Nick watched as a woman collapsed over the form of a young boy. His throat knotted. No, not Lucy. She was alive somewhere in this carnage. He moved as quickly as he could, stepping gingerly to avoid the injured. Other than the boy, there seemed to be remarkably few dead, but unfortunately the more gravely wounded might find holding on to life difficult. Infection, disease—enemies far stronger than soldiers with bayonets—must now be faced.

Nick was within ten yards of the speaker's platform when he saw her. Her bright curls stood in relief against the dullness of the stone beneath her head. She lay motionless, and for a long moment he couldn't move, could only pray with a fervor he'd known only once before. *Dear God. Dear God, why do you never take me instead?*

"Lucy!" In three long strides he was beside her, hardly able to breathe. He dropped to the ground and rolled her onto her back. Lowering his cheek to her mouth, he begged heaven for the feel of her warm breath against his skin. For once in his life, the Almighty was listening.

"She breathes," he said, but there was no one else to hear. Her right temple was bruised and bleeding where it had hit the stone. "Lucy. Lucy, open your eyes." His voice was not as commanding as he'd intended, hardly more than a whisper. He ran his hands over her limbs and her belly, checking for other injuries. He felt no weaknesses, no blood, no breaks. If he was a very, very lucky man, and God was feeling gracious, Lucy might only be concussed.

"Oh, princess," he said, sighing. "This was not the way I intended to win this wager."

Very carefully, Nick lifted her in his arms and moved back across the square. Guilt, that familiar burden, seemed to weigh more than the unconscious Lucy. It would be too much to hope that the surgeon was still in front of the bakeshop, but Nick asked God for it anyway. For Lucy. Surely the Almighty had a soft spot for reformers. After all, his own Son had been one of them.

Nick passed the grieving mother who still rocked over the body of her child, passed underneath the celebrating gentry on the alehouse balcony. One of them called down some imprecation, but Nick's ears were deaf to the taunts.

Inhumanity knew no social class, no level of privilege. He had learned that much this day.

The surgeon was still there, bent over the woman on her bed of flour sacks. The babe must have begun to cry again, for Tom had scooped him up and was awkwardly bouncing the infant. "Lady Lucy!" Tom's cry of relief quickly died away when Nick placed her limp form on another bed of flour sacks.

"When you're finished, sir," Nick said to the surgeon, "if you'd examine this girl, I'd be in your debt."

The surgeon, a grizzled old man, gave the bandage he'd wrapped around the young mother a final smoothing and stood. "I'm done with her."

Nick cringed at the finality in the man's tone. "Is she dead?" Had he sacrificed precious time, and possibly Lucy, all for naught?

"No, thank God. Perhaps I've managed to save one today. The pressure stemmed the flow of blood, otherwise she'd not be so lucky." The surgeon paused to run his hands over the babe in Tom's arms. "You will not have to give up your mother's milk quite yet, little one." He looked at Tom. "Do you know this woman?"

"No, but I'll find her people. You may leave her to my care, sir."

Nick watched as Tom seemed to mature in an instant, and his estimation of the youth rose several notches. If it weren't for the younger Selkirk fetching the surgeon, Nick's losses this day might have been more than he could bear. They still might be.

"Then let's see about this girl." The surgeon, accustomed to dire wounds, did not linger over his success. Nick stepped back as the man examined Lucy. For long, anxious minutes, the only sound Nick could hear was the echo of his own breathing. Finally, when he thought he couldn't stand another moment of not knowing, the surgeon looked up at him.

"I can find nothing wrong aside from the bump on her head, but I'm concerned she's not come around yet." He reached into his kit and brought out a small vial. With a deft hand, he waved the smelling salts under Lucy's nose. She winced and started to rouse, but then fell back against the flour sacks.

"Damn." The surgeon tucked the salts back into his kit. "Head injuries can be tricky. She needs to be somewhere warm and dry. Normally in these cases, the patient will rouse within twenty-four hours."

Nick couldn't miss the apprehension in the surgeon's voice. "And if they don't?"

"Then there is no knowing. I once had a patient lie insensible for a month, but when he awoke he was as fit as a fiddle."

"Then she will awaken?" Nick refused to allow fear to creep into his voice. Lucy would be well. She must be. He could not bear to lose her, not when she'd become as vital to him as the beating of his own heart.

"Warm and dry. Don't take it too hard, man. I have hope she'll recover." The surgeon paused. "She is your wife?"

"No," Nick answered. "But the moment she awakens, she will be."

The surgeon hoisted his kit. "That's the spirit, young man. No sense in waiting, not when life is so uncertain." He turned toward the square and looked back at Nick. "Is it bad, then?"

"Like a battlefield," Nick said.

The man's shoulders sagged. "I was at Waterloo, you know. I came to Nottingham for a bit of peace and quiet."

"And instead found reformers?"

"No. Instead, I found that the men who saved England are now treated like enemies. God save the poor mad king and damn the Regent. This would never have happened in Farmer George's day." The surgeon walked away, and Nick, feeling strangely shamed, turned to Tom Selkirk.

"Would your resourcefulness stretch to finding a cart, Tom? It's the only way I know to get these ladies home."

Tom nodded, handed Nick the babe, and took off down the narrow alleyway. Nick cradled the baby and waited, his eyes never leaving Lucy's face.

A day that had seemed so full of promise to the people of Nottingham ended in more tragedy than they'd be able to bear, Nick thought as he sank back on the stone bench that had literally been carved from the wall of Mrs. Selkirk's bedroom. He ached with exhaustion, but no amount of persuasion could move him from his perch beside the bed. Lucy lay very still. The injured mother and her child had been given a pallet in the main room, and Nick had insisted that the Selkirks tend to the woman and babe while he kept vigil over Lucy. Night had fallen at last on the long summer day, and Tom appeared at the doorway with a candle in hand.

"You'll want this when she wakes. She might be afraid if she finds herself in the dark."

"Thank you." He accepted the candle from Tom and set it on the bench beside him. Strange how tragedy could forge friendships between antagonists.

"She'll be all right," Tom reassured him. "Lady Lucy is strong, far stronger than you'd expect from an—"

"From an aristocrat?" Nick finished the youth's sentence with a tired smile.

Tom dipped his head and then grinned sheepishly in response. "Yes, I suppose so."

Nick rubbed his aching eyes with his fingertips. "We're not so different, you and I, Tom. I've learned that much this day."

Tom sagged against the doorway for support. "You're gentry, too, aren't you?" The question was casual, curious, with no hint of hostility.

"Royalty, actually," Nick responded before he thought the better of it.

"I'm not surprised," Tom said with a laugh. "You have that princely arrogance about you."

Nick nodded. "I suppose I do, Tom. I suppose I do."

For a moment, both were silent.

"She'll wake soon." Tom meant to reassure him, but the young man's doubtful gaze did not match his words.

"Within the hour, no doubt," Nick responded, but with little success at injecting optimism into his voice. With each hour that passed, his concern grew. The surgeon had specified twenty-four hours, but Nick couldn't bear to wait that long.

"Call me if you need anything," Tom said and then, with a lift of his hand, left the doorway.

"The only thing I need you cannot give me, young Tom." Nick shot a glance toward the door and then eyed the wide space beside Lucy. The cold stone bench was not an inviting bed, and more than anything he wanted to be close to her. He'd rather not shock the Selkirks, but they'd be shocked enough when Nick's identity was revealed.

With the ease of much practice, Nick divested himself of his boots, circled to the other side of the bed, and slid beneath the counterpane. How he wished he could undo the events of the last few days, and that he could start again from the last time he'd shared a bed with Lucy, when they'd been trapped in the fairy bower at Madame St. Cloud's.

Chapter Sixteen

A gentle buzzing near her ear woke Lucy from a heavy sleep. Reluctantly she opened her eyes, and the world swam before her. Despite the blurring, she recognized the bedroom; it was Mrs. Selkirk's. The counterpane beneath her fingers was the same one that had covered her the night before. A candle burned by the bedside, providing some illumination in the darkness. From beyond the half-closed door, she could hear voices.

Lucy gingerly turned toward the door to hear what they were saying, and her head throbbed in response. Gently, she reached up and fingered her temple. She could feel a swath of bandages over her brow. Slowly, she traced the neat edges of the soft linen. She must have struck her head. Gradually her vision grew clearer, and the low buzzing grew more annoying. She turned toward its source, away from the door, and felt every inch of skin tingle when she found Nick's face no more than a foot from her own.

Lucy's heartbeat accelerated, which exacerbated the pounding in her head. He was snoring again. His face was relaxed in sleep, but where repose made most men look boyish, he appeared more mature and handsome than ever. The candlelight lent soft shadows to his face, obscuring the tops of his high cheekbones and the firm line of his chin. She tried to lift her head from the pillow, prepared to protest his presence in the bed, but a wave of nausea rolled over her and she sank back instead.

Was she destined to spend her life trapped in a variety of beds with Nicholas St. Germain? The thought held a distressing appeal.

Since she couldn't move, and Nick showed no signs of waking, Lucy took advantage of the opportunity to gaze her fill at his devastating face, memorizing each plane and angle. He had the face of an ancient Caesar, the high forehead and strong line of his jaw, the aquiline nose. And though he could look extremely proud, he never lost that air of smoldering sensuality that had so threatened the defenses around her heart.

Indeed, time and time again, he'd breached the walls she'd constructed in the wake of her father's scandalous death to keep others at bay. Against good looks alone, she might have held fast. She could steel herself against charm. But when those things were combined with generosity to climbing boys and a heartfelt grief for a lost mother and sister, what could be done? Lucy was lost, had been lost, for longer than she cared to admit. She was thoroughly, irrevocably in love with him.

His repeated offers of marriage were all too tempting. Surely, though, after the previous day's rally, his convictions would be softened and she would win their wager and they would part company. She only hoped her untimely accident had not detracted from the effects of a peaceful reform rally. Perhaps she would even travel to Santadorra for the day when Nick granted universal suffrage in his realm. The thought cheered her, even as she knew that once they parted, it would be too painful to see him again.

She was deep in her reverie, distracted, and so it was a

moment before she noticed that the snoring had stopped and Nick had opened his eyes.

"Hello, princess."

The appellation brought tears to her eyes, but Lucy silently reprimanded herself. She had no more desire for a future with a prince than she had believed one possible with a gardener.

"Why are you here?" Prickliness was her only defense against his delicious closeness and her own unruly feelings.

"So that I can watch over you." He smiled ruefully and rubbed his face with one hand. "Not the most effective keeper of a vigil, I must admit." He levered himself up on one arm so that she looked straight up into his warm mahogany eyes. "How are you feeling?"

She willed the tightness in her chest to ease, because Nick, caring and concerned, was far too tempting. "Rather woozy, I'm afraid. But I can manage. Is it morning?" She didn't want to think about how she felt, physically or otherwise. Feelings were too dangerous, too disconcerting, especially when they centered on Nick St. Germain. Especially when she knew that it was time to let him go.

Nick glanced toward the candle and then in the direction of the half-open door and the voices coming from the main room. "It must be dawn. Or nearly so."

"And why isn't Mrs. Selkirk in here beating you with her broom? Or ordering Tom to throw you out the front door?" In Lucy's experience, Mrs. Selkirk was as high a stickler in her own way as the patronesses of Almack's.

"She had her hands full with the other young woman, I suspect. I told her I'd stand guard over you."

"Other young woman?" His words made no sense. "Nick, what's happened?"

He hesitated, and the candlelight revealed the indecision in his eyes.

"Nick, is something amiss?" Panic stirred within her. Her head injury, Nick in her bed, another woman in the

Selkirks' main room. Something must have happened at the rally, but what?

"How much do you remember?" His question was carefully phrased, and Lucy paused to consider her answer just as carefully. Even with a bruised head, she could play verbal cat-and-mouse.

"Remember about what?"

"About the rally."

Lucy was silent for a moment, and she frowned so that he would think she was searching her memory. In truth, she recalled very little, but obviously something quite important had happened, and Nick wanted to use her lack of information to his own advantage. Had she hit her head in the square? Her last memory was of pushing through the crowd as she hurried to the speaker's platform. Perhaps she had tripped and fallen.

"So you don't remember the rally, then."

"I remember moving toward the front of the crowd."

"But nothing after?"

He started to turn away but Lucy reached up and captured his chin in her fingers. His skin was rough with a night's growth of beard. For a brief moment, she considered running her palm over the stubble across his jaw. For an even briefer moment, she made the mistake of looking into his eyes. His gaze caught hers, and he tensed beneath her fingertips.

"Please, Nick. This is too important for games. What happened at the rally?" Lucy dropped her hand, willing away the power of the attraction to him that made her heart beat in double time.

"The dragoons were called in." His voice was even. Too even.

"How could they have known? There was no public declaration beforehand. Lord Sidmouth would hardly have sent troops unless he had direct confirmation. There were no spies involved in the planning. I am sure of it."

Nick's face was impassive. "Surely you realized the risk that something like this would happen."

"Did a riot break out? There was concern about the men from one of the other shires. They have been unruly elsewhere, but their leaders swore an oath they would not disrupt the rally."

"No, Lucy. The lads caused no trouble."

She wished she could tell what he was thinking behind that unemotional mask. "What then? Tell me, Nick." Her head throbbed, worry and tension knotting her neck and shoulders.

"I didn't see the cause of the trouble. I was trapped behind Mrs. Selkirk."

His veiled expression gave nothing away. "Then the rally was cut short? Well, we will try again, perhaps in another place, although Nottingham was ideal."

"Lucy, it was a great deal more than cut short."

Her heart seemed to stop. "What do you mean?"

Nick looked troubled, an unaccustomed expression for him. "The troops charged the crowd."

Lucy's breathing stopped as well as her heart, and then she sat up, ignoring her swimming senses. She must go to the square. It required little imagination to envision the damage that mounted soldiers could inflict upon an unarmed peasantry.

"They must be stopped." She swung out of bed, reaching for the bedpost and then realized there wasn't one. Her hand swung through empty air and she pitched forward. She braced herself for impact against the stone floor, but at the last moment a pair of strong arms caught her, and she was hauled against Nick's chest.

"You're shivering," he said. With one hand, he jerked the counterpane from the bedstead and wrapped it around her. "You need to be in bed."

Lucy clung to Nick as if he were the only solid thing in the world. "Were they hurt, then?" Her voice sounded small in her own ears. She despised it when her voice sounded small.

"The Selkirks? No."

"Not the Selkirks. The people."

225

"Which people?"

"Any of them."

He hesitated. Dear God, it was worse than she'd feared. "Are there dead? How many injured?" She wanted to pound his chest, to force him to tell her, but she doubted Nick would respond to such measures and she was too weak to hit him properly.

"Two dead. A boy, and one of the speakers who got tangled in the bunting and fell from the platform." The platform to which she'd been determinedly moving, Lucy thought, choking back tears.

"And injured?"

"A great number."

It seemed unreal. A thing not to be believed. They had planned so carefully. The soldiers had acted without provocation, she was sure of it. The mere threat of the common people assembled sent Sidmouth and his ilk into panic. But how had the Home Secretary known? He would never act on mere rumor. Someone, someone creditable, had communicated the reformers' plans to Whitehall.

Lucy dropped her fingers from Nick's shoulders and stepped back, willing strength into her limbs. "At least now you see the justice of my cause." She had wanted to win the wager with Nick, but never would she have imagined proving victorious in such a horrible manner. "A terrible price to pay to win a mere wager, but at least some good may come of it," she said, wiping her eyes with the back of her hand. "The men of England must return home and wait for justice another day, but their brothers in Santadorra will join the ranks of voting men."

Nick dropped his arms, and Lucy missed the warmth of his embrace keenly. "What are you assuming, princess? That the irresponsible actions of a company of soldiers will change my views? Surely I've shown myself more steadfast than that."

Cold enveloped her, sending chills through her chest and down her limbs. She clutched the coverlet more tightly about her. No. He could not take the part of the soldiers. There was no justification for violence against those who were defenseless.

"When soldiers attack their own citizenry without provocation, then it is indeed time for reform. Even you cannot argue that point."

He arched a brow. "Without provocation? A thousand men assemble in a town to demand the repeal of established law, and that is not cause for the government to worry? After what happened to the aristocracy in France, it is only prudent."

Lucy could hardly believe her ears. "You have not changed your mind, then?"

He shook his head. "I have not, and tomorrow we will wed as our bargain decrees."

White-hot fury ripped through her. "I will not marry you, Nick. I will maintain my betrothal to Mr. Whippet."

His lips tightened into a firm line. "A commitment you have no intention of honoring. You made this wager of your own free will, Lady Lucy. It is not very becoming to accept the consequences so churlishly."

Lucy flushed. He was right, even if he was not just. She could acknowledge that, but she was not yet ready to concede. She needed time to think, to plan. Her head ached, not just from her injury but from the complicated mess her life had become.

"If we are to be held to a gentleman's standards, Your Highness," she drawled his title, "then let us be held to them indeed. Your presence in this room is unseemly."

"Unseemly?" His cheeks reddened with anger, but the effect did not last long. He quickly brought his response under control. "I suppose you are right, princess. Filled with irony, but right nonetheless."

He turned to go, and Lucy's heart ached. Why couldn't he see? Why wouldn't he believe the evidence of his own eyes and ears? The past should never have that strong a hold on the present. Despair settled over her, enveloping her as surely as the coverlet covered her from head to toe. If the devastation he must have seen in the market square could not change him, then nothing could.

"Are you certain you still want to wed?" she called after him and winced at the fear in her voice. "You do not have to marry me, Nick. I release you from the wager." How could she bear it, to be married to a man whom she loved desperately but who did not love her?

He turned in the doorway, his fingers curled around the frame. "But I do not offer you release, Lucy. At least," he paused, and his gaze held hers, filled with dark promise, "at least, not yet."

Nick passed through the main room as quickly as possible without glancing at any of the occupants. Mrs. Selkirk called after him, but he continued through the door and out into the gray dawn. He should have brought the leather vest that fitted over his smock, for the morning air was quite cool. Perhaps it was just as well. Waking up to Lucy Charming in his bed had made him altogether too warm to begin with.

She would be the ruination of him. He saw that now, and could even smile at the humor of it. Their first meeting had been highly symbolic, and he would have been better prepared for this eventuality if he'd understood the symbolism at the time.

No more wagers, he'd bragged to Wellington. No more heroism, and less than ten minutes later he'd been forced to eat his words when he'd bashed the burly thug over the head with a flowerpot. Lucy Charming was the cause of each transgression, and now she'd been the cause of his biggest sin of all. It was a sin against honor, and one from which he'd always prided himself on abstaining.

Still, he had lied.

He had lied to her, to the woman he loved.

Nick did not lie on principle. It was dishonorable, and too easy a path to dishonor at that. But principles were gone, and he'd lied to Lucy, lied grievously, and lied so that she would be joined to him for a lifetime. Old ghosts, damp caves, lifelong convictions—all held no sway when he'd stood in the midst of the crowd in the market square and watched the soldiers thunder toward the speaker's platform. For a fraction of a moment, he'd felt like the child he'd been in Santadorra when the peasants and the French soldiers had stormed the palace, but the screams of terror from around him had quickly pulled him back to the present. The terror-filled eyes of the young woman who'd thrust her baby at him had been his mother's eyes. The older woman who had keened over the body of her son had wept as bitterly as his mother must have when they'd snatched four-year-old Josephine from her arms. Nick clutched his midsection, for the thought was like a physical pain. But he was not a boy any longer. He was a man, and it had been a man, not a frightened boy, who acted in the Nottingham market square. The young woman stood a good chance of recovery in the Selkirks' care. The grieving mother could never be comforted, and so there was nothing more he could do. Most of all— thank God, most of all—Lucy was safe and for the most part unharmed. If her anger at his falsehoods was any indication of her returning strength, she would soon be as well as she'd ever been.

But he would still be a liar.

Nick turned back between the little cottages carved into the hillside and mounted the uneven stairs he'd climbed two nights before. He strode up the slope until he came to the log he and Lucy had occupied that night. She'd shown him no pity then. That was one of the reasons he loved her, he supposed. Despite his fears that he would become one of her reform projects, she hadn't turned his transformation into a civic duty. Perhaps it would have been better if she had.

Nick sank down on the log. He was not altogether converted to her cause, he admitted to himself as he rubbed his arms to keep warm. He still saw the dangers of mass gatherings. He still believed that the nobility held a sacred charge to govern their lands. Yet now he understood, as he supposed he should have understood before, what it meant to be without a voice in determining one's own destiny. He'd already known how it felt to stand at the wrong end of a bayonet, but he had not known the feeling of injustice when soldiers attacked an unarmed populace. He had known what it meant to diminish his belief in his religion for the sake of social acceptance, but he had not known how it felt to understand that a place in the social order would forever be denied him. She had changed him, damn her eyes, when he had not wanted to be changed. It was too difficult. Much easier to find solace in whiskey and wagers and little acts of heroism.

Still, he had not capitulated to his instinct for self-preservation—the instinct to run as far as possible from Lucy Charming. Instead he had lied to her, to keep her safe, and though she would marry him, she would despise him. Nick wiped his suddenly damp hands on his worn breeches.

When the whole charade had begun, he had not cared whether she loved him. She was entertaining. She was a challenge. He wanted her, and she would irritate his father. All that had seemed enough, if he were forced to settle for a bride. Now, though, in the cold light of dawn, none of those things mattered anymore. Boredom, self-indulgence, even spiting his father could all be satisfied in a myriad of ways. His love for Lucy could only be fulfilled if it was returned, and his lies would prevent her from ever opening her heart to him.

Despair filled him, and he slumped on the log. He had spent most of his life trying to escape who and what he was, to avoid his destiny, but alone on a hillside above Nottingham, he could no longer elude himself. Nicholas St. Germain, Crown Prince of Santadorra, was, like many men before him, forced to accept that the situation he'd created was his own doing, and his own responsibility.

Mr. Twickenham was the curate of the parish and did the real work of tending to the flock while Mr. Whippet danced attendance on the duchess. Lucy could tell from his pursed lips that he was scandalized by the whole affair, for who had ever heard of a royal wedding held in a cave?

Mrs. Selkirk's cottage, though, proved adequate for the small wedding party. Lucy hid herself in the bedchamber, ostensibly to don the dress that Tom Selkirk had borrowed from one of the neighbors, but her real purpose was to avoid Nick.

He had lied. The more she considered it, the more certain she grew. How could he have witnessed the devastation in the market square and still remain unchanged? Tom Selkirk had told her of Nick's heroics, not only his rescue of her but of the woman with the babe. Besides, a flicker of guilt had flashed in Nick's eyes when he'd claimed the victory of their wager. His gaze had not quite met hers, as if he were hiding something.

Mrs. Selkirk opened the door to the bedchamber, her smile as broad as her ample middle. "Come now, dearie. 'Tis time."

Lucy put a hand to the bandage on her forehead and willed the fluttering in her stomach to subside. Unfortunately, the Selkirks, having learned Nick's true identity, were pleased beyond reason that their beloved Lady Lucy had snared a handsome prince. Visions of happily ever after danced in Mrs. Selkirk's eyes especially. Only a prince would have been fine enough for the motherless miss who had stood on a stool in her kitchen at Charming Hall to stir the puddings and soups.

Lucy refused to cry for herself, but her feelings for the Selkirks as her surrogate family threatened her equanimity. She gave her homespun skirt a final brush and moved toward the door. "The sooner we start, the sooner it will be done."

Mrs. Selkirk put an arm around Lucy's shoulders as she brought her into the main room. "Tut, tut, my dear. 'Twill not be so bad. At least you will be out of your stepmother's clutches."

Lucy couldn't echo Mrs. Selkirk's sentiments, though,

for she was sure that life as a crown princess would be far more onerous than even she suspected. They moved to the center of the room, and Lucy looked over the company. The groom stood patiently by the fireplace while what was surely the most unusual party ever to grace a royal wedding assembled in a half circle around the curate. In the corner, the woman Nick had rescued lay on a makeshift pallet and nursed her baby to keep him quiet. Tom Selkirk begrudged the groom a bow and then stood as best man. Mrs. Selkirk, her work-roughened hands hidden in her apron, stood next to Lucy to attend her. Mr. Selkirk sat at the rough table, ready with ink and quill so that the couple might sign the special license as soon as possible.

Lucy heard very little of the ceremony until the waspish little curate said, "Do you, Lucinda Eleanor Charming, take this man to be your lawful husband?"

Her throat closed when she opened her mouth to answer, and no sound emerged. How could she do this? How could she sacrifice her love for reform? But how could she not, for it was a debt of honor she owed to Nick. And in truth, she could not deny the longings of her own heart, however disastrous they might prove.

Perhaps, at least for a short time, she could have the man she loved. The thought filled her with both hope and despair. Because for whatever brief joy she might fifind, she knew that devastation would surely follow. They were so unsuited, so different in their aims and purposes and beliefs. Marriage was the worst mistake they could make.

She couldn't look at Nick, or at anyone else for that matter. If she were going to leap from a cliff onto the rocks below, she would simply shut her mind to the consequences and jump. "I do," Lucy said, the words slightly breathless.

The curate continued. "Do you, Nicholas Alexander Leopold St. Germain, take this woman to be your lawful wife?"

"I do." Nick's thunderous affirmation left no room for doubt, but he said the words as if they weighed twelve stone.

Another few moments and it was done. There was no kiss, for Lucy turned her face and moved away from Nick as quickly as possible. Mrs. Selkirk produced a great quantity of cakes, and Tom carried a plate and a mug of milk to the woman and baby in the corner.

Not the most romantic of moments, Lucy thought, but it would suffice. Mr. Selkirk dipped the pen in the inkwell and offered it to her, and Lucy signed her name with deft, bold strokes, binding herself forever to the man she loved. It was folly of the worst kind, and the most exasperating bit was that she could not deny that she wanted Nick. She only feared what would happen now that she had him.

They were not to spend their wedding night at the Selkirks', Lucy learned shortly after she signed the special license that Nick had brought with him from London.

"Mr. Selkirk has agreed to drive us into town in his cart." Nick held himself as stiffly as he had during the ceremony, as if any sudden movement might unleash a disastrous torrent of feeling.

"Into town?" Lucy was surprised. "Is it safe with the dragoons there?"

"The soldiers left yesterday, and the market square has been put to rights." Nick's face was impassive, but Lucy could hear the sadness in his voice. "There is little left to evidence recent events."

Nick had refused to take her to the square to view the aftermath of the soldiers' attack, and she'd been angry. Secretly, though, she'd been relieved as well. No one wanted to view her dreams as they lay in ruins.

"Very well," she said, suddenly nervous. She'd been so intent upon the wedding ceremony that she'd not considered the wedding night. "We need our rucksacks."

"Tom put them in the cart before the curate arrived."

Lucy wiped suddenly damp palms on her borrowed skirt. "We should help Mrs. Selkirk with the washing up. She has enough to manage with a sick guest and an infant."

Nick's brow furrowed in frustration. "Lucy, you are the bride. Mrs. Selkirk would not want you up to your elbows in suds."

"Oh. Of course not. You're right, certainly." She tried to think of another reason to delay, but no inspiration occurred to forestall what was to happen next. Their good-byes took no time at all, and Lucy soon found herself once more riding in the back of an ox cart with Nick. She heartily wished for the presence of the other men who had accompanied them from London. Anything to distract her from—

"Lucy . . ." Nick began to speak and then stopped. She waited, glad for the quantity of hay separating them. It had happened so quickly, the wedding, but there'd been no point in procrastinating. Nick was not going to release her from their agreement. She could see it in his eyes. And in the most secret corner of her soul she was glad. She had just married the man she loved. It was sure to be a disaster. He would never be able to understand the dearest wishes of her heart, and ahead she could see only division and the ruin of her hopes. Perhaps he would divorce her or have it annulled, but for now the marriage lines were there, tucked in the pocket of his vest, an irrevocable fact. She had just married, and now she was to have a wedding night with a man she loved, a man who would surely put an end to her dreams.

Lucy sighed and glanced at the sky. It was still not yet noon and hours to go before the late summer sun would set and darkness would claim the sky. How did one survive such a quantity of anticipation of what might prove to be both a disaster and a fantasy?

Mr. Selkirk drove them to an inn on the London road and pulled into the busy yard. The native stone of the long, low building glowed with the patina of age.

"We'll return to town by post chaise in the morning," Nick informed her as they climbed from the back of the cart. Lucy would have preferred to prolong their journey instead of facing the reality of her new marital state. Her steps faltered. Nick reached out and grasped her hand as they crossed the coach yard.

"What will we do, then, 'til tomorrow?" she asked, and the look he shot her almost melted her bones. Lucy blushed at her poor choice of words. Gathering her courage, she persisted. "Until nighttime, then. What shall we do until it grows dark? If we are hiring a post chaise, we might be halfway to London before nightfall."

Nick opened the door to the inn's taproom and ushered her inside. "Has anyone mentioned waiting until dark?" he whispered in her ear, and her insides turned to jelly. Why wasn't she fighting her fate with greater passion? Why was she not railing at the unfairness that had taken her destiny from her own hands? Instead, she stood meekly by as her new husband bespoke a room, paid the innkeeper with a few guineas, and then led her up the staircase to a wooden door. The innkeeper had given Nick a heavy iron key, and when he placed it neatly in the lock it turned with a soft click and the door swung open.

Lucy stepped forward, but Nick stopped her by sweeping her into his arms and carrying her across the threshold. "I only plan to marry once, Lucy," he murmured in her ear, and his warm breath was like the caress of a soft, moist breeze. "Let's not eschew any of the niceties."

Lucy's heart almost stopped at the seductive promise of his words. He kicked the door shut behind them with his boot and crossed the room to the lumpy-looking bed. Thankfully, instead of laying her across the mattress, he released her legs and allowed her to stand upright. The room was dim, for only a small window allowed the late-morning light to invade the interior. The chamber was far from luxurious, barely comfortable in fact, but for all its inadequacies, it was exactly where Lucy Charming did—and did not—want to be.

"You should have had flowers," Nick said and stepped toward the window. Lucy had expected him to move toward her, not away, and disappointment flitted through her.

"Nothing about our acquaintance has been anything like the usual courtship," Lucy said with as much equanimity as she could manage. "Why should our wedding be any different?"

Nick turned back from beneath the window and smiled slightly. "I suppose this is the point at which I should do the honorable thing and allow you to refuse me a husband's privileges."

"Are you going to? Do the honorable thing, I mean." Lucy found herself slightly breathless, fearing either answer and unsure which she preferred. Why was she so confused? It would be much simpler if her feelings for him were not so complex.

"I've not managed to do an honorable thing since I met you, princess. Why should I begin now?" Despite his words and the sensual undercurrent of them, he remained immobile by the window.

"Why, indeed," Lucy murmured. She felt like a tightly coiled spring. Blast the man. Why didn't he simply kiss her and let nature take its course? She was nervous enough without this need for conversation.

He straightened. "Tell me to get out, Lucy, if you've no desire for what lies ahead. Tell me now, and say it with conviction. With passion." He stopped and rubbed his temple with thumb and forefinger. "No, not with passion. With indifference." He looked up at her, his brown eyes full of something she didn't quite dare to name. "Yes, with cool, disdainful indifference."

"What would you have me say?" She wasn't a tightly coiled spring after all. She was a woman standing on the edge of a precipice, and the wind was blowing against her back. She could turn away if she wanted and, despite everything, he would let her. He was an honorable man, no matter how he thought of himself. Telling him to leave would be the wise course. The prudent course. Small wonder she couldn't follow it, but then she never had before.

"Would you have me lie?" She forced herself to speak firmly to belie the fact that her knees threatened to knock together. "I am not indifferent, Nick. How could anyone be indifferent to you?"

Her words lit a low flame in his eyes. His hands rose and he quickly shirked his leather vest. "Then what are you, princess, if not indifferent, because I confess I do not know."

What was she, indeed? A telling question, and the answer was just as revealing. She had no intent of making that particular revelation in Nick's hearing. "Perhaps I am angry."

Nick moved toward her, his steps muffled by the dusty carpet beneath their feet. He crooked one finger and placed it beneath her chin, and his touch singed her skin, flame against flesh. For a long moment, he examined her, turning her head one way and then another. Her knees threatened to buckle instead of knock.

"You don't appear angry," he said in a soft voice, and his closeness set her heart to pounding. "Your cheeks are not red. Your eyes sparkle, but not from fury. And though your breath seems to have quickened, you are not tensed to strike out at me. No, you are not angry."

Lucy wanted him down to the darkest depths of her soul. It was a painful realization, and an even more painful admission, but it was the truth nonetheless. She had a vague idea of what occurred in the marital bed. She had an even clearer idea of the demands of her own body, and something within her longed to learn the demands of his.

"Perhaps I am repulsed," she snapped, her frustration rising even further. "The mere idea of the marriage bed may be repugnant to me."

He smiled then. He did it so rarely that its effect was

all the more devastating. Strong, even teeth. Mobile lips. Faint lines around the corners. Repulsive was not the first word that sprang to mind.

"I've seen you repulsed, princess. When you find a man repellent, you swing a scythe at him. Or fling a teakettle in his midsection. But I daresay you do not stand this near to him"—he moved even closer—"and allow him to touch what he has so long dreamt of."

She would surely melt under the warmth of his gaze. His hand grazed her shoulder and then lightly, softly, continued down her arm until his fingertips reached the curve of her breast. Lucy gasped and thought her heart might leap from her body. He had touched her there before, that night in the maze at Carlton House, but the gentle pressure felt as fresh and thrilling as it had the first time. Would it always be this way? With Nick, she feared so.

"No," she admitted weakly. "I am not repulsed."

He rewarded her by leaning forward and placing a soft kiss on her mouth. Their lips clung for a long, heart-stopping moment, the fulfillment of every girlish dream she'd ever had, and then he pulled away. "Then what are you, Lucy Charming?" he murmured, his face mere inches from hers. "For I should dearly love to know."

She was in love, was what she was, but she would never admit it to him. He held far too much power over her as it was.

"I am a wife, as our wager dictates," she replied as calmly and evenly as she could manage. "That is all." Nick hesitated, his eyes searching hers, and then seemed to accept her answer.

"Then come to bed, wife." She expected him to grab her wrist, as he was so wont to do, or at least take her hand and lead her to the bed. Instead, he stepped to the side, tugged back the bedclothes, and gestured toward the lumpy expanse of the mattress.

Lucy swallowed hard. She would not turn craven now. "Perhaps I should undress first?"

Nick reddened, and she realized he'd forgotten that detail. A little thrill of pleasure shot through her. The debonair rogue had overlooked the obvious. Perhaps his sangfroid was not as complete as it appeared.

"An excellent idea," he said, and his eyes traced her from lips to toes, shifting the balance of power back in his favor. "Where would you like to begin?"

Chapter Seventeen

Lucy hesitated, her fingers crumpling her skirt. She was only Lucy Charming, forgotten daughter of an eccentric duke. She was a reformer by night, a mistreated stepdaughter by day, but when it came to Nick, she had no idea who she was or what she was supposed to do. How did one go about being a wife? Her ignorance was appalling.

"Princess?" His teasing smile faded. Her fear must show in her eyes. "I know you, princess. You would not be standing here with me if you did not wish to be. Are you frightened?"

Terrified, but she'd rather perish on the spot than admit to it. He knew everything that was about to occur, while she could only guess. And hope. And dream.

"Kiss me." She meant to sound commanding, but the words came out rather breathlessly. Her husband, though, seemed not to notice anything untoward, for he bent with alacrity to perform the task.

The feel of Nick's lips on hers was so intense, so alive. Keen awareness enervated every part of her body. How strange, and how delightful, that the simple act of mouths meeting should produce such wonder. In another moment, his tongue reached out to trace her lips, and she willingly parted them, allowing him access to the richness and depth of a full lovers' kiss. He groaned, and the purely masculine sound brought a heavy sensation to her womb. Her thighs clenched and she instinctively pressed her body against his.

His sure hands found the soft places beneath her jaw and the smooth line of her arms before encircling her shoulders. She felt the tips of his fingers glide along the back of her dress, searching for hooks and buttons.

"In the front," she breathed, when his lips left hers for the slightest moment.

He hesitated, and Lucy moved to distract him by splaying her fingers across his chest. The rough linen of his borrowed shirt contrasted pleasantly with the firm, muscled smoothness of his skin. She wanted to stroke him as she would a cat, but the soft growl in her ear reminded her not to confuse a tiger with a house pet.

"Undress for me," he murmured against her ear, and then he moved a step away. Lucy's throat went dry. For all that society might brand her a hoyden, undressing in front of a man in broad daylight was not a thing to be taken lightly. Even if that man was her husband.

Slowly, not meeting his eyes, Lucy reached up and unhooked the bodice of her gown. It parted, and she allowed the sleeves to slip down her arms. The corset and chemise she wore underneath retained her modesty, but the simple undergarments revealed her breasts and the curve of her hips.

With a strangled moan, Nick lifted his hands and tentatively cradled her breasts in his palms. Lucy gasped. His touch felt incredibly good, and with only the thin linen separating them, she tingled where the warmth of his skin met hers. With a mesmerizing slowness, his fingers moved, caressing first the tops of her breasts and then the sides. Lucy swayed but remained upright until his talented hands cupped her fully and his thumbs brushed her nipples. Their response was instantaneous, and the weakness that had threatened her knees since she had first glimpsed Nick's handsome face finally took its toll. She swayed into his touch, and Nick groaned in approval.

He caught her, steadied her, and then, seeming to think better of trying to keep them both upright, turned her until she felt the mattress against the back of her knees. She fell, and he fell with her. The length of his body on hers was more erotic than she'd imagined. If it hadn't felt so wonderful, she would have been frightened out of her wits.

Sharing thoughts and feelings did not come easily to Lucy, but physical intimacy was apparently another matter altogether. If nothing but unhappiness could lie ahead, then she would make the most of this moment. She returned Nick's kiss with abandon, her hands reaching up to stroke his hair. The feel of the thick curls beneath her fingers was a sensual delight. She tugged on them lightly, and he groaned again. Her fingers moved eagerly, curiously, wanting to learn the feel and texture of every inch of him.

He reared up long enough to tug his shirt over his head and cast it to the floor behind him. At Nick's urging, she lifted her hips so that he could slide her gown past her waist and down her legs. It followed his shirt to the floor. Lucy drank in the sight of him and couldn't decide whether she most wanted to stare at the lean, lightly furred planes of his chest or trace their contours beneath her fingers. Nick reached down and took her hand and slowly, gently, placed her fingertips on his breastbone. "Touch me, Lucy."

She needed no further invitation. Eager to explore, she allowed her hands to roam and took pleasure in the breathless sounds her touch elicited from Nick. He half-reclined above her, braced on one elbow, which left his other hand free to caress her hip through the thin chemise. Lucy had never known such delight. No wonder men and women of all sorts, society and peasant alike, made such fools of themselves over love. If she'd had any idea of the pleasure to be had, she would have made an idiot of herself long before.

Except that before, she wouldn't have known Nick. Before, she would never have had any desire to remove her gown in the presence of a man. And before, she would not have been married and thus felt herself free to follow a man down such a wickedly sensual path.

But there was still more pleasure to be had, as Lucy was to discover. The heat that arched between them continued to grow, and Lucy found herself divested of her corset. Nick pulled away long enough to shed his boots. His breeches quickly followed. Clad only in linen small-clothes, he pulled her to a sitting position and slipped the straps of the chemise down her bare arms. Each touch of skin, each brush of fabric burned like a flame but left no mark. The sheer lawn of the chemise fell to her waist, and Nick eyed her as if she were a banquet table set before a starving man.

Lucy knew that at least once in her life, every woman should see that flame of desire in the eyes of the man she loved. Whatever happened to her, whatever happened to Nick, no one could ever take away this moment, when her husband held her and caressed her as if she were the answer to his prayers.

He knew where to touch her with an instinct that was almost frightening. Lucy felt the longing within her build to a fever pitch. Nick stroked her stomach, her thighs, before venturing lower. She parted her legs reluctantly, afraid to continue but terrified to stop. Instinctively, she tensed against the pain. Someone had told her once there would be pain. But there was only the absolutely glorious sensation of Nick's fingertips spreading her legs and sliding through the softest, most intimate part of her body.

It was criminal the way he fed her every need. She should stop him, reclaim her modesty, but her brain had relinquished control to her aching body. He drew wetness from her until she was thick with it. And yet for all the pleasure, there was an ache as deep and as full as it was empty. She needed him.

"Nick." She whispered his name, although it sounded like a shout to her own ears. Drawing himself up, he covered her body with his own. She had been afraid that she would feel diminished or overpowered. Instead, she felt a thrilling sense of freedom and purpose as she pulled him closer. His hands urged her knees apart until she was completely open and vulnerable.

"I'm sorry for the pain."

She wanted to tense against what would happen next, but his hand returned to its wicked rhythm against her core and she could only arch into the undulating pressure. He kissed her, hard and long, and then she felt the length of him, foreign and unfamiliar, press inside.

Nick tried not to panic. He'd never made love to a virgin. God, was he even doing it properly? It was too fast, but she must be ready. Her body gave too much evidence for him to be mistaken about that. Lucy Charming let him in at last, and he slid into her until he felt the barrier of her maidenhead. Knowing she was not the sort of woman who would want to be coddled at such a critical juncture, he surged ahead. The sensation was exquisite. Even as Lucy gasped in pain, Nick could not hide the pleasure of finding himself deep inside her. She was peace, recompense, absolution, and tears stung his eyes. She was his wife.

"I'm sorry." He traced the rim of her ear with his tongue and blew softly on the faint wetness. Perhaps he could distract her from the discomfort. Her fingers dug into his shoulder blades and her legs wrapped around his own. She was no whimpering maiden, his princess. Despite her inexperience and her discomfort, she clutched him as fiercely as a warrior would his sword. Slowly, tentatively, he withdrew and then settled back into her. She cried out, pain mingled with pleasure. "I'll stop," he whispered in her ear. "Tell me, Lucy, and I'll stop."

"No." Her legs wound more tightly around his own. She was a woman who gave no quarter, and so she asked none. "I want this. I want you." She whispered the fierce words against his neck, and he would have given anything to see her face, to look into her eyes. This was more than passion. It would have to be, he realized with a shock, for Lucy to allow him such intimacy. She could call it wifely duty, or she could say she was simply bowing to the inevitable, but only a woman in love clutched at her husband as if she were drowning and he was her lifeline.

The realization both thrilled and terrified Nick. He loved her. He'd known that for some time now. And here was proof that she loved him. He moved inside of her, rocking back and forth, attentive to signs of her discomfort. Two people in love. Was there ever such a recipe for disaster?

Nick couldn't maintain his tender pace for long. The tiny moans she made kept him from focusing on anything but the needs of his body. With a grunt, he increased his pace, working swiftly toward his release. Lucy arched beneath him and cried out in fulfillment. When Nick's release came, it struck with a blinding intensity that swept away thought and allowed him to sink into blessed oblivion.

Later, with a satisfied sigh, Lucy nestled closer to her husband's sleeping form. She'd fallen asleep herself, and from the slant of light through the small window, they'd both slept for some time now. She wanted to stretch, but more than that she wanted to preserve this momentary idyll. The future loomed large and uncertain, and she had no desire to face it just now. No, much better to hug this precious moment tightly, because it would likely be wrenched away soon enough.

Nick mumbled a few words in his sleep and then, to Lucy's dismay, rolled away from her, taking the bedclothes with him. She shivered and reached down beside the bed, capturing her chemise with her fingers. She pulled it over her head and let it settle around her hips. Not wanting to disturb Nick, she left the bed.

A pitcher of water and a cracked basin rested on a low, rickety table. A small amount of much-mended linen sat beside them. Thankful for a sleeping husband and a modicum of privacy, Lucy washed away the evidence of their coupling. The cool water soothed her skin, and she could not help but smile with satisfaction. She had never expected to lose her virginity to a husband whom she loved. For the moment she would allow herself to think of nothing else. Humming softly, she dressed.

The jingle of harnesses in the inn yard accompanied her low tune. Lucy marveled that the rest of the world would remain ignorant of the momentous event that had occurred in this room. She felt older now than she had when she'd entered the bedchamber. One of life's great mysteries had been solved, and her new knowledge made her feel powerful. She refastened the hooks that held her bodice in place and settled on a nearby footstool to straighten her stockings and don her half boots. Her stomach rumbled with hunger, and she decided to go in search of food. With deft hands, she bundled her hair at the nape of her neck and anchored it with hairpins. Surely the cook would spare her some bread and cheese. When Nick awoke, she would have a tray waiting for him.

She descended the stairs and entered the taproom. The low-ceilinged structure, much older than the bedchambers, held only a few travelers and a handful of locals. The innkeeper stood behind a long bar, filling mugs with dark brown ale.

"Pardon me." Lucy spoke in a low voice, hoping to remain inconspicuous. The innkeeper looked up, his bland face filled with disinterest.

"Miss?" He slid the mug he had finished filling down the length of the bar to a waiting customer. The man caught it and slid a coin back in return.

"Could I trouble you for a small tray of bread and cheese? My husband and I . . ." Lucy stopped, fumbling for an excuse. "That is . . ."

"Wore him out, did ya, lassie?" The graying workman at the end of the bar roared with laughter, and Lucy felt herself go red to the roots of her hair. "Best keep up his strength, then, my dear, for it's not dark yet. If he fails ye, call for Old Jedidiah and I'll be happy to stand in for 'im."

The other men joined in the laughter, and Lucy wanted to sink through the packed earthen floor. She scanned the room, afraid she might see a fellow reformer. As the daughter of the late duke, she had a wide acquaintance among both the gentry and the peasantry of Nottingham.

The outside door swung open and slammed against the wall. Lucy turned to find Mr. Selkirk and Tom silhouetted in the opening. Sweet heavens, now her embarrassment would be complete. Behind them lurked another figure, a faintly familiar one.

"Lady Lucy." Mr. Selkirk looked relieved as he crossed the room. Tom's face lit up at the sight of her. "We're not too late, then."

At the revelation of her identity, the good-natured laughter in the taproom died away, leaving an uncomfortable silence. The trio in the doorway moved closer, and in that instant, Lucy recognized the third member of the party. She would never forget his face, not when she'd swung a scythe so close to his crooked nose.

"Tully," she breathed the name.

"At your service, miss." He smiled, an expression that sent prickles of unease down her spine. Hadn't Crispin put him on a transport ship? And what was he doing with Mr. Selkirk and Thomas?

"Is your husband still here?" Mr. Selkirk asked, and Lucy blushed.

"Yes. Above stairs. Whatever is the matter?"

"You'd best come with us, Lady Lucy." Mr. Selkirk extended his hand. "We've something to tell you."

"It's too late, Jack," Old Jedidiah called from the end of the bar. "He's already had his pleasure of her. You can tell from her blushes."

"Quiet, you fool," Mr. Selkirk barked. "Do you know who this is?"

"No," Lucy protested. "Please, let's step outside."

She led them toward the door. Outside, the inn yard was eerily quiet. Lucy crossed it with trepidation. When they reached the hedgerow that bordered one end, Mr. Selkirk stopped. Lucy eyed Tully with suspicion and distaste but she was safe enough. Her friends would forestall any nefarious designs the thug might have on her person.

"Do you know this man, Lady Lucy?" Mr. Selkirk asked.

Lucy grimaced. "I do, indeed. But I had thought him bound for the colonies, or Australia. He is one of Sidmouth's men."

"Aye, but he is one of us as well."

Lucy's mouth opened, but no words emerged. Mr. Selkirk nodded. "It's true, my lady."

The world tilted beneath her feet. "I don't believe you. He followed me that day, from the meeting, and he planned to take me from my stepmother's home. His loyalty is to Lord Sidmouth," she insisted.

"No, my lady. He might take Sidmouth's gold, but he believes in the cause of reform as much as you or I. Ain't that so, Tully?" The thug nodded in smug agreement.

Lucy shook her head. But how? It made no sense. "Then why did you attack my husband? Why did you follow us to Madame St. Cloud's and then to Lady Belmont's?"

Tully scowled. "After the way you defended 'im, I figured your friend the gardener must be key to the reformers." His resentment of Nick flared in his eyes. "Who was to know that the Crown Prince of Santadorra 'ad dressed 'imself up as a servant?"

Lucy still refused to believe the evidence Mr. Selkirk

was offering. "How did you escape transport? Lord Wellstone saw you safely aboard a ship."

Tully's grin emphasized his missing teeth. "And the captain saw me just as safely ashore again when I made meself known to 'im."

Lucy turned to Mr. Selkirk and Tom, chilled. "Do you believe him?"

Mr. Selkirk removed his cap and scratched his head. "Begging your pardon, my lady, but Tully is my cousin on my mother's side."

Lucy's empty stomach pitched. There had to be more to their presence than simply revealing Tully's identity. "There is more, is there not?"

"Yes, my lady. I am afraid so."

"Well, tell me then." She braced herself for their news.

"Tully appeared shortly after you and Prince Nicholas left. Thanks to him, we've discovered who informed Sidmouth of the rally," Mr. Selkirk said.

Lucy's shoulders sagged with relief. This was good news, then. She had been afraid that—Well, it really wasn't worth thinking about, was it? She'd been wrong.

"Who is the traitor?" She felt sorry for the man, because his life would no longer be worth much in Nottingham. He would be forced to flee in disgrace, all for the price of the paltry number of guineas Sidmouth would part with.

"My lady . . ." Mr. Selkirk's voice trailed off, and Tully showed his evil grin.

Tom kicked the dirt with the scuffed toe of his boot, and then, as if he could contain himself no longer, the words burst forth. "It was your husband, my lady. He was the informer. His treachery brought the dragoons."

Lucy's head swam. "No." A giant weight pressed against her chest. Nick was not sympathetic to the work of the reformers, but even he would not coldheartedly bring troops down upon them. "You must be mistaken."

"No mistake," Tully growled and spat on the ground. "I 'eard 'im tell Sidmouth meself."

"If my husband had seen you, sir, he would have told me."

Tully laughed. " 'Twas in the anteroom of Sidmouth's office, waiting for me purse."

It could not be true. The man was lying to even the score with Nick. "And you have a grudge to bear against him." Lucy turned, appealing to the Selkirks. "Nick bested him twice. He is lying."

Mr. Selkirk shifted uneasily. "I don't believe he is, my lady, but there's one way to find out."

Lucy's stomach sank. Despite Tully's unsavory character, his words had the eerie ring of truth.

"You will wait here for me," Lucy ordered the three men, her heart in her throat. Tom started to protest, but she waved away his words. "My husband will do me no harm, and I'll quickly have the evidence to disprove this man." She shot a look at Tully.

"All right, then, my lady," Mr. Selkirk answered. "We'll wait, but only for a quarter hour. If you don't return, we'll come to find you."

Lucy nodded in agreement. "It will take far less time than that to untangle this mess, I can assure you." She whirled and marched back toward the inn.

Nick yawned and stretched, replete with well-being. The room was dim, but enough light peeked through the small window to reveal Lucy's absence. Nick frowned. Rolling onto his back, he cursed the lumps in the mattress. The next time he made love to Lucy, it would be in a proper bed, with a proper mattress, although, truth be told, he'd not noticed the condition of the mattress earlier. He smiled a delicious smile, full of satisfaction. He doubted Lucy had had any complaints at the time either. He was in the process of scooping up his breeches and smock from beside the bed when the door opened and she entered. He smiled at her and knew himself a man besotted.

"Dare I hope you've brought anything to eat?" His pleasure at the course of events felt too marvelous not to share, but she was holding her head high and her tense shoulders rested very close to her ears. Something was wrong.

Nick was a master at bored indifference. He wiped the smile from his face and calmly, without hurrying, swung his legs over the edge of the mattress to pull on his breeches. He stood and buttoned them before he slipped his arms into the sleeves of the smock and pulled it over his head. Dressed, he turned toward her but kept his distance. "Is something the matter, princess?"

She looked confused and scared, and that was not how she had appeared when he'd finished making love to her earlier. Nick stepped toward her and Lucy lifted her chin higher. Always a very bad sign.

"The Selkirks are here. I met them in the taproom when I went down to request a tray."

"Is Mrs. Selkirk ill? Or is it more trouble with the soldiers?" Guilt knotted his stomach. "We can return to Nottingham if necessary."

"No." Lucy waved off his question. "It's nothing like that. They simply brought someone to speak with me."

"You appear to have seen a ghost."

"Not a ghost. A thug. Our friend Tully, to be exact. Tully of the red cap."

Nick's pulse accelerated, and his muscles tensed. If the man thought he would take Lucy from him now, he was sorely mistaken. He'd bested him more than once and he could easily do so again. Nick reached for his boots. "Why the devil isn't he in Australia or the colonies? Crispin assured me he'd seen him aboard ship."

Lucy remained by the door, and alarm bells pealed in Nick's head. She seemed strangely unafraid of the thug's presence.

"Apparently he convinced the captain he was in Lord Sidmouth's service and was released. What I've learned today is that he is in someone else's service as well."

Nick frowned. "He's either extremely brave or incredibly foolish to play both ends against the middle with Sidmouth."

"You've not asked me where his other loyalties lie."

Nick paused. There was something disturbing in her tone, but her face was impassive. "For whom does he work, princess?"

Her lower lip quivered for an instant, and fear shot through him with an icy flame. She bit her lip to stop it from trembling. "He works for the cause of reform, Nick. Just as I do."

Nick sank back down onto the mattress, confused. "Then why did he pursue you so doggedly? I don't understand."

"The more interesting question is why the Selkirks brought him here today."

"And why did they?" A sudden, fine sweat broke out on his forehead. He'd been discreet in his contact with Sidmouth. It had been the dead of night. Whitehall was deserted, and Nick had traveled unaccompanied in a plain carriage.

"Tully knows who informed Sidmouth about the meeting. He was there, in an anteroom, when the information was shared."

Nick was glad he was sitting. His knees felt weak. "Whom did he name?"

"Need you ask?"

For a long moment, there was silence.

"No. I guess not." Oh, God. He'd not known his chest could hold so much pain. He'd been accused, tried, and convicted within the space of a moment. His pulse thundered in his ears. There was no point in denying his guilt, and certainly little use in offering explanations. He had offered all the reason a man needed that night in the dark above the Selkirks' home.

Lucy's shoulders, which had been so stiff, now sagged with pain. "Why, Nick? Why would you endanger innocent women and children in such a manner?"

His spine stiffened, even as a yawning pit of despair

opened in his midsection. Knowing his story, could she not see why he'd been compelled to act? "I did nothing to endanger the reformers. It was for their protection, actually. You are naïve, Lucy, to think that such a meeting held no possibility of violence."

Her cheeks were stained pink with anger. "The only violence was that committed by the king's soldiers."

"There was no way to know that." And it was true, but even as he justified his actions, he couldn't force the picture of the grieving mother keening over her dead son from his thoughts.

Lucy studied him pityingly, as if he were a small, dumb animal. Resentment stirred, but it was mixed with guilt and a foreboding sense of doom. Of course it must end badly. Things always did for him.

"If what you did was so sensible, so honorable, then why didn't you tell me of your visit to Whitehall?"

Her question pierced him, and he could only stare blankly at her for several moments. "You don't know what it's like, princess." Nick felt as if he were sinking, the water rising with each passing moment. He must make her understand or else he would lose her. He had not fought so hard and conceded so much only to lose his princess.

"I refused to risk losing you, Lucy. It was too dangerous not to inform Sidmouth. I protected you the best way I knew how."

"Protection?" She laughed bitterly. "Funny, Your Highness, but I don't feel protected. I feel distinctly betrayed."

As he'd known she would. It was the very reason he'd kept his secret to begin with. Now he could see that his choice had not been between Lucy's safety and his losing her, as he'd thought, but between Lucy's safety and her love. Much higher stakes, but he would follow the same course again without hesitation. With pain, he saw in his mind's eye the young mother thrusting her babe toward him, begging for his assistance, and suddenly the rightness of his decision did not seem so clear.

"We can resolve this, Lucy." Strength had returned to

his legs as he willed it to, and he rose from the bed, mov
ing toward her. "I know you feel I've betrayed you—"

"Betrayed me?" Her eyes flashed with incredulous, bit
ter laughter. "Oh yes, Your Highness, you have betrayed
me, and I might someday be persuaded to forgive you for
that. You are my husband, after all—for better or for
worse, is it not?"

Hope shot through Nick. "I did what I believed to be
right."

Lucy continued without any heed for his reply. "But
your betrayal of me is nothing to your betrayal of the
reformers." Her words slapped him, and he stood
stunned.

"You are angrier that I've betrayed your cause than that
I've betrayed you?" Nick couldn't hide his incredulity.

Lucy's face, which had reddened, now paled. "You
don't understand what you've done, do you?"

Her accusation stung. "I am not a simpleton, Lucy. I
am aware of the cost of my actions. It was I, you'll recall,
who walked through that square in the aftermath, search
ing for you."

"You think the aftermath is finished? Do you think the
dead and wounded from the rally are the only conse
quences?" She stepped toward him, her fists clenched at
her sides. "Now that the soldiers are gone, the local mag
istrates will begin their investigations. Arrests have already
been made. Men will be transported, if not hanged,
merely for their presence at the rally, and their wives and
children will be left to starve."

Nick's stomach felt like a ball of lead, but he refused
to show remorse. He would not grovel in apology, not for
protecting the woman he loved, even if she rebuked him
for his actions.

"They knew the risks when they attended the rally."

"The committee assured them it was safe."

"Then the committee is exceptionally naïve."

"I am one of the committee."

"I rest my case."

He should not have said the last, he knew it instantly. Beyond his own guilt, he could see Lucy's remorse in her eyes. She felt as responsible as anyone, perhaps more so.

"Then you are not sorry? You have no regrets?" she asked.

"None."

He wanted her to rail at him, to scream and fling the basin and pitcher at his head. He wanted the passion she'd revealed to him earlier, in their lumpy marital bed. Instead, she fixed him with an icy stare. "I'm returning to Nottingham with the Selkirks."

"The devil you are!" Nick exploded. "It would be foolish in the extreme, if arrests are being made. I'll see you to London, and we will be extremely discreet until the uproar has died down."

"No." The word was quiet but implacably final.

His heart raced. "Lucy, you are my wife."

"You may change that as soon as you wish."

"How? By divorce? By annulment?" Surely she did not mean it. "We have lain together as man and wife, and I have no desire to end our marriage."

"And I have no desire to begin it." She turned toward the door, her hand on the knob. "You will release me from the wager."

She didn't want him. The truth struck him between the eyes with the glancing force of a blow. And alongside her rejection came another revelation: There was no way to bridge the difference between them. She could not understand his most deeply held convictions, and he could not accept hers. What common ground could they possibly find?

"You are leaving me, then?"

"Yes." She paused. "The marriage lines—if they were to be lost, there would be no proof of our union. My stepmother can easily persuade Mr. Whippet and the curate to blot our names from the parish register." She smiled cynically. "He has done it before, when the reward was sufficient."

Nick watched, dumbfounded, as she slipped quietly from the room. The door closed behind her with soft finality, and Nick stood immobile. He could not betray his beliefs merely for the pleasure of her love, any more than she could forsake her convictions for his. Dear God, she had left him with an escape, and he might run if he wanted. How was he to find happiness in such a marriage? Would it not be better to end the torment for both of them now and save them years of pain? Since the moment she'd struck him with the door, his life had been spinning out of control, but the same woman who had sent him reeling had just given him the means of righting himself.

It would only cost a small part of his soul.

Nick fell full-length on the bed. With a growl, he turned and began pummeling the blasted mattress into submission.

Chapter Eighteen

Lucy clutched the edge of the wagon seat as Mr. Selkirk's oxen rumbled over the earthen track that led to his cottage. If thrown into a pond, she would surely sink, for the horrible truth of Nick's betrayal weighed in her stomach like a stone. Nick had no understanding of what he'd done. Or he comprehended but was too blind to accept the consequences of his actions. He was not a stupid man. What could possibly have possessed him to inform Sidmouth of their plans?

But she knew the answer to that question all too well, and her heart ached with the knowledge. His past had shaped his decision, wrong-headed as it was. Lucy wanted to hate him. She wanted to despise him, and she could for a few minutes, but her fury was difficult to sustain. It kept entwining itself with vivid images of a young boy hiding in a cold cave, his mother's body buried beneath a pile of stones not far away.

Lucy knew why Nick had done it. She even understood his typically masculine reasoning. The question was not whether she could understand. The question was whether she might come to forgive. And if she forgave him, could she forgive herself for depending upon a man destined to betray her?

The cart ascended the hill, and she smiled wanly at the sight of a candle burning in the Selkirks' window. Tom bounced from the back of the cart even before it stopped moving, but Lucy waited until Mr. Selkirk drew the oxen to a stop. It was then that she noticed the horses. They stamped restlessly, their bridles jingling. The four beasts had been tethered to a post and were jostling for position near the grass that covered the side of the Selkirks' cottage.

"Stay here, my lady," Mr. Selkirk admonished her, but Lucy took no heed. She followed him as he approached the cottage and ducked under the lintel.

"Are you Jack Selkirk?" A tall soldier stepped forward from the fireplace, and Lucy cast a quick glance around for Mrs. Selkirk. She spied her at the end of the long dining table, wiping her eyes with a corner of her apron.

"Aye, I am he." Mr. Selkirk drew up his bony shoulders and Lucy's stomach sank even farther.

"Jack Selkirk, by order of His Majesty, the Prince Regent, the occupants of this household are to be placed under arrest and taken to London."

Lucy gasped. London meant Newgate. Mrs. Selkirk burst into tears, and Lucy went cold. "What are the charges, sir?" she demanded, stepping forward.

"Sedition, inciting a riot, the usual list." The soldier seemed almost bored. At that moment, Tom, who had been caring for the oxen, appeared in the doorway.

"You can't arrest Mr. Selkirk," Lucy protested. "He's done no wrong."

The soldier bristled. "We can arrest him, miss. And you as well. We're under orders to take up the entire household."

His words hung in the air, and then in a heartbeat the main room of the cottage burst into a frenzy of motion. A second soldier grabbed Lucy's arm, and Tom leaped forward to fight him off. Mrs. Selkirk screamed. Lucy fought as the soldier dragged her from the house. In another moment, she was thrown over his saddle, the breath knocked from her lungs. The horses reeled, and the party set off into the darkening night.

Nick determined to leave immediately for London. Let Lucy Charming have her precious reform and leave him in peace. In fact, he descended to the taproom for the purpose of settling his account with the innkeeper, but in a desperate bid to squelch the pain of losing Lucy, he allowed himself to be waylaid by one tankard of ale, and then another, until the sky grew dark and he was too foxed to travel, even by hired carriage.

The innkeeper must have poured him into the lumpy bed, he deduced the next morning when he awoke with a pounding in his head. He stumbled to the washbasin, poured water from the pitcher, and shoved his face beneath the cool liquid. When he came up sputtering, his head still pounded, but he was awake.

Unfortunately, he was also awake to the memories of the past few days and bitterly aware of their consequences. At some point, he would have to retrieve Lucy. As he dressed and dried his face and hair, this inevitable truth stared him squarely in the face. As a point of honor, he could not bribe Mr. Whippet to blot their names from the parish register. Annulment and divorce were out of the question as well. Honor prevented him. That, and the fact that he was desperately in love with her. Honor forced him to admit that, too. He had lost enough already. He did not intend to lose Lucy as well. Nick sighed. A better man would release her from her vows. He had not turned out to be quite so heroic after all.

He had expected the taproom to be rather deserted at this mid-morning hour, but a buzz of voices greeted him as he crossed the threshold. A large group of men clustered near the bar, their voices echoing off the inn's thick stone walls. The innkeeper saw him, raised a tankard questioningly, and chuckled. Nick's stomach rolled and he shook his head.

"Thirty or forty at my count," a barrel-chested man was informing his listeners. "The soldiers rounded 'em up last night. Some women, too. Mrs. Selkirk even, God bless her soul. If the old duke were here, he'd not stand for it, no matter that they said he was queer in the attic."

Nick's chest constricted, and his heart began to pound as furiously as his head. Mrs. Selkirk? Soldiers?

"The gaol won't hold them all," another man said.

" 'T'ain't Nottingham gaol where they've gone. The magistrate ordered them sent to London to be tried for sedition."

This information was greeted with a gasp and an air of resignation from men who knew all too well the ways of the ruling classes.

"That's it, then, isn't it?" a younger man asked, looking at the others, all of whom were older than he. "They've gone to Newgate. It'll be Australia or the rope."

"Or the colonies."

Nick's throat went dry, and he wished he'd accepted the innkeeper's offer of a pint. What had happened to Lucy when the Selkirks were arrested? Surely she would have possessed the good sense to seek refuge at her family's estate. Even with the duchess in London, there must be servants there who would look out for her. Where else would she go?

"Can you tell me how to find Charming Hall?" he asked the man nearest him. His request brought all other conversation to a standstill.

"They won't be hiring, lad, more's the pity," the man replied. "The duchess turns off more servants than she takes on. Best look for employment in town."

"No. I must find the estate." At Nick's insistent tone, the other men eyed him with interest.

"Are you looking for someone, then?" the man asked, measuring Nick with an appraising eye.

"A member of the family."

"The family is in London. Except for Lady Lucinda, and she'll be in London shortly as well, I expect."

Nick's shoulders tightened. "What do you mean?"

The man paused. "What's your interest in the Charmings? We hold great store by Lady Lucinda. All we have left of the old duke. Is it her you're wanting to speak with?"

Nick decided that the truth would serve him better than a lie. "Lady Lucinda is my wife."

The laughter that erupted from the group was long and hearty. "Aye, of course," the youngest man said, wiping tears from his eyes, "and I myself am married to Queen Charlotte." The men shared the joke, slapping one another's backs with enthusiasm.

"What do you mean she is shortly to be in London?" Nick demanded, patience at an end. He grabbed the man by his jacket. "Tell me where my wife is!"

The laughter died. "Easy, lad," one of the older men said. "I did hear a rumor that Lady Lucinda married some foreign fellow two days ago. But I gave it no credit. Some folderol about a prince that filled my wife's head with foolish dreams."

Nick drew himself up to his full height. "I am Nicholas St. Germain, Crown Prince of Santadorra. And Lady Lucinda is my wife."

One man started to laugh, and the others hushed him. The original speaker, evidently the leader of the group, stepped toward Nick.

"Have you proof of this claim?"

Nick reached into his vest pocket and pulled out the marriage lines, pressing out the wrinkles and displaying them for all to see. The signature of the curate, together with the bishop's name, provided proof of the marriage.

"Where is my wife?" he demanded.

The leader peered at the paper and then into Nick's eyes. "Could be a trick."

Nick reached into his vest once more and pulled out a large, golden coin. He held it out to the man. "It is my likeness, commissioned by my father on my twenty-fifth birthday for the dorrian, the coin of Santadorra."

The man studied the dorrian and then Nick's face. "I'll be damned," he muttered.

"One hopes not," Nick answered, putting the coin back into his pocket, "but it couldn't hurt your cause with the Almighty if you'd tell me the whereabouts of my wife."

"She's with the others," the youngest man offered, his face now pale. "The magistrate ordered her especially taken straight to London. Said she had betrayed the ruling classes, just like her mad father before her. They'll clap her in Newgate until she's hanged or transported for sedition."

Nick stiffened. "Not if I have any say in the matter."

The innkeeper insisted that Nick be given the fastest horse in the stable. Nick clasped the man's hand and could only offer his thanks. The touch of the innkeeper's roughened grasp humbled him. Before Lucy had opened his eyes, he had thought such men quite content with their lot. Now he knew the injustice of denying honest men a role in their own governance.

Lucy was the woman who'd opened his eyes, just as she had wagered him she would in an alleyway somewhere between Mayfair and Spitalfields. Lucy. The horse's hooves beat a rapid tattoo on the London road, but they were no match for the furious hammering of Nick's heart or the ache that filled every corner of his being. She'd involved him in everything he'd sworn against—wagers, heroism—and he'd been redeemed. But at what price?

He could not lose her. He would not lose her. For if he did, he would truly be as worthless as his father had always said. No, Lucy Charming had changed him, despite his resolve to remain unaffected. One mere wisp of a girl, a curly-headed hoyden in heartbreakingly snug breeches, had worked her way so far underneath his skin there was no getting her out. Truth be told, her hold on him was far more than skin deep, for the moment he'd slid inside her virgin body, she'd become embedded in his soul.

By Jove, this time he *would* rescue her. Nick grasped the reins more tightly. Failure would not be countenanced. He would remove her from Newgate and after that . . . well, there was no use thinking about that. Santadorra it would be. Dwelling on the inevitable would not change the course of events that must follow.

He pushed his mount hard until both horse and rider were drenched with sweat. After a long night in the saddle, he reached the outskirts of the city and then turned the horse toward Mayfair.

Nick had always kept his bachelor's establishment small, not merely because of his meager purse but also to keep his father at a distance. The Cromwell Hotel was barely respectable, but it was considerably cheaper than the Pultney or the Grillon and the landlady was most forgiving when he was late with the rent. At the entrance to the hotel, a fresh-faced young tiger took his horse, and Nick flipped him his last coin, the golden dorrian. The tiger looked at it curiously and then bit it before shrugging and slipping it into his pocket. Nick passed through the empty lobby, pounded up the stairs, and walked briskly to his rooms, for he hadn't a moment to waste.

The door to his apartments stood ajar, and a frisson of wariness prickled along his spine. Nick stopped just outside the threshold and listened. Perhaps it was only the maidservant changing the linen, except that he had not been at home for several days and there was no linen to be changed. With a soft touch, Nick pushed against the door until it swung open.

"I say, Nick, you've been gone a devil of a long time with no word to anybody."

Crispin lounged in Nick's favorite chair, a book in one hand and a brandy in the other. His immaculately polished hessians gleamed in the light that streamed through the window. "Your father's called twice today, and I was at a loss for any further explanations to account for your whereabouts."

With an oath, Nick entered the room, shut the door behind him, and wasted no time in hastening to his bed-chamber beyond. "My father deserves no explanations," he called over his shoulder, pulling off the vest and smock as he went. He flung the garments in a corner and opened the small wardrobe. With impatient hands, he pulled out a well-made but shabby coat.

Crispin came to stand in the doorway. "Shall I summon your man?"

Nick shook his head. He intended to be gone before they could fetch the valet from his favorite tavern. "No time." He had dressed quickly before—at school to avoid a caning or later when fleeing from the bed of a scheming, marriage-minded lover. His fingers stumbled in his haste, and he let out another oath.

Crispin laughed, and Nick shot him a quelling glance. "Don't, Cris. It's far too serious."

His friend sobered. "Would you care to enlighten me?"

"Lucy's in Newgate," he blurted out as he pulled on a clean shirt. He looked up to find that Crispin had gone as white as the shirt.

"I find that jest decidedly lacking in humor," Crispin shot back and turned to leave.

"Cris! Wait!" Nick forced himself to take a deep breath and slow his movements. "It's no jest. I've been in Nottingham with Lucy. There was a reform rally, and the king's men and local militia routed the people."

Crispin stepped inside the room, his brow furrowed. "Yes. The papers are filled with the news."

"Lucy was arrested."

Crispin slapped the doorframe. "Arrested? How in the name of all that's holy could you let her be arrested, Nick? For God's sake, you're a bloody prince!"

"At the time I was one of the mob. She's being held on charges of sedition." Nick jerked a neckcloth from a drawer. He managed to settle it properly around his neck, but his frantic fingers made a mess of the knot, creasing the linen.

"Here." Crispin shoved his hands away and, with precise expertise, crafted a splendid mathematical knot. "I'll tie, you talk."

"She was arrested with the Selkirks."

"Who are they?"

"Former servants of her father's. The father and son are heavily involved in reform. We were married in their house."

Crispin looked as if he'd been shot. "Married?" There was a moment of silence, and then Cris chuckled. "Well, perhaps I've not lost my touch after all."

"You will most definitely have lost your touch if my bride ends up hanged before I can get to her." Nick motioned impatiently toward the cravat. Crispin finished off the knot, straightened it, and stepped back.

"There. You appear every inch the prince." The look of satisfaction on Crispin's face nettled Nick. Crispin sensed his friend's prickliness. "They won't hang her overnight. You've time to concoct a scheme. How do you mean to retrieve her from the prison?"

Nick had an idea, but it was complicated. He tugged at the sleeves of his jacket and straightened his cuffs. "I have devised a plan, but I need help."

Crispin nodded. "You know, of course, that I'm entirely at your disposal, and I'm sure your father will assist you in any way he can."

Nick froze. "I have no intention of going to my father."

"Whyever not?" Crispin looked perplexed. "Pride is one thing, Nick, but a wife is another matter altogether."

"Yes, well, as she is my wife, I shall see to her care."

"And was she under your care when she was arrested?"

Nick ignored Crispin's gibe. Instead, he brushed past his friend, snagging a beaver hat and cane from a stand just inside the sitting room door. "Are you coming with me, then?"

Crispin grabbed his own hat and stick. "Of course.

We'd best stop at the banker's on the way. You're going to need pots of money as a start."

Nick froze. Bribes in Newgate took money, and he had none until his next quarter's allowance. "Cris?" He did not have to speak the plea. The one word and a mutual look of understanding were all that was required.

"After you, Your Highness."

Nick turned and held out his hand. "You have ever been my friend."

Crispin clasped his hand for a brief moment and then stepped away. "Yes, well, it can't hurt to have a prince in one's debt."

Together, the pair clambered down the stairs and out onto the street.

Lucy had heard of the horrible conditions of the women and children confined to Newgate Prison. She had even contributed some of her pin money to the work of the women who were taking the leadership of prison reform. But for all that she had known her involvement in reform projects might prove risky, she had never expected to find herself on the receiving end of her own charity.

She glanced down at the blanket on which she sat in a corner of a cramped common room. The matted straw beneath the ratty wool was as old as tyranny but she had no money for fresh bedding. The regular ration for each prisoner was one small loaf of bread a day. Lucy's bread had been snatched from her fingers that morning almost before it had touched her outstretched hand. Her stomach growled, a persistent reminder that she'd not eaten since leaving Nick in the bedchamber of the inn at Nottingham. Nick. The thought of him brought a fresh wave of pain.

She crossed her arms across her empty middle and refused to cry. Two days was not so long, really, to go without food. The people of Nottinghamshire had gone without for much longer during the darkest days of the Luddite activities. The next day she would be much quicker, and far more territorial, when the gaoler appeared with the rations.

Even in the far corner of the room, there was no privacy. The cold stone walls ran with water, and the smell of the chamber pots sometimes forced her to cover her mouth and nose with a corner of the musty blanket. Despair lurked at the edges of her thoughts, but Lucy refused to acknowledge it. Surely someone would come to her assistance. Not her husband, of course. But someone.

"Here, love." An older woman sat a few feet away on a similar blanket. She twisted her small loaf in half and extended a portion to Lucy. "You need some bit of comfort, don't ye? 'Tis always hardest on the young ones."

Lucy stared numbly at the bread and at the dirty fingers curled around it. Her eyes returned to the woman. A moment ago, Lucy would have sworn she was quite elderly, but a closer study revealed that above the missing teeth and deep crow's feet, the stranger's eyes shone with the strength of a woman not much above thirty.

"Thank you, but I could not deprive you of your ration." Lucy's situation was dire, but it was not without hope. This woman, though . . .

"It's all right, love. I won't be needing it. I'm called to the dock on Sunday."

"The dock?"

"Aye. In the chapel, to hear the condemned sermon."

The woman's words struck Lucy with the force of a blow. "You're to be hanged?"

Her short cackle of laughter brimmed with amusement. "What dock did you think I meant? Portsmouth?" The woman laughed again, and Lucy shifted uneasily. The older woman seemed not to notice her discomfort. "I pinched a petticoat. Fancy dying for a petticoat." Since Lucy had refused the bread, the woman tore off a bite, stuffing it in her mouth. "If I'd known I'd swing for it, I would have taken the pantalets as well."

Other women in the area joined in the dark humor.

" 'Twould have been a bit smarter, Anne, if you'd

waited until your mistress wasn't wearing the garment to filch it."

"Lor', and they won't even let you wear it when you hang," another added. "At least then you'd leave 'em with a dainty view of your legs swinging amid that fine linen cloth."

Lucy's stomach revolted. She turned toward the wall, and let the silent spasms rack her body. If they would hang a woman for a petticoat, then Lucy was sure to swing for sedition.

Just then, the clank of the heavy bolt on the door of the cell rang out. Lucy heard a murmur and the rustle of feet in the straw.

"Get back, you!" The gaoler, a burly, ham-fisted man, did not hesitate to strike any woman or child in his path. Lucy had quickly learned that much. "Get back! This here's quality, and not for the likes of you."

An excited murmur rose from the women in the room, and two of the children shrieked. Footsteps sounded, coming closer to Lucy. The cluster of females in front of her parted, and Lucy looked up into the appalled faces of her stepmother, stepsisters, and Mr. Whippet. Relief flooded her body, so intense she thought she might die from its effects.

"I might have known." The duchess's sharp features tightened as she curled her lip in distaste at the sight of Lucy. "I had hoped it was idle rumor, but such lunacy is in the blood." She turned to the vicar. "I told you, did I not, Mr. Whippet? 'Tis a madness, passed to each generation by the one before."

Lucy scrambled to her feet, weak with relief. Her stepmother might berate her as much as she chose, but Lucy did not care. She only cared about escaping this hell on earth.

The gaoler marshaled the other prisoners toward the opposite wall, leaving her face-to-face with her betrothed and her family. Mr. Whippet surveyed her from head to toe, lips pursed in an expression of fastidious distaste.

Bertha appeared bored. Esmie had the grace to appear uncomfortable, and her stepmother eyed her with triumph.

"Yes, indeed," the duchess said to no one in particular, "blood will tell, however blue it may be."

Lucy opened her mouth to defend herself but Mr. Whippet spoke first. "Clearly, your grace, she is mad," he said, addressing her stepmother as if Lucy were not even in the room. "There can be no other explanation for it, and consequently the betrothal cannot stand."

The duchess smirked. "Of course the betrothal will stand, you fool. It will stand until she is either hanged or transported, at which time we will petition the Crown for her marriage portion and divide it equally; I as her mother and you as her betrothed." The vicar opened his mouth to protest, but the duchess dismissed his arguments with a wave of her calfskin-gloved hand. Her gaze returned to Lucy. "You look hopeful, my dear, but let me set your mind at ease. We have not come to rescue you." The words were icy, meant to chill, and they had the desired effect on Lucy. The brief flicker of hope that had ignited at the sight of her family abruptly died.

"Then why have you come?" Lucy fought back tears. She refused to cry. Refused to give her stepmother the satisfaction. "Merely to say good-bye?"

Her stepmother looked over her shoulder to where the gaoler had corralled the other prisoners at the far end of the room. Then she moved forward, lowering her voice. Her words were thick with the malice she normally disguised. "I came to be certain it was you, my dear. I came to ensure there was no mistake. You have never been anything but a trial and a vexation, a curse upon me. First, you were your father's favorite. Then your beauty outshone my girls'. But weak blood will always tell, and you have certainly proven yourself a Charming."

Lucy stiffened. "If I have proven myself to be my father's daughter, then my efforts will not have been in vain." She refused to be cowed.

"You are as mad as he was," the duchess hissed. "But even more so, you are a fool." One set of clawlike fingers reached out and grasped Lucy's neck. Lucy's first instinct was to slap them away, but she willed herself to be still. The duchess made no further move, merely rested her hand lightly around the column of Lucy's throat. "You could have married a prince. You might have paid back some of the forbearance I've extended to you over the years." The fingers began to squeeze slightly. Lucy's heart pounded. "Yet you threw away my girls' futures for a few knitters and some filthy animals like the Selkirks."

"The Selkirks are not animals!" Lucy's head snapped up and she grasped her stepmother's wrist. With one quick movement, Lucy pushed the bony hand away.

"They live in a cave, do they not?" Her stepmother smiled, an evil expression, and the duchess let her hand drop to her side. "Like the animals they are."

"They are fortunate to live anywhere after you turned them off the estate."

"They are criminals, and deserve to swing alongside you." The duchess reached into her reticule for a perfumed handkerchief and held it to her nose, inhaling deeply.

"How did you find me?" Lucy would not give in to the despair. She would not lose hope. Someone else would come. Surely there must be someone.

The duchess lowered the handkerchief. "Tom Selkirk reached London this morning."

"Tom? He is not in the prison?" Hope rose within her.

"He was not then, but I insisted that the footmen restrain him until the authorities could be summoned." She waved a hand toward the door. "He is here now somewhere, I suppose, with the other felons and miscreants."

Lucy had not known a heart might break more than once. Hers felt as if it had been shattered, the tiny shards piercing her with each breath she drew. "Why? Why would you revenge yourself on Tom Selkirk?"

The duchess sniffed. "Because I despise you."

"Because my father loved me?"

"Because there has been no one else to punish."

"Punish for what?"

The duchess's eyes narrowed. "You really don't suspect?"

"Suspect what?"

Her stepmother's laugh was an annoying trill that set Lucy's teeth on edge. "Have you truly believed the rumors all these years, then?" she asked.

Lucy straightened her shoulders. "I have ignored the gossip about my father."

"But you do know society does not believe your father died of an accidental gunshot."

Lucy felt her cheeks grow crimson. "No. They believe he took his own life."

"Took his own life! Ridiculous, isn't it?"

"Yes, it is ridiculous," she answered, but her words lacked conviction.

Her stepmother's smile now bared crooked teeth. "So, you believe it as well. How delicious. I only wish I'd known of your doubts all along. I could have enjoyed tormenting you in a much more thorough and delightful manner."

"Then . . . he did not . . ."

"Kill himself? Of course not." The duchess inhaled the perfume of her handkerchief again. "Though he was shot."

Lucy's jaw sagged with disbelief. "By whom?"

The duchess laughed and then cast a cautious glance over her shoulder. "By Mr. Whippet, my dear, but then, the vicar was only defending his property, weren't you, good sir?" She cast a sidelong glance at the clergyman. "He had an interest to preserve, given his investment in the knitting frames the Luddites were smashing. Your father was a threat to those interests, to all of our interests."

Lucy felt numb. "I don't understand."

Her stepmother snorted. "Your demented father was not merely sympathetic to the Luddites, my dear. He would have been out there with them, if he could, smashing frames. Instead, he was preparing to introduce a bill into the House of Lords that would have been even more effective at dismantling the frames than hammers and clubs. With his influence, he might have even been able to ensure its passage."

Lucy's shoulders sagged with relief, but her stepmother mistook the movement for shame. The rumors of suicide that had haunted her for eight years had not been true after all. Her father had not abandoned her. Dear God, she had not been wrong to depend upon him after all.

Her stepmother continued. "Yes, well, imagine how it was for me, spreading lies to cover up his intentions and then the shooting. I did not wed a duke so that I might continue to smell of the shop."

Lucy looked at Mr. Whippet. "Murderer!" she breathed.

The vicar drew a snuff box from somewhere within his tightly fitted jacket. He flicked the box open, removed a pinch of the shredded tobacco, and inhaled deeply. His eyes watered, and he coughed twice. Then, returning the box to his pocket, he turned his flushed face to Lucy. "Am I? What proof have you?" His look of triumph made Lucy's skin crawl. "You realize, of course, madame, that I must request you release me from our engagement." His eyes traveled around the squalid room and he shuddered with distaste. "This is more than I can bear, even for my share of ten thousand pounds."

"Don't be a fool," the duchess hissed.

"My peccadilloes are unfortunate," he said to Lucy, ignoring the duchess, "but they are nothing compared to your indiscretions or those of your father. And you're scarcely creditable now. The daughter of a duke practically in chains. Say what you like about me. No one will believe your claims."

"I am the daughter of the Duke of Nottingham." Confidence and release from the long-held secret flooded Lucy's voice as they flooded her soul. "My friends will believe me."

"Daughter of the duke?" Her stepmother snorted. "A kinship that never mattered to you one whit until now. You have disgraced the family name so vilely I wonder you dare claim it."

"Disgraced it?" Anger, clear and true, poured through Lucy's veins and gave her strength. "I have not been the one to shame my father's memory with toadeating and simpering. I have not indebted the estate to remove the stench of trade."

Her stepmother's neck went rigid. "I have taken my rightful place. You have renounced yours, just as your father did before you, and you will meet the same end."

Lucy had never felt such despair and yet such relief at the same time, as if one door had been slammed shut and another thrown open. It was finally over, this strange half-life where she belonged neither to the *ton* nor to the world of the Selkirks and the other working people. Of course, there would be no escape from Newgate. Her heart raced at the thought. Her stepmother would renounce her, the Selkirks were in chains themselves, and Nick . . . He would condemn her actions for his own reasons. She could not hope for help from that quarter.

And yet . . . Her spirits lifted. Her father had not killed himself. The weight of a great burden lifted from her shoulders. For years she had carried the secret, only to find that there was no shame after all. He had not left her purposely, and he had been more than a mere advocate for reform. His passion and his persistence had cost him everything. The last thought sobered her. Well, she might be unsure of her own place in life, caught between her aristocratic birth and her reformer's principles, but if nothing else, she was her father's daughter.

"There is no need to stay any longer," she said to her stepmother. The duchess's eyebrows rose at Lucy's dismissive, regal tone. "You may leave me to the consequences of my actions."

"I had no intention of doing otherwise," the duchess snapped. She turned to her companions. "Come, Esmie,

Bertha, Mr. Whippet. We will leave *Lady Lucinda* to the gaoler's hospitality and her chosen squalor."

Lucy stood in the matted straw and watched the small party make its way to the door. Esmie was the only one who looked back, her face bleak and eyes filled with regret and shame, an acknowledgement that the Duchess of Nottingham had finally gone too far. Fear squeezed Lucy's heart, but she refused to beg them to come back. The odor of unwashed bodies rose up again in her nostrils, and she put a hand on her stomach to calm it. Her father had not been a coward after all. He had not left her of his own will.

Lucy sank down on her blanket. Her father had been a man of integrity, a man willing to pay the price for his beliefs. She, too, was a Charming, and she could do no less.

Chapter Nineteen

Nick spied the Duchess of Nottingham and Mr. Whippet emerging from Newgate and sank lower against the squabs of the plain black carriage. The vicar minced alongside the duchess, while Lucy's two stepsisters followed like goslings behind their mother.

"How did they learn her whereabouts so quickly?" Crispin asked. He lounged with deceptive ease on the seat next to Nick. The hackney cab had stood outside the prison for more than an hour, and it was everything Nick could do not to leap from the carriage, run to the door, and pound upon it until he gained entrance. Crispin had counseled caution and he had been right, though Nick chafed at the restraint. Every detail of the plan must be methodically plotted and executed.

"Someone must have sent word to the duchess from Nottingham." Nick wondered who it had been. "Their visit will be convenient for our purposes."

Crispin nodded his assent. "I'll pay my respects to the gaoler now." He snapped his fingers, his eyes alight with devilment. "I'll say I'm acting on behalf of the duchess."

They had refined Nick's scheme over the last hour until Nick thought it might have a chance of working.

"Be careful, Cris. And don't let Lucy see you. She might give away the ruse."

"Don't worry, Nick. Of all the times I've known you to play the hero, you've never failed. This plan will be no different."

Nick felt a tightening sensation in the area of his heart. "Oh, but I have failed, my friend." He grimaced. "I failed the most important test of all. I don't intend to do so a second time."

Nick opened the carriage door and stepped down. Crispin followed. "They must move her to the State apartments, Cris, if we're to have any chance at all."

Crispin frowned. "If this works, you know you'll have to flee England. It may be doubtful that you can ever return."

"If this works," Nick answered with an air of finality, "I will have no choice. Lucy must go to Santadorra, and I must go wherever she does."

Crispin started to speak and then apparently thought better of it. With a mock salute, he turned toward the prison. Nick watched him ring the bell at the gate and then disappear inside.

It was a complicated plan, requiring the cooperation of far too many people, but he'd had no choice. He could only hope to complete each step as it presented itself and pray that no one would betray them. Nick was rather out of practice when it came to prayer, but since he had met Lucy, the habit was becoming far more common. He closed his eyes and addressed a few pleas to the Almighty.

"Lucy Charming!" The gaoler's voice rang out in the crowded room. Lucy jumped at the sound of her own name, for she had been lost in an impossible daydream about Nick. Her palms grew damp. So soon? Surely they could not bring her to trial yet. She had only been brought from Nottingham the day before.

She rose, picked up her blanket, and moved toward the door. The huge gaoler eyed her with some curiosity. "Leave it," he said, pointing toward the blanket. Lucy froze. They couldn't hang her until she'd been called to the dock, at least that was what Anne had said, so it must mean she was to be transported.

She shivered.

"Come along."

With no choice but to follow the massive shoulders of the man who'd summoned her, Lucy stepped out into the hallway. The door swung shut behind her and he threw home the bolt. "This way." He jerked his chin toward the long hallway that lay to the right.

Although conditions within the prison had been improved of late, low-pitched moans and strangled cries echoed through the passageways. The mixture of damp and stench filled her nostrils. Better to become accustomed to it, she thought. No doubt a transport ship would smell worse. They turned again into another passageway and then climbed a flight of stairs. As they went, the cries of the prisoners faded. The damp dissipated as well, and she even heard muffled laughter from behind a door.

"Where are you taking me?"

"You'll see soon enough."

At last they stopped before another door. The gaoler opened it and thrust Lucy inside. She stumbled and almost fell. "Be thankful as ye 'ave friends," he muttered before shutting the door in her face and turning the key in the lock.

Lucy spun around, prepared to face yet another scene of squalor. Instead, to her surprise, she found herself in a drawing room that could have passed for one in any respectable part of London. She had heard of the State apartments in Newgate, where wealthy and aristocratic prisoners were held. No doubt that was where she was. Who could have arranged for her to be brought here? Nick's chocolate eyes flashed in her thoughts, but she hardly dared hope. Indeed, she would not hope. Not anymore. She would merely take each moment as it presented itself until the noose tightened around her neck.

The carriage rumbled through the streets of London, its circuitous route meant to lose any spies who might have followed the conveyance from Newgate. Nick frowned as he glanced at the list Crispin had handed him. In all, twelve men and one woman had been brought from Nottingham to Newgate.

"You are certain that the gaoler moved her?"

Crispin nodded. "Lucy is comfortably ensconced in a State cell, and I spoke with all of the Nottingham prisoners." He nodded toward the list and flipped Nick the empty purse. "Conversation in Newgate is not to be had cheaply. The guards must retire at a young age to the seaside with the bribes they receive."

"Mr. Selkirk?" Nick asked.

"He was worried for Lady Lucy and concerned that Tom was nowhere to be found."

"Why was Tom not taken by the soldiers?"

"Evidently he slipped away before they could catch him. In the confusion, it was several hours before they noticed he was missing."

"What of Mrs. Selkirk?"

"Taken to the gaol in Nottingham but released."

Nick rubbed his forehead. At least Mrs. Selkirk had been spared the humiliation of Newgate.

The carriage pulled to a stop in front of a familiar shabby edifice. Crispin nodded toward the building. "Do you think she'll help us?"

For the first time that day, Nick smiled. "When has she not, my friend? If it were not for her, we'd both have been fleeced of our purse, if not our fortunes, the moment we came down from university."

The two men climbed from the carriage and strode up the walk toward Madame St. Cloud's. Halfway to the door, Nick stopped. Seated on the steps of the brothel was Lucy's stepsister, Esmerelda Fortune.

At the sight of Nick and Crispin, the girl rose to her feet. Deep shadows beneath her eyes dominated her gaunt face.

"Your Highness," she began, her lips, hands, and knees all trembling uncontrollably.

Anger, thick and fierce, filled Nick's chest. The duchess had no doubt sent her unfortunate daughter on some errand of extortion, but he would not listen. Without so much as a lift of a finger of acknowledgment, he brushed by her.

"I know where Lucy is."

Nick continued up the stairs, refusing to listen. He already knew anything the girl had to tell him.

"And I know where Tom Selkirk is as well." Esmerelda Fortune raised her chin in defiance and Nick stopped in his tracks.

Crispin looked puzzled. "How could you possibly know that?"

The girl blushed. "I was there, when he made his way to Nottingham House."

"He is there? At your mother's?" Nick moved back down the steps and planted himself in front of Esmerelda.

"No. He is in Newgate, just as Lucy is." She cringed when she delivered the information, as if expecting him to strike her. As much as he disliked her, Nick felt a brief flash of pity. Was she truly there to offer information or had she simply yet to name her price?

"Why should I believe you? Perhaps your appearance here is part of some stratagem that the duchess has conceived?"

The girl had the grace to blush. "I have been complicit, Your Highness, in many sins against Lucy Charming, but even I know that my mother has gone beyond the pale this time." The determined set of her jaw lent conviction to her words.

Nick stood silently for a long moment, his eyes boring into the girl's as he waited for her to tear her gaze away.

Her eyes, though, held his steadily until even he was satisfied of the veracity of her statement.

Crispin stepped forward. "This information may help us with our plan."

"Yes." Nick rubbed his chin. "Tom's presence may be just the thing to help us free Lucy." Lucy. He ached to hold her, and he did not dare allow his mind to imagine what might have happened if Crispin's bribes had not worked. As it was he could barely remain inside his skin thinking of her in the relative safety and comfort of a State apartment.

"You will free her, then?" Esmerelda asked. "She does not deserve this."

"You have my word, madam." Nick could perhaps have been more kindly to the girl, but he was still too appalled at the family's treatment of Lucy to be very forgiving.

"Then I will go." She stepped between the two men and walked toward the street.

"A moment, madam." Nick might despise the girl for her complicity in her mother's sins, but he could hardly let her go traipsing across London alone. "My carriage stands ready. It will convey you to Mayfair and can set you down near Nottingham House without undue notice."

Esmerelda's cheeks flushed with gratitude, and Nick saw a glimpse of what the girl might have been like, had she not been so worn down by her termagant of a mother. Esmerelda murmured her thanks and then disappeared into the waiting carriage. Nick turned to Crispin once again.

"I've half a mind to find my gardener's smock and bribe my way into Lucy's cell tonight."

"You can't, Nick." Crispin laid a hand on his arm. "Not unless you want to jeopardize her freedom. I know patience appears to be a very small virtue at present, but you must be high-minded a bit longer."

Nick's shoulders slumped as they turned toward Madame St. Cloud's door and lifted the knocker. Patience had never been numbered among his strongest attributes.

A moment later, the door opened and Henny squealed with delight at the sight of her two favorite customers.

It took the better part of two days to put the plan into place, and Nick felt every hour of the forty-eight as if they were his last. The only thought that saved his sanity was the knowledge that Lucy rested comfortably in two well-furnished rooms inside the prison. For a healthy bribe, the State prisoners were allowed to receive visitors freely and even entertained, some with food baskets ordered from Gunther's. Nick's plan was costly, and his debt to Crispin mounted with each passing hour. A basket of food, a dress, a bottle of brandy—one by one each found its way to Lucy Charming's new abode.

At long last, though, the preparations were complete. Late in the morning of the fourth day since Lucy had been imprisoned, Nick and Crispin emerged from Madame St. Cloud's, hailed a hackney, and set off for Newgate.

The summer sun grew increasingly warm as the day lengthened, but Nick's restlessness had passed. Now that the rescue had begun, his nerves were as calm as the surface of a Santadorran mountain lake on a still day.

"There's another one," Crispin said as they watched a young boy, dressed in the familiar black clothes of a chimney sweep, slip through the doors to the prison.

"How many in all?" Nick asked.

"Fifteen. Mr. Cartwright said that every boy in the school demanded to be a part of the rescue."

Nick glanced at Crispin. "Are you sure you want to be a part of this? It's quite illegal."

Crispin laughed. "Illegal it may be, but I began this bumblebroth with my matchmaking schemes, and I will see it through."

Nick could not match Crispin's lighter tone. "Thank you, my friend." He forced a smile. "Perhaps someday I might play matchmaker for you."

"You always were the vengeful type," Crispin shot back with a grin, and then his face grew serious. "Be happy with her, Nick. She was made for you, you know, and you for her."

A knot formed in his solar plexus. "I'm quite aware of that, my friend. I can only hope that the lady has come to the same realization, along with a generous measure of forgiveness."

A sharp rap on the carriage interrupted their exchange. Nick glanced around and came face-to-face with his father. Without waiting for an invitation, King Leopold wrenched open the door and vaulted into the hackney.

"Cris!" Nick knew who the culprit was immediately.

Crispin did not flinch. "Humor me. I seem to be having a streak of good fortune when it comes to furthering alliances."

"Good morning, Wellstone," his father said, nodding to Crispin. "Nick." The one syllable managed to convey a lifetime of parental disapproval.

Crispin cleared his throat. "I know what you said, Nick, but be reasonable. Your chances of leaving the country greatly improve if you can use your father's consequence as a smokescreen."

The king regarded Nick with concern. "Lord Wellstone has told me everything."

Nick wanted to ignore his father but the truth of Crispin's words rang in his head. Which mattered more, his pride or Lucy's life? He'd already answered that question when he'd accepted that he must return to Santadorra.

"Splendid." Nick tried to keep the sarcasm from his voice, but old habits died slow deaths. "Then we shall have plenty of time for you to lecture me regarding the proper behavior of a prince. It will be another half hour, at least, before all of the climbing boys are inside the prison."

"Good. Then that will give me ample time to say how pleased I was to discover that my son had married a reform-minded hoyden in an Anglican ceremony, without consulting his sovereign and father."

Touché, Nick thought. "You wanted me wed. You and Prinny concocted the scheme. I merely saw it through to its completion."

The king barked with laughter. "You ask no quarter, do you, lad? But then, by Jove, you give none either."

The words brought Nick up short. He'd so recently thought the very same about Lucy. They were alike, he realized, in a flash of clearheaded insight. Neither of them willing to compromise. Both passionate, in their own ways, in defense of their beliefs.

"What's done is done."

"Bedded her, have you?" The king eyed him shrewdly.

Nick bristled. "Have a care. She is my wife."

"I do not seem to be the one who needs to have a care for your wife," his father shot back. "It is not my bride in Newgate."

"No, yours is buried nicely beneath her funeral pyre." The caustic words shocked even Nick, but he met his father's gaze without flinching. They had avoided the past for far too long, he could see that now. He had fled from Santadorra, and his father had let him run, sending him to England to school. Then it had been too painful for them to share their feelings. Now it was in all likelihood too late.

"Enough, Nicholas. I came to mend fences, not to topple them. Still, if you are untrained in the art of reconciliation, the blame lies at my door."

His father's matter-of-fact words stopped Nick cold. "And you, sir, are the expert peacemaker who might teach me the trade? Pray, tell me where you learned your craft, for I should like to study there myself."

His father's cheeks reddened. "I learned in Santadorra, where you have not set foot in almost twenty years. I learned as I rebuilt my life and re-established justice for my people."

His father might try to make Nick feel guilt over the

abandonment of his country, but it would not work. "You know my feelings on that matter."

"And yet you married," the king remarked, his eyes narrowing. "Why is that, Nicholas? You have always informed me your intention was to allow the line to die out. With no heir, Santadorra will revert to Spanish control. And yet you have married and you have bedded the girl. An heir may already be on the way. I confess I find such behavior extremely puzzling at best, and inconsistent at worst."

Nick bristled. "It is you, sire, who let the line die that night in the palace. You sent your family alone into the mountains. Surely you knew what the outcome would be."

For once, his father did not respond with an angry outburst of his own. Instead, silence reigned inside the carriage for several long, cold minutes.

Nick watched his father, who turned to the opposite window of the carriage and gently drew back the curtains. His gaze was fixed on whatever foot traffic passed in front of the shops.

"There was no hope for you in the palace." His father's voice was flat, and he did not turn to face Nick.

Nick spoke before he could stop himself. "A fortunate happenstance, then, that you should emerge unscathed."

"Unscathed!" The king jerked the curtains closed and the sound of ripping cloth rent the air. "Wife and daughter dead, son lost in the mountains, and a knife wound in my belly. I would hardly call that unscathed."

"Compared to what Mother and Jo suffered, it was nothing." The wound that had festered for so long opened, and Nick could contain it no longer. His father's shoulders slumped then, and he looked old. The sight jolted Nick.

"Why do we continue to do this, Nicholas? After all these years, one would think our bloodlust would be sated, but we cannot even occupy the same carriage without the urge to draw each other's cork."

Nick shrugged to hide the pain that knifed through

him. Time and time again his father had made politely worded requests for forgiveness. Nick had always thought them insincere, but now, with the passage of time, and with his own sins against Lucy weighing heavily on his mind, he began to doubt his assessment of his father's pleas. Perhaps the king had regretted his actions. Perhaps . . . but no. The price was too great. To admit that he might have been in error about his father would be to acknowledge his own fault in their long separation.

"If you do not care to offer me your assistance, you may tell me so at once," Nick said. His father turned from the window, and in the clear light of day, Nick could see the signs of age that lined his brow. Looking into his father's countenance was like staring into his own face several decades into the future, as sure a resemblance as the one on the dorrian. It was an eerie feeling.

"You have always been and will always be my son."

"Yes." Nick acknowledged ruefully. "For good or ill, our lives will always be bound together."

Crispin, who had been silently observing the interchange, spoke. "The last boy has entered the prison. I'll slip around the corner to speak with Mr. Cartwright." He looked at Nick. "Then we may begin."

Nick nodded, and Crispin slipped from the carriage. His father eyed him thoughtfully. "You have set yourself a herculean task, have you not? Tell me, how does your radical wife feel about being a royal princess?"

A smile sprang to Nick's lips, but concern for Lucy smothered it as quickly as it came. "Let us just say she has yet to . . . accustom herself to the role."

His father chuckled, a sound from Nick's childhood, and one fondly remembered. "She sounds a great deal like your mother."

Nick inhaled sharply, and his father nodded in sympathy. "We may speak of her, Nick. She is only dead, not damned."

"Only dead? You say that very casually." The carriage seemed to be growing smaller by the moment.

"No, I say that peacefully. Once you have accepted the past, that it cannot be changed, then it becomes much simpler to let it go."

"Of course no one can change the past," Nick said stiffly.

"You believe that you can."

His father's words caused him to shift restlessly in his seat. "What a ridiculous notion."

"Is it?" The king's gaze pinned him like a butterfly in a schoolboy's collection. "Then why all the rescues, I wonder? Why the incessant need to play the hero?"

Nick hated that his motives were so transparent, especially to his father. "Practice makes perfect, perhaps?" he asked and then winced. The quip revealed too much.

"Yes. I suppose so." His father turned toward him. "You know, Nicholas, there was nothing either one of us could have done differently."

"You could have come with us."

"And then they would have killed us all."

"You don't know that."

"Son, I am the King of Santadorra. The rebels had no eyes for anyone else. Their purpose was to murder me and my family. By staying behind, I gave you, your mother and sister a chance to escape."

"You ordered the guards to remain with you." The words were a weak attempt to resurrect the walls that had shielded him for so long. The blame he had always heaped upon his father was melting away, and Nick felt unprotected without it, like a knight without armor.

"And I instructed your mother to take clothes from the servants' hall and travel incognito. A contingent of the Santadorran guards at your heels would have ruined the disguise."

Nick swallowed at the deluge of memories that threatened to swamp him even after all this time. "Instead, our costumes made us easy prey for the renegades from the French and Spanish armies," he said, no longer arguing with his father but with himself.

"Yes." His father's head dipped. "I did not think of them at the time. Only of the French soldiers pouring into the palace."

Neither said anything for several long moments. The rumble of traffic from the street floated on the air.

"Where the devil is Crispin?" Nick twisted in his seat to look out the opposite window.

His father ignored the question. "The Royal Guards will be waiting for you on the Portsmouth road." He reached for Nick's hand, and Nick surprised himself by not shrinking from the contact. He had not felt his father's touch in more than fifteen years, and yet it was as familiar as if they had embraced only the day before. "Come home, Nick, and we will put the past to rest. I think we are both ready now to do so."

At that moment, the door to the carriage swung open and Crispin stuck his head in the opening. "It's time."

Nick's father clapped him on the back. "Good luck, son. By nightfall, we will be halfway across the Channel."

Nick looked at his father, and for the first time since the cold night on the mountain, he allowed himself to hope. "Santadorra will hardly seem like home."

The king smiled. "In time, son. In time."

Nick climbed from the carriage, and he and Crispin crossed the street to the entrance of the prison. The guard nodded at Crispin and extended his hand for the proffered coin.

"The boy?" Crispin asked, and the guard grunted.

"I'll take ye to 'im myself."

For the price of a few more coins, they gained admittance to the room where Tom Selkirk was held. The young man's shoulders sagged with relief when he saw Nick and Crispin. Nick kept his expression stern, careful to hide his true feelings from the guard.

"Selkirk." He nodded at the youth. Tom looked puzzled, until Nick managed a surreptitious wink.

"Sir." Tom, a quick study, bowed formally and appeared to be shaking in his boots.

"You will come with us," Nick ordered, and Tom bowed and scraped. His humility seemed to satisfy the gaoler.

"I'll take you to the lady, then, but 'ide the lad if anyone looks suspiciouslike."

The walk from Tom's cell to the more genteel part of the prison seemed to take forever. Nick concentrated on placing one shabbily booted foot in front of the other. No one said a word, and, thankfully, the passageways were deserted. His head spun from his conversation with his father, but he could ill afford distraction now. Lucy's future depended on his clear-thinking resolve.

The guard inserted a key into a heavy wooden door and pushed it open. " 'Alf an 'our, and no more," he instructed. Nick stepped across the threshold, Crispin and Tom close behind him. The door slammed shut with hollow finality.

Nick glanced about. The small drawing room lay empty. His heart pounded in his chest. "Cris?" He looked to his friend for reassurance.

Crispin arched an eyebrow. "I would offer to look in the bedchamber myself, but perhaps that is a husband's prerogative?"

Nick laughed ruefully. "I'll go."

For a small drawing room, it took a surprisingly long time to cross. He opened the door on the other side and stepped into the dimness beyond.

His eyes, unaccustomed to the dark, required a moment to focus. They cleared, just in time to see a large object hurtling toward him. Nick ducked, and a washbasin shattered against the wall behind him.

"Hello, Lucy," he said wryly. He saw her then, outlined in the dimness. Never had there been a more welcome sight. Her only response to his greeting was to fling the pitcher at him as well. It, too, crashed against the wall when he nimbly stepped to the side.

"Get out." Her cheeks were flushed, and Nick breathed a sigh of relief that she appeared unharmed.

"Out of this place? Gladly." Her face fell, and Nick

breathed a sigh of relief. "But not without you," he added. Her spine stiffened and she raised her chin. Nick felt warmed from head to toe. As he'd known the day he proposed, if she were set against forgiving him, she'd not be displaying such a bounty of indignation.

"You are mad to think I'd go with you." She turned up her nose.

"Me? Mad? I'm not the one refusing a way out of this hellhole," he pointed out quite reasonably. Lucy glanced around for something else to throw. It was time to put a stop to the missiles, Nick decided, and moved toward her.

She refused to cower, which was one of the things he loved most about her. "Pardon me if I fail to express my gratitude properly." Her tone was scathing. "But as I recall, you're the reason I'm in this predicament to begin with."

She had him there. Nick cleared his throat.

"You have every right to despise me, Lucy." The words were difficult to say, despite their truthfulness. "I betrayed you. Whatever my purposes or reasons, it was a betrayal nonetheless."

Her eyes widened at his confession. "Then you admit your error?"

"I admit my actions," he said evasively, "but what's done is done." He moved a step closer, and she did not shrink away. "I can't change the past, Lucy. I've finally learned that lesson. But I can change the future, and I have no intention of seeing you hang or allowing you to be thrown aboard a transport ship."

She stiffened, and he saw in her eyes the toll that the fear of the last few days had exacted from her. "Sidmouth will never allow my release."

"I know." The bold statement of fact and its implications hung in the air between them. "I've come to rescue you, Lucy, if you might allow me that privilege one last time."

"What do you mean?" Her eyes narrowed.

Beth Pattillo

"If you come with me, you will have to leave more than Newgate behind."

"I don't understand."

Nick wondered if she truly did not understand or if her stubborn will refused to accept the inevitable. "You must leave England, princess. There is no possible way you can remain. Sidmouth is a powerful man, and he will not rest until you can no longer trouble him."

Her eyes flashed. "Why does he care? I am nothing to him, and very little to the cause of reform. I could understand if I were Wilburforce or Orator Hunt, or even Mr. Benton, but I am no one."

"On the contrary. You are the daughter of a duke, and that makes you the worst of traitors in his eyes."

Nick could almost see the gears of her mind turn as she thought over the implications of his statement.

"Where . . . where would I go?"

Nick wanted nothing more than to sweep her into his arms, but now was not the time. She must decide for herself, with no other form of persuasion than his most logical arguments.

"You must come with me to Santadorra."

"No." Her chin rose.

"Be reasonable, princess. At the moment, your only protection lies in my country."

"As your wife."

"Yes, as my wife."

The next few moments were the longest of Nick's life, longer than the time he'd spent huddled in the cave, longer than the moments he'd spent staunching the flow of blood from the woman he'd rescued from the market square while agonizing over Lucy's whereabouts. Any hope for happiness, for a future, dangled in the balance.

She looked as if she might spit in his eye, and then suddenly, remarkably, Lucy began to cry. Her face crumpled, and Nick's heart broke in two. It was everything he'd feared. To Lucy, he had literally become a fate worse than death.

"You will force me to come with you," she said between sobs. "Here." She extended her arm.

"What?"

"Here. You are forever grabbing at me, pulling me about. Here." She lifted her arm higher until her wrist was almost beneath his chin.

"No." By Jove, what did she expect of him? Was he not her husband? Was it not his duty to care for her?

"What is to stop you?" she demanded. "Do as you have done every time before. Grab my wrist and tow me about like a child in leading strings."

Images flashed through his mind. Fleeing the duchess's town home. The night in the maze at Carlton House. Lucy was right. Since the moment they'd met, he'd been grasping her and pulling her against her will.

"No," he said again and took a step back. Her arm dropped to her side, and she wore a look of unhappy satisfaction.

"Then I will remain here." She raised her face to his, and the tears shining in her eyes pounded what remained of his heart into dust.

Without another word, Nick lifted his hand and extended it toward her. He held it, palm up and fingers loose, as if he were making an offering to the gods.

"I lied." The words were thick and hard to say, but he managed them. "When you asked me how I could not be changed by what happened in the square, I lied."

Lucy went white. "What do you mean?"

Nick swallowed hard. "You did convince me, with your Orator Hunt and your reform rallies. You convinced me with your climbing boys and the Selkirks and your passion for the truth. Reform is not without reason. I see that now."

Lucy clutched the bedpost. "No."

"Yes. I lied at the Selkirks' so you would be forced to marry me." Nick's pulse pounded in his throat.

"Why?" Lucy looked as if she'd been struck. "Why would you want to marry me?" Then, as if she'd comprehended her own question, she nodded. "So you could rescue me, of course. Your damnable tendency to play the hero."

"No." The denial sprang to his lips. "No. I told myself at the time that was my reason, but I lied even to myself."

Lucy moved around him, and he had to let her go. She had refused his hand. "Don't lie," she said, "not now. It doesn't matter. You feel responsible, and your overdeveloped sense of guilt will not let you rest until you set things right."

Nick's throat was tight. "I can never set things right."

She whirled to face him. "What do you mean?"

"Lucy, you must come with me." He extended his hand once again. "I can never give you back what I have cost you. You must relinquish your country, your friends, your cause, but I will do everything in my power to make you happy. I will bear you company, if that is what you wish, or I will banish myself from your presence forever. You have only to say the word."

Her mouth was a thin line. "But the word will have to be said in Santadorra. That is what you mean."

"Yes." His fingers continued to hang in midair, and his arm grew heavy with the effort of holding it out toward her. "That much I cannot change."

Her lip trembled. "I have no choice, do I?"

"Very little," he conceded.

The moment stretched into a lifetime. Then, Nick watched as with agonizing slowness, her hand lifted, and she reached out and laid her fingers atop his own.

"If there is no other way," she whispered, and Nick would have given any future kingdom to take her in his arms and offer her comfort. Pride, though, and respect for Lucy prevented him. Perhaps one day . . .

"We have little time to waste." With his free hand, Nick flicked open the buttons of his coat and began to work at the fastenings of his waistcoat. Lucy jumped back with a gasp.

"You are disgusting."

"What?" Nick looked at her in confusion. He began to unwrap the clothing he'd concealed beneath his garments. First a worn pair of breeches, followed by the distinctive black shirt and vest of a chimney sweep. Last of all came the familiar cap that covered her curls so well. "We've no time for missishness, princess. The royal yacht awaits us at Portsmouth." He thrust the clothes into her arms.

Lucy blushed, and Nick realized what she'd thought. He stilled. "Am I truly such a cad, then?"

"No," she whispered, her eyes luminous. "No, you are not."

The moment was suspended between them, as fragile as crystal. Nick looked into her amazing eyes, and for the first time since the debacle in Nottingham, he felt hope blossom in his chest.

Chapter Twenty

Seductive hope curled through Lucy, wrapping itself around her heart. Her husband had left her to don her boys' clothes, and her stomach lurched as she tucked her hair under her cap. God, could she risk betrayal again? Could she open herself to more pain, even at the expense of the joy of being in Nick's arms? She understood what had prompted Nick's actions, even if she did not agree with his decisions. And he had confessed to his change of heart about reform. Perhaps he would still honor the terms of their wager and grant the men and women of Santadorra the vote. He was a man willing to bend, though he might need a bit of persuasion and hard experience to do so. He was a man on whom she could depend, a man not easily swayed. Did she have the courage to risk placing her heart in his keeping?

Lucy sighed. Really, it was too late to even ask that question, for her heart had been his for some time now. He had come to rescue her, not to bend her to his own will or to his own views, but because he kept his vows. She could depend on him without becoming dependent upon him. He would be strong enough to allow her a sense of independence, but she would have to allow him to worry about her welfare and to protect her from time to time. The thought held a warm appeal.

Lucy emerged into the sitting room to find Tom Selkirk seated on a chair, wearing her gown. He was a good sport, as well as a satisfactorily pretty girl, but she decided to refrain from sharing that information with the young man. He pulled at Lucy's gown where the ripped seams had been repinned to accommodate his broader shoulders. With a shawl draped around his neck, he might sit with his back to the door and prove a most effective decoy until the guards came to bring her dinner.

"Are you sure, Tom?" Guilt tore at her. They had no way of knowing exactly what might happen to him when the ruse was discovered.

"Lord Wellstone's solicitor has already begun work on my family's behalf. When we are freed, Prince Nicholas has promised us a new life in Santadorra. Besides, once you bind my hands and tie me to the chair, I have a fair enough story to hold them off with." He grinned, enjoying his part in the drama. "Now fix my hair, my lady."

Lucy reluctantly did as he instructed. She placed the blond wig that had been tucked inside Crispin's hat upon Tom's head and then tied a kerchief around his mouth to gag him.

"You will be welcome in Santadorra," Nick added from the corner. "You and all the Nottingham reformers. The solicitor has instructions to provide you with funds for travel."

Tom, since he was gagged, made no reply, merely nodded in Nick's direction and gave him a broad wink.

Crispin stood watch at the door. "The guard is coming."

Outside, a nearby clock tower chimed the hour. Lucy felt as if she might be sick. Nick stepped toward her. "Are you sure you can do this?"

"How can I not?" Her love for this complicated man threatened to overwhelm her, but now was not the time for giving in to emotion. Nick had come for her. He had admitted his lie regarding their wager and his feelings about reform, but more than that, he was clearly willing to sacrifice his pride and his fear of the past to see her safely from England. Lucy rubbed her hands against the leather of her breeches. "You and Lord Wellstone have exceeded the very heights of deviousness. I would not be the one to be the failing of such a foolproof plan."

Nick regarded her intently with his chocolate eyes. "I only hope it will work as we envisioned." He adjusted Lucy's cap, lowering it over her eyes, and she tingled at his nearness. She had been so busy trying to transform Nick into someone he was not that she had failed to see the man he was, but in the confines of Newgate, her eyes had been opened.

The door to the room swung open and Nick stepped away from her. "Come along, boy," he commanded in such stern tones that Lucy jumped. The guard laughed and gave her a shove as she passed by him and into the corridor. Lucy saw Nick's fists clench at his side, but he said nothing.

"The boy 'as to return to 'is cell now," the guard said to Nick's back. He cuffed Lucy on the ear. Nick paused, glanced back, and Lucy wondered if he might lose control, but he only shrugged and continued walking.

"Take him, then." Nick waved a dismissive hand. "We've no more need of the lad."

Lucy's heart clenched as Nick and Lord Wellstone continued down the corridor, but the guard grabbed Lucy's elbow and pulled her down a side passage. It took every ounce of strength not to wrest her arm from the man's grip and flee after Nick, but she mustered her courage and played the part of Tom Selkirk. In no time at all, she found herself returned to the common area of the prison. The guard shoved her into a room—heavens, but she was tired of being thrust about—and she fell to her knees. Rough hands jostled her, and she looked up to see the faces of an entire room full of men glaring at her.

Lucy fought panic. Before she could open her mouth to speak, a slim figure emerged from the group. He was dressed in breeches, black shirt, and cap identical to her own. "Let me 'elp you, boy."

Lucy gratefully accepted his assistance and he pulled her to her feet. "Now, then," Mr. Cartwright's pupil said with a cheerful, crooked grin, "shall we begin?"

Nick had made her memorize the complicated routes and patterns of their charade. It had not been easy to do, in the few moments before the guard had returned to her room, but she had managed. Now she mumbled them to herself as she slipped in and out of the various chambers, each time trading places with another of Mr. Cartwright's boys who was "visiting" someone in the cell. The identical black shirts caused no notice as Lucy wove her way from one room to another. Nick had given her sufficient gold for her own bribes, which she slipped into the bulging paws of guards who locked and unlocked doors. Before long, she was just another of a swarm of climbing boys who had descended on Newgate that day to visit parents, uncles, aunts, and cousins. Each of the boys gave her a smile and a press of the hand for luck as they performed their intricate minuet the length and breadth of the prison, and Lucy would have defied Sidmouth himself to keep track of which boy was which. Finally, leaving the last cell behind, she hurried toward the main gate and, at the gruff signal of one of the guards, emerged onto the street. She dared not stop to look about, although her heart was beating like thunder. With a long sigh at the warmth of the sun on her face after four days within the prison, she turned her steps eastward.

Nick paced the length of the carpet in the fairy bower bedchamber at Madame St. Cloud's. He had wanted to wait a short distance from the prison with a carriage, but Crispin had insisted they leave Lucy to find her own way. They had gone to far too much trouble to escape notice to rouse suspicion with the sight of a climbing boy clambering into a hackney.

He glanced at the casement clock and wondered if it had stopped. Twice, he strode to the window to survey the street below. Once, he saw a flash of black dart along the pavement, but he couldn't be certain it was her. At long last, footsteps sounded on the stairs, and he heard women's voices. He tried to convince himself that it was only two of Madame's girls preparing for their role in the daring plan, but he could not squelch the hope that rose unbidden.

The door swung open and Madame entered the room, followed by Lucy. She pulled off her cap, shaking out her golden curls, and Nick's breath stopped. God, he loved her.

"Henny will assist you with your bath," Madame said to Lucy, the two of them ignoring Nick as if he were a sofa instead of a husband. "The servants will bring up the water *immediatement.*"

"Thank you, Madame." Lucy pressed the older woman's hands between her own. Nick wished that the Frenchwoman would simply leave. He wanted Lucy in his trembling arms as soon as possible. Not for nefarious purposes, although he did cast a longing look toward the incredible bed. That would have to wait. No, he merely wanted to reassure himself she was all right.

Madame left, and the door clicked shut behind her.

"Well done, princess." He stayed where he was by the window, not wanting to rush his fences.

"It was a brilliant plan." She smiled shyly, and his heart lurched. "Even Sidmouth does not employ enough agents to follow all of Mr. Cartwright's boys."

"It's not finished, though." Nick knew the dangers that still lay ahead. "We must reach Portsmouth."

"We will." She seemed almost unnaturally quiet for Lucy Charming. That worried Nick. The servants knocked at the door and brought in the water to fill the hip bath behind the screen in the corner.

"I'll go," Nick offered when the servants had left. The scent of rosewater permeated the room, and Nick's imagination needed no prompting to envision Lucy naked in the bath, her skin covered with soft lather. His body hardened at the image.

"No. Stay." Lucy spoke the words so softly Nick thought he might have imagined them, but when she looked him boldly in the eye and began to remove her clothing, he knew he had not.

"Lucy, don't torment me," he breathed, and she smiled with pleasure, damn her eyes.

"You lied," she reminded him, and he nodded, wary.

"I did."

"To protect me?"

"Only in part." He shifted his stance to disguise the effect of her body on his own. The woman did love to torture him.

"And the other part?"

"I think you know." Why was she toying with him? He was afraid she had only accepted his help because she had no other choice.

"I have hopes, but I need you to speak the words."

Nick's breath caught in his throat, and for the first time, he dared to believe that the smile curving her lips hinted at the future—their future. "You are a hard woman, Lucy Charming."

"Quite the contrary." She grinned cheekily. "I think I'm very soft." To demonstrate, she removed the last of her clothing and stood before him in all her nakedness. Nick tried to swallow but his throat would not cooperate.

"There's only one point on which we need clarification," Lucy said, and Nick wished she would quit talking. He stepped toward her. Was there room enough for both of them in the hip bath? Perhaps he would content himself with merely watching her bathe. Perhaps he would assist her by rubbing the scented soap over her body until she arched with pleasure and cried out in release. Yes, that thought held definite appeal.

Lucy swatted his hands when they came too close. "Let us be in perfect accord about one thing, Nick. I won the wager."

He groaned, grabbed her, and pulled her against him. "Yes. Yes. You won the blasted wager."

"And the men and women of Santadorra will receive the vote when you are king."

"Yes. The men will receive the vote. Now, can we quit talking?" He caught her head between his hands and proceeded to angle her mouth so that he could slake his thirst for her. She pressed a finger against his lips.

"And the women?" she prompted.

"The women may take a bit longer. Now be quiet, princess. We've very little time, and I have no desire to waste it on something as frivolous as conversation."

"No desire?" She pressed against him, and he groaned. "I wouldn't say that, Your Highness."

To his delight, Nick discovered there was room for both of them in the hip bath, provided they were joined in the most intimate of ways. Later, when the water had cooled, he lifted her from the bath, led her to the bed, and scooped up something from beneath the pillows. Lucy eyed him curiously. "What's that?"

Nick extended the object forward, allowing it to dangle from his hand. "I believe you are familiar with these?"

With a squeal of delight, Lucy snatched the wrist irons from his fingers and proceeded to clamp them around both his wrists.

"Lucy! Wait!" Nick protested, but it was too late. She held him prisoner, and he would not have had it any other way.

"I love you, Lucy Charming," he whispered when she had pushed him back into the pillows and was pressing kisses to the side of his throat. His manacled wrists rested uncomfortably between them, but he didn't mind. It was a bondage he had chosen, both literally and figuratively.

"Of course you love me." She slid her way down his body, kissing him as she went. Nick waited for her to repeat the affirmation, but instead she tortured him by trailing her tongue across his stomach.

"Lucy!" He tried to sound regal and commanding, but she simply smiled and slid her body back up along his until her lips were a mere inch from his own.

"You deserve to be tortured, you know." She moved against him.

"Yes, well, you're doing a more than adequate job. Now tell me, by Jove. Do you love me or not?"

"What do you think, Your Highness?" With only the briefest of kisses on his lips, she began to work her way down his body once more until he thought he might die from pleasure.

Nick accepted that answer as a yes.

Unfortunately, there was little time to linger in the luxurious chamber. Lucy stretched, her body tingling with pleasure, and climbed from the bed. She enjoyed Nick's eyes upon her as she crossed the room and disappeared behind the screen. A yellow muslin walking dress and spencer hung on a peg. Lucy donned the garments and pinned up her hair. By the time she emerged from behind the screen, Nick had dressed as well and was pulling on his boots.

"Are you ready, then?" He looked at her hungrily, and the strength of his gaze made Lucy shiver.

"Yes."

Ten minutes later, they had gathered in the foyer with a bevy of young women, all dressed in matching primrose gowns. Mr. Cartwright's aging seamstresses had managed to ply their needles one last time.

"Quiet, then. Quiet." Crispin was desperately trying to impose some sort of order on the chattering fray. Lucy watched as he and Nick exchanged a meaningful masculine look. With a laugh, she plunged into the midst of the group. In the middle of the chaos, she found Henny holding a fat blond pug.

"Wellington!" The other woman handed the dog into

Lucy's arms, and he wheezed and licked her cheek. Lucy cuddled him close. "I never thought to see you again."

"Lord Wellstone brought 'im," Henny said, patting the pug's head. "Thought he might as well go along. His mistress, Lady Belmont, won't be back in London for ages."

Lucy smiled, tucked Wellington into the crook of one arm, and hugged Henny with the other. "My thanks to you as well."

"Thanks?" Henny looked genuinely surprised. " 'Twas a mean-spirited trick I played that day, scaring you and forcing you to listen to Mr. Whippet."

Lucy laughed. "If nothing else, you saved me from a husband who crawled on all fours."

Henny smiled and glanced at Nick. "You have brought this one to his knees, my lady, but no farther."

"No, no farther." They shared a smile, the kind of conspiratorial exchange only two women can know. "Good luck, Henny."

In another moment, they were filing out the door, one by one. Each girl had instructions to proceed to a different posting inn and from there to a seaport to book foreign passage. With a backward glance at Nick, Lucy followed the last girl out the door.

It felt good to be free, and Lucy enjoyed the walk to the nearest stage stop. Even being forced into the crowded confines of the mail coach did not dampen her good spirits. At the second stop, she alighted from the coach. Across the yard sat an impressive carriage, complete with the royal crest of the King of Santadorra. The door to the carriage swung open, and Lucy moved forward nervously to greet her new father-in-law.

The Royal Guards escorted them to Portsmouth, where the king blustered at the customs officials until they were too intimidated to ask to see official traveling papers for the sovereign's new daughter-in-law. A short time later, the Crown Prince and his companion, accompanied by King Leopold and Lord Wellstone, boarded the royal yacht. The captain quickly weighed anchor.

Lucy did not breathe a sigh of relief until the coast of England grew quite small in the distance. Nick stood beside her at the rail, his arm draped around her shoulders. Her stomach pitched in rhythm with the deck beneath her feet, and she clutched her husband for support. Excitement at what lay ahead combined with a strong sense of loss. Her life would never be the same.

"Steady." Nick pulled her closer. "Are you feeling ill?"

"No." She hesitated, unsure whether to share her thoughts. Despite their mutual declaration of love, their relationship still seemed somehow unsettled. "No, I am not ill."

"Then you are regretting your decision." His face was impassive, but Lucy heard the worry in his voice.

"Yes, I am regretting it."

He stiffened and began to pull away, but she wrapped her arms around his waist and refused to let him go. "Yes and no. It is difficult to leave England, especially under these circumstances. To say good-bye to the only life I have known."

They watched the disappearing coastline in silence for several long moments, until Lucy could put her feelings into words. "You were right when you said that one day I would have to choose whether to live in the world of my birth or the world of my cause. But I have lived so long in that in-between place that making the choice frightens me. It was much easier to be one reformer among many than it will to be the Crown Princess of Santadorra."

Nick grinned at her. "I have no fears on that score. You will leave your own distinctive mark on the monarchy."

Lucy bristled. "I will not relinquish my passion for reform."

Nick laughed and brushed her cheek with his fingers. "I would never expect you to change, princess. In fact, I fully expect that you will plague me about the business for the rest of our lives."

Lucy's heart caught in her throat. "I fully expect that I will, too."

"Good." Nick pressed a kiss against her lips. "A man always likes to know that there's something in this world on which he can depend."

Lucy gave herself to another kiss, and it was several long, breathless moments before they came up for air.

Nick set her back from him. "Just promise me one thing, princess."

"What?" Lucy eyed him warily.

"Promise me you'll stay away from garden doors."

"Oh!" Lucy reached out to swat him, but he caught her hand and scooped her up in his arms. She was still pummeling his chest and shoulders when they disappeared below decks.

Crispin leaned against the railing of the yacht and watched as they sliced through the waters of the Channel. King Leopold stood a few feet away, his gaze locked on the horizon.

"I have a feeling that the people of Santadorra are in for a great shock when they meet their new princess," the king said, and Crispin could only smile.

"Will we not see them above decks the entire voyage?" he asked.

"Somewhere about Portugal, I should think." The king laughed and clapped Crispin on the shoulder.

Crispin suppressed a twinge of disappointment. "That's several weeks at least."

"If my memory serves me correctly, several weeks should be adequate."

"Adequate? For what?"

The king barked with laughter. "No wonder you are not yet wed, Lord Wellstone. When we reach Santadorra, we shall have to look about for a bride for you."

Crispin felt his stomach shift, and it wasn't due to the waves. "My talent is not wedding them, Your Majesty, only matching them."

"And a fine talent it is, sir. I never thought to see my son return." King Leopold turned toward him. "I owe you my thanks, as do the people of Santadorra."

"Yes, well, it is one talent I hope never to need again," Crispin replied and vowed to himself that his days as a matchmaker were finished. As the sun descended, the royal yacht rode the crests of the Channel, carrying the small party into the future.

And as for the happily ever after . . .

Epilogue

Santadorra, 1844

Twenty-four-year-old Crown Prince Leopold, the heir to King Nicholas and the Ivory Throne, stood with his family on the balcony of the palace overlooking the crowds gathered below. Bright sunshine and clear blue sky marked a historic day for the tiny kingdom. The official ceremony being enacted was a momentous one, so Leo strove to look properly dignified—despite the fact that his parents, the ruling monarchs, were paying more attention to each other than to the reading of the historic proclamation. After the fierce battles over the last ten years within the young parliament on such a hotly debated issue, one would think his mother and father could stop gazing at each other with such intensity and attend to the moment.

Ten trumpets rang out, and Thomas Selkirk, the captain of the Royal Guard, stepped to the balcony railing and unrolled a large scroll. "Be it known throughout the land," he cried, "that on this day, the year of our Lord eighteen hundred and forty-four, King Nicholas and the duly elected parliament of Santadorra do extend suffrage, and all the rights associated with the same, to the women of this realm."

Feminine cheers rose from the crowd, and Leo heard the groans of more than a few men. How would the day's events shape his country in the years to come? Rumor had it that a number of women of independent means and progressive thinking from as far away as England and Germany planned to descend upon the kingdom en masse and establish residence where they could enjoy the right to vote.

A kingdom full of women. The very thought made sweat bead on Leo's brow. Without a doubt, his parents would welcome them all. Leo would have to as well. He glanced over at his sister, Sophie, and shuddered. If he didn't prove properly hospitable to such forward-thinking women, his sister would cut up his peace to no end.

Leo groaned. Sometimes it was hard to be a man, especially when one had a weakness for lost causes. For the last several years, he'd noticed a growing tendency within himself to try to rescue every waif and damsel who crossed his path. Leo shifted with discomfort as he thought of the pledge he'd made the day before. Coal for the orphanage had seemed harmless enough; he'd never dreamed it would come to almost half the total of his quarterly allowance. Perhaps he should seek advice from his father regarding the management of this alarming tendency to heroism.

Leo glanced behind him to where John Davidson, his manservant, stood with as much dignity as any of the royal personages. Two years Leo's elder, John had been rescued from a rioting mob as an infant by King Nicholas. John and his mother had traveled to Santadorra with the Selkirks, and Leo had gained not only an exemplary manservant but a friend and confidant as well. His father's heroism seemed to have reaped its own rewards. Perhaps Leo's would as well, although his purse still felt considerably empty.

Leo turned toward his parents as the cheers of the crowd faded. A low sound caught his ear, and Leo frowned. If he hadn't known better, he would have said the muffled clank of metal came from where his mother and father stood, smiling into each other's eyes, their hands obviously joined behind the cover of their ceremonial robes.

How odd. Leo sighed. Sometimes parents were the very devil to understand.

KATIE MACALISTER
NOBLE INTENTIONS

Noble Britton suffered greatly at the hands of his first wife, and he refuses to fall into the same trap again. This time he intends to marry a quiet, biddable woman who will not draw attention to herself or cause scandal. Gillian Leigh's honest manner and spontaneous laughter attract him immediately. It matters little that she is accident-prone; he can provide the structure necessary to guide her. But unconventional to the tips of her half-American toes, his new bride turns the tables on him, wreaking havoc on his orderly life. Perpetually one step behind his beguiling spouse, Noble suffers a banged-up head, a black eye, and a broken nose before he realizes Gillian has healed his soul and proven that their union is no heedless tumble, but the swoon of true love.

____4965-1 $5.99 US/$7.99 CAN

Dorchester Publishing Co., Inc.
P.O. Box 6640
Wayne, PA 19087-8640

LYNSAY SANDS
The Reluctant Reformer

Everyone knows of Lady X. The masked courtesan is reputedly a noblewoman fallen on hard times. What Lord James does not know is that she is Lady Margaret Wentworth—the feisty sister of his best friend, who has forced James into an oath of protection. But when James tracks the girl to a house of ill repute, the only explanation is that Maggie is London's most enigmatic wanton.

Snatching her away will be a ticklish business, and after that James will have to ignore her violent protests that she was never the infamous X. He will have to reform the hoyden, while keeping his hands off the luscious goods that the rest of the ton has reputedly sampled. And, with Maggie, hardest of all will be keeping himself from falling in love.

___4974-0 $5.99 US/$7.99 CAN

A Rogue's Promise
PEGGY WAIDE

Eighteen years ago, deep in the mountains of China, Lady Joanna Fenton's father found a sacred statuette. The two-headed dragon is reputed to beget prosperity, but for Joanna, it brought nothing but heartache. Her father was obsessed with the piece until his death. Now, the artifact itself has disappeared.

Her search takes her to the darkest establishments of London, and from those rat holes steps a friend. He is a smuggler, a man who has forsaken his noble heritage for the shadows. A man who sees that she does not belong. And when MacDonald Archer swears to aid her, Joanna realizes the secret to true happiness is not in Oriental charms or spells, but in love.
